Andres & Blanton

Cafenova

S. Jane Scheyder

Andres & Blanton
Niantic, Connecticut

Cafenova

Published by Andres & Blanton
Niantic, Connecticut

ISBN 978-0-9830318-0-2

Printed in the United States of America

www.andresblanton.com

10 9 8 7 6 5 4 3 2

In Memory of Ted

Acknowledgements

My sincerest thanks to the following people, without whom this book would never have left my computer:

* Jacob, who not only believed and insisted that I could write this story, but also painstakingly edited and updated the entire manuscript. This is an immeasurably better work because of you.

* Paul, who never wavered in his belief that this was a worthy project, and who gave me much insight into the details of remodeling and renovation; and Michael, Daniel, Mary and Hannah, who let me disappear to the imaginary land of Clairmont more frequently than any mother should ever leave her children.

* Jan, my first editor and critic, who saw this project through to publication; and Karen, my copy editor, who was willing to take a chance and invest her time and talent in a new writer.

* Jessica, who makes me feel like I can do anything, and helped me to understand Maddy a little better; and Carol, who was one of the first people to picture Clairmont, and kept me inspired with beautiful photographs of the Connecticut coast.

* Charlie, who told me about the workings of crews and remodeling; and Dan and Diane, who shared their renovating skills and knowledge.

* Linda, Cathy, Sandy, Halli and Puja — my first reviewers. Thank you for your insight.

* Loring and Ruth, who championed my first book and gave me a place in their home to write some of this one, as well as exposed me to the wonders of the Maine coast; and Dave and Lynn, whose beautiful Victorian home in Maine has been a place of respite and inspiration!

* The Whaley family, who introduced me to their dog, Sherman, who is Burt's inspiration.

* The staff at the *Inn at Harbor Hill Marina* in Niantic, Connecticut, the beautiful B&B where I stayed, wrote and explored; and Ellen M. Plante's book, <u>The Victorian Home</u>, (Courage Books © 1998), which gave me insight into Victorian decorating.

* Finally, my mom, Judy, and Becky, Diane, Linda, and Jisue, who prayed me through this entire endeavor.

Cafenova

A Renovated Romantic Comedy

Andres & Blanton

prologue

Maddy stepped out of her office and walked to the conference room. Phil had called a meeting, and she wondered what necessitated the entire staff's presence. Glancing down at her legal pad, she smiled at the list of wedding details she'd discussed with her mother the night before. She tore it off and folded it, inserting it somewhere in the back of the pad. Taking her usual spot near the head of the table, she wrote a new heading on the top sheet and waited, nodding at the others as they filed in.

Phil arrived last. "I'm going to cut right to the chase," he said.

The room became very quiet as all eyes turned to him. "I've sold out my shares to Buckingham. I think this is the right time, and you should all consider doing the same."

The silence was profound. Some eyes turned to Maddy, but hers were on Phil.

"I've decided to start another company down in San Diego." He avoided looking at Maddy as he continued his well-rehearsed speech.

She didn't hear the details. Phil was leaving; the company, and apparently her. Now all eyes, except Phil's, were on her. She could feel the layers of sympathetic gazes. It made her nauseous.

"You going alone?" someone finally asked.

"Kathy's coming with me."

The eyes turned to the account manager. Maddy's heart dropped, and for all practical purposes stopped beating. Nothing was said for a moment, and then she pushed her chair back and stood. She took off Phil's ring and placed it quietly on the table. She picked up her pad, and her list fell to the floor as she left the room.

one

There was no getting around it; the house was a dump. Maddy Jacobs was no longer in the business of deceiving herself, and she faced the unsettling truth head-on. Seven days into her new life and the picture was bleak. From the grossly over-painted woodwork to the alarmingly thick layers of carpet, from the battered shelving to the mysterious holes in the walls, Maddy knew she had invested in an unqualified dump.

Potential, the real estate agent had repeatedly assured her. Indeed. The house was huge, it was old, and it definitely had character. Maddy exited the outdated travesty that was her kitchen and walked onto the shabby, if sprawling, porch. The screen door *banged!* in her wake, and for some reason, the sound made her smile. She pulled the salty air into her lungs and beheld the majestic Atlantic beyond her rocky beach of a front yard.

Yes, her new home had potential. The fact that it needed so much work was the only thing that made it affordable for a 29-year-old former software consultant. Maddy would return it to its former glory as a seaside inn. She would need a great deal of help, of course, but she would do it. She crossed her arms with determination as her eyes swept the glorious expanse of water.

A heavy, muffled, slapping sound brought her out of her reverie. She looked down at her housemate, Burt, sprawled under the white plastic table. Her Irish wolfhound continued to thump his tail in greeting, but was too tired to do more. He'd spent the morning exploring the rocky beach and was replenishing his energy for the next run.

"Poor baby," she grinned, leaning down to scratch his ears.

"Hello, Miss Maddy!"

Maddy stood and waved at her elderly neighbor approaching across the sand.

"Otis, how are you?" she called out, glad to hear a voice other than her own. She really needed to get out and meet some people.

Otis Jensen ambled up the steps and gave Burt a friendly pat. "I'm doing just fine, Maddy, my dear. And how are you?"

"Fine, as long as I stay on the porch," she replied. "Can I get you a drink?"

"No, thanks. I just came over to see if you needed anything downtown."

Maddy could easily visualize her shopping list. "Thanks for the offer, but I need to get out of the house. I was planning to take Burt out, anyway."

Otis nodded. "Don't forget to stop at the farmer's market in the square," he reminded her. "Every Saturday. They have the best zucchini."

"Thanks, Otis." Maddy smiled as he waved over his shoulder and walked back down the steps to the beach.

Turning to her ever-present pad on the table, she flipped past the "To Do" list, which had grown by a page and a half just that morning. With a sigh, she updated her "To Buy" list and nudged Burt with her foot.

"Let's take a walk."

He stood up and cocked his head expectantly.

"Over your morning fatigue, are you?"

They walked through the house, and Maddy caught her reflection in the front-hall mirror. She hesitated, considering the woman looking back at her. She adopted a more natural style when she moved to Maine, and it suited her. Her wavy, sometimes curly, light brown hair had a few blonde streaks, and when it behaved, it could be rather pretty. More often than not, she kept it pulled back. Her blue eyes were probably her most striking feature, though she had to give credit to the years spent in braces, which left her teeth nice and straight. Her winter skin could definitely use some beach time, she observed as she finished her quick appraisal by adding a touch of lipstick.

All in all, she was satisfied as she closed the door behind her and started down the walkway. She'd make a decent impression if she ran into any good-looking men in the produce department.

Maddy never made it to the produce department. Before she even reached the grocery store, she literally ran into a jean-clad Greek god at the post office. It was hardly what she had expected when she made that quick detour, but there he was. She had been looking back at Burt, contemplating what she would do with him while she ran inside, when she turned and came face to chest with a dusty T-shirt. It was a muscley, dusty T-shirt; not an altogether unpleasant collision.

"Oh – sorry!" Maddy backed up and had another collision, this time with Burt's snout, and she almost tumbled over backwards. "Burt!" she scolded, at which point he sat down in the threshold of the post office with a snort.

"I'm so sorry," she said again to the interesting stranger, who had taken a step back and waited patiently for them to clear the doorway. "We're new in town," she rattled on a little nervously, "and he still doesn't understand that he can't just follow me every-where." Maddy rolled her eyes in exasperation, and to keep herself from gawking.

He was tall, she figured that out already, and once she caught a glimpse of his face, she had to make an effort not to stare. She searched her brain for a cliché other than "rugged good looks" but nothing else came to mind. Disgusted with her incompetent fantasy vocabulary, she decided to stick to the facts: Hazel-colored eyes – great eyes; sandy brownish hair that curled in charming disarray around his ears; square, unshaven jaw…

Maddy quickly turned her attention to moving her dog out of the doorway.

"Daddy?"

A small head peered around the dusty jeans – curly hair, green eyes, not quite waist-high. Maddy couldn't readily determine his age, but the relationship was clear. All of her fantasies about meet-ing a handsome, single New England lumberjack – in the post office — were brought to an abrupt end. It was a sweet, albeit brief, dream.

"It's okay," the lumberjack said, stroking the blond curls gently. It was a good voice; deep and smooth.

"Can I pet it?"

Another little body suddenly appeared, and his father caught his shoulder as the boy lurched forward. This body was even smaller than the first. He had brown hair and big, brown, mischievous eyes.

"Maybe another time."

Yeah, another time when we run into a strange woman with a wolfhound buying stamps, Maddy smiled to herself.

"Honestly, he's very gentle," she said. "Just scratch under his chin; he loves that." She managed to move Burt back from the doorway, and stood to his side so the little boy could come forward if he wanted to — if his dad would let him.

The boy looked up at his father, and when his dad's hand released him, he ran right up to Burt.

"I'm Parker," he said, glancing briefly at Maddy. "And I like your dog!"

"I'm Maddy," she answered with a smile. "And I like anyone who likes my dog." She knelt down and took Parker's hand and gently guided it to Burt's furry throat. "This is Burt."

Parker looked up at the dog and then straight into Maddy's eyes. "He looks like a monster."

"Oh, he's not a monster — just a big dog," Maddy laughed. "And I think he likes you."

Parker grinned as he continued to pet the animal looking down at him. "See Dad, I'm not afraid!"

His father watched the exchange with interest, but not with particular ease. "You are very brave, Parker. I'm not even sure I want to pet Burt." He grinned apologetically at Maddy.

She shook her head with a smile and turned to the other child. "What's your name?"

"I'm Blake." He walked cautiously toward her and extended his hand.

Impressed, she took it. "I'm very pleased to meet you, Blake.

Would you like to pet Burt?"

Blake considered the invitation carefully. He slowly put his hand out and let Burt get a good whiff.

"You're definitely missing out." Maddy turned to the father, who continued to watch his kids with wary amusement. At least he had closed the gap and was standing somewhat closer to their little group.

"I guess we know who the coward in the family is," he said, making way for a petite, elderly woman leaving the post office.

The woman absently patted the dog on the head as she walked by. "Nice doggie," she cooed, continuing down the sidewalk.

"Okay, I'm going to have to get this big brute out of here so people can get through the door," Maddy said. "Maybe I'll see you another time."

The boys reluctantly peeled themselves away from Burt and returned to their father.

"Did you need something in there?" he asked, not sounding particularly willing to watch her dog if she did.

"Just stamps," Maddy shrugged. "I'm sure I can get them at the grocery store."

"Yeah, I think you can." He glanced at the dog, wondering if she'd really solved her problem.

"Oh, he'll be fine," Maddy assured him. "The other day I just hooked his leash on one of the posts out front while I ran inside. He tends to keep other shoppers away so I can have the place to myself," she quipped.

"I'll bet," he answered, a little too readily. "Well, it was nice to meet you."

"Thank you, and I enjoyed meeting your sons. Parker, Blake – you guys take care." Maddy started pulling on Burt's leash to get his momentum going.

For the second time, the tall, dusty form blocked her path; this time intentionally. Maddy stopped and looked up, feeling something wonderfully uncomfortable ripple through her insides when their eyes met.

"I beg your pardon," he said, suddenly formal. "I'm John." He extended his hand and added, "and I like your dog." A small grin turned the corners of his mouth.

Maddy smiled and then laughed, glad for the distraction as she put her hand in his. It was a good strong hand. *Maybe he really is a lumberjack.* "I'm Maddy."

He regarded her a moment more. "Good to meet you, Maddy." With that he dropped her hand and grabbed those of his sons.

"Time for the hardware store," he said to them. "Say good-bye, boys."

"Bye, Miss Maddy," they chimed, and they were off down the street, in search of tools.

Maddy watched them as they bounced off, talking and laughing. They seemed so happy to be out with their dad. It was a sweet picture, she thought as she turned to walk in the opposite direction. *I'll bet their mom would love it.*

"Let's go, Burt," she said, trying to remember what she needed at the grocery store. Who needed groceries when there were hammers, nails and paint to be purchased?

John pulled the sandpaper from the hardware store bag and put a fresh piece on the small hand sander. He turned back to the old Adirondack chair, and crouched low to finish the backside of one of the panels.

"I see you, Daddy!"

John squinted through the slats and grinned at Parker, squatting and staring back at him from just inside the patio door.

Delighted with his discovery, Parker said, "Okay, now I'll hide. You count." Before John could object, his son jumped up and ran around the side of the house.

Blake, arranging a rock collection on the edge of the patio, watched his brother with a smile. "Guess you're playing, Dad."

"Guess I am," John agreed. "How about you?" Blake hesitated only briefly before taking off after his brother.

"... Twenty-eight, twenty-nine, thirty... Ready or not, here I come!" John took in the backyard with a sweeping glance. There was no sign of movement around the swing-set/fort that he built for the kids two summers ago. He made his way toward the side of the house where he prepared to jump on the nearest victim. No one was giggling among the neatly trimmed bushes, but he could hear someone rustling up near the garage.

"I can hear you hiding…" he called ominously as he walked slowly and heavily toward the front of the house. He heard a gasp and a giggle as at least one small hider realized that discovery was imminent. John jumped around the corner and crouched down, sending Parker squealing from his spot behind the garbage can. John grabbed him and swung him up onto his shoulder.

"Blake, help!" Parker yelled.

"Yes, help, Blake!" John roared, marching around the yard with Parker flailing on his shoulder.

"Let me go!" Parker giggled.

John set Parker down and growled, "Stay here while I go find your brother." Parker lay laughing in the grass, and then quickly jumped up to hide again. John approached the front porch and almost tripped on Blake, who had hidden near the bushes.

"I give up!" Blake shrieked, immediately wrapping his arms around his dad's legs.

John returned the hug with a laugh and grabbed Blake's hand as they continued to circle the house.

"How about we just let Parker keep hiding, and we go have supper?"

John eyed Blake with a barely concealed grin. "How about we find him and make him finish sanding Grampa's chair?"

"That's even better," Blake agreed. "I bet he's in the fort."

Rounding the house into the backyard, they heard a loud giggle, confirming Blake's guess. John fired up the grill and Parker came down and sat on the deck in the unfinished chair, looking rather like an undersized king on a throne.

"Do you think Miss Maddy's dog could come over sometime?" he abruptly asked.

John looked up, surprised. "I don't know, Parker," he answered. "Miss Maddy and her dog are new to town, so they might not feel comfortable just, you know, coming over and hanging out with us."

"I was thinking just her dog," Parker clarified.

John shook his head with a smile.

"If they just moved here, they probably need some friends," offered Blake.

"Burt is so hairy!" Parker exclaimed. He sat back and kicked his shoes together. "Miss Maddy's pretty."

"Did you think so, Dad?" asked Blake.

"I agree on both counts," John answered carefully. "So, do we make these chili dogs or what?"

He retreated into the house for supplies. Yes, he'd noticed the post office girl, and his mind had drifted back to her pretty, laughing face several times throughout the afternoon. She'd been wearing jean shorts, a T-shirt and sneakers; nothing fancy. *Nice legs*, he recalled.

"I want cheese, too!" Parker called after him, then added, "Cheese, *please*, Daddy."

"You got it, buddy."

Blake followed him inside. "I'll pour drinks," he offered.

"That would be great." John pulled chips out of the cupboard, and thought again about the encounter downtown. She'd been a little flustered at first, but had recovered quickly. He liked how she interacted with his sons; there was something very natural in her manner. He smiled to himself as he put the simple meal together. It had been a long time since he'd felt a flicker of interest like this.

"You okay, Dad?"

"Oh, I'm fine. I just can't find that can of chili, and you can't have chili dogs without chili."

"It's right there." Blake pointed to the shelf in front of his father. "You're funny, Dad," he added as he walked out of the kitchen.

The church was very quaint, and though the benches were a bit hard, Maddy liked the feel of the place. She loved the setting of the historic building, and had walked past the old white church several times during the week. Curious about what it looked like inside, she decided to attend the Sunday morning service.

The walls were whitewashed and all of the woodwork was

stained dark brown. The area in front was uncomplicated and, for some reason, it appealed to Maddy. A large wooden cross adorned the wall behind the altar, and wide windows along the sides of the church offered a view of the surrounding property.

She supposed she had no business in their church; or perhaps, it was business that she had, and little else. She needed to start establishing some contacts, and it seemed like as good a place as any to begin. Besides, she'd never been in a church that old.

The room was about three quarters full, and the families with young children sat toward the back. Maddy felt a familiar pang as she watched young mothers wrestling with their little ones, trying to get them to behave. She wondered where Parker and Blake were. Did their family go to church?

"This seat taken, young lady?" Maddy jumped and turned to see Otis sitting down next to her.

"I didn't know you went to this church, Otis," she said, moving over for him.

"If I'd had the nerve to invite you, I could have offered you a ride," Otis said ruefully. "I'm afraid I find it a little bit difficult to extend that invitation sometimes."

"So do I," Maddy agreed. It had been a long time since she'd attended church, much less invited anyone else to go.

She looked back at the service folder in her lap. As happy as she was to see a familiar face, she didn't like the idea of deceiving Otis. Maddy turned at the sound of the pastor's voice as he welcomed the people to worship.

"You'll like him," Otis whispered. "He knows the Word and he gives it to you straight!" He settled back with a satisfied smile.

Maddy smiled politely, but had no intention of getting to know the stranger in front of them. She was beginning to regret the impulse to attend church. Otis would assume that they had some weird religious bond, and worse, he'd expect her to come back.

As soon as the service ended, Otis invited Maddy to the fellowship hour in the basement.

"Oh, no thank you," she replied. "I should probably get back and check on Burt."

"Come on, neighbor," Otis encouraged her. "The donuts are always good, and I promise I won't make an announcement that you're new in town."

Maddy's determination started to crumble, and she paused long enough for him to grab her hand.

"Not that they won't know, already," he smiled back at her as they walked down to the basement together.

Maddy rolled her eyes and followed, nodding at the friendly greetings from the people they passed along the way. She had so wanted to make a quick escape. The connections she thought she should make now seemed too personal. She searched her mind for another excuse so that she wouldn't have to extend her mistake through an endless cup of coffee.

"Miss Maddy! Look, Daddy, it's Miss Maddy! Hey, I rhymed! Daddy and Maddy!"

Parker ran back around the corner as soon as he saw her, and returned a moment later, dragging his father with him. John appeared with an apologetic grin, which didn't stay sorry-looking for long.

"Good morning, Miss Maddy."

Wearing khakis and a casual shirt, he definitely hadn't lost his earthy appeal. Maddy was momentarily and uncharacteristically mute. Parker walked in circles around them while Blake stood quietly at his father's side, holding a cup of punch.

"Good morning, John," Maddy finally found her voice. "Hi, Blake and Parker. I didn't see you in church this morning." She groaned inwardly at the needless revelation.

"Oh, we just come for the coffee." John answered so seriously that Maddy looked up in surprise. He immediately smiled, and Maddy tried not to stare at his beautiful teeth.

Braces, for sure, she thought.

"Would you like a cup?"

"A cup of…" Maddy replied absently, despising her verbal ineptitude.

"Coffee," he gently supplied, putting his hand on her shoulder to guide her to the refreshment table. "Clearly, you haven't had any yet."

"Clearly, not enough," she agreed, as she allowed herself to be led through the gathering crowd. Suddenly, she remembered Otis, and turned to see him standing where she'd left him, watching her with a smile.

"Otis, I'm sorry!" She spun away from John and returned to her neighbor, grabbing him by the hand. "Otis, this is my new friend, John. John, this is my... also new friend, Otis."

John extended his hand. "John Fordham. I've seen you around church. You're usually up in the summer, right?"

"Actually, I've become a full-timer," Otis replied. "Name's Otis Jensen. Maddy, here, is my date this morning."

John raised an eyebrow and nodded. "Of course."

"Miss Maddy, where's Burt?" Parker had stopped running in circles and nibbled on a small frosted cupcake. He dotted his nose with the frosting as he tossed in the last bite.

"They wouldn't let me bring him in," Maddy answered with a sigh. "He'd sure like this part of church, though." She glanced at the crumbs covering Parker's shirt. "He'd be your best friend right now."

"Is he outside waiting for you, like at the grocery store?" Parker looked ready to investigate this possibility.

"Oh, no," Maddy replied. "He had to stay home. I really should go and check on him."

"And miss out on coffee?" John asked. "How do you like it?"

Where's the quiet lumberjack from yesterday? "I'll need some cream."

"Got it," John said. "How about you, Otis, do you like your coffee the way your girlfriend does?"

Otis chuckled. "She knows just how I like it. Don't you, Maddy?"

"Black, but lots of sugar," Maddy directed. "At least that's how he likes it first thing in the morning," she added, her voice low with the implied scandal.

John paused and eyed them both. That voice both surprised and intrigued him, and he wasn't sure how to reconcile those feelings in the church basement. He turned to get their coffee.

"So, how did you like the service?" Otis asked.

"Oh, it was fine," Maddy replied.

"I like Pastor Rob!" Parker piped in with enthusiasm. "He lets us come in front of the church and tells us funny stories."

"Really?" Maddy didn't recall that part of the service.

"Yeah, but not always."

"He seems very nice," Maddy said, nodding with a smile as John returned with their coffee.

"He is. Do you want to meet him?" Blake asked politely.

"Yeah!" Parker answered for her as he began to circle her, again. He pulled on her skirt and said, "He's coming to our house for lunch today, and you can come, too. Right, Daddy? And bring Burt!" He looked from one adult to the other.

John gently pulled his son away, but before he could speak, Parker added, "Remember we wanted to invite her over yesterday?"

John's face colored slightly, which Maddy found surprising and a little charming. She focused on Parker.

"I'd love to visit sometime, and meet your pastor, too." It seemed like the right thing to say. "But I've got to go and take care of some things at home. I have friends coming over this week to help me with my house, and I need to be ready for them."

Parker sighed. "You have *more* new friends? Are you having a party?"

"Oh no," Maddy smiled. "It will be a long time before I can have a party at my house. It needs a lot of work to fix it up, so I'm having some worker friends come over to help me."

"That Mason family tore your place apart, but good," Otis chimed in. "It was such a nice little inn before they bought it. Not one of us in the neighborhood regretted it when they moved to Florida. A loud bunch they were, and those kids were so unruly." He put his arm around Maddy and smiled. "But now look who the Lord brought to the beach!"

"So you two are neighbors," John deduced, his momentary embarrassment replaced with interest. "And you bought the Mason place? Are you hoping to turn it back into a Bed & Breakfast?"

"That's the plan. I wouldn't want to stay in that big old house by myself," Maddy replied. "Of course, it will be a while before anyone will actually want to come and stay there with me," she added with a rueful smile.

John doubted she'd have any trouble filling her inn. He felt oddly uncomfortable with the idea, and agreed that it would probably be quite a while before she could reasonably expect guests.

"It sounds like a big job," he concluded casually.

"Yes, and thank you for reminding me." Maddy grimaced at him, which had the unnerving effect of making him smile with those beautiful teeth. She could feel the heat in her face and quickly turned to her neighbor. "Otis, if you're ready to go home, I'd love a ride. The walk was a bit of a challenge in these heels."

two

Maddy woke suddenly, and not very cheerfully, when the doorbell rang early the next morning. Tired and confused, she wrestled with her blankets as she tried to get out of bed.

"Figures, the doorbell works," she muttered, finally stumbling down the stairs.

"Move, you big horse!" she grunted as she shoved against the door that Burt was accustomed to sleeping against. "Can't you hear the doorbell? I can't get through!" With one last push, she got Burt to move out of the way. He got up with a sigh, and then stretched his long body. Having awakened, he began to greet Maddy with his customary energy.

"Good morning to you, too," Maddy grinned, scratching his ears. "You need to go outside, so I can see who's at the door." She pulled on his collar and pushed him out onto the porch, and then made her way back to the other side of the house. *Who would stop by at this hour?* she wondered as she fumbled with the lock.

Glancing in the mirror, she was half-pleased with her sleepy and disheveled reflection. Whoever was on the other side of the door was going to know that they woke her up. The lock released and she pulled the door open, preparing a little scowl for her visitor.

Standing on the other side of the screen door, with two steaming cups of coffee from the bakery downtown, was John Fordham. He took in her tousled hair and white cotton robe and was at once embarrassed and delighted. He cleared his throat and put on his professional smile.

"Hello, Maddy."

Immobilized, Maddy felt only embarrassment. Delight had no place on her emotional radar as she beheld her handsome new friend, even if he was holding coffee.

John noticed that she had definitely improved on her scowl from the day before. "I brought you coffee," he said. Then after a moment, "I'm here to look at your house." It sounded more like a question than a statement.

A dozen questions flooded Maddy's mind, not the least of which was how she managed to get the date of her meeting with the builder wrong. The most pressing was apparently not a question at all; *the lumberjack is my contractor?* How had she not known? She slowly opened the screen door for him.

"I'm the contractor," he tried again, stepping inside. "You know, one of your 'worker friends?' "

"You're the contractor? You're a builder then?"

"More of a renovator," John qualified. He would have offered her his card, but his hands were full. "I work primarily on restoration jobs," he explained, shifting his weight slightly and looking over his shoulder, as if hoping the rest of his crew would suddenly materialize and back him up. *Maybe it wasn't such a good idea to surprise her like this...* He hadn't counted on her not expecting anyone at all.

Maddy's mind was still spinning, but one little detail finally came into focus: John Fordham of Fordham-Davidson Renovations. That's why his name had sounded familiar the day before. She'd just latched on to the 'FDR' in her previous contacts with him. *So this is Mr. F...*

"What time is it?" she suddenly asked.

"A little after eight."

"Eight o'clock! I missed the sunrise!" Maddy turned and ran back through the house, leaving John standing in the doorway.

He looked around uncertainly, expecting to be attacked, or at least greeted in some way by her monster of a dog. No one came to meet him, however, as he maneuvered the door shut with his foot and proceeded through the house. He glanced into the rooms he passed, starting a mental list of repairs. Finding his way to the kitchen and through the back door, he found Maddy standing at the railing of her porch. Her robe moved around her ankles in the morning breeze, and John contemplated this distracting sight as he walked out to join her. Then, remembering his fear, he looked around for the dog. Puzzled, he set the coffees on the table.

"Where's Burt?" he asked, half hoping he'd imagined the beast a few days earlier.

"Right behind you," Maddy answered.

Burt lumbered up from behind the wicker sofa and sniffed John's back pocket. He stiffened slightly under the gentle assault.

"He won't hurt you." Maddy turned to face John, who was decidedly pale. She couldn't help but smile; he really was afraid of her dog. "So, one of these is for me?" she covered a yawn and reached for a cup.

"Help yourself," John replied, trying unsuccessfully to ignore Burt.

Maddy picked up one of the cups and sipped it gratefully. "I'm sorry I took off like that. I have this thing about sunrises."

"Don't worry about it," John shifted, looking down, somewhat, at the dog.

"Put your hand out so he can see it, and then just pet him under the chin." Maddy lifted the lid from her cup and blew gently on the steaming liquid, smiling as she watched John gather the courage to touch her dog.

"You make it sound so easy," he mumbled as he slowly let the dog smell his hand. "He could have me for lunch."

"Oh, I'll be sure to feed him before then," Maddy responded playfully. "Besides, you don't exactly look like the helpless type." She eyed him for a moment. "You could probably outrun him. Burt's not that fast, at least not here on the beach." She paused, then added, "You don't want to get him out in the open, where he can really take off. Then you wouldn't stand a chance."

"Thanks, that's reassuring," John said dryly, eyeing her with a look she would soon come to find familiar and unsettling. She found that she couldn't hold his gaze when he directed it at her, and later named it 'the look' for quick reference.

"You're welcome," she said quickly, sliding a chair out. "Now, have a seat and tell me again. You're the contractor. We must have spoken on the phone… I thought you were coming tomorrow."

John lowered himself into the chair across from her, while Burt continued to stand next to him, his muzzle alarmingly close to John's shoulder.

"We spoke about a month ago, while you were still on the West Coast, I believe," John explained, looking at the dog, and sliding his chair over. "I've mostly dealt with your agent, obviously, but we touched base briefly after I worked up the initial proposal."

"Wow, that was *you*?" Maddy tried to place his phone voice. "So you must have known yesterday that we might be working together," she concluded, leaning back and directing her own 'look' at him. "You might have mentioned that."

"Oh, it took me a while to figure it out," John answered with a grin.

"Yeah, right," she replied. "Why would I have thought the meeting was *Tuesday*?" she wondered aloud. "I'm usually more attentive to those kinds of details."

"You've got a lot on your plate," he said.

"I think, maybe, I locked onto the date. I had the tenth in my head, and today must be..."

"The ninth."

"Right, well, I guess we should get started, but I'd like to get dressed, first."

"Probably a good idea," John replied, half of his grin still evident.

Maddy scowled and got up from the table. "I can't believe I slept in today. I haven't missed the sunrise since I moved here. I'm usually up way before this." The coffee was definitely kicking in. "I'll be back in a minute," she said. "You and Burt can bond."

The grin left John's face as Maddy walked to the door.

"Burt, stay," she said as he tried to follow her inside. She wanted John to be the uneasy one, and his discomfort with the dog helped. Burt sat down and regarded her sadly as she walked through the door and it *banged!* shut behind her.

"I can fix that," John called after her.

"Don't you dare! I like it that way."

ଓଃ୭ଠ

It didn't take Maddy long to get dressed, but it felt like forever to John, who refused to move as long as the dog sat staring at him.

"So, you think you can run faster than me?"

Burt understood this as an invitation to approach, and he lumbered over to John and slumped down in front of him. John shifted in his chair to accommodate the large animal at his feet.

A few minutes later, Maddy appeared wearing jeans and a T-shirt, her hair pulled back in a pony tail.

John forgot about the dog and smiled. "That was fast."

"I was motivated. I find that people don't take me as seriously when I'm in my bathrobe."

"I imagine that's true."

Maddy grimaced, and John continued. "So, why don't you tell me what you're thinking? I have a pretty good idea of what you need, but I'd like to get your take on things before we walk through."

Maddy's head spun; she had hoped to be more prepared for this meeting. Sitting down across from him, she pulled her pad in front of her.

"I hardly know where to begin." She flipped through the pages. "I figure we should start upstairs. It's a mess. One room needs … well, I call it the 'hole-room.' You'll see what I mean. I think someone pushed a dresser through the wall, or something. All of the rooms need repair of some kind or other." She sighed. "The wallpaper needs to be stripped. It seems to be hung indiscriminately throughout the house, and where there isn't paper, the walls are pretty beat up. Then they'll all need painting, of course."

She paused to catch her breath. "I would like all the carpet pulled and the floors refinished. There's some beautiful wide-wood flooring. I'm not sure if that's what you call it, but I like it, and I'd like to see if it's worth restoring."

John nodded, grinning.

"What?" She couldn't possibly have displayed some amusing lack of knowledge about remodeling already.

"Oh, nothing," John chuckled. "It's just that what you said rhymed; flooring and restoring. I just had this vision of you making your whole list rhyme."

Maddy regarded him, and then broke into a smile herself.

John enjoyed the transformation. "I'm sorry. Most of my reading is at a four-year-old level right now, so a lot of it rhymes... Please, go ahead."

"I'm afraid the rest of the list isn't so entertaining. The bathrooms are a mess, and I don't have any hot water. I think something's terribly wrong with the water heater in the cellar, but I haven't hung out down there long enough to check it out." She shuddered and sheepishly added, "That's the one part of the house that kind of creeps me out."

John grinned. "We'll take care of the water heater."

"Thanks." Maddy was beginning to sense the lifting of a monumental burden. It was a more welcome feeling than she could have imagined. She looked back at her list.

"Anyway, I figure if you get the bedrooms to the point where I can take over with decorating, then I'll keep busy while you guys work on the lower level. This floor has its own challenges." She took a deep breath. "All of the rooms need paint, and a lot of the woodwork needs to be stripped and refinished. You probably noticed the dining room on your way in; it looks like someone spray-painted with guacamole. I can't imagine why they picked that color, or covered that beautiful woodwork."

"I've asked that same question many times."

Maddy continued. "I'd like to put up new wainscoting throughout the lower level, and again, I'd like to find the wooden floor under all the carpeting. The kitchen needs a whole lot of updating, but it's functional." She looked up. "How does that sound for starters?"

"Sounds like fun," John replied, pleased by Maddy's energy and vision for the house. Many of the homeowners he worked with were difficult and often clueless about the demands they made.

"I'm guessing this is going to take a while," she said. "You mentioned having a three-month time frame with your crew, and I'd love to be open by Labor Day. Do you have any idea if that's realistic?"

"It's hard to tell – it depends on the extent of the repairs, among many other things," John answered. "I have a partner and two guys who work for me over the summer. My plumber comes and goes as the job dictates. I do have a few others that I use for work that may need to be contracted out, if we get in a pinch." John glanced at her pad. "New roof – that's a big job in itself."

"Yeah, I didn't get to the outside list."

"We do roofs," he assured her, standing up. "Okay. This is where you give me a little tour, and we decide what it's going to take to get you up and running."

"Sounds good," said Maddy, pushing away from the table. "Brace yourself, it's not pretty."

They stood in the kitchen and looked from one end to the other. It was a large room, and it needed a lot of work. The floor needed replacing, and the cupboards were pretty beat up. The sink was original and had the accompanying charm and limited functionality. The appliances were dated, dented and ugly; replacing them would be a priority before Maddy opened for business.

John jotted down notes as she made her observations about the room.

"I don't know if it's practical, but I'd like to keep the sink the way it is, if we can just clean it up and check the plumbing. I like the idea of keeping as much of the original house as possible."

John nodded and wrote in his notebook.

"Same thing with the cupboards," she continued. "I know they aren't very up-to-date, but the wood seems nice and solid, and I'd like to make them work." She looked back at John and found his eyes were on her instead of the cupboards, a thoughtful look on his face. "Something wrong?"

"Oh, no," John smiled. "I'm just surprised; pleased, but surprised."

"About what?" What could possibly make him happy about her dirty old cupboards?

John walked over, opened one of them and looked inside. "Most people just want to scrap the old stuff and put in new." He ran his finger along one of the hinges and turned to her. "We do it all the time, and it's really a shame. Like you, I prefer the idea of preserving the original as much as possible. It takes longer and it's not always cheaper, but it's what real restoring is about."

"Would this be a bad time to tell you that I want to change the color?"

John chuckled. "Just don't tell me you want them avocado green."

Maddy smiled. "I just want them lightened up. This dark wood makes the kitchen look smaller, and, I don't know, less inviting. I think a light cream color would be nice."

John looked around the room and nodded. "It will brighten the space considerably."

"I'd also like glass panels in some of these upper cupboards."

John agreed. "That will help open up the space, too. You might even consider leaving the doors off altogether here, and here." He pointed along the wall and Maddy tried to visualize his suggestion.

"There will be no hiding anything, will there?"

John smiled. "We've done it in some of our restorations by necessity, but I've come to like the look of the open space." He wrote something down, and looked up again. "You've got plenty of time to decide."

They went on to discuss the appliances and flooring, and then John gestured at the ceiling. "It will take some effort to restore the tin; what do you think?"

Maddy followed his gaze. *Tin ceiling?* She hadn't noticed the ceiling at all, and she didn't have any idea if it was worth restoring. "I'll have to give that some thought, too," she stalled, determined to hide her ignorance about Victorian home restoration for as long as possible.

They moved to the large living area that shared the ocean view with the kitchen. An enormous fireplace took up half of the interior wall. Windows made up most of the rest of the perimeter of the room, allowing for the breathtaking water view from just about any vantage point. Their footsteps echoed across the wooden floor as John checked windows and gave the fireplace an initial inspection. Maddy watched him and wondered what kinds of things made it onto his list.

"This is a great fireplace," he said.

"Yeah, I thought so, too." Maddy joined him in the middle of the room.

"You'll be glad you have it in the winter."

"I'll be glad if I can build a fire by then."

John turned to look at her. "You don't know how to make a fire?"

Maddy shrugged. "No. But I'll figure it out."

"You know it gets cold up here? Really cold?"

"I believe it."

"I'll show you how to make a fire."

Maddy smiled sweetly. "We'd better see if you want this job, first."

John shook his head as he followed her out of the room. *Does she have any idea what she's in for?* Living on the coast of Maine was not just about sitting on the beach. He hoped she would make it through her first winter before hustling back to the West Coast.

They crossed back to another room behind the kitchen, which Maddy figured would be her bedroom, eventually. The carpeting was old and worn and the walls reflected its shabby state. Still, the room had possibilities, and Maddy liked the fact that a door led out to the porch that wrapped around the beachside of the house.

The tour continued through the rest of the lower level, which included a front hall, a large parlor and a smaller sitting room, the dining room, two bathrooms and a laundry room. John continued to write detailed notes, and Maddy made a few of her own.

"Are you ready to go upstairs?" she asked hesitantly.

"Sure."

They walked back through the kitchen to the rear staircase.

"I'm only using the kitchen stairs right now," Maddy explained as she opened the door. "You saw that I have the front staircase blocked off so that Burt won't go upstairs while it's under construction, so to speak."

John nodded, visibly relieved that he didn't have to ask for that little perk.

They walked through four of the five bedrooms that filled the second floor. These rooms shared a large bath, which needed a new tub, among other things. Maddy began to worry, again, about the size of the job that she had taken on.

John gestured up to the third floor. "Attic?"

"Yeah, we can take a look," Maddy said, leading him up the steps.

"You could easily finish this at some point," John said, looking around. "The ceiling is high enough, and you've got plenty of windows."

"I was thinking the same thing," Maddy replied. "It will have to wait a while, but I think this would be a great living space. I'd need a bathroom installed, and a porch," she pointed to the ocean side.

"Some interesting possibilities," John agreed. "What's next?"

Maddy led him down the steps and on to the master bedroom. John walked in and whistled.

"Well, you certainly have the view." He took in the simply decorated but orderly room and the incredible seascape just beyond the windows. "This is very nice."

The large room was sparse, but warmed up by the bedding, curtains and floor rugs Maddy had chosen. There was a massive four-poster bed against the wall opposite the windows, which seemed to fit the house but looked out of place with the rest of the furnishings. Other than the small bedside table, there was an antique dresser that needed refinishing, an old rocker and a floor lamp next to the window. A hope chest, equally old, lined the wall further down. Neatly labeled boxes stood in the corner to his right, and to the left a wall of built-in bookshelves and cupboards needed serious attention.

"So, I can't help but notice that you have almost no furniture in the house, and yet you have this huge bed," John observed. "I don't suppose you moved that across the country?"

"Oh, no. I found this beautiful thing at an estate sale the day after I arrived." Maddy ran her hand along the smooth wooden post. "I wasn't really expecting to start shopping so early, but the sale was in the neighborhood, so I thought I'd check it out. I got my kitchen table and chairs there, too."

"That's convenient."

"Yeah. The guy had his sons deliver the furniture and set up the bed for me. It was nice."

John walked to the bathroom door. "Mind if I go in here?"

"Go ahead." Maddy crossed the room to join him. "Isn't it beautiful?" She gestured at the claw-foot tub. "If the view hadn't sold me, I think the tub would have," she mused aloud.

John grinned. "It's a great bathtub." He looked up in the corner and pointed with his pencil. "You're going to need that leak repaired; no telling what's behind that stain."

"I'm afraid to find out," Maddy replied, following his gaze. "I have a feeling I'll be saying that a lot."

"The sink will need to be replaced," John continued. "But you probably knew that."

"The big crack in the basin was a pretty good clue."

John walked out into the bedroom, taking in the ocean view. "You'd make good money on this room."

"Oh, I know I'll have to give it up," she agreed. "I'll use that room off the kitchen downstairs. I just figured I'd take advantage of this one while I'm restoring the place."

"I'd do the same thing. Do they work okay?" He nodded at the double doors leading onto the balcony.

"They stick a little, but I've used them every day, until this morning, that is. We can go out if you like."

Maddy opened one of the doors and stepped onto the balcony. It was roomy enough for the table and chairs she envisioned for the space. For now, it just held two plastic lawn chairs; all that she really needed to enjoy the exquisite view.

"This is my favorite part of the house," she said, leaning out over the railing and relishing the sea breeze on her face.

John resisted the urge to pull her back. "It is beautiful, but it's just as nice from back here."

"You're not afraid of heights, too?" she teased.

"No, I'm just used to protecting little bodies from leaning, jumping and even just standing where they shouldn't." He grinned. "Sorry about that. I guess you can handle yourself."

Maddy turned back to the railing with a smile. "I figure I can sand and paint these rails and the deck area up here."

"Every bit that you can do will help." John closed his notebook. He didn't say that to every homeowner, but Maddy seemed up for the challenge. Looking out over the water, he said, "You have a beautiful spot here."

"Oh, I know, this is absolutely a dream." Maddy hesitated. "Think you can help me out?"

John looked at her for a moment. "I'm sure we can help, but I'll need to give you a more detailed bid and see if you're still interested in working with me."

He gave her a half smile, which Maddy found almost as unnerving as 'the look.' "Is there anything else you need from me before you can do that?"

John flipped through his pad. "I should probably have a look at your water heater in the cellar. Are you game?"

"Absolutely. I'll follow you."

Maddy walked Burt slowly through the center of town, noting the various stores that she would visit later. She was happy to see at least two antique places, some interesting gift shops and a used book store.

As she walked, she replayed the morning and her meeting with Mr. Fordham. As intriguing as he was, she wasn't sure it was particularly wise to have someone like him under her roof all summer long. She knew of several other contractors, but they all worked individually on smaller jobs. Fordham-Davidson Renovations at least had a crew, and she had a feeling it would take a small army to get her home ready for guests by the end of the summer.

She was, admittedly, pleased with his approach so far. He had asked a lot of questions and taken as many notes. He didn't seem put off when she didn't have answers, and wasn't condescending or patronizing. Deep down, she hoped that his bid would be reasonable. She checked her watch again. He had said he'd be back with the contract before five. A few more hours, and she'd have a pretty good idea how she'd be spending the rest of her summer.

Unfortunately, Maddy wasn't ready for John the second time he stopped by, either. She'd decided to start sanding the rails on her porch, a fairly demanding task that she figured would effectively employ the energy she would otherwise have spent pacing while she waited for him to return. She completely lost track of time, and it wasn't until John appeared on the beach that she realized how consumed she'd become with her project.

She stood up a little stiffly. "Welcome back." She tried to brush the paint chips off of her arms. "Sorry for the mess."

John smiled. "Guess I'll adjust my quote. Did you get that hole fixed upstairs, too?"

Maddy laughed. "Can I get you a drink?"

"That would be great." He sat down at the table while she went in to wash up.

She poured lemonade, took a deep breath and went back out to join him.

"So, Mr. Fordham. How does it look?"

"Not too bad."

They sat down with the contract, which took almost half an hour to review. Maddy wanted to make sure she understood what John was charging for his services, as well as how expenditures would be approved along the way. She basically trusted him, but knew better than to put too much stock in a handsome face. At five-thirty, they shook hands, and Maddy signed the contract.

"I'm more relieved than I can say," she admitted as she walked him to the door.

He smiled. "I'm looking forward to working together."

Maddy could have kicked herself for blushing. He probably made that remark to every homeowner who signed a contract with him. Fortunately, Burt came up and pushed his way between them.

"I guess Burt wants to say good-bye."

John slowly put his hand out, and Burt nudged him with his nose. He obliged the dog and pet him tentatively, while Maddy watched with a smile.

John exhaled and said, "Okay, well, we'll be here bright and early. Are you sure you want to get started tomorrow?"

"Definitely," Maddy agreed. "I'll be ready for you this time."

three

Maddy awoke to the sound of a woodpecker tapping on the window. It took her a few minutes to realize that this didn't make sense, but she was glad that whatever it was had awakened her. *The sunrise!* She sat up and immediately felt the muscles pull in her legs.

"Ow!" she moaned, as she tried to drop her limbs over the side of the bed. She reached for her robe and a stab of pain pierced her right arm. Letting it hang limp at her side, she slid off the bed and stood still, willing some of the pain coursing through her body to stop. Feeling ridiculous and unfit, she hobbled out onto the balcony. The sky was light gray-blue and clear; a few stars were still visible.

"Ow!" she yelped with more feeling. A shell or some small object had flown over the railing and landed on her little toe. Too tired to be alarmed, but still curious, she limped to the edge of the balcony.

She didn't really expect to see anyone when she peered over the side, and she jumped back in surprise at the sight of someone looking up at her. Her aching legs did not accommodate this sudden movement well, and her expression showed it when she slowly leaned back over the railing. There was no mistaking the person smiling up at her from below. It wasn't that dark out.

He spoke before she had a chance to think. "Morning, Maddy. I came to make sure you didn't miss the sunrise again."

Maddy, a little pleased and a little furious, couldn't believe that John had awakened her two days in a row. *Is there something I don't know about East Coast people?*

"I know, you can't believe I'm doing this again. Neither can I." He stood there with his hands in his pockets and shrugged. "I just felt compelled to help you start the day with the sunrise." He looked like a not-very-sorry little boy trying to talk his way out of getting punished. "I brought more coffee," he added, nodding toward the porch. "Get dressed and come join me."

"Thank you for that option, at least," Maddy finally found her voice. "If you didn't have coffee I'd send Burt out after you."

She walked back inside with no choice but to get dressed and share the sunrise with her new contractor. She gingerly pulled on some jeans, and limped into the bathroom to comb her hair and brush her teeth. No makeup for John this morning.

"We'll see if he keeps coming back at the break of dawn," she muttered.

She made her way slowly down the steps and into the kitchen where Burt was standing at the door, looking through the window and wagging his tail.

"You should be barking at him," Maddy complained. Cupping Burt's face in her hands, she said, "He's a *stranger!* Aren't you supposed to protect me from people like him?" Burt wrenched his face free and looked back out of the window. Maddy sighed and opened the door, happy to let the dog out ahead of her.

John smiled at her and then steeled himself, putting his hand out as Burt energetically approached. The dog sniffed him approvingly and then waited to have his throat scratched. John gestured to the coffee on the table.

"Help yourself."

"Thanks," Maddy said, reaching with her left hand and holding the wonderfully warm cup between her fingers. "So," she said, "you're here again."

"Well, you knew I'd be back, of course. I just got here a little early." At this, John had the decency to look a little sheepish. "You just seemed so sad when you missed the sunrise yesterday, and I knew you'd be tired this morning…"

"Why would you assume that?" Maddy dropped her limp body into a chair. "I just did a little sanding."

"Yeah, I noticed. Nice job, too."

"Thanks."

"I figured you'd be paying for crouching for hours, not to mention your sore arm and shoulder," John continued, sitting down across from her.

"Thanks for reminding me."

He smiled. "Believe it or not, I don't plan to wake you up every morning. But the next few days are supposed to be overcast, not great for watching the sunrise, so I took a chance that you'd forgive me if I made sure you didn't miss this one."

"So now it sounds like I'm supposed to thank you."

"That's probably more appropriate."

Maddy grinned over her cup.

"And I brought you coffee," John pointed out, glad the smile appeared.

Maddy turned her attention toward the horizon; the sky was brightening up. "You can't expect to charm your way through life with coffee. It won't always work."

"It's the only way I know."

"I'll bet." Maddy gave him a tired version of her 'look.' "Well, this is three days in a row, Cafenova." She was immediately horrified at the pun, which won her a wide grin from John.

"Did you just call me 'Cafenova?' "

"I can't be responsible for poor puns this early in the morning." Maddy slunk lower in her chair and held her coffee in front of her face.

"No one's ever called me Cafenova before. So, what does that mean, exactly?" It was John's turn to watch Maddy squirm. He enjoyed it immensely.

"It means you try to seduce women with caffeine, I guess."

"So you think I'm here to seduce you this morning?" John leaned back in his chair and regarded her.

Maddy was mortified. "No, of course not!"

"Maybe at church the other day?" John tried to look serious, but her distress was just too entertaining. "I usually try not to seduce women at church, especially if they already have a date."

"Okay, can we please talk about something else, maybe something that will horrify you, instead?" Maddy eased out of her chair and stood at the railing, waiting for the sun to come up over the water. *Why is it taking so long?*

"Of course. I'll let you pick the subject," John replied, clearly enjoying the upper hand early in the morning.

"I already told you I can't think this early," she replied, focusing, instead, on the sun edging into the day. "Here it comes!" Maddy was rapt as she stood by the railing. Nothing else mattered as the sun slowly eased above the water line.

John got up from the table, and they watched in silence together. He glanced at her as she took in the spectacle; her face delighted and yet utterly peaceful.

"I will never get tired of this. It's absolutely beautiful." The sun had risen to the point where it appeared to rest for a moment on the horizon. It sent a shimmering trail across the water and seemingly right up to Maddy's own beachfront.

"I sometimes feel like I should be able to walk right down that golden track back to the sun." She turned to him with a sheepish grin. "I guess that's a little corny, huh?"

"It is an amazingly precise path," he agreed.

"I'm surprised that I never see my neighbors out watching the sunrise," she observed, relieved that he hadn't given her a hard time. She liked her shiny sun path, and didn't want anyone making fun of it.

"Most of them probably aren't here yet," John answered. "The season doesn't really get started until later in June. Water's too cold."

"That's the other thing I don't get," Maddy continued. "How can people afford to own these homes and not actually live here? It was all I could do to buy this place, and I only got a hold of it because it's such a mess."

"Too much money out there," John mused. "I do get a little frustrated, helping people spend a fortune fixing up a home they only live in a couple of weeks out of the year. Of course, a lot of these places get rented out, which helps make the mortgage payment, if there is one." He paused, and then said, "Many of them don't seem all that happy with their money." He shrugged. "Anyway, it's not a problem that I share."

"Me neither. I keep wondering if I'm crazy for doing this. I have limited resources. When those are gone, I'm going to have to start making money on this place, or I don't know what I'll do."

"So, no tips, huh?"

"No way. You'll be lucky to get a paycheck."

"I guess I'd better get to work then," John said. "'Although I wouldn't mind stretching my legs. Are you up for a quick walk?"

Maddy smiled as Burt's head shot up at his favorite word. He lumbered to his feet, wagging his hind quarters and almost knocking John back into his chair.

"I guess that's a yes."

"Whatever made you choose a dog this big?"

"I didn't choose him, he chose me."

"Really?"

"Yep." Maddy started to jog involuntarily as Burt began his walk with considerable energy. "Burt – wait!" she called, but he was too happy and distracted to listen. Maddy let the leash go and Burt took off down the beach.

John caught up to Maddy, smiling as he watched the dog lope around between the rocks. It was a comical sight, with Burt's long limbs flailing, but managing to keep his body generally moving forward. John could almost imagine developing some affection for the animal, although he definitely preferred him at a distance.

"I figure the neighbors can't get too mad if they're not actually here to see him running loose," Maddy said. "We're going to have to start behaving when they get here."

"Good luck with that," John replied as they maneuvered slowly around the rocks. "You were going to tell me how Burt chose you?"

"Oh, that. Well, a friend of mine had a litter, and..."

"Those things come in litters?"

" 'Those things,' are Irish wolfhounds. Honestly, you act like you've never seen a dog before." Maddy pushed the hair out of her eyes, and then rolled them expressively at him. "So he's big; big deal. You're not exactly tiny, but I'm not freaked out at your size."

Really, Maddy? You just said that aloud? Biting her lower lip, she ventured a look up at him.

He returned her gaze thoughtfully.

"I guess I never thought my size freakish," he answered. "It's served me rather well. But I guess it's a fair analogy; just because your dog is big, doesn't mean that he's not just a dog, after all."

"Exactly my point," Maddy jumped at the opportunity to make any sense of her comment. "And I don't think you're freakish, by the way."

"Thank you. So, about your friend's litter…"

"Oh, yes," Maddy returned to her story. "There were just two puppies."

"Makes sense."

"Usually there are more."

"Really?"

"Sure, sometimes five or six. Anyway, I went to visit and Burt just wouldn't leave me alone. He kept nuzzling me and climbing into my lap; it was crazy."

"And a bit uncomfortable, I imagine."

"Well, he wasn't nearly so big. They are fairly small puppies."

John looked at her doubtfully.

"Really. Anyway, I hadn't planned on taking him home with me, but I did, and he's been with me almost three years. I don't know what I'd do without him."

"How'd you come up with his name?"

"The vet did that. I'd planned to call him Brute, but she read his chart wrong." Maddy smiled at the memory. "From that point on, he was Burt."

They circled around and headed back to the house. "You'll be glad to have him out here," John said.

"That sounds a little ominous."

"Oh, it's not like the community isn't safe," he quickly explained. "It's just that the summer people can be a bit unpredictable. Don't forget, you'll have a fair amount of renters out here. Those who can afford these houses," he gestured, "may behave all right, but a lot of the smaller cottages get rented out to kids who are… Well, they're kids, and it'll just be good to have him around."

"You and Otis are a pair – both convinced that I can't take care of myself."

"I never said that. But you're a single woman, running a business where strangers come and stay in your house. It just makes sense to have a little extra protection."

"Who said I was a single woman?" Maddy inquired.

"I assumed…"

"How nice."

"Then I guess I'm a little surprised that your husband let you go for a walk on the beach at dawn with another man," John remarked dryly. "Maybe you should introduce us? He might have a thing or two to say about the renovations we're planning,"

"I'm pretty sure you've already met," Maddy replied, looking past him onto her porch. John turned to see Otis waving down at them.

John laughed and Maddy grinned as Burt led the way to say hello.

Otis shared a cup of coffee with Maddy, but left before the others arrived, missing the spectacle of Burt greeting the crew at the door. Maddy almost missed it herself, but came upon the scene shortly after Burt found them. Whining and wagging his tail with fervor, he was fairly determined to find his way out to join the newcomers. The guys on the porch seemed somewhat amused, and more than a little relieved that at least a screen door separated them from the animal.

"I'm so sorry!" Maddy called out as she ran to meet them. "He's harmless, really; he's just big. You can come right in." She came up behind Burt and grabbed his collar. "It's okay, Burt. These are friends."

No one moved for a moment, and then John's partner, Frank, noticed John coming up behind Maddy. "Okay, come on, guys. You first, Tom." He grinned and shoved one of the men in front of him.

Three young men preceded Frank and filed into the house, smiling at Maddy and doing their best to avoid the dog. Brief introductions followed, and John lost no time in leading them back through the house to get an overview of the job.

Maddy returned to the kitchen and sat at the counter to look at her lists. She knew that she'd have to face her railing eventually, and hoped that some degree of dexterity would come back when she did. A little while later, the men came through the kitchen, nodded their hellos and headed out to their trucks. Maddy stopped John on his way through.

"So, what do they think?" she asked.

He smiled. "They think they're going to keep busy this summer."

"That's a good thing?"

"Of course," he said. "We're starting on that wall upstairs. It's going to get noisy."

The guys returned a short while later, and Maddy listened as the house began buzzing with the sounds of hammers, drills and power tools that she couldn't identify. Burt eventually came to terms with the commotion and resumed his nap on the kitchen floor.

Not to be outdone, Maddy got her supplies together and went out to the porch. She'd completely stripped five rails when John opened the door from the kitchen. *Only seventy more to go,* she thought with a moan, regretting the impulse to count them earlier. She looked up and forced a smile.

"I'm heading down to the hardware store. Do you need anything?" he asked.

"I can't think of anything right now, but I do have a question for you."

"Shoot."

"Do you know what your guys are planning to do for lunch? I'd like to feed them, but I don't know what your routine is."

"I try to have lunch with Blake and Parker as often as I can," John answered. "The others usually bring theirs."

Maddy thought for a moment. "Can I offer you all lunch tomorrow, as a kind of welcome?"

"Yeah, that would be nice," he replied. "But just this one time. Don't spoil us."

Maddy smiled. "Okay, so what would you like?"

"You want to pick up some grinders?"

"Okay," Maddy hesitated.

"Problem?"

"Oh, no. It's just that… I don't know what a grinder is."

John laughed. "It's a sub-type sandwich. I don't know what you call them in Seattle."

"A sub-type sandwich."

"Brilliant."

"I know. Okay, please tell the guys that I'll provide grinders tomorrow," Maddy said.

"Thanks, I will," John replied. "I'll be about an hour. I've got my cellphone if you need anything."

Maddy smiled at the familiarity of the phrase. "That would be helpful if I actually had your cell number."

"Check your list," John said, opening the door carefully and looking up at the simple spring mechanism that had long since given way.

"Don't even think about it," Maddy warned.

John smiled and walked through the house.

The crew arrived promptly at eight the next morning, and Maddy offered them some of her very best West Coast coffee. It was duly appreciated, and they lost no time in getting to work upstairs. Maddy lost a little time; it took a while for her body to loosen up enough to get back to what now seemed an endless sanding job.

At noon she picked up grinders at the highly recommended Theo's Deli and served them on the porch with lemonade. John helped himself to a sandwich and then excused himself to go see his sons.

"Thanks for the grinder, Maddy," he smiled at her, and then turned toward the others. "I'll be back in half an hour. Don't get too comfortable."

Maddy, quickly distracted by the porchful of interesting young men, had them re-introduce themselves. They went on to explain how each had come to work for Fordham-Davidson Renovations.

Frank Davidson insisted that he was both the F and the D in FDR. He was the computer guy and in charge of all things electrical. He looked to be in his mid-thirties, and was the most likely to kid around and keep things light.

Travis and Tom were both college students who spent their summers working for FDR. Travis, red-haired and generously freckled by the summer sun, was a bodybuilder and not at all shy about displaying his strength, especially in front of Maddy. Tom, a bit shorter than Travis, was dark complected with brown hair, and probably spent the same amount of time at the gym. He was the serious one of the bunch. Willy, the plumber, worked on select jobs for John. He was tall and lean, and always smiling.

"Can I get you guys anything else?" Maddy asked as they finished their meal. They declined with contented smiles, just as John came up the steps from the beach.

"Don't you all look relaxed?"

They did. Willy had his long limbs propped up on the newly sanded railing. Travis was tipped so far back in his chair, it was uncertain which way he'd land when he came down. Tom was sitting closest to Maddy, and Frank sat in the rocker grinning. John found himself unaccountably irritated by the whole scene.

"We are discussing important renovation details," Willy assured him with a grin, making no effort to adjust his rather unbusinesslike pose.

"Well, I hate to break up your meeting, boys, but we have to get back to work. Thank you for lunch, Maddy."

Maddy looked at him, a little surprised. Where was the guy who'd pegged her balcony with shells the day before? John met her gaze with a brief, professional smile, and turned to talk to Frank. With groans of protest, the others got to their feet and collected the remains of their lunches. John led the way back upstairs and they followed, smiling at Maddy and adding their thanks.

By quitting time, Maddy was thoroughly stiff. The day had warmed considerably, and though she'd covered herself with sunscreen, she knew that her arms and neck had taken another hit. She'd regret that later. Having finished the sanding, she finally sat down in her rocker and let the breeze lift the hair from her temples. Not long after she stopped her work, she heard the rumbling of feet descending her stairway into the kitchen. The men filed out onto the porch for a debriefing.

"Help yourself to iced tea or whatever. I can't move," Maddy groaned, vaguely remembering and momentarily dismissing her determination to be tough and relentless in her work pace.

The boys met her with a chorus of teasing concern and offers to get her a drink, a pillow or whatever else she might need.

Putting the back of her hand against her forehead she whimpered, "Why, I would so enjoy a cold drink."

Three grown men nearly fell over each other to meet the need. Frank watched with amusement, while John rolled his eyes.

"I'll never get another decent hour of work out of them. They'll be killing each other to wait on helpless Miss Maddy," he observed wryly.

Maddy dropped her arm and drawled, "I'm paying good money for your services, Mr. Fordham, and I do appreciate the attention to detail."

Travis was the first on the porch to offer Maddy a glass of tea. She accepted it gratefully, flashing him an altogether dazzling smile that almost kept John from commenting. He pulled his eyes away, turning his attention to Travis.

"Hey, Travis, there are two other thirsty people out here. One of us signs your paycheck."

"Willy's got you covered, John. Frank, you can expect Tom to wait on you." He looked back at Maddy and winked. "I won."

"I had no idea that restoring a house was going to be so much fun," Maddy replied with a contented yawn. She was too tired to do anything but enjoy sharing her porch with five interesting men, who for the moment were willing to do her bidding. How long could it last?

"It'll be fun, alright," John interrupted her pleasant, self-absorbed reverie. "We'll be short two of our crew tomorrow, so we could use your help tearing out the old carpeting upstairs." He smiled at her wickedly.

Maddy considered her contractor. He was not being nearly as charming as he'd been earlier in the week. "I think I'll leave you boys to the inside jobs," she decided. "Maybe I'll start stripping the shingles off the roof instead."

This brought a laugh from the others, and John shook his head with a smile. Maddy was ridiculously appealing, even when she was a mess.

He stood up and finished the last of his drink. "Thanks for the tea, Willy. Gentlemen, why don't we clear out so that Ms. Jacobs can rest?" He glanced her way and couldn't help but grin as she started to pull herself out of her chair. He extended a hand to help her up, but she waved him off.

"Oh, I'll be keeping up with you guys. A warm bath, and I'll be good to go," she braced herself on the table as her knees started to buckle beneath her.

"About that," Willy said. "You know you need a whole new water heater, right? I ordered one, and we're hoping it comes in sometime next week."

Maddy's countenance fell with an almost audible thud. *Next week!* She hadn't really expected it to be fixed so soon, but *next week?* She dropped back into her chair. She simply didn't have the energy to haul buckets of hot water through the house, which was her only hope for a warm bath. She wished she'd thought of that before she spent her last ounce of energy on the stupid rails.

John almost felt sorry for Maddy, she looked so forlorn. "We'll get it in as soon as possible," he assured her.

"Don't worry about me. I'll just go jump in the ocean," she replied with a grimace. "I'll see you guys tomorrow."

The men said their good-byes and began filing back through the kitchen. Tom was the last to leave, and he stopped and regarded Maddy.

"If you need a hot shower," he began.

Maddy looked up, surprised. Too tired to think better of it, she played along. "Just give me an address…"

Tom's look wasn't playful. "I can just hang out here and wait for you."

Maddy was spared responding to this suggestion by a call from the doorway. "Tom, got a minute?"

He turned with a shrug. "Later, Maddy," he said, and walked into the house.

Maddy sat back in her chair, convicted and irritated. Of course, John heard their conversation. Would he come out and reprimand her, too? She bristled when she heard the door open. Apparently, the answer was yes.

"Maddy?"

She turned to him with a bit of an attitude. "Yeah?"

"Tom shouldn't have started that conversation," John said carefully, "but you might want to," he hesitated, "just be a little careful."

Maddy was too tired to express the defiance she felt. "I think I can handle myself with these guys."

John was more bothered than he cared to admit, but he wasn't going to argue with his employer. "Okay, I'm heading out. I'll see you on Friday."

Maddy's defiance dissolved into concern. "You won't be back tomorrow?"

"I have a job up in Augusta," he said. "Travis and I will be there most of the day. We might get back tomorrow afternoon."

"Oh," Maddy replied. "I'll see you when you get back."

"See you then."

Otis stopped by a few minutes later while Maddy was still brooding. She thought about asking to use his shower, but apparently she'd behaved scandalously enough for one day. She sighed with frustration as she tried to muster a smile.

"Hey, Otis. How's it going?"

"Doin' good, Miss Maddy. How are you?"

"I'm tired."

"You look like you've put in a long day," he said gently.

"I have. And I just got scolded by my contractor."

"Scolded? Surely not by John?"

"I surely did," Maddy replied. "He says I need to be more careful around the crew."

"In what way?"

"I don't know. How I talk to them, I guess."

"Now, that's probably good advice."

Maddy rolled her eyes.

"Well, you hardly know them, and it's probably best to be a little cautious," Otis said, watching her scowl grow. "Now, don't get offended. I worry about you over here with a houseful of men." He shook his head. "I just don't want anyone harassing you."

"You can be sure John won't allow that," Maddy replied, half in frustration, half in she knew not what emotion.

"He seems a decent fellow," Otis conceded. "I guess he'll look out for you."

"And don't forget Burt," she reminded him. "Oh, I forgot Burt!" She'd shut him in the room off the kitchen during lunch and never let him out. She ran into the house.

"Oh, Burt, I'm so sorry!" she cried as he trotted off as quickly as his big form would allow. "How could I have forgotten my dog? Why didn't he bark?" She watched Burt meander down the beach, happy with his freedom.

"Oh, he'll be alright. He probably had a good long nap."

"I hope so."

"I won't keep you," Otis said. "You get yourself some rest tonight." Doing his characteristic wave over the shoulder, he called out, "See you tomorrow."

Maddy plopped down into the rocker and watched her dog start to chase a seagull and then think better of it. He ambled back up onto the porch a few minutes later and greeted her with his forgiving dog smile. Maddy scratched his ears and hugged his neck. "I'm so sorry, Burt. I'll never forget you again." She eased herself out of the chair and remembered the cold bath awaiting her.

"That should make Mr. Contractor happy," she mumbled as she slowly climbed the steps to her room.

Maddy awoke on Thursday morning with a vague feeling of discontent. The feeling of discomfort was much more acute, but at least she was getting used to that. She wandered out onto her balcony and considered the dark horizon that stretched out before her. The discontent slowly revealed its source, and she wondered if John was as bothered by their last interaction as she was.

He's probably used to all kinds of difficult homeowners, she decided. She was just one of many eccentric people he dealt with all the time. This observation did not comfort her at all.

She shivered. It was definitely chillier this morning, and it smelled like rain. She remembered John's prediction and wondered what rain did to a sunrise.

Maddy decided to spend the morning at the library, looking for resources on Victorian renovation. She marveled at the information available; there was one whole book on porches alone. *There's no excuse for being uninformed now.* She selected several volumes and a few magazines and sat down to read.

She was completely immersed in the complexities of the tripartite wall when she looked at her watch and realized it was noon. She couldn't believe how quickly three hours had sped by, and was glad to feel a little more knowledgeable about the job she was undertaking. She packed up and walked down the street to Theo's and ordered a sandwich.

While her food was being prepared, she looked around the small store at the many pictures on the walls. Some were framed newspaper articles; others were black and white photos of the lobster industry from decades earlier. Maddy scanned the display with interest, and the young man at the counter had to call her name twice when her order was ready. She thanked him and left with her meal, happy that even the lunch stop had been so enlightening.

Back at the house, the men were sitting on the porch, eating their lunches and planning the afternoon's work. Maddy greeted the crew and went in to set Burt free. The guys cleared a path for him so that he could head down to the beach.

"Don't you worry about him wandering off?" Travis asked.

"I guess I should," Maddy speculated. "He's just always been so good about sticking close to me. I've never really worried about having him on a leash unless there are people around, and then it's just for show." She shrugged. "He tends to stay pretty close to the house unless I'm with him and he comes when I call him. If he's upset enough not to, then no leash could hold him back anyway."

Willy shuddered dramatically. "I hope I never upset your dog."

"I hope you don't, either," Maddy grinned.

Moments later, Burt strolled up, and Frank bravely stepped forward to scratch his ears.

"See, he's not so scary," Maddy said, impressed. "I don't think John cares for him much."

"I'm not surprised," Frank answered. "He had a run-in with a dog at a house he was restoring last summer. It was supposed to be empty," he added. "The dog didn't take kindly to John letting himself in."

There were groans around the porch, and Maddy grimaced. "I guess I'll have to stop teasing him." She walked her dog to the door and pushed him inside.

"Oh, don't stop teasing him," Frank replied. "Keeps him humble – it's good for him."

"Keeps who humble?" The object of their discussion came up the steps from the beach, and everyone but Frank looked guilty as John and Travis joined them. "Gotta be me, by the looks on your faces," he acknowledged.

Maddy immediately colored; she didn't know John well enough to read his face. Normally, she would have taken Frank's advice, but she had John's advice to consider as well. She held her tongue.

"Oops!" Frank answered remorselessly. "How are things up in Augusta?"

"Everything's on schedule," John answered, content to change the subject. "How did you do here?"

"The plaster's drying and we got some of the wallpaper stripped. We started on the carpet in room four, just to see how the floor looked. So far, it seems to be in decent shape."

"That's great," Maddy and John responded simultaneously.

Frank looked from one to the other of them, grinning speculatively. "Anyway, no surprises so far."

The men got back to work upstairs, and Maddy buried herself in finances, which eventually took her downtown to the bank. She didn't get home until after everyone had left for the day, and she immediately went upstairs, eager to see what they had accomplished. The walls were stripped and significant repairs made. Splotches of Spackle covered nail holes and other dents and cracks that were made in ways that she couldn't begin to imagine. Every spot had been sanded smooth and was ready for primer. She ran her hands over the walls and smiled. They were doing good work.

The carpet had been removed from the four bedrooms, and she was glad to see that it was out of the house altogether. Someone must have hauled it to the dump because she hadn't seen any evidence of it outside, either. She looked at the floors and agreed with Frank; the damage underneath was minimal. There were still a lot of nails around the periphery that needed to be removed, but the floor looked salvageable.

She thought of the moment that John and she had responded identically, and smiled.

four

When John arrived the next morning just ahead of the others, Maddy was ready for him. She met him at the door with, "Good morning, John. We need to talk." She looked up at him expectantly, conciliatory coffee cup extended.

John took the cup and thanked her. "What's up?"

"Come out to the porch," she directed him. "I can think better out there."

John followed, and Maddy turned as the door *banged!* behind them. Looking up into his eyes, she lost a little steam, but pressed on.

"I'm sorry I reacted negatively to your warning the other day."

"Maddy," John began.

"No, please, I need to say this." She took a deep breath. "You made a good point; I know better than to feed that kind of interaction. It won't happen again."

John smiled and regarded her with interest. "Thank you."

"You're welcome." She smiled a little back.

"I'm sorry if I came on too strong with the advice."

Maddy rolled her eyes. "It's okay."

"I think we were both pretty tired."

"And irritable," Maddy added.

John nodded.

"Especially you," she qualified.

John's eyebrow went up. "Me?"

"Sure," Maddy answered. "The rest of us were having fun, but you were just," she paused, "not."

John gave her his 'look,' and Maddy studied her newly sanded railing.

"Maddy."

She looked back up at him, hands on her hips, determined to muster her elusive confidence.

"I just feel responsible for how they behave around you," John explained. "I don't want them encouraged to take any more liberties than they're inclined to take already."

"Wow. That was unnecessarily complicated. Why don't you just say 'don't flirt with the crew'?"

"Don't flirt with my crew, Ms. Jacobs."

"Don't tell me what to do, Mr. Fordham."

John locked eyes with her and then grinned. "Look, I basically trust these guys, and appreciate their work, but I can't guarantee that they'll always…"

"Always what?"

"Well, behave," he finished, for lack of a better word. He'd talked to his guys in the past about boundaries, but it had never been a serious issue.

Maddy gave him a coy little smile. It didn't help him remember his point. "Maddy, these guys can get sidetracked." He paused, but she simply waited, so he continued. "The first day, it was kind of funny, how they tried to get your attention, or made some excuse to talk to you or be around you."

"They did?"

"Oh, please." John sighed. "Travis walked through the porch at least four times on the way to his truck, which was parked, as you know, on the other side of the house."

Maddy laughed. "I guess I was into my railing," she said, "I didn't notice." She turned as Burt began to whine and wag his tail, indicating that someone else had arrived. She looked back up at John with a smile that he'd missed the day before. "I'll be good," she promised, and left to go greet the others.

Maddy spent the morning at the library again, and checked in with the crew when she got home after lunch. They were in the former hole-room, or more accurately, in the hole-room closet, admiring their handiwork from the other side, and discussing some additional repairs that were needed. Maddy looked at the bedroom, now primed, the floor clear of all carpeting evidence.

She was very pleased as she crossed the room to join the men. "Party in here?"

Frank started dancing, and John shook his head as they walked back into the room.

"This looks great," Maddy said.

"It's coming along," John acknowledged. "The floors will need a lot of work, but we'll get there."

"Well, I'll let you finish up," she replied. "Lemonade's out downstairs."

She slipped out and went across the hall to the next bedroom. Here, too, the floor was relatively bare, but the walls had not yet been primed. The two others were the same. She could hardly be disappointed; she had no idea how long this phase took.

Maddy changed into shorts, and then ran into John in the hallway as she emerged from her room. She looked up at him, momentarily unable to think of anything to say.

"Have you got a few minutes?" Apparently John didn't share her impairment.

"Let's see ..." Maddy consulted her busy mental calendar. "Yep, I've got the whole afternoon free. What's up?"

"I need to touch base with Willie, but then I'll need your input on a few things."

"I'll meet you on the porch; I have a date with the rain."

Maddy called her dog and went outside to put her feet up. Settling herself in her rocker, she watched and listened to the rain fall over the water. It was wonderfully soothing, and she leaned her head back and closed her eyes.

A short time later, John came out to the porch, where Maddy was sitting in the rocker with her feet propped on the railing – asleep. He checked his advance, smiling as he looked down at her peaceful face, her hands folded in her lap. He glanced at Burt, who was also napping, but somehow managed a brief wag of his tail between gentle snores.

John took advantage of his unusual opportunity to study the features of his new employer. Her face was nicely proportioned. Her eyebrows, which could form an excellent scowl when necessary, were relaxed and framed her eyes well. Her nose, although a little sunburned, was otherwise unremarkable, which, as noses go, was probably a good thing. Her lips were very nice, he thought, especially when she smiled. A few strands of her wavy, sun-streaked hair blew gently around her face as she rested.

Pretty and peaceful as she was, John thought he'd enjoy the privilege of looking into those lively eyes while her smile was fully engaged. She was, without a doubt, one of the most animated women he'd ever met. She displayed her changing moods very effectively. *But when she smiles...*

John looked out over the water. The falling rain was very soothing; Maddy had picked a great spot for a nap, whether or not she intended to take one. Venturing another look at her, he tried to guess her age. Late twenties, he guessed. She had to be at least that old to have worked long enough to be able to afford the porch on which she was now napping. She didn't seem like the type that had grown up with a lot of money.

She turned slightly and John took a step back. He walked quietly to the door, opened it, and then let it *bang!* Maddy-style. This had the desired effect of making her jump and wake abruptly.

"Hey there," he said, a little too loudly. "Enjoying your date with the rain?" He walked over and pulled a chair out from the table. "We need to talk about your roof. Are you up for that?" Opening a folder, he began pulling out some information and brochures and laid them on the table.

"Sounds pretty serious," Maddy said, trying to stifle a yawn. "What's to discuss?"

She watched as John ran his fingers through his hair while he contemplated how to broach this terribly serious subject with her. She was distracted by the curls and colors. Was that a little bit of silver mixed in with the sandy brown near his temple? *How old is he?*

"We can go with twenty, thirty, or even forty-year shingles."

"What? Really? I'd say forty," she answered more quickly than either of them expected. "I think thirty's too young, or whatever …" She burst out laughing at John's expression.

"Thirty is too young?"

Maddy continued to laugh. "I'm sorry, my mind was wandering." She eased her body out of the rocking chair, still feeling a little stiff from her workout earlier in the week. She walked over to the table. "Okay, tell me all about your shingles."

This unusual invitation provoked another giggle as she fell into the chair next to him.

John continued to regard her display in puzzled silence, which, of course, only made Maddy laugh more.

"I'm so sorry, I don't know if I can do this right now." She pulled her chair up and tried to look at his pictures, but kept erupting in giggles, making it very hard for either one of them to concentrate.

"I had no idea that picking out roofing materials could be so funny," John observed.

"Neither did I. Didn't I tell you that renovating was going to be fun?" She smiled up at him, and he couldn't help but meet her grin.

"It's definitely more fun with you than with most people," he conceded.

Maddy's eyes cleared a little and she gave him her most unaffected smile yet. John met her gaze and completely lost his train of thought. Maddy tilted her head, and then patted his hand.

"So how do I pick my shingle age?"

John cleared his throat. "It depends on when you want to do all of this again."

"Probably never. Let's go with the forty-year-olds and see if they outlive me," she said playfully.

"Not likely, for a number of reasons; the biggest one being the toll taken by your proximity to the ocean. So, while you'd like them to last until your eightieth birthday, it probably won't happen."

Maddy slapped his arm. "So you think I'm forty! Do I look that old?" She started to get up from her chair, and immediately buckled back into it.

"Well," he answered slowly.

She gave him one of her very best scowls. "Nowhere near, for your information."

He grinned at her. "I'm just kidding, but you could set the record straight, if you like."

"No," she held up a hand and turned her head. "If you want to think I'm old like you, go right ahead." She continued to look out over the water, but the smile that spread across her face was evident in profile.

"Touché," he said. "Maybe we'd better get back to the shingles. The forty-year shingles are the best, but they're expensive. I can get you a deal on the thirties, and I'm inclined to go with those," he explained. "They're on sale at Builders' Supply, which is why I thought I'd look into it now. I don't plan to do the roof until August, when I can be relatively sure of a dry spell."

"Thirty is perfect," she smiled at him, "in so many ways."

"I'm glad you approve. They sound a little young, but they'll probably do just fine."

Maddy laughed and asked, "So what else do I have to decide?"

"Well, now that we're working with the thirty-year group, we can look at the colors."

"Colors?"

John pushed the paperwork in front of her. "They look pretty bland here, but it makes a difference when you see them on your roof. You can go to the store and see some of them displayed on their sheds. It helps to visualize what your roof will look like."

Maddy looked down at the endless variations of rusty brown and gray shingles. "I can't imagine how I would choose," she said. "Do you have any recommendations?"

"I'd suggest either the pewter gray or charcoal, or maybe even the slate blend," John pulled out another sample page and pointed out the color. "I think you had mentioned going with a white exterior?" he asked, and Maddy nodded. "Then I think those colors would be your best bet. The sale runs through next Saturday, so if you could take a look at them sometime during the week, that would help."

"I'll drive out this afternoon," she offered.

He looked through the papers again, and pulled out another

sheet. "While you're there, check out the two different styles – traditional three-tab and architectural, and see what you think."

"I had no idea this would be so complicated," Maddy replied. "I can't imagine really caring one way or another. No offense," she quickly added. "I appreciate all that you're doing."

"Don't worry about me; I'm just letting you know your options. Some people feel strongly about these things, and I have to give them the opportunity to share their input. It's your money," he shrugged and sat back in his chair.

"Do you like either one of these better than the other?" Maddy looked at the pictures and tried to visualize the different styles on her roof. She wasn't sure which one best fit the character of the house.

"I would lean toward the architectural style," he offered. "There's a little more texture to it, and I think it's more interesting."

"Well, we don't want a boring roof."

"That would be unfortunate," John agreed soberly.

They looked at each other for a moment, and smiled.

In her former life, weekends were for traveling, so on Saturday morning Maddy decided to take off and explore. Awaking to another beautiful sunrise, she figured it would be a good day to see the coast. She also knew it would be a good day to work on her rails since the weather was dry, but that option just didn't have the same appeal. Aware of the fact that her house would not be filled with people working on a Saturday, she felt not relieved but a little lonely. It was time for a road trip.

She decided to head south, driving along the coast as much as possible, and visit every antique store and souvenir shop along the way. She mapped out a route and then packed a few things, figuring she'd spend the night somewhere and come back Sunday evening.

As she started to back out of the driveway, she looked in her rearview mirror and saw that John was pulling in. She got out to greet him, not particularly disappointed about the delay, but wishing she'd at least put some lipstick on before getting in the car with her dog.

John waved as he pulled to the side of her drive, and Maddy realized that Blake and Parker were in the truck with him. She decided to get Burt so they could have a full-out reunion.

"Hey, Dad! It's the ugly green house!" Parker yelled, running toward Maddy. Blake came up alongside his brother, and they both reached up to pet Burt.

Blake remembered his manners first. "Hi Miss Maddy. I like your house."

"Thank you," she answered, wondering if he felt compelled to make up for his brother's candid observation.

John came up behind Parker and whispered in his ear.

"But it is!" Parker said earnestly. He looked up into his dad's eyes, sighed and turned to Maddy. "I'm sorry I said your house is ugly."

"It's okay, Parker. Anyone can see it's ugly." She smiled and shrugged. "That's why I have your dad."

John grinned. "Sorry to stop by without a heads-up. I need to check out how much cement you have in your shed before we go to the hardware store this morning. I want to be ready to repoint your porch and fireplace when we get around to that job."

"Oh," Maddy replied, trying to remember what 'repointing' meant. "You don't have to apologize for coming over here. You're welcome any time."

"We were going to be spies," Parker told her. "I was going to jump out of the truck and run behind the bushes!"

"Wow, that sounds like fun," Maddy said. "I'm sorry I ruined it by being here to catch you."

John looked over at her car. "Are you leaving? We don't want to keep you."

"I'm in no hurry," Maddy replied. "Do you guys want to come inside for coffee or juice, or something?"

"Yeah, Dad, let's go inside!" Parker jumped at the invitation.

"I'd really like to see her house," added Blake.

Maddy smiled and watched John be a dad.

"Hang on, guys," he said. "Remember how we weren't going

to disturb Miss Maddy?" He looked down into their disappointed faces, and then over to Maddy, who raised an eyebrow expectantly.

"Okay, we'll stay for a few minutes."

Parker jumped and squealed in response, and immediately ran up to the porch, Blake in tow.

They walked through the lower floor, the boys enjoying the sound of their echoing voices in the empty house. Making their way upstairs, they found themselves, finally, in the hole-room. John tried to point out the work that had been done to repair the wall, but the boys were more interested in the closet.

"This isn't even the best part," Maddy insisted, grinning at John, who returned a puzzled smile. Satisfied that he would be surprised by her revelation, she got down on her hands and knees, and gestured at the boys to follow.

"There's a secret panel under this shelf," she said, sliding it back with some effort. She squeezed through to a tiny room beyond, and the boys followed. Maddy had found it several days after she moved in, only because she'd had trouble removing a box that had been lodged in the space in front of the "door." She hadn't yet gone in herself and momentarily regretted the urge to squeeze through the tiny portal.

"This is so cool!" exclaimed Blake, showing as much emotion as she'd seen from him.

Parker walked around the periphery and hollered, "Dad, come in here! You gotta see this!"

"Sorry guys, I don't fit," John replied with some chagrin. He crouched down to peek in, but his shoulders wouldn't allow him any further into their hideout.

Maddy smiled. "This is where we can come and have secret meetings without your dad."

"Yeah!" Parker agreed.

John pulled back from the hole, noting the relationship developing between Maddy and his sons, and really wishing he could get into that room.

"You go ahead and have your secret meetings," he called out. "But just remember what a good spy I am."

Maddy laughed. "Okay, let's go and join your dad before he

gets too lonely."

"Oh, man," Parker sighed.

John helped his boys to their feet, smiling as Maddy wriggled out after them. She ended up flat on her back, looking up at him.

"Need help?"

"This wasn't the graceful exit I had planned," she replied, turning and pulling through. "Okay, so maybe that spot isn't made for me, but I still think it's really cool, don't you guys?"

The boys agreed wholeheartedly as they went back downstairs. Blake and Parker were fairly anxious to explore, so John took them out to the beach while Maddy made coffee. She heard his cellphone as he walked onto the porch, and he came back a few minutes later, looking rather pleased with himself.

"Your water heater is in at the hardware store," he announced. "They'll even deliver it today if we want them to."

"That's great!" Maddy answered.

"I can get Frank to come over and help me install it."

"I don't want you to have to work today," Maddy protested. "Can they just leave it in the shed?"

"It would be good to get it in place before the rain comes," John replied. Noting her look of concern, he added, "We're used to deliveries at unusual times. We take things when we can get them."

"Well, I'll stay and help."

John grinned. "You're going to help move the water heater into the cellar?"

Maddy smiled back. "Maybe."

Frank was available to come over and help out, so Maddy entertained the boys while the men opened the bulkhead and cleared a path for her new appliance. By mid-afternoon, the heater was delivered and installed, and except for a faulty thermostat, ready for use. Willie would be able to fix it first thing Monday morning, John assured Maddy over a late lunch.

"So what do you guys think of my house, now that you've had the tour?" she asked the boys.

"It's awesome!" Parker answered enthusiastically.

"It's really, really big," Blake observed.

"Yes, it is," Maddy agreed. "Your dad's working hard to fix it up for me." She smiled at John, and he raised his glass of lemonade in response.

"Yeah, my dad works really hard," Blake replied proudly.

Maddy nodded. "So, what are you doing this afternoon?"

"We're going to look for a baseball glove," Blake said happily.

"Yeah, and go to the park!" Parker added, amping up the excitement level.

"Yeah, and mow the lawn!" John mimicked his son's enthusiasm.

Maddy laughed. "Sounds like fun."

They continued to talk about the day ahead, eventually agreeing that the day ahead was getting behind them. They said their good-byes, and Maddy waved as they left, happy with the turn her Saturday morning had taken.

five

Maddy heard the rain Monday morning before she even attempted to get out of bed. It was very soothing, and she was happy to be lulled back to sleep. When her "emergency" alarm went off at 7:45, she woke with a start. She got dressed and went down to the kitchen and greeted her dog.

"I'm afraid we can't go for a W-A-L-K this morning, what with the rain."

Burt looked at her and wagged his tail furiously.

"Not this morning." Maddy stroked his head and shook her own at his puppy-like excitement. "You can go out, but you're on your own," she said, opening the door.

Burt looked out of the door and whined.

"You've got to be kidding. There's no way I'm going out there with you."

He looked up at her and wagged some more.

"You are one strange dog," she muttered as she closed the door and went over to get her coffee ready.

John stood looking out over the beach through the rain, wondering where Maddy could possibly have gone. She was obviously home from her trip; apart from her car in the drive, the coffee was fresh and the cream was still out on the counter. He looked at the hook where Burt's leash hung. She hadn't planned on walking the dog, which didn't surprise him. The fact that her absence bothered him so much was unsettling.

The others didn't seem terribly concerned. Frank enjoyed watching John worry, but suggested they get to work. "She'll show up, and I'm sure she'll check in with us when she does."

"How's that water heater coming?" Travis asked Willy. "She's gonna need to warm up when she gets back, if she's out in this rain."

"I picked up the thermostat this morning," Willy answered. "I'll take care of it first thing."

None of the men heard Maddy's sloshy arrival about ten minutes later. Willy was the first to discover her when he emerged from the basement. She was huddled over the sink drinking coffee, and she looked up with a rueful smile.

"Remember what Travis said about my dog wandering off?" Her gaze fell on the offending creature and her smile became a glare. Burt, oblivious, panted happily on his mat in the corner.

"He took off this morning after something – I still don't know what – and I was stupid enough to chase him." She shuddered again. "I don't suppose…"

"All set," he said. "You should have hot running water now."

Maddy all but hugged him, she was so happy. Then her smile faded. "Are the others…?"

"Conveniently working in your room on the book cases," he finished with a grin. "At least two of them are," he qualified. "Want me to go and chase them out so you can try your most recent re-novation?"

"I hate to do that," she answered, her teeth chattering.

"That's why I'm going to do it for you," he bowed chivalrous-ly. "Sit down and catch your breath, and I'll see if I can steer them in another direction."

"Thank you," she whispered.

It wasn't long before just one set of footsteps sounded down the stairs. Hoping Willy was returning with good news, Maddy blew her nose and looked up.

John came through the door and stopped in his tracks. Maddy was drowning in an oversized, dripping sweatshirt, and her wet hair was pasted to her head. Pale and shivering, she'd never looked so awful, and all John could think about was holding her and warming her up.

Instead, he wrinkled his nose at the smell of wet dog in the room. "I hope that's not you."

Maddy focused her limited energy on a rather potent scowl.

John grinned and walked over to her anyway. "What were you doing out there?"

"You don't want to know," she replied with a side-long look at her pet.

"You need to get out of those clothes," John said. He immediately looked embarrassed and Maddy couldn't help but smile. Then she sneezed.

"I'm sorry. You know what I mean," John continued. "You're going to get sick. It's chilly out there this morning."

"Yeah, I noticed that," she said with another sneeze. "Do you actually get summer here in Maine?" she whimpered.

"Eventually," he smiled, relaxing. *Poor baby.*

"How's it looking for getting into my bathroom?" she asked. "I don't want to interrupt your project..." She hated herself for begging, but she really felt miserable.

"Frank's just cutting some wood, and then we're going to work on the shelving in the other rooms."

They heard more footsteps coming down the steps and the rest of the gang joined them. Everyone had a good laugh at Maddy's expense, and then assured her that her room was clear.

"You're going to take the dog, right?" Travis asked, holding his hand over his nose.

"I'm so sorry, he's not allowed upstairs," Maddy said with absolutely no regret, and disappeared up the steps.

She reappeared half an hour later and found the men working in the hole-room. She was about to thank them when John spoke.

"You don't look so good," he said, getting to his feet.

Maddy preferred to misunderstand him for the sake of the audience. "Aren't you just so charming?" she sniffled.

"I'm glad you think so." He turned her gently and walked her back down the hall. "You need to get some rest."

"I'm perfectly able to decide when I need a nap. I never sleep during the day," she added, trying to be irritated with him for being bossy.

He ushered her into her room. "Yeah, I noticed that Friday afternoon."

"Oh, well," she hesitated, "that wasn't typical."

"Neither is this," he said. "I'm not trying to tell you what to do, but if you want to rest, we can keep busy downstairs." He stood in the doorway, more or less blocking her exit.

She put her hands on her hips and looked crossly at him, but didn't reply. Truth was, she wanted more than anything to climb back into her big warm bed. *Why am I so tired? Why am I arguing?*

"Do you have any chicken noodle soup?" he asked, switching tactics.

"I'm sorry?" She was trying to figure out a way to win the argument and still end up in her bed. *What is he saying about chickens?*

"I was just thinking that you might have some canned soup or something that I could warm up for you." It seemed like a good idea until he verbalized it – twice.

"I think I do, but I can heat up my own soup. I'm not paying you to be my nursemaid." At the look on his face, Maddy decided to make an effort to be civil. "I'm sorry, John. You're right. I need to get some rest before I become really evil. I'll eat a little bit later, okay?" She looked away toward the window. "I'll be asleep in no time with this rain."

She glanced back up at him, and John finally smiled. She grinned back with glassy eyes and a red nose, and it was his turn to look away. He tried to contemplate the rain but could only think about his overwhelming desire to take care of her.

"We'll probably work in the dining room," he said. "Stripping the woodwork will take at least a week. There's no quick way to get around those edges and preserve the lines. Will you mind the mess if we start that project?"

"Not at all. I rarely go in there, so have at it." She started to pull back her covers and then stopped.

John took the hint and put his hand on the doorknob. "Right, well, we'll sand quietly. I hope you get some rest." He glanced briefly at her and then closed the door quietly behind him.

Maddy snuggled under her goose-down comforter, wondering only momentarily why it felt so good in the middle of June.

She awoke much later to a light tap on her door. It took her a minute to figure out why she was in her bed in the middle of the day, but then her head began to throb and she remembered. The tap came again.

"Come in!" She wondered briefly how she looked; she sure didn't feel any better.

The door opened and Frank peered inside. "Sorry to bother you," he began. "I just wanted to let you know that we're finished for the day. Do you need anything before we go?"

"No, thanks for asking," she replied, slowly waking up. *What time is it? Where's John?* "I'm okay, really," she continued with a little more clarity. "I just need to take care of my dog." She started to maneuver out from under her covers.

"Believe it or not, John took him for a walk when it stopped raining a little while ago," Frank said. "He didn't look too happy about it, but Burt was thrilled."

"That was brave of him," Maddy replied, surprised. She pulled her feet back up under the covers. If Burt was okay, she had a few more minutes to rest. "If he's still here, please thank him for me."

Frank hesitated. "Do you want me to send him up?"

Yes! No! Maddy's face regained some of the color it had lost during the day. "That's not necessary. I'll see you all tomorrow."

"Okay, take care," he said, closing the door as he left.

Maddy listened to the faint sounds of the men talking and cleaning up downstairs. After a few minutes, she heard a final slam, and then all was quiet. Not for the first time, her house seemed very lonely.

⊂⊃

Maddy slept through the sunrise Tuesday morning, but managed to be up, dressed and ready to greet the crew at eight. They unanimously voted that she should go back to bed.

"Hey, Maddy, you look pretty grim. Rough night?"

"I'm sorry you didn't sleep better."

"I hate it when my face blows up with a cold like that."

And her favorite: "I think you looked better yesterday."

John was the only one who wisely held his tongue, but the look on his face made her almost as mad.

"Wow, thanks guys. And good morning to all of you, too."

The follow-up apologies fell on plugged-up ears. She turned on her heel. "I'll be in my room."

She marched up the stairs, simply unable to appreciate any concern they might have genuinely felt. Much as she hated to admit it, her vanity had taken a serious hit. No woman, sharing a room with five good-looking men, wants to hear talk of her looking tired, or *grim*, of all things, however kindly motivated the comments.

She walked into her room, and a well-timed moment of restraint kept her from slamming the door. She climbed back into her bed, wishing she'd at least brought her coffee when she'd stomped out of the kitchen. No matter what they said, she wasn't tired, and if she was being sent to her room, she at least wanted something to drink while she read a book. She sighed with frustration. There would be no dignity in revisiting the kitchen; she'd just have to do without. She picked up her book and leafed through it.

Hearing footsteps, she stopped and listened. Would they work upstairs today? She looked at the bookshelves they had started overhauling the day before. It probably drove them crazy to have to stop in the middle of a project.

A knock on the door made her jump.

"Come in," she grumbled.

The door slowly opened, and John stepped in. Maddy crossed her arms and rolled her eyes, and then realized that he was holding her coffee. *How sweet is that?* To her dismay, she began to tear up and squeezed her eyes shut. The fact that she teared easily was a constant nuisance. The last thing she wanted was for John to think she was over-emotional.

"Are you alright, Maddy? Can I get you anything?"

His attention was at once endearing and unsettling. Remembering how she'd treated him the day before, Maddy tried to be polite.

"Just my coffee," she said with a weak smile. "I was really wishing I'd brought it up, but I wasn't about to go back for it."

John smiled, relieved, and set her mug on the bedside table, which was considerably lower than the bed. He processed this, looking between the two, and said, "We're going to have to do something about that."

"Oh, I know I need new furniture for this room," Maddy acknowledged. "This is all mismatched."

"Eclectic is the popular term for it," John reminded her as he turned to rummage through the wood that had been cut the day before.

He grabbed a few like-size, small boards, and stacked them neatly on the table, raising her coffee cup a good six inches. Maddy looked on, bemused. Not yet satisfied, John pulled out a few more pieces and adjusted her new table until her cup was easily within reach. Maddy shook her head and smiled at him.

"I'll bring lunch up later," he said decisively. "Try to get some rest."

With that, he left the room, and Maddy was left without opportunity for reply as she stared at the closed door.

When John returned with lunch, he didn't stay long. After knocking lightly, he delivered a chicken salad sandwich and a water bottle, and asked if she needed anything else.

"This is perfect. Thank you, John."

He seemed a little embarrassed. "You're welcome." After a brief pause, he said, "We're making good progress in the dining room. I think you'll be pleased with the wood we're uncovering."

"I can't wait to see it."

"Well, wait a little longer," he said with a slow smile.

"I will," Maddy promised, feeling her face warm up. She probably looked feverish as she added, "But I'm feeling better, much better than this morning."

"I'm glad to hear it," John answered, walking back to the door. "I'll check in before I leave this afternoon."

Maddy felt so much better Wednesday, that she started washing the kitchen windows. The additional light that streamed in through the clean glass was remarkable, and very motivating. She tired of that job fairly quickly, however, and decided to spend a quiet afternoon at the library doing more research.

After flipping through a book on window treatments – the curtain layering was shockingly complicated – Maddy decided that she really wasn't into research. She wanted to be outside in the sunshine, so she packed up and walked downtown.

It was a beautiful afternoon, and she enjoyed seeing the town come alive with vacationers and summer people. She smiled at the thought that she'd be considered a "townie." She hardly knew the small village.

Happy to be doing a different kind of research, Maddy wandered into a little antique shop. Within minutes, she found a handsome desk that would fit perfectly in the alcove of the room off her kitchen. She tried not to appear too anxious as she approached the clerk.

"We just got that piece in and my husband hasn't priced it yet," the woman said, coming around to get a closer look at the desk. "I'll give him a call."

Maddy walked toward the back of the shop to give the clerk some privacy.

"I don't know why you didn't price that desk. I knew it would move fast," the woman said irritably into the phone. "There's a lady here who wants to buy it – one of those summer people," she guessed, eyeing Maddy through the aisles.

Maddy turned away with a smile. *I guess I'm not a townie yet.* She walked slowly around the store and returned when the woman finished berating her husband.

"We'd like a hundred-fifty for it," she said, looking ready for a fight.

"That sounds fair," Maddy replied. "I think it will fit in my car, so I'd like to take it now."

The woman's face softened a little. "That's fine," she said. "How would you like to pay for that?"

"I'd like to pay with a check, if that's okay."

"I'm sorry, we only take local checks."

Maddy smiled. "That's the only kind I have."

The woman, surprised, slowly smiled back. "Welcome to town, Ms.," she glanced at the check, "Ms. Jacobs. I hope you enjoy your desk."

Maddy made one more stop and then hurried home. The men were leaving as she pulled in, and she backed out into the street to make room for the exodus. John's truck didn't move, so she parked next to him.

He got out to check in with her. He thought she looked a little flushed. "Hey. How are you feeling?"

"I'm fine, thanks. Here, I bought you something." She handed him a bag before she could change her mind.

Pleased and puzzled, he took it from her. "What's this?"

"Just a little 'thank you' for taking care of me," she replied.

John pulled a stainless-steel coffee mug out of the bag. "This is perfect," he said, removing and replacing the cover and then linking the cup on his belt loop with a clip on its side. He was like a little kid playing with a new toy. "Thank you, Maddy."

He pulled out some chocolate-covered espresso beans. "I love these." He tucked them inside the cup. "You didn't have to get me anything," he said, apparently pleased that she did.

"Well, you didn't have to take care of me while you were fixing my house," Maddy reminded him.

"It was my pleasure."

Otis came on the scene a moment later. "Hey there, neighbor!" he called out. "How are you feeling?"

Maddy smiled. She had never gotten so much attention over a cold in her life. "Much better. Thanks for asking."

"Hello, Otis," John greeted him and shook his hand. "I'll let you two catch up. Maddy, I'm going to be in Augusta again tomorrow, but I'll be back here on Friday."

"Oh, okay." She cleared her throat. "What will the others be doing?"

"They're going to work on the fenced area for Burt."

"I didn't realize you were ready to start that project."

"I picked up the fencing today," John explained. "It should go up pretty easily."

"That's good," Maddy replied, wanting to prolong the discussion about the dog fence, but not sure what else could be said.

"Of course, it'll come down pretty easily, too, if Burt decides to walk through it," John finished with a grin.

"I don't think he will," she smiled, "but it'll be interesting to see how he adjusts."

"Yes, it will."

"So, I'll see you Friday?"

"See you Friday." He nodded at Otis and got into his truck.

Maddy looked back at her neighbor. "How about some lemonade?" she asked, linking her arm in his as they walked up the steps to the house.

Thursday morning dawned and Maddy contemplated what to do with her day. *John won't be here*, she remembered with something bordering on dissatisfaction. *What's so important up in Augusta?* She got up and played hostess for the rest of the crew, and then got to work on the windows. The men continued the tedious job of stripping the wood in the dining room.

The afternoon was spent installing Burt's "play area" on the side of the house, an endeavor that was not fully appreciated by the intended recipient. Upon its completion, Maddy invited Burt inside, and he followed her willingly enough, sniffing the familiar bushes and trees and then looking inquiringly at her. When Maddy attempted to leave, he followed, and it took significant effort to get him to stay within while she secured the gate. She couldn't help but feel sorry as he stood inside the fence and regarded her sadly.

"Walk away, Maddy," Travis suggested. "He'll be okay, and you can't give in every time he makes those big eyes at you."

Maddy scowled a little and then remembered that thanks were

in order. "You're right, Travis, and thank you for all of this. I'm sure my neighbors thank you, too." She looked at Burt, whispered a quick word of comfort, and then joined the men on the porch.

They left a short while later, and Maddy immediately returned to her dog, who had remained at the gate. She let him back into the house, where he reclaimed his mat in the corner of the kitchen and settled down with a sigh.

six

Maddy spent most of Friday doing errands, finishing her business at the bank just before five. Rounding the corner of her street, she was pleased to see the trucks still parked in her driveway. Otis was sweeping his porch, and waved as she pulled in.

"How's it going, Otis?" she called out.

He strolled over to chat with her. "More research today?"

Maddy nodded at the stack of books in her arms. "I can now tell you the difference between chintz and brocade. That's a big deal for me."

They walked into the house, and Maddy stopped to look at the progress in the dining room.

"Look at the difference," she marveled. "I mean, I know it's a mess, but look at what they've uncovered. Who would hide this?" She ran her fingers along the wood, intrigued by the detail.

"People do strange things," Otis replied. "Mostly, they don't want to take the time to care for the wood, so they paint over it. It's a shame," he shook his head. "So, do you have dishes to display in here?" He gestured at the glassed-in shelves along the wall. "Some of that colored glass would look mighty nice."

"I know. That's what I was envisioning, too. I'd love to find an old tea set and some vases..." She looked around the room.

"An art glass panel would be perfect in that window," Otis pointed out.

Maddy considered her neighbor. Did everyone know more about the Victorian era than she did?

"And what might that be?"

"It's like stained glass," Otis explained. "It may even be clear, but when the sun shines through, it sends rainbows around the room. You'd catch the morning sun beautifully in here."

"Sounds interesting," Maddy agreed. "I'm hoping to check the antique stores, or some yard and estate sales; see if I can get some bargains."

"There are a couple of sales going on tomorrow in town. Saturday's usually a big day for those," Otis said. "How about we go out shopping together?"

"I think I could probably use your help."

Things began to quiet down up above, and at least one pair of work boots made its way downstairs as Otis and Maddy walked into the kitchen. John came through the door and Maddy smiled in greeting.

"I'll head over early," Otis was saying, "and I'll bring some muffins. Afternoon, John," he said, walking out onto the porch with a wave.

Maddy pulled the iced tea out of the fridge and filled a glass for John. The day had warmed up, and he was flushed from the work and increased humidity. His hair curled at the sides of his temples, framing his face nicely. Maddy found something very interesting to look at on her stovetop.

"So what did you guys get done today?"

"Well, you saw the dining room, and the bookcases in your room are rebuilt and primed. They'll just need a coat of paint, which you could do this weekend if you like."

An interesting commotion in the stairwell drew Maddy's attention to the door, which burst open as Parker and Blake tumbled into the room.

"Hi, Miss Maddy!" Parker greeted her enthusiastically.

"Hello! What are you guys doing here?" Maddy got the lemonade and set out two more cups.

"Daddy picked us up early so we could come and see you and your big house. Then we're going out to eat!" Parker began racing around the kitchen with the car he'd brought along with him.

"Easy, there, buddy," John said, scooping him up as Parker lapped the room. "No running in Miss Maddy's house." He clamped his son onto his lap, and Parker giggled and wriggled to get free. John held him firmly and finished the explanation. "I hope you don't mind. I've been promising I'd bring them by all week." He smiled a little awkwardly over Parker's head.

"You guys are always welcome," she replied. "So, have you been painting, or what?"

"No, we were just upstairs with Uncle Frank," Blake answered.

"We showed him our secret hideout!" Parker exclaimed.

Maddy smiled at his sense of ownership. "I hope he doesn't try to go in there."

"We told him he wasn't allowed," Blake replied matter-of-factly.

"I see," Maddy nodded. "Oh, look who's back."

The boys immediately ran to open the door for Burt. He licked them in turn while they giggled and scratched his ears.

A few minutes later, after the rest of the crew had left, they re-grouped on the porch to enjoy their drinks and the evening breeze. The sun had come out again, sparkling on the water and on the various boats that were beginning their weekend excursions. The mood was very companionable as the four of them sat together, and Maddy had a feeling of contentment that she hadn't known in a long time. She didn't want the afternoon to end.

"This swing is awesome!" Parker exclaimed, intent on propelling it to greater heights than Blake was comfortable with.

"I'm glad you like it," Maddy replied. She'd never seen it move that way before.

"We're going out to eat tonight!" Parker reminded her. "Don't you want to come with us?" The swing was really going now, and John looked ready to grab it and keep it from launching over the railing onto the beach.

"Parker, ask Dad!" Blake whispered, holding on tightly.

John got up to slow the swing, and turned to look at Maddy. "We'd love to have you join us."

She returned his gaze thoughtfully. It might be smarter and safer to keep the relationship simple, but what was wrong with a little dinner, especially with two small children in the mix?

80C3

Maddy looked into her closet and contemplated what to wear on her "date" with John, Blake and Parker. She didn't want to get too dressed up, but she wanted a different look from the work clothes she'd worn all day, all week, and pretty much since she'd met John. Her Winnie the Pooh T-shirt would please Parker, she decided. Probably Blake would like to see her in a suit. What would John like? She pulled out her favorite black cocktail dress and smiled.

It would definitely make an impression, she thought as she held it up and looked in the mirror. Not long ago, she wore that kind of thing regularly. She couldn't deny that she'd enjoy seeing the look on John's face if she came down the steps in that dress. It was something she wore well. She hung it back up in her closet. Blake would most likely disapprove.

She finally decided on capris and one of her favorite summer blouses; not too fancy, but not too plain. A quick glance in the mirror revealed that the color had returned to her cheeks after her cold. She brushed through her hair and decided to leave it down.

Her dates were patiently waiting on the porch with Burt, and they turned around together when she walked through the door. Parker, not untypically, was the first to comment.

"You look pretty, Miss Maddy!" he said, running up to hug her. Surprised, she hugged him and tousled his hair.

"Thank you, handsome!" she responded. Parker giggled, and Blake smiled. "So, what's for supper?"

The restaurant was small and dimly lit, and boasted the best pizza in town. Maddy slid into a booth, and Parker climbed in next to her; John and Blake sitting opposite. Maddy took a deep breath and told herself to relax. She only jumped a little when John's knees knocked into hers.

"Sorry about that. Long legs."

"The booths are a little tight," she said as she shifted for him, "but from what I hear, the pizza's worth it." She smiled at Blake, who nodded.

"We come here a lot," he acknowledged with a shy smile, and

then looked down at the activities on his place mat.

"I want pepperoni, Dad," Parker announced as he began coloring with the crayons the waitress had given him.

"Excuse me?" John replied.

"Pepperoni," Parker said again, not looking up.

"Excuse me?" John put his menu down, and gave Parker his full attention.

"My dad can't hear so good," Parker explained, looking up briefly from his coloring.

Trying to hide her smile, Maddy watched the little family drama unfold.

"Dad wants you to say 'please,'" Blake explained. "You always forget."

"No, I don't!" Parker defended himself. "Don't I, Dad?"

John grinned at Maddy while he tried to untangle the negatives in his son's question. "You don't always forget, Parker, we just have to keep working on remembering."

"Okay, then I'll please have pepperoni, Dad."

"What do you like on your pizza, Miss Maddy?" Blake asked.

"Oh, I like lots of things," she answered thoughtfully. "Mostly, I like mushrooms."

Blake gave his dad a somber look and Parker gasped.

"My dad *hates* mushrooms!"

John shook his head and closed his menu. "This will never work," he said with an exaggerated frown. "Maybe Miss Maddy will have to sit at another table."

Maddy, momentarily taken aback, had no time to respond before Parker started packing up his crayons and announced, "I'll go with her!"

Maddy laughed and stopped him. "No, Parker, you're staying right here with me. Your dad and I are going to have to work this out together."

"Okay," Parker answered cheerfully.

Blake seemed to think about Maddy's answer, while his father looked pleased. Maddy regarded them both, and then leaning forward slightly, locked eyes with John. They were great eyes.

"You want to take this outside?"

John laughed, and Blake's surprised face relaxed. John then turned 'the look' on Maddy and leaned forward himself. "That won't be necessary. You can have whatever you want."

Maddy smiled and sat back, putting proper distance between them again. "What I really want is a Diet Coke. Maybe that won't be so controversial?"

"I'd like root beer, please," added Blake.

"Me too, me too!" Parker agreed, and then catching his dad's eye, said, "Me, too, Dad, please."

John signaled the waitress, who came over and took their order. The conversation continued comfortably as they awaited their food. Maddy asked what the boys had been up to during the week, and they were happy to fill her in on their summer activities. After the drinks arrived, the conversation centered on her and how she liked her new home.

"So far, I like it very much," Maddy told them. "I like my house, I like Clairmont, I like Maine, and I like my new friends." She lifted her glass of soda with a smile.

The boys enjoyed taking turns clinking cups with her, and then Blake asked her, "Do you miss your old friends?"

"Yes, I do, Blake. It's always hard to leave friends behind." After a moment, she added, "You know who I really miss right now?"

"Who?" Parker asked, wanting to be in on the conversation.

"I miss my mom," Maddy answered. "She's not quite so far away as my other friends, but for some reason, I miss her the most right now."

"My mom is gone, too," said Parker, still coloring.

Maddy looked up at John abruptly, apologizing with her eyes for having opened up this potentially difficult subject. "I'm so sorry," she said to Parker.

"It's okay," he replied. "She comes back sometimes."

Well, here's the story at last. Maddy could have kicked herself for inadvertently bringing it up.

"No, she doesn't, Parker." Blake looked solemnly at Maddy. "My mom left when I was five," he explained quietly. "She has some problems."

"Yeah, we pray for her," added Parker.

"That's a good idea," Maddy answered somewhat mechanically. She looked again at John, wondering how to save him the embarrassment of any further revelation.

His face reflected his concern about how his boys were processing this difficult situation. His expression, however, was frank as he explained. "It was a little over two years ago." He paused, then continued, "Blake's right. She had, *has*," he corrected himself, "some things to work through. And Parker's also right," he looked over at his son. "All we can do right now is pray for her."

Maddy was struck by how he seemed to be at peace with whatever he'd been through. "Well," she answered slowly, "I hope she, I hope you all…" she hesitated, not sure how to finish. Did she really hope they worked it all out? Whether she did or not, was it even fair to express that sentiment to the children?

"Thanks for the thought," John gently interrupted her, "but we are living very separate lives now, and," here he hesitated again, "that won't change. It's hard, but it's what's best."

The waitress walked up with the double-cheese pizza, and set it down on the table with some plates.

"I'll be back with more napkins," she gushed at John.

He nodded his appreciation and turned his attention back to the table. "Why don't you guys run to the bathroom and wash up?" he suggested. They quickly jumped down from the booth and made their way through the familiar restaurant.

John reached across the table and put his hand on Maddy's. "I'm sorry to share all of this personal information with you so suddenly. It's a lot to absorb at once."

Maddy nodded as she looked at him, unsure what to say. Somehow, in all of this revelation, John seemed more worried about her than himself. She focused on his hand covering hers. His story wasn't as hard for her to absorb as he thought. She wished it sounded unfamiliar.

"So," she finally ventured, "are *you* okay? I mean, you seem so composed about it all."

"It probably sounds strange, but I've found my peace with it." John paused. "It's complicated, of course, but we're okay." He looked up to see his boys running back to the table. He pulled his hand away and called out, "*Walk*, guys!"

"I think I'll go wash up, myself," Maddy said, sliding out of the booth. "Please, go ahead and start."

She walked across the room and looked back as she rounded the corner into the hallway. The Fordhams had their heads bowed. *Praying*, she thought to herself. *For their food? For their mom? Probably both*, she decided, and continued down the hall.

After dinner, they decided to go to Checker's Ice Cream Shop. Maddy listened to the boys' animated discussion of ice cream flavors, absorbing their excitement at the prospect of dessert. It occurred to her, and not for the first time, that it must really be fun to be a parent. At least some of the time. Most of it was a complete mystery to her.

They walked several blocks to the popular ice cream place and found long lines, which neither surprised nor deterred the Fordhams. The choice of flavors was unending, and Maddy listened dutifully to the advice of everyone in her party before ordering a hot fudge sundae with peanut butter cup ice cream. She tried to pay for dessert since John had paid for the pizza, but he shook his head.

"You can have us over for dinner sometime," he suggested.

"You have no idea what you're asking," she countered, tasting the hot fudge and whipped cream and closing her eyes to savor them.

John smiled and started on his own sundae, grabbing a handful of napkins for the road.

They took their treats to a park bench and sat down together. There was an awkward moment as they worked out who got to sit next to Maddy, but it was soon resolved. The privilege was granted to young men under the age of ten, and they squeezed on accordingly. The ice cream was wonderful, as promised, and this time as they ate, they talked about an upcoming vacation that John and his boys would be taking in New Hampshire. All in all, it was a wonderful evening, and everyone over the age of twenty-five was especially sorry to see it end.

CRRO

Late the next morning, as Maddy and Otis were on their way to yet another sale location, Maddy found herself increasingly distracted.

She felt happy, yet guarded about her developing relationship with the Fordham family. One minute she was anxious to see them again, and the next she was relieved to have a break from John. She could never think clearly when she was around him. Apparently she couldn't think clearly when she was away from him, either. She didn't know what she wanted, and it was wearing her out.

Otis, cheerful as always, continued to have high expectations for the morning. "Maybe we'll find a treasure here," he said hopefully, as they walked toward the garage.

"You've said that every time," Maddy said with a tired grin.

"Still possible," he answered as they started sorting through some dishes on a table. "Now, here's a piece," he said. "You see how there are no lines at all; it's just one smooth piece of blown glass."

Maddy studied the vase in Otis' hands. "It's beautiful," she agreed. "I wonder how much they want for it?"

"I'll find out," he offered, and shuffled out to the yard where the homeowners were chatting with shoppers.

Maddy sighed and wondered if the Fordham boys ever went to yard sales. She found herself looking up every time a new car pulled in.

She wandered to another table and picked up an interesting plate. John said he'd be ordering the shingles today. Would he need to ask her any questions about what she'd selected? Maybe she should have gone with the charcoal instead of the slate. She had an unreasonable urge to finish her antique shopping at the Builder's Supply store.

Otis returned. "They only want a dollar. I'd grab it."

They spent the next half hour picking out some of the more unique pieces on the table. Ten dollars later, Maddy had a boxful of pretty glassware to display in her dining room. Her mood began to lift, and she thanked Otis for his help.

"I know I haven't been great company this morning, but I'm really happy we found these. You have a good eye," she said, loading her treasures into the back seat of her car.

"I enjoy looking around, too," he answered. "Are you getting hungry?"

They drove downtown and bought some sandwiches from Theo's and sat on a bench in the park to eat. Down the street, lines formed at Checker's; not surprising for a Saturday afternoon. Maddy smiled when she thought about the seating arrangements on the bench the night before. John didn't have a chance.

"You do seem a little preoccupied today," Otis said, biting into his turkey and cheese. "You alright?"

"I'm fine, really. Maybe a little tired."

Otis nodded and worked on his sandwich.

Maddy hesitated a moment, then continued. "I went out for pizza with John and his boys last night."

"Well now, I bet that was fun."

"It was," Maddy admitted. "It was really fun. Those kids are wonderful, and John, well…"

Otis chuckled. "That didn't take long."

" 'That,' " Maddy replied emphatically, "has yet to be defined. But I'll be honest, I'm…" she searched for the word, "definitely intrigued. John can be very charming, and he's great with his kids, and he's funny, when he's not bossing me around my house," she quickly qualified. "I don't know; I really enjoy his company." She looked off in the distance. "When I moved here, I was determined not to get involved with anybody for a long time, maybe not ever." She stopped, lost in thought. "It didn't take long to bring down that wall of resolve."

"Kind of like Jericho," Otis observed with a smile.

"I'm sorry? Who?"

"Jericho. You know, Joshua and the children of Israel?"

Maddy vaguely remembered the Bible story from her childhood. "You'd better refresh my memory."

"The Children of Israel were entering the Promised Land, and Jericho was a big walled city that stood in their way. So, God told them to march around the city a whole bunch of times and the walls came tumbling down," Otis half sang the last part of his explanation. "There's a song that goes with it," he added with a grin.

"I think I remember," Maddy smiled at him. "I'm not sure that John's really doing any marching right now," she said thoughtfully. "At least not that he's aware of."

"He doesn't seem like the type to mess around with a woman's heart," Otis answered, patting her knee.

"I'm inclined to agree. Still…" She looked across the park at nothing in particular, then spoke with more confidence. "Anyway, the city hasn't been taken yet. I still have a few defenses."

"That's all well and good," Otis said, "but if the Lord means to take down those walls," he paused and looked at her, "they're comin' down." With that he stood up and took his empty cup to the nearby garbage can. Maddy followed and walked back to her car, deep in thought.

seven

Otis knocked on the door at nine the next morning. Maddy had been up since the sunrise, but hadn't planned on going anywhere. She looked at how Otis was dressed and, trying not to appear surprised, she invited him in.

"Oh, no, I won't come in right now. I'm going to run downtown. I just wanted to let you know that I'd be leaving for church in about forty-five minutes, if you'd like a ride," he offered.

Maddy considered this. Church meant seeing John, a confusing, but intriguing prospect. Struggling only briefly with this questionable motivation, she said, "Sure, Otis, I'll be ready in half an hour."

Otis left, and Maddy went upstairs to see how her wardrobe stretched to fit the church scene. She didn't have much of her professional wardrobe left, but she had a few skirts and summer dresses. She smiled as she passed the black dress, and then chose a simple white sundress. She took special care with her makeup and hair, too. So what if Otis teased her? It was alright *not* to look like one of the crew for a change, at least while she went to church.

John walked his kids into the sanctuary, involuntarily searching the room for Otis and his date. His eyes rested on a couple, mid-way up the church on the left-hand side. The back of Otis' balding head was unmistakable.

John ushered his boys into a pew several rows behind, finding it hard to take his eyes off Maddy's back. Her hair was pulled up in a clip, and the white straps of her sundress criss-crossed her nicely tanned shoulders.

"Hey, that's Miss Maddy!" Parker whispered in a voice the whole church could hear.

More heads than Maddy's turned in response, but hers was the only face John saw. She bestowed a dazzling smile on Parker, and waved discreetly at the three of them. She faced forward again a few seconds later, giving John the opportunity to put an end to what must have been an undignified stare. Maddy was wearing earrings and a touch of makeup, and although he had always liked her natural style, this other side of her had its appeal.

"Miss Maddy looks nice today, doesn't she?" Blake asked in a much more effective whisper.

"She sure does." John leaned over to make sure he had Parker's attention. "We'll talk to her *later*. Let's try to think about church now."

He opened his service folder and tried to get his head where it belonged. Pastor Rob interrupted his efforts with an invitation for the people to stand and greet one another. John stood and shook hands with the couple next to him, wondering if he could work his way up a few rows without making a scene.

Parker wasn't concerned about making a scene. He got down on the floor and slithered under the pews, army-man style, until he came up between Maddy and Otis. John was surrounded, so he could only look on in dismay as Maddy jumped back in surprise at Parker's indecorous arrival. Otis laughed and helped the boy to his feet. John watched with mixed alarm and envy as Maddy leaned down to say hello.

"Dad, do you see Parker?" Blake asked unnecessarily. "We'd better get him back."

"Let's go," John agreed, inwardly grinning at Parker's determination. He walked up to Maddy's row, Blake in tow.

"Good morning, Otis, Maddy, *Parker*."

"Hi, Dad!" Parker beamed, completely unaware of the possibility of having misbehaved.

Maddy extended her hand, first to Blake and then to John. "I see you guys prefer the conventional route."

John took her hand and returned her smile. "I was tempted, but the last time I tried it I got stuck."

Maddy laughed quietly, then noticed a deep scratch at the base of his thumb. "Oh, are you okay?"

John looked down at his hand, turning it slightly. "One of the perils of my trade," he acknowledged. "My present work site is particularly dangerous."

"You can say that again," Maddy replied, her eyes flickering away almost as soon as she met his gaze.

People were returning to their seats, so Maddy dropped John's hand and sat down, giving a small wave to the boys as their family went back to their pew.

Otis leaned over and whispered, "The idea is to greet more than one other person."

Flustered, Maddy tried to find her place in the service folder. "Maybe next time you could warn me that we're going to have a greeting free-for-all before the service starts."

"He doesn't always do it, so you never know," Otis said with a smile.

After worship, Maddy decided she might like a donut. "So, Otis," she said casually, "are you staying for coffee, or do you want to get home?"

"I'd love a cup, if you're not in a hurry to leave," he replied.

Facing the back of the sanctuary, Maddy noticed that the Fordham family was no longer in their pew. Most of the people were just starting to leave, and she was puzzled. *Had they left early?* The fellowship hour immediately lost its charm, and she suddenly remembered that she'd had quite a lot of coffee before church.

"Let's go on down," Otis interrupted her thoughts. "I'd like to introduce you to the pastor."

He took her hand as he had the first week, and Maddy found herself walking down to the fellowship hall, once again doubting if she had any real business there. *Great. Now I'm meeting the pastor. This is what she got for using church and coffee hour to indulge her juvenile boy-chasing.*

Entering the fellowship hall, Maddy found herself at once pleased and vexed. The Fordham family had not left the building; John was across the room, serving coffee. It looked as though several attractive women were having a hard time securing their own cups, and he was graciously helping them out. One of them was tall and too voluptuous for the church basement, Maddy decided. The other one was just too… blonde.

"Cafenova," Maddy muttered under her breath.

"I'm sorry?" Otis asked, searching the room for his pastor.

"Nothing."

The room was getting crowded, so Maddy had a few minutes to process her dissatisfaction with the scene before Blake and Parker discovered her. They grabbed her hands before she even realized that they were in front of her.

"Hi, Miss Maddy," Blake greeted her. "We're serving the donuts this morning. Come visit our table."

"We have jelly-filled!" Parker added excitedly.

The boys began pulling her across the room toward the coffee table. Maddy was trying to muster her aloof look for John when he caught her eye. A smile spread across his face, and the women with him turned to look at the object of his obvious pleasure. Their reaction to her wasn't nearly as warm.

Maddy smiled briefly in return, and soon found herself at the donut display. Accepting the rather full plate that Blake and Parker prepared for her, she turned as Otis came up behind her.

"Sorry I took off like that," she apologized. "I got swept away by these charming donut servers." Blake and Parker grinned in response.

"Can't have donuts without coffee."

Maddy jumped at the voice behind her.

"Thank you, John," Otis said. "I'll take the black one. I was just trying to talk Maddy out of some of her donut holes."

Maddy reached for a cup. "Thanks, Coffee Man."

He smiled, watching as she sipped her coffee. "How does it taste? I've never made fifty cups at a time before."

"It's fine," she said quickly lowering her cup. "Not as good as the donuts, of course."

"The competition is rough down here," John admitted with a grin. "How are you guys doing?" he turned to his boys. "You keeping up with the crowd?"

They assured him that they were enjoying their powerful position of donut rationing. John excused himself to get back to his coffee serving, and Otis and Maddy said their good-byes as well. Blake waved as Parker hustled around the table to give Maddy a sticky hug.

"See you later, Parkerpants," she laughed.

Monday morning dawned overcast, so there was no spectacular sunrise to tempt Maddy out of bed. She enjoyed the extra time to burrow under her covers and contemplate the day ahead. She finally got up and dressed, admiring the new bookcases as she left her room. Walking through the other bedrooms on the second floor, she noted the improvements, as well as the work still necessary. How soon would she be able to decorate and make the rooms inviting?

Another unsettling thought struck her. What would it be like when the work was done and her house was no longer filled with the sounds of the crew and their projects? It had been an adjustment initially, but she had grown accustomed to all of the noise and commotion. It was going to be very quiet and a little lonely when they finished.

Maddy walked down to the kitchen, and her dog's distracted greeting told her that at least one of the guys had arrived. She let Burt out while she made the coffee. The men were now accustomed to knocking briefly and letting themselves in. She couldn't identify the footsteps that she heard coming through her dining room minutes later. She knew that they weren't John's boots anyway. She watched the door with interest as it opened.

"Hey, Tom. How are you?"

Frank was surprised to see that he'd arrived before John, and hurried in when he realized whose truck was parked alone in the drive.

Abruptly opening the door into the kitchen, his forced smile evaporated. "Everything okay?"

"We're fine," Tom muttered, backing away from Maddy.

Maddy shot Frank a grateful look, and turned to pour his coffee. "Hey, Frank."

She held out his mug, but he was looking hard at Tom. Slowly facing her, he said, "John will be here soon."

"Great," Maddy replied, attempting to sound cheerful. She was, in fact, very glad to hear it.

They heard Willy's laugh a few minutes later as he entered the house with Travis and John. The trio made a noisy entrance, and Travis announced, "I need some of Maddy's coffee!"

John entered last and immediately sensed the tension in the room. He and Frank exchanged glances, and John's look turned grim. Maddy busied herself with pouring coffee, while Travis continued making small talk with no one in particular.

Maddy set the mugs on the counter. "Help yourselves," she invited them. "So, what are we doing today?"

Tom walked outside, and Burt pushed past him into the kitchen, growling quietly. He walked over to Maddy and stood between her and the others.

Travis stopped jabbering long enough to drink his coffee, and John carefully approached Maddy, petting Burt as he came to her side.

"Are you okay?"

"Sure," she said, feeling relieved with him standing near. He wore a blue denim oxford, open at the collar, and she could see little tan stripes in the buttons. She looked up at him. "I'm fine, really."

He searched her eyes, and then said to the others, "We'll be working upstairs. Frank, why don't you do your computer thing with Maddy this morning?"

"Sounds good," Frank replied.

The others took their coffee and went to work, John giving Maddy a nod as he left the kitchen. Tom walked in and set his mug on the counter, avoiding eye contact with anyone as he followed them upstairs.

Frank immediately turned to Maddy. "Did Tom…?"

"He just asked me out," Maddy replied awkwardly. "I told him we probably shouldn't go there, and," her voice trailed off.

Frank waited for more, but when Maddy wasn't forthcoming, he didn't push. He knew John would be the one to address the situation, if necessary.

They spent a comfortable morning together, working on computer-related issues. At noon, John talked briefly with Frank, and then excused himself to check on his sons. Maddy joined the younger men on the porch, while Frank finished some work inside. The day was clearing up, bringing the warm temperatures with it.

They ate for a while in silence, and then Willy said, "You did a nice job stripping and priming those posts, Maddy. They'll look really nice with a fresh coat of paint."

"Thanks," she answered. "I had no idea how much work it was going to be. I went back and bought the expensive paint so it will last a long time. I'm not interested in doing this job again any time soon."

The others nodded their agreement. They'd seen a lot of shortcuts that hadn't paid off.

"Well, I'm going to get back to work," Willy announced. "I have to leave early today, so I'd better get at it."

Travis got up to join him, and Maddy followed, staying in the kitchen to clean up while they went upstairs. She was relieved when she heard familiar boots crossing her dining room.

"Hey," she said as John walked in.

"Hey," he answered, walking over and sitting on a stool opposite where she was working.

"How are the boys?" Maddy gently lifted his hand and wiped the surface beneath him. "You could help me out here," she suggested.

"The boys are great," John said, enjoying her simple touch. "They send their greetings to you, of course."

"I'm still washing yesterday's greetings out of my dress."

"Don't tell me," John grimaced. "Jelly?"

"Yep," Maddy answered.

"And it was such a nice white dress," he said sadly.

"You noticed?"

John watched her wash the counter. "I was working on *not* noticing your dress."

Maddy turned a pretty shade of pink. "You looked so busy, I didn't think I was even on your radar."

"In church?"

"No, not in church. I would hardly expect you to notice my dress in church," she scolded, fully hoping he had noticed her dress in church. She shook her head. "*After* church."

"During the fellowship hour?" he ventured.

Maddy slapped him with her dishtowel. "Yes, during fellowship hour, when you had half a dozen helpless women around you who couldn't pour a cup of coffee."

"Ah," he said with a slow smile. "I'd forgotten about all those helpless women."

"Well, it was a bit of a spectacle," Maddy assured him. "I noticed it briefly, but then my attention was taken by two handsome young men, and then I had no more time for you."

"Is that right?"

"Yes, and one of them," she leaned over the counter, confiding in a low voice, "one of them even embraced me." She pulled back, folded her towel and laid it next to the sink.

"Really?"

"I know you're jealous," she sighed.

"Wait until I get my hands on that guy…"

The door *banged!* and Tom entered the room. He walked up to the counter and put his glass down. He looked from Maddy to John, definitely sensing more familiarity than he expected.

"She's busy on Saturday night," he said to John, whose eyes narrowed at Tom's tone. "And she likes to keep her business relationships *clear cut.*"

John stood up slowly. "Get back to work, Tom."

Tom stared at Maddy a moment longer and then disappeared up the steps. John watched him leave, and then came around the counter. "I'm sorry about that."

"It's not your fault," Maddy said quietly.

"I hired him."

"Well, you warned me that this kind of thing could happen."

"I hoped it wouldn't," he said earnestly. "I can barely get Tom to show up on time. How early did he get here this morning?"

"Not noticeably early, but then he's never arrived before you, so I guess that was a little odd."

"Frank said he asked you out."

"Yeah." She looked up at him. "I said no."

"I hope so." John's face grew serious. "Anything else?"

Maddy rinsed her cloth. "He got a little pushy, but Frank came in before…"

"Before?"

"Before anything else happened."

"Maddy, if you felt at all threatened by him, I need to know."

"It was uncomfortable, that's all. I'll just keep my distance."

"You shouldn't have to do that. I'll talk to him, and if anything else happens…"

"I'll let you know," Maddy promised.

John opened the fridge for her so she could put the lemonade away. "Maddy?"

She faced him again. "John?"

He smiled. "Are you really busy on Saturday night?"

Maddy colored a little. "Too busy to go out with Tom."

"Right."

Maddy raised an eyebrow. "Any other questions?"

"Well, the boys wanted me to invite you over to the house for a cookout."

"The boys did?"

"Yeah. Pushy, aren't they?" he grinned.

Maddy smiled. "Good thing they're so cute."

"So, what should I tell them?"

Maddy thought for a minute. "You should probably tell them to ask me themselves next time."

John smiled. "Maddy, *I* would like you to come over for dinner on Saturday night."

She was unprepared for the direct attack. "Really?"

"Really."

"Well, then tell the boys I accept."

ഓരെ

The rest of Monday passed uneventfully, and Maddy was happy to have exactly half of her rails painted by the end of the afternoon. John made sure he was the last to leave at the end of the day, though he didn't stay long. After starting the first of their weekly finance discussions, a call came in from another work site and cut the meeting short. Agreeing to finish up on Tuesday, John left, greeting Otis on his way out.

Maddy invited her neighbor in for a cup of lemonade and a peek at her beautiful railing. Otis was duly impressed. They talked companionably over their drinks, and Otis mentioned that her neighbors on the north side had arrived. He promised to introduce them the following day, and pointed out that the beach would start to fill up since it was getting into the latter part of June. Maddy, glad that Burt now had a fenced-in yard, hoped he'd be satisfied with the transition from roaming the entire beach to hanging out in his little pen. She also hoped he wouldn't learn how to bark.

Otis left a short time later, and Maddy got ready to camp out in her new office. She looked up area B&Bs online and took pages of notes on prices, room decor, room names and menu ideas. The last list was very short. Maddy had no plans to cook for her guests, a little detail that might become troublesome later on. Acquiring that skill was relegated to her "To Do" list.

The rest of the week passed much like Monday afternoon. There were no further incidents with Tom, who apparently decided that he wanted to keep his job. He and Travis spent the week removing the last vestiges of green paint from the dining room. Frank went through the house checking wires and dealing with various electrical issues, replacing outlets and switches as necessary. Willy worked his magic in the bathrooms, replacing a tub in one and a sink in another, and otherwise getting the plumbing in order. By Friday, he was tearing into Maddy's bathroom ceiling to find out what had caused the leak in there. She didn't want to know.

Maddy finished painting her railing Wednesday morning, and

then kept busy running errands for John and the crew. While she was out, she began to price window dressings and visited a few antique shops to get an idea of how she might decorate the bedrooms. It was overwhelming at first, as everything seemed to be, but once she got into a rhythm, she began to enjoy the challenge. She made list after list: to do, to buy, to look up online, to make, to ask Mom about.

Furniture was another consideration; so much would be needed to fill her large house. She hoped, eventually, to fill the rooms with antiques and estate-sale treasures, but that would take time. Everything took lots of time, and Maddy was slowly learning patience. Life in Clairmont contrasted sharply with the world of technology she'd lived in for so long, where information was immediate, and waiting was unheard of.

When Friday afternoon rolled around, Maddy did her grocery shopping and hustled home before the crew quit for the weekend. Pulling into the drive, she noted with some disappointment that John's truck was gone.

She unloaded her groceries and put Burt on his leash. Starting down the beach, she noticed that more of her neighbors had arrived and were getting out their boats, lawn chairs, grills and other indicators of summer beach living. She marveled that this was all a part of her life now. Some of the people introduced themselves, and Maddy was glad to start making connections. No one seemed overly terrified of her dog; not yet, anyway.

Back at the house, Frank reported that all of the molding in the upstairs bedrooms had been stripped and lacquered. The next step would be to paint the rooms, and then the floors would be sanded and coated with polyurethane. When that was dry, all of the bedrooms besides Maddy's would be ready for her decorating touch. She was anxious to see the progress, and Frank accompanied her upstairs.

Maddy was delighted with the striking molding surrounding the windows and doorways, and was equally enthused that the painting phase was just around the corner. She could hardly wait to see how the rooms would look. It was all very exciting, and she said so to Frank, probably a half-dozen times.

"John will be glad to hear that you're pleased."

"Is he coming back this afternoon?"

"I don't think so," Frank said. "I think he was picking his boys up early today."

"Oh." They started walking down the steps together.

"Of course, he'll probably be in touch with you to discuss… whatever," he finished with a smile.

Maddy tried to ignore the overtones of teasing in his voice as she said good-bye. Frank was probably accustomed to homeowners falling for the contractor; not a particularly comforting thought.

eight

Maddy sat on her balcony with a cup of coffee and watched as the blue-gray predawn gave way to the rose and peach hues of the newly sunlit sky. This grand display started the day a little early. She'd hoped to sleep in, and not have quite so much time to focus on her dinner plans.

She got busy, now sanding the paint off the balcony rails, alternately looking forward to the evening, and then reproaching herself for having any "date-like" thoughts about her host. The tedious work left her brain far too available for speculation.

After lunch, she walked Burt and chatted with a few more neighbors, then spent some time weeding the gardens surrounding her house. She observed with satisfaction that the flowers were coming in nicely.

A few hours and a leisurely bath later, she was parked in John's driveway, considering the white ranch with black shutters. An occasional colorful toy broke up the green carpet of lawn, and a basketball net hung over the garage, the backboard low over the door.

As if on cue, Parker ran around the side of the house and raced up to her car. "You're here! You're here, Miss Maddy!" He jumped up and down at the window.

His father called him off from across the yard. "Hey, let Miss Maddy out, buddy!"

Parker skipped away from the door, but right back into the space as soon as Maddy opened it. He gave Maddy a hug and said, "We haven't seen you all week! Remember when you called me 'Parker-pants?' Where's Burt?"

Maddy laughed. "Oh, I didn't think to bring him."

John walked up behind his son and put his hands affectionately and strategically on Parker's shoulders, effectively getting him to move out of Maddy's way and stand still.

"Can you go back and get him, please?" Parker looked first at her, then up at his dad. "I said, 'please.' "

"Let Miss Maddy come into the house, Parker. We'll have Burt over another time."

John and Maddy exchanged untypically formal greetings and then walked up to the porch to meet Blake. They had barely said hello when the boys insisted on taking Maddy on a tour of the house.

"Our house isn't so big," Blake warned her, "but it's nice."

"Yeah, and we have a *huge* fort in the backyard!" Parker added, fairly dancing in anticipation of showing it to her.

"Let's show her our room first," Blake suggested, and they all but dragged her down the hall to show her their toys and books. John followed and leaned in the doorway, watching as Maddy patiently looked from one treasure to the next, trying to focus and comment on everything they put in front of her.

"Come on, guys," he finally interjected. "Let's show Miss Maddy the backyard, and let her sit down."

The deck was large, with a table and chairs, a grill, and room to spare. A single step led down to the yard and the wonderful fort and swing set. Once again, the boys took her hands so she could get a closer look. Parker scrambled up a climbing rope and called for her to join him in the little fort above the slide.

Maddy laughed. "I'm afraid I can't climb up there in these clothes." She looked a little regretfully at the casual, long skirt she'd decided to wear.

Parker giggled and threw himself down the slide, while Blake showed off by swinging across the monkey bars.

"I'm very impressed. You guys have a great fort."

That was all they needed to hear, and they continued to put on a show, yelling, "Look, Miss Maddy!" at regular intervals.

John smiled and invited her to sit down and have a drink. "We have soda and lemonade," he offered, "or would you like a glass of wine?"

"A glass of wine would be great."

He returned a few minutes later with a bottle of red from a local winery and poured two glasses. "Cheers."

She smiled and touched his glass with hers. They sipped their wine and watched the boys play. The evening was still quite warm; summer had definitely arrived.

"I'm glad you came tonight," John said, watching Parker swing higher and higher. "I have to tell you, my boys have never been so persistent with a new friend. They really like you."

"The feeling's mutual," Maddy replied honestly. "I haven't spent that much time with children. I'm surprised at how easy it is to be with them."

"They're definitely out to charm you," John admitted. "They aren't always so well-behaved." He turned to her and set his glass on the table between them. "So, time to get to know my employer. What did you do out in Seattle?"

"Computer stuff," she answered. "Websites mostly. I worked for a small company, so I had the opportunity to do a little bit of everything."

"So why give that up?"

Phil... "Basically, a bigger company bought us out. We had the opportunity to stay on as they expanded, or..."

"Buy a Bed & Breakfast?"

Maddy smiled. "Yeah. I've always wanted to run an inn, something on the water." She stopped for a moment, lost in thought. "I looked online at inns for sale, all over the country really, and a few over in Europe. I decided that I wasn't ready to go overseas, so I settled for the coast of Maine."

"Some people think that Maine is pretty foreign."

"Yeah, well, my friends did give me a hard time for moving out to the 'sticks,' " she admitted with a laugh.

"It's got its own charm," John pointed out. "More and more people are finding their way up here, so we must have something going for us." He got up to uncover the grill.

"Have you lived here all your life?"

"Most of it," he answered. "We moved here from upstate New York when I was in grade school. I lived in Portland through high school, then went to college back in New York. After I graduated, I found my way here to the coast, just like you did. I've been in Clairmont for about eight years."

"So, pretty much right from college, huh?"

"Pretty much right from grad school."

"Grad school? Really?"

"Yeah. It's a long story."

Maddy was intrigued. "So, you moved here after grad school?"

"That's right."

So, Mr. F, you're around thirty-two, I'd say…

"Something funny?"

"Oh, no. Do you ever think about living in another part of the country?"

"Not really. This is home, and it's a good place to raise the boys."

"Well, I grew up in the Midwest, but I've always dreamed of living right on the ocean. I had hoped to make it happen eventually, but I didn't expect to do it before…" she stopped and smiled.

He turned and looked at her quizzically. "Before what?"

"Oh, I don't know," she stalled, "before September, I guess."

He gave her 'the look' and Maddy grinned. She took a sip of her wine and focused on the boys.

Supper passed pleasantly, with talk of the fort and how John built it with the boys' help. Parker served cupcakes for dessert, and John plugged in some patio lights, including a string of plastic lobsters.

Very festive, Maddy thought as she tried to negotiate the huge pile of frosting on her cupcake without wearing most of it.

"Miss Maddy, why did you move to Clairmont?"

Blake caught her off-guard with the question. She set her cupcake down, glad to have a reason to put off that task for a while.

"Well, Blake, this is kind of like a dream come true for me. I really like your town, *our* town," she corrected herself with a smile, "and I've always wanted to open up an inn like your dad is helping me to fix up."

"Did you work at an inn where you used to live?"

"No, I worked for a computer company," she replied, smiling at John, who was getting the story for the second time.

"Did you have a hubson at your other house?"

"I'm sorry, a what?" Maddy looked at Parker, who had suddenly entered the conversation.

"A husband," John clarified with a little grimace.

Maddy's smile was slightly pained. "No, Parker, I don't have a husband."

"Do you have a boyfriend?" Parker rephrased his question with a giggle. This was funny stuff for a four-year-old.

John shook his head and started to intervene, but Maddy answered. "Yes, Parker, I did have a boyfriend."

Blake listened carefully, while Parker, who started the conversation, focused on his frosting. John looked up, obviously curious.

"In fact," she continued, taking a deep breath, "we were going to get married, so he would have been my husband."

"What happened?" It was Blake, again.

"Blake," John began.

"It's okay," Maddy said. She turned to Blake. "He had some things to work through, and… he had to go." She knew that the tears would well up in her eyes, but was relieved when they went no further.

Blake sensed her sadness, so he backed off with his questions. Parker, who had finished with his cupcake and was oblivious to her pain, asked, "Do you pray for him?"

"Not as much as I should," Maddy answered, *or at all…* She looked at John, now silently welcoming his intervention.

"Okay, guys," he said. "Let's go inside and get away from these bugs. If everybody grabs something from the table, we should be able to make it in one trip." He sent the boys ahead and turned to Maddy. "Will you stay for coffee?"

Maddy was fairly sure that she wasn't going to be great company. "I think I should probably head home," she replied, a little catch in her voice.

John wasn't surprised. "I'll walk you to your car."

"It's okay," Maddy replied. She could feel the tears surfacing, and didn't want to make any more of a spectacle. "I'll just say good-bye to

Blake and Parker." She picked up her purse, took a deep breath, and looked at John again. "This was fun tonight. Thank you for inviting me. I'm sorry; sometimes it just hits and I..." She expelled a breath and blinked. She wasn't going to last much longer.

"Please don't apologize," John quietly interrupted her. He wanted to tell her that he understood – to comfort her somehow – but he knew that she needed her space. "We're glad you came tonight. Maybe we can do this again?"

Maddy nodded with a small smile. John walked her through the house and helped to expedite the good-byes with his boys. They watched from the porch as she pulled out of the drive.

"I wish she could stay and play Uno," Parker sighed.

John squeezed his shoulder. "We'll have her over again."

"With Burt, right?" Parker regained his enthusiasm. Blake seemed to perk up too.

"We'll see, guys," John answered. "Right now it's time to get ready for bed."

Once she was in her car and driving down the street, Maddy's defenses gave way, and the tears flowed freely. They continued as she walked into her house and absently greeted Burt. She dropped her keys and purse on the floor, and leaned against the wall. She closed her eyes, unsuccessfully fighting the awful memories. Sliding down the wall, she sat on the floor, her arms wrapped around her knees, looking sadly up at her anxious dog. She finally dropped down and wept. Burt lay down next to her and sighed. Maddy wrapped her arms around his neck and cried some more. He kept his post patiently until her grief was spent, and then licked her face when it reappeared from the tangle of her hair.

nine

Otis stopped by after church the next morning. Tired as she was, Maddy was glad for the company, and led him to her porch.

"I've got a special delivery," he said, pulling a bundle of napkins out of his pocket. He laid it on the table. "Hand-picked by Parker, and wrapped by Blake," he said with satisfaction. "John wanted to send coffee, but I don't have those fancy cup holders in my truck, and I didn't think it would travel well in my pocket." He tried to get a smile out of Maddy.

"Thanks, Otis," she said. "Can you stay for lunch?"

"I don't know," she said as they finished their sandwiches. "It sounds easy, the way you talk about it, but it's really... hard," she finished, for lack of a better argument.

"Forgiveness came at quite a price. I figure God has the right to tell us how to do it."

"I can't argue with that," Maddy said softly. She hadn't forgotten everything she'd learned in Sunday School. "But what if you feel like part of your issue is with God? I mean," she hesitated, struggling to express herself. "Sometimes I feel angry with Him for letting this whole thing happen."

She knew she wasn't alone. Many of her friends were disillusioned, and had abandoned any religious practices that they'd grown up with, and God along with them. Some of them, if they were honest, didn't actually reject the concept of God, they were angry with Him.

"The trouble is," Otis replied slowly, "people have this idea that God owes them something, as though creating them, redeeming them and promising them a perfect eternity weren't enough." He shook his head. "Jesus never said that life on this Earth would be easy. In fact, He assured us that it would be hard. Most of us have it so good that we can't comprehend suffering, and when it happens, we're shocked and angry with God." He stopped and looked out over the water.

"Somehow we've come to believe in this image of God as a sort of genie figure who grants our wishes when we pray. That's fine, as long as everything goes our way. But as soon as something goes wrong we get angry, because that doesn't fit our image of how we think God should behave.

"People don't take the time to get to know God the way He chose to reveal himself, and that's through this," Otis put his hand gently on his Bible. "The truth is all in here, and everything we need for sorting it out when life hurts." Otis sighed. "I guess people don't want to work that hard."

Maddy knew she hadn't been willing to work hard at it. It was much easier to assume that God was unfair, and reject or ignore Him altogether. Another thought occurred to her, and she looked at her friend, aware that he'd also experienced his share of pain.

"Otis, you don't have to answer this, but when your wife…"

"Louisa," he supplied.

"Yes, Louisa. When she died, when God took her from you," she added, "weren't you angry with Him?"

"I was devastated, without a doubt," he conceded. "She got so sick, and I hated to see her suffer." The tears slowly formed in his eyes. "But if you're going to talk about God taking her from me, then you've got to follow it through and acknowledge that He also gave her to me. I didn't deserve that, either," Otis said quietly.

Maddy ached for him. "I'm sorry to bring up something so painful."

"Believe it or not, it helps to talk about her," Otis answered. He turned earnestly to Maddy. "I know that you feel like something was taken away from you. I don't know what you went through with that boy in Seattle. What was his name?"

"Phil."

"I don't know what that Phil put you through, but it must have been pretty bad to make you feel like you looked this morning."

Maddy nodded grimly. She was a wreck when Otis stopped by to pick her up for church. He hadn't argued at all when she declined to go.

"But as long as we're talking about God giving and taking, did it ever occur to you that God took *you* away from *Phil,* and for good reason?"

This concept bewildered Maddy. The way her relationship had ended, it felt an awful lot like she was the one who came up empty-handed.

"Again, I don't know the fellow," Otis pressed, "but knowing what you know about him now, can't you at least acknowledge that maybe God did you a favor by taking him out of your life? Maybe it didn't happen in a very nice way, I don't know, but did you ever think that God allowed that, so when you finally healed up inside you would never second-guess whether that boy, that Phil, was really the right man for you?"

Maddy sat quietly, her mind spinning in a new direction. "You're probably right," she said.

Otis nodded, not sure what else to say. He hadn't expected to challenge her like that, and he certainly hadn't expected to be 'probably right' so soon.

Maddy continued to be pensive, so he got up and stretched his back. "I'd better go home and take my nap," he declared. "Preaching makes me awfully tired."

Maddy smiled a little and stood up with him. "I'll give some thought to what you said," she promised.

"You do that," Otis replied, squeezing her hand. He started down the steps and then turned. "You taking a day of rest?"

"Actually, I was thinking of doing some Spackling."

Otis waved her off with a grin and made his way home. Maddy went inside and got out her tools. She might as well put her body to work while her mind reeled.

ဿ

John arrived at Maddy's house a few minutes early Monday morning. He'd missed her the day before, and had a restless night thinking about her. By the time he walked up to her porch to start work, he felt like he'd already put in a full day.

He was about to knock when he noticed a suitcase just inside the door. His mind raced with the possibilities: *She's going back to Seattle, she's going to her parents', she's leaving for a week, for a month, forever...* He stopped to get his head together before going in. Whatever her suitcase was doing there, there was a reasonable explanation.

He heard footsteps, and Maddy appeared at the door.

"Hey," she said. "Come on in."

"Morning," John replied. She looked a little tired, but he thought she looked good.

"You look awful," she observed.

"Thanks, Maddy."

She grinned. "You just look so tired. Let me get you some coffee."

"I think I need some." John followed her toward the kitchen. "You look nice. Going somewhere?"

Maddy stopped and turned, but in his weary state John ran right into her with a fair amount of force. He grabbed her waist with one hand and the doorframe with the other, effectively keeping them both from falling to the floor.

The threat having clearly passed, they remained very still and very close for several interesting moments.

Maddy finally broke the spell. "Sorry about that. I don't think I drew blood." She patted his shoulders where she'd grabbed him.

"No, it was my fault," he insisted, slowly releasing his grip on her. "I didn't sleep much last night, so my reflexes are a little slow."

"Well, you kept us both from hitting the floor." She was still smoothing his shirt. It was smooth from his collar, all the way across his shoulders. *A considerable distance*, Maddy decided.

While John appreciated her concern, the effect of her smoothing was anything but calming. He gently took her hands. "I'm sorry, Maddy, but if you comfort me anymore, I'm going to forget why I'm here and start behaving... unprofessionally. I'm going to walk *way* over there and pour myself some coffee, okay?"

With that he squeezed her hands, and then gently dropped them and walked past her into the kitchen. Maddy leaned against the counter and watched him pour his coffee. *Good thing I'm getting out of town.*

John sat down and smiled at her over his mug. "Too frank?" he asked with an impish grin.

"Frank, or not, it was probably smart," Maddy breathed, walking over to get her own mug. She stood on the other side of the counter. "So, why didn't you sleep? Are you okay?" She'd slept like a baby, which she really needed after the awful night before.

"A lot on my mind, I guess," John answered. "So, you going out of town?"

"Yeah, I thought it might be a good idea," Maddy began.

Here we go, he thought, steeling himself.

"I'm heading up the coast to do some antique shopping."

That's it? "For how long?"

"Oh, I don't know, most of the day, probably. I packed a bag in case I get involved and decide to spend the night along the way."

That's it? "What will you do if you find something big?"

"I thought of that," Maddy replied smugly. "Otis is lending me his truck. He'll use my car if he needs it."

"Right." It made sense. She needed to start decorating the house, and antiquing along the coast of Maine was the way to do it.

"Otis and I had a really good talk yesterday. Well, he talked and I listened," Maddy qualified. "He gave me a lot to think about, and I figured it would be good to drive for a while and think and process, and shop," she added with a smile.

John nodded and yawned.

"Am I boring you?"

He stretched his arms, grinning. "I think you should stay home."

Maddy sipped her coffee. "You're funny when you're tired." She walked over to get her keys and purse, but John caught her hand as she passed. She stopped and looked at their joined hands and then at him.

John stood up. "Be careful, okay?"

"Be careful, yourself," Maddy replied. "Are you sure you're going to be safe working with tools?"

John dropped her hand. "I'll be fine. I'll just make Frank do all the hard stuff."

"Well, you'd better get some sleep," she said, backing out to the porch to get Burt's leash. "Burt, come!" she called over her shoulder.

She let her dog into the kitchen as John refilled his coffee. "I'm going to take him over to Otis' house. You'll be sure to lock up when you leave tonight? I don't know when I'll be back."

"Of course," John said, following her through the house.

Maddy picked up her suitcase and walked down the steps to the drive, Burt trotting happily beside her. John watched as she climbed up into Otis' dusty truck in her sundress. She put her suitcase inside, and Burt tried to follow, which resulted in an entertaining little scuffle between them. John grinned at her efforts to manhandle Burt, who was obviously intent on accompanying her. She got out of the truck and tried to drag her dog over to Otis' house.

"Do you need a hand?" John called out, walking down the steps.

She looked up in exasperation. "I should have just left him at home," she said. "Now he knows I'm going somewhere, and he's being impossible."

"He's going to miss you," John commiserated, taking the leash from her. Burt stopped straining and sat quietly.

Maddy looked from one to the other of them, finally meeting John's sympathetic gaze. "Oh, quit feeling sorry for him; he'll sense your weakness." She scratched Burt's ears and then asked, "Do you mind taking him back over to the house for me?"

"No problem," he answered. "I'll deliver him to Otis when I leave this afternoon." They walked back around the truck together.

"You might consider jeans the next time you borrow this vehicle," John suggested, holding the door for her as she climbed behind the wheel.

She smiled and rolled her eyes. "See you later," she called, and backed out of the drive.

~ ❧ ~

Maddy glanced at her map as she drove through town. Confirming her route up the coast, she settled in for the drive. Otis' radio came in sporadically at best, so she gave up trying to tune in a station. She settled for the sound of the seagulls as Clairmont disappeared behind her.

In the first little town she encountered, she found one antique shop on the main street. The store carried more craft-type decor than antiques, so after looking around briefly, Maddy headed to the next town. Thirty miles on the map took almost an hour on the winding back roads, which often paralleled the rocky ocean coast. Maddy marveled that this scenic area was now her home.

She pulled into the next town and found three antique shops. In the first store, furniture of all shapes and sizes filled the multi-roomed shop, some of it arranged into little sitting areas but most of it just crammed haphazardly wherever it would fit. Smaller chests sat on top of larger ones, and old dishes and odds and ends filled the shelves, countertops and cupboards. Some pieces were obviously very old and in varying degrees of disrepair. Many had potential, but a few just needed to be hauled to the dump. Still, Maddy felt like she had entered a world of long ago, and she took her time wandering the aisles. This was the kind of place she had imagined when she set out in the morning.

She had taken measurements of the bedrooms, and had a general idea of the furniture she wanted. Nothing significant in the first store caught her attention, but she did pick up a beveled mirror, a pitcher and bowl, some candlesticks, and a beautiful old quilt rack. The owner wrapped each item carefully, and a teenage boy brought them out to the truck. Maddy thanked the young man as he finished loading, offering him a tip, which he refused with a shy grin.

She drove around the corner to the next store, and there she found a headboard that she really liked. It was expensive, so she tried a bit of haggling, which she found didn't come very naturally to her. The clerk wasn't ready to give much on the price, and Maddy returned to her shopping, contemplating another approach. She was delighted to find a sleigh bed in the back of the store, and decided to make an offer on the two together. This went over much better with the surprised clerk, and Maddy left the store very satisfied. Two of her rooms were underway.

She found the last store on her way out of town. It was a light-brown aluminum building, and she pulled hesitantly into the parking lot, which was almost empty. The sign on a free-standing marquis out front advertised an "antiq e inven ory blo out ale."

Inside, Maddy observed that most of the inventory had already been blown out, and the leftovers were composed of an alarming amount of worn wicker. She circled the store, trying not to look as dismayed as she felt, and then left again, deciding she'd had enough antique shopping for one day.

Just after the supper hour, Maddy pulled into a quaint little B&B and parked near a freshly painted red barn. *Parking*, she reminded herself. She had plenty of room, but she would need to mark the area better for her guests. She'd have to ask John what he thought about paving the lot. Getting out of her car, she admired the lovely gardens surrounding the house. Someone around there definitely had a green thumb.

Maddy walked up onto the front porch, taking in all of the details as she knocked on the door. She liked the large planters that held a variety of flowers. A number of hanging baskets also adorned the front of the house, and Maddy admired the purple flowers that hung from them.

A woman in her sixties, Maddy guessed, came to the door.

"You must be Miss Jacobs," she said warmly. "Please, come in. I'm Carolyn Evans," the innkeeper extended her hand. "I'm glad you found us."

"Your directions were very good," Maddy assured her. "Thank you for having me on such short notice."

"You never know from one day to the next what kind of availability you'll have," Mrs. Evans informed her. "We just had three couples leave this morning."

"Your house is lovely," Maddy said, taking in the decor and the unique aura of the entranceway. It was more ornate than she liked, but it certainly made a statement. One that many people appreciated, judging by the thick and well-used guest book on the table. She'd have to remember that detail, too.

"Thank you so much, dear," her hostess answered. She took Maddy's suitcase and set it by the stairs. "I'll have David take that upstairs to your room later. Why don't we go into the parlor and have tea?"

Maddy followed her, mentally taking notes. *Interesting curtains, love that table, weird couch — can't be comfortable.*

She passed the next two hours hearing how Carolyn and David Evans started their inn ten years ago, the changes it had undergone, business in their part of Maine, and other details as they occurred to the rather disorganized but very friendly mind of her hostess. Mr. Evans joined them mid-evening, and after a few brief stories of his own, reminded his wife that it was time to let their guest turn in. Maddy was grateful.

"We've given you our nicest room," Carolyn said as she led Maddy up the steps. "It has a lovely view of the ocean in the distance; you'll see it better in the morning."

She pointed out a few of the amenities, and was especially proud of the bathroom with its one-of-a-kind claw-foot tub. Maddy smiled and gushed accordingly, admired the soaps and the wallpaper, and wondered if Mrs. Evens was ever going to leave.

When she found herself alone in the rose-themed room, Maddy set her laptop on the desk. It was a beautiful piece in dark wood, with dainty little drawers and tiny brass knobs. It was definitely a woman's desk, and Maddy wondered what kind of women had sat in the very same chair over the years to do their work. She looked at her screen and then shut the computer down and put it away. Pulling her pad out of her bag, she began making notes.

The sun pouring through the sheer curtains on the other side of the room woke Maddy the next morning. She'd evidently missed the sunrise. She stretched and turned to look at the clock, contemplating the day ahead. Burrowing back down into the crisp sheets and soft blankets (no expense had been spared there) she wondered if she would be able to handle Mrs. Evans before she had coffee. As the only guest, she was bound to receive lots of extra attention.

Finally pushing the covers back, Maddy got out of bed to check out the view. The view was really only that; the ocean was a fair distance. It didn't compare with the sight, sound and smell, sometimes even the taste and feel of the ocean from *her* bedroom window. Maddy smiled a smug little smile. If she was keeping score, her B&B would have won that round.

She dressed and went down to greet her hosts. The house smelled wonderful, and Maddy could only imagine what awaited her at the breakfast table. She noted this fact with mixed feelings. Round two – Mrs. Evans.

She liked the dining room better in the daylight, especially when she beheld a lovely coffee urn. She made a mental note to get a cool-looking coffee dispenser, and wasted no time in helping herself. She smiled contentedly and looked around. Fresh flowers adorned the hutch and the middle of the table. A breeze gently blew the white lace curtains into the room.

Mrs. Evans came in a few minutes later with some apricot scones. "Good morning, Miss Jacobs," she said cheerfully.

"Please, call me Maddy."

"How did you sleep, Maddy?"

"Very well, thank you." The bed had been comfortable, but the pillow was a little stiff. She'd made a note about that.

"I'm so glad. Please help yourself to the scones," her hostess beamed. "The Belgian waffles will be ready shortly."

"Thank you so much; they smell wonderful," Maddy said, taking a scone and a seat. She'd brought her notebook along with her, so she'd be ready with questions when her hostess had some time to chat. She had a feeling that she wouldn't be waiting long.

ten

It was interesting to walk into her house after having been gone. It smelled of wood and stain, and Maddy was happy to see the dining room well underway. Cans, brushes and tarps covered the floor, and she recalled Mrs. Evans' dining room with the lace curtains and fresh flowers. She wondered if her own dining room would ever compare.

Burt continued to demand attention as she walked into the kitchen, and she smiled as she scratched his ears and picked up a note from John. It referenced the painting of the bedrooms, and the fact that he would be in Augusta the following day. The disappointment that she wouldn't see him for another whole day was fairly acute, and Maddy stood in her kitchen, more perplexed than she cared to admit.

Determined to think about her house instead of her contractor, she hurried upstairs to see the newly painted rooms. The smell of paint was strong, though the windows were open for ventilation. She went from one room to the next, marveling at the transformation. It was starting to look inviting, and now she had furniture that she could picture in the rooms as well. Delighted, she went back down to the porch with her dog to get some fresh air.

She sat for a few minutes, breathing in everything that was wonderful about her front yard, when the phone rang. She wasn't terribly familiar with the sound. Her land line had only been hooked up for a week, and not many people had called her on that phone in the interval. Few people even had the number. *Maybe it's John?*

"Becky?" she said with surprise when she picked up the receiver. "How are you?"

Maddy felt particularly happy to wake up in her own bed the next morning. She made coffee and greeted the crew, then went back up to work on her balcony.

So, Becky's coming up for the weekend. Her younger sister had said she'd visit in July, but Maddy hadn't put much stock in the promise. Becky's plans tended to change, especially when her family was concerned. And how was it the Fourth of July already? She'd completely lost track of time.

Maddy continued to scrape the paint off the wooden boards. Becky had suggested that she have a picnic. *As long as I'm coming, why don't we have a little party?* Maddy sighed and scraped. Becky didn't know what she was asking. She was hardly ready to entertain, and who could come on such short notice anyway? John and the rest of the crew probably already had plans for the day. Besides, a beach party meant Becky in her string bikini and butterfly tattoo on her...

"It looks good," Frank observed, having suddenly materialized in the doorway. "I'm glad you're taking your time."

Startled, Maddy nodded as she tried to redirect her thoughts to the project at hand. She wasn't sure she could do it any faster if she tried. Better to let him think she worked slowly on purpose.

"You know we won't be working on Friday, right?" he continued. "Fourth of July?"

"Oh, right, I figured as much," Maddy replied. She hesitated, and then said, "Say, Frank, I was thinking of having a cookout on Friday. No work, just relaxing, maybe some beach time. I'd love it if you could come and bring your family." She smiled tentatively.

"That sounds like fun. We have a party at my brother's house, but we'll probably stop by. What's your time frame?"

"Maybe in the afternoon? I'm just making this up right now."

Frank chuckled. "You can let me know tomorrow."

ॐ

Maddy didn't sleep well during the night, but when the sun began to rise, she was out like a light. She never heard the men arrive, and woke only when she heard voices in the next room.

Looking at her clock, she sat up in bed with a start. How had she slept through her alarm? She squinted at the clock again, and realized that she'd unset it. She rarely used it anyway. Running her hand through her wild hair, she wondered how long it would take to make herself look human enough to greet the crew.

Maddy got up and stumbled into the bathroom, gasping at her reflection in the mirror. What had happened to her during the night? She threw cold water on her face, trying to revive it. Sighing, she brushed through her hair and pulled it back into a ponytail. A little bit of makeup would be necessary to make it look like she hadn't slept the morning away.

This was not the way she'd hoped to greet John after three days. Resigning herself to their unseemly reunion, she opened her door and walked down the hall.

Someone was in the hole-room; it sounded like Frank and John. *Maybe I can just sneak down the stairs and pretend that I've been busy ... somewhere else.*

It was worth a try. She started quietly down the steps when she heard footsteps in the hall above.

Immobilized, she turned to see John standing at the top of the stairs. *He* looked awake and completely composed. His hair was perfect in its unruly way, and there were no frightening bags under his eyes. He held his mug of coffee and grinned at her, and Maddy's heart melted down into her stomach.

"Hi," she said simply.

"Late night?"

John walked down the steps, unable to take his eyes off her face. She looked a little sleepy, but something else, too. He couldn't quite put his finger on it. He met her halfway, and they stood for a moment in the stairwell.

"Couldn't sleep," Maddy answered. "Until about four a.m., but no problem ever since. I missed the sunrise."

She was fidgeting, and John was thoroughly charmed. "I'm glad you're back."

Maddy smiled. "Me, too. Sorry I wasn't up to make coffee."

"I managed," John replied stoically. "Ten cups is definitely easier than fifty. Let's go get you some."

Maddy decided to spend the morning weeding the gardens. If she was having a picnic, people would be outside, and that's where she needed to spend her energy. She looked out over her front "yard" and smiled at the fact that no mowing was necessary. That part of her property was low maintenance at least.

Burt followed her around throughout the morning, finding shady spots to lounge in while she got good and dirty. She weeded and pulled the remains of past-their-bloom flowers, working her way around the house.

So much for taking the time to clean up this morning. She was sweaty and dirty, and at least once she'd rubbed dirt into her hair while slapping at a bug. All that remained was for John to have some urgent matter to discuss with her before she had a chance to clean up again.

It didn't take long for that little fantasy to be fulfilled. Just before noon, John walked out through her "office" door. Maddy, down in the garden to the side of the porch, squinted up at him; the sun was almost directly overhead.

"Hey," John smiled down at her. The right side of her face was streaked with dirt, as were her arms and legs.

Maddy stood up and stretched her back with a grin. "How's it going inside?"

"Fine, the floors are looking good. We're just about to break for lunch. Can we get you anything at Theo's?" John could hear himself rambling. *Focus*, he told himself. *Just don't look at her.* He walked over to test one of the hooks that supported the swing. It looked like it could use some tightening, especially with the way his boys had swung on it.

Maddy tried to push a strand of hair out of her face with her dirty garden glove. "I'm all set, but thanks for asking."

John walked back toward her, gesturing toward the door. "You're planning to move into this room eventually, right?"

"Yeah, I'm actually kind of excited," she replied. "There's a lot of space, and I like the fact that there's a door to the porch."

"That doesn't bother you at all?" John asked.

"Why would it?"

"Well, do you think it's a good idea to have outside access to your bedroom?" He shifted uncomfortably. "I mean, what if you're sleeping and someone comes prowling around?" He stopped when he saw the look on her beautiful, dirty face.

"I have Burt," she reminded him. "No one's going to mess with me, but thank you for planting that little seed of fear." The gardening metaphor seemed appropriate.

"Sorry," John said. "I'm sure you'll be safe, but," he hesitated. "Maybe you could use one of the upstairs rooms?" He liked this idea much better. "How about the hole-room?"

"I need immediate access to my sunrise," she reminded him. Then, changing the subject, "So, anyway, I've decided to have a little picnic for the Fourth of July. I promise we won't work at all. We could cook out and play on the beach; that kind of thing. And bring the boys, of course."

"Sounds like fun," John answered. "What can we bring?"

Maddy's heart did a little dance. "Let's see. I invited Frank and his family, and Otis, and my sister will be here, too." This last was added with mixed emotion.

"Your sister's coming?"

"Yeah, she lives in the Boston area. She called last night and reminded me that Friday was a holiday and told me to have a party." Maddy shrugged. "So I guess I am. She'll fly into Augusta late tonight and spend the weekend here."

"It'll be nice to meet her."

Maddy tried to feel enthusiasm about the impending introduction. "If you wouldn't mind bringing a dessert, that would be great," she replied. "Otis is bringing a pasta salad, and Frank said he'd bring some sort of watermelon bowl."

"He's famous for those," John said with a grin. "The boys will help me think of something appropriately sugar-filled," he assured her. "Anything else?"

She smiled up at him. "Just yourself."

ಬಾಜ

The drive to Augusta took longer than Maddy had expected, and she hoped that Becky could keep herself entertained. She shouldn't have doubted that inevitability. Maddy found her sister at one of the car rental booths, the man on the other side of the counter fairly drooling. She was leaning seductively over the counter, making the most of what little cleavage she had by the way she folded her arms. Becky's propensity to be tall and thin had only that one disadvantage; she wasn't particularly curvy. Still, her model-like stature was definitely striking.

It always took Maddy a moment to rein in her critical eye and prepare herself to greet her sister with what she supposed was a warmth that came naturally to everyone whose sister wasn't Becky.

"Hey, Becky," she called out.

Becky turned slowly – it was part of the persona – and waved. Maddy knew that she was receiving the same appraisal that she'd just given her sister, and felt sure that Becky would be gracious enough to point out areas of potential improvement.

"Hey darlin'!" Becky floated in her direction.

Maddy smiled, still happy to see her, for all of the baggage that came along with Becky's brand of sisterhood. "How was your flight?" she asked, picking up one of Becky's suitcases and leading her back through the airport.

"Boring; no one fun to talk to," Becky complained. "You look fabulous, by the way. You're getting lots of sun." She sounded a little envious. "I'll have to catch up this weekend."

"It's supposed to be nice for the next few days," Maddy replied, wondering what kind of strange beachwear was forthcoming.

"Perfect," said Becky. "Those sandals are adorable. Didn't you get those last year?"

"Yep. I was delighted to find that they still fit me, so here they are again."

"Oh, you're so funny," Becky giggled.

"So, how did your show go?"

"It was okay," Becky answered a little flatly. As an art teacher, she'd had some of her paintings featured at a show with those of other Boston-area teachers. "We can talk about that later. So, what's the deal with your contractor?"

Where did that come from? Maddy didn't think she'd mentioned John to Becky. In fact she was sure she hadn't.

"I'm not sure what you're asking," Maddy answered carefully. "He's doing a very nice job, if that's what you want to know." She was not about to give away the tenuous position of her heart with regard to John. That would be a bad idea on so many levels.

"Like I care about *that*," Becky rolled her eyes. "I mean, what's going on between you?"

"Nothing," Maddy absolutely lied. "Why do you ask?"

"Mom said there might be something…"

Maddy considered this. It was unlikely that her mother had implied anything. It was more likely that Becky was looking for drama and determined to find it, and complicate it if possible.

"I can't imagine why she'd say that." They arrived at the car and loaded Becky's bags into the trunk. Maddy was glad for the distraction. She really didn't want to talk about John with Becky.

"So, is he hot or what?"

Maddy sighed. "He is very nice-looking."

Becky looked at her wickedly. "Really? How old is he?"

"Too old for you."

This won an honest laugh from her sister as they pulled out of the lot. Maddy wasn't completely comfortable with that reaction.

"So, is he married?" Becky pressed.

"No, but he does have two sons from a previous marriage."

Becky showed the first signs of disinterest at this bit of information. It wouldn't last when she saw John, but it was a momentary deterrent. They spent the rest of the ride home catching up on family news. They had plenty to cover, and the trip passed quickly.

Becky marveled appreciatively when they finally pulled into Maddy's drive. The outside of the house definitely looked better at night.

"This is fabulous, you lucky girl!" Becky smirked. "I can't wait to see the inside."

Once they were in, Becky greeted Burt with affection, and then proceeded to ask for a cork screw.

"I brought along a fabulous Shiraz," she told Maddy. "You'll love it."

A tour of the house, which Becky apparently could wait to see, gave way to a glass of wine on the porch. The latter wasn't so bad for Maddy. The porch was, after all, her happy place. The wine might help Becky seem a little less menacing as well.

They sat with the lights off, watching the moon on the water. It was very peaceful, and they talked companionably for some time. Becky launched into the details of her recent jobs, relationships and jewelry purchases, and Maddy sat back and listened. She tuned in to the professional references, but didn't get too involved in the rest. The story rarely changed, or perhaps it changed too often. Either way, Maddy had learned not to get too invested.

"So, who's coming to the party tomorrow?" Becky stopped to draw air.

"I'm inviting my neighbor, Otis," Maddy said, and then slapped her sister's arm when she saw the questioning look in her eyes. "He's eighty years old, Becky."

Becky smiled demurely. "Who else is coming?"

"Two of the guys from my crew *and their families*."

"No one single, huh?" Becky pouted.

"Only John." Maddy found herself bristling at her sister's unabashed interest.

"He's the one with the two kids?"

"Yep."

"Well," Becky stretched languidly in her chair. "We'll just see how cute he is."

She sipped her wine and grinned at Maddy, who only sipped her wine. Maybe tomorrow her world would fall apart again.

eleven

Maddy woke early Friday and slipped out to her balcony in time for the sunrise. At first, the clouds on the horizon threatened to interfere, then their pale outlines blazed into fiery orange clarity with the emerging sun. She watched, mesmerized, letting the morning unfold peacefully around her, and willing herself not to worry about the day ahead.

The party, due to start around two, would include badminton and beach time. Swimming was also an option, but the water seemed terribly cold. For dinner, she'd cook steaks and burgers on the grill. She had also picked up some sparklers and other small fireworks for later on in the evening, if her guests stayed that long. All in all, she felt prepared for whatever the day might bring.

John called mid-morning, and their brief conversation ended in an invitation to his sister and her daughter to join their party.

Maddy sighed; *more sisters.*

When Becky rolled out of bed around eleven, Maddy started a fresh pot of coffee. Untangling the badminton set had dominated her morning, and her hopes that Becky might help with the rest of the preparations were short-lived. Her sister planned on taking a run on the beach and then a long soak in Maddy's antique bathtub.

"After all, I'm on vacation," Becky reminded her cheerfully.

Otis arrived promptly at just before two while Maddy was finishing a cheese-and-cracker tray. She brought it outside just as he walked up the steps.

"Hello, Maddy," he said. "Great day for a picnic!"

"It's perfect," she agreed with a smile.

"How is your sister?"

"Becky is Becky," Maddy replied. "She took Burt out for a run, and she's not back yet. She knows people could get here any time." Maddy poured Otis a glass of lemonade. "Anyway, I'm determined to have fun at my first party. I tend to get tense when she's around, as though I'm responsible for her behavior. I have to let that go."

"Easier said than done."

Maddy nodded. *Wise Otis.*

He lifted his glass to her. "You make a lovely hostess," he said. "This vocation suits you. It brings out the color in your cheeks."

Maddy smiled, clinking her glass with his.

The doorbell rang, and Maddy found Frank and his family at the door. He introduced her to his wife, Linda, and their six-year-old daughter, Kelsey. Maddy walked them out to the porch, where they met Otis. Not long after, John and his boys arrived, and Maddy's first party began.

John greeted the others and then went down to the beach to spell out the water rules for the kids. Maddy poured lemonade and watched as he knelt down to talk to them, putting his hand on Parker's shoulder and pointing out to the ocean. She couldn't hear what he was saying, but the gist was clear.

Becky then came jogging up the beach with the dog, perhaps a little faster than she would have liked. Burt knew exactly whom he was running to greet. The boys ran up to Becky because of the dog, and John stood to greet her. Maddy watched from the porch and poured lemonade on the table.

"Shoot!" she said, drawing the attention of her guests.

Linda got up to help, and the others resumed their observance of the pretty runner. They could hardly help but watch her.

Maddy, trying to smile, told them, "That would be my sister, Becky."

Frank gave a low whistle, and Linda smacked his arm. He grinned at her, and kissed the hand that slapped him.

Maddy took a deep breath and prepared herself to formalize the introduction. She walked down the steps to the beach, and Otis watched approvingly as she neared the couple.

"Hey, Becky," she called out, shading her eyes as she approached them. "I see you've met John."

"Have I!" Becky gushed. She put her hand on his forearm and said, "Maddy, I have half a mind to get my apartment refinished!"

Refinished? Maddy agreed with the half a mind part. "Good luck with that." She turned to John. "This is my sister, Becky." She boldly looked up, fully expecting to wait for John to pull his attention away from the dazzling jogger.

John met Maddy's gaze immediately, nodding as he gently removed his arm from Becky's grasp. "She said she ran all the way to the public beach and back. I'm impressed."

That was all Becky needed to hear. She chattered on about running, Burt and the seagulls, shells in her shoes, and then acknowledged that she needed a nice long bath. She smirked coyly at John, who looked to see where his boys had gone with the dog.

"Come on back, Blake!" he called. "That's further than I want you to go." His boys turned and ran back toward their father.

"They're so good," Becky simpered.

"Thank you," John said. "I'd better go over the rules with them again. Excuse me." He smiled at Maddy and joined his kids.

"He's fabulous!" said Becky, barely lowering her voice.

Maddy gritted her teeth into a smile. "I'll introduce you to the others, and then you can go and get cleaned up."

"Seriously, Maddy, how do you concentrate when he's around? Did you see his…"

"Here we are!" Maddy sang out as they stepped up onto the porch. "Otis, Frank and Linda, I'd like you to meet Becky."

Otis stood and Frank followed suit. Becky greeted them all effusively and then excused herself.

Maddy watched her leave. "Okay, who's up for badminton?"

John and Linda, along with Kelsey and Parker, took on Frank, Maddy and Blake. Otis relaxed at the table and played referee.

They volleyed for a while, and then Frank said, "Enough of this. Let's start some serious competition, here."

"Sorry, Maddy," Linda said. "This was bound to happen with these guys."

Maddy smiled at Linda, and then looked through the net at John. He grinned and shrugged, but his stance had definitely changed. He crouched and looked ready to spring. She briefly took in what she could see of some very nice quads. She'd never seen him in shorts.

"We'll let you guys have the serve," she decided, bouncing the birdie and then tossing it to John. "Let's see what you got."

"As you wish," he replied formally. Moving back into position, he announced, "Zero serving zero!" and sent the little birdie like a bullet over the net.

Frank dove, but didn't have a chance. Spitting sand, he said, "Okay, lighten up, Johnny boy. No spiking on the serve." He got to his feet and resumed his "ready" position. Linda rolled her eyes and Kelsey giggled at her dad.

Maddy just stood looking at John, who grinned and got ready to serve again. Winding up the same way, he let the birdie float gently over the net. Blake hit it back, and Kelsey made a successful connection, much to her mother's delight. When Frank ripped it over the net, John just barely got under it. Maddy returned it, and Linda sent the birdie high in the air.

Blake waited for it, and then popped it back over. This time Parker tried to send it back, but didn't quite connect. John ran up behind him with a growl and scooped him up. Parker squealed with laughter, forgetting his missed shot. John spun him around and then set him down, jogging back to his spot. Frank served, and the play continued.

Half an hour later, they were finishing their second game. Maddy's team lost the first by two points, and they were determined to win the second one. There had been some ominous talk of the losers of the match taking the first dip in the ocean, willingly or otherwise. Maddy was not about to be among the reluctant swimmers.

Then Becky showed up. She was dressed to the nines; every detail was flawless, from her movie-star sunglasses down to her ankle bracelet and French-manicured toenails. She sauntered out to the group and stood by the sideline, watching.

Maddy knew that she should probably invite her sister to join them, but decided to finish the game first. Too much was at stake. She wished Becky would sit with Otis, but instead she hung out right by the pole, marveling over every other play. Finally, she called out while Maddy was serving.

"Maddy, I hate to interrupt, but something's wrong with your tub," she drawled. "The water won't turn off."

Maddy stopped and looked at her sister. "Really? Why didn't you tell me right away?" She threw the shuttlecock to Blake. "I need you to take over for me, buddy," she said, leaving the court.

"Let me check it out, Maddy," John offered.

"No way. This is not a work day," she insisted. "I'll figure it out."

She tossed the racket to her sister, who squealed and let it drop at her feet. "Why don't you take my place, Becky?"

Maddy ran to the house and upstairs into her bathroom. The water was running lightly, so she gave the handle a good crank, and the water shut off. She sat down on the edge of the tub, trying to get a hold of her frustration. It wasn't just the games that her help-less sister played that made Maddy so crazy. She'd seen them a hundred times before. Even the one time Becky met Phil she had shown little restraint, but it hadn't bothered Maddy this much. She knew it was irrational. She reminded herself that she didn't have any official claim on John.

Maddy sighed. It was Friday afternoon and Becky was staying until Sunday. How much damage could be done in a weekend?

John's sister and her daughter arrived later in the afternoon, just as Frank and his family were leaving. They exchanged greetings on the porch, Frank mentioning that they might return for the fireworks. The town put on a display at the public beach, and they would have a great view from Maddy's house.

John introduced Karen and her daughter to the others, and Annie immediately ran off to play with her cousins.

"You have a great spot here, Maddy," Karen observed.

"Thank you," Maddy replied, adding Karen's tray of chips and dip to the other snacks on the table. "This salsa looks wonderful. Did you make it?"

"As a matter of fact, I did." Recipe banter ensued, and John excused himself to go swimming with his boys.

"Can somebody help me with this blender?"

A call of distress sounded from the kitchen, where Becky had gone to make daiquiris. Maddy was only mildly surprised that her sister couldn't operate the machinery necessary to complete the task. She went in to see if she could do any better.

Karen was the only taker, besides Becky, when they reappeared with drinks a few minutes later. The women sat with Otis and talked while John played with his boys and their cousin in the water. Becky was itching to discuss John with Maddy, but refrained while his sister was with them.

An opportunity presented itself after a few minutes when Karen walked down to the beach and Otis went home to get his sunglasses. As soon as they had the porch to themselves, Becky opened up on her sister.

"Will you look at him, Maddy?"

It was an unnecessary request. Maddy was acutely aware of the fact that her contractor was half-dressed in her front yard.

"He's gorgeous! Check out his abs. I bet he works out."

"Hmmm," Maddy replied.

"I don't suppose he dresses like that while he works?" Becky sighed.

Maddy was jarred back into the conversation. "No, Becky, he doesn't wear his swim trunks while he's working on my house."

"I know *that*. I mean, it must get hot, though, and I don't know what I'd do if I had a bunch of half-naked construction workers wandering around my house." Becky knocked back her daiquiri, her eyes on John. "I'd never get anything done with him around."

Maddy held her tongue.

"Are you sure there's nothing going on between you two?"

"I don't know why you keep asking that."

"I don't know; he smiles at you a lot. I can't believe you haven't noticed."

A lot? I hadn't noticed. "We're good friends, nothing more."

"Well, if you're sure…" Becky got up and carefully removed the little cover-up jumper she'd been wearing, unveiling her scanty bikini and tattoo. "Maybe I'll just go out and get some sun."

Maddy bristled. "Come on, Becky, don't you think you're being a bit obvious?"

"I hope so," Becky smiled, strolling down the steps.

Maddy rolled her eyes, not wanting to watch the scene unfolding in front of her, yet perversely unable to look away. She cleaned up the snack table and watched as Parker and Blake jumped over the waves rolling in. John stood hip-deep between them and the deeper water. Focused on being a watchful dad, he probably had no idea of the distraction he was causing.

Otis' return spared Maddy further private reflection on the situation. He stood next to her and followed her gaze out to the beach. "How is it that you two are so different?"

"I don't know," Maddy answered slowly.

Becky had reached John, who was herding his boys out of the water. He immediately became very interested in the castle the kids had been working on, and Maddy had to smile. *Such a gentleman.* He may not want to gawk, but he'd have to start doing somersaults to keep from looking at Becky. She was sure to make every effort to stay in view.

"Becky didn't buy into many of the reasonable life lessons our parents tried to teach us," Maddy explained. "She's always worried them. Not that we haven't all done our share of that," she conceded after a moment.

"She's a pretty girl, but I don't think she's John's type," Otis said, cutting to the chase and patting her hand. Maddy smiled at him, and he continued, "I think I'd like to go get my feet wet, young lady. So if you're finished here, why don't you join me?"

Maddy, Otis and Burt made their way out to the rest of the party on the beach. John looked up to see them approaching and stood.

"Hey, boys, Miss Maddy's coming out for a swim!"

Parker cheered without looking up from the moat he was carving out of the sand. Blake stood up and grinned.

"No, I'm just coming out to see your castle," she corrected him. "I'm not dressed to swim," she further pointed out, observing with some concern the look on John's face.

"Sure you are." He took a few steps in her direction, and Maddy checked her advance. Becky watched from beyond the sand castle, pouting, and Karen knelt in the sand with her daughter, looking on the scene with a half smile.

"John…" Maddy tried to think of a way to threaten her guest.

He smiled and continued walking calmly toward her.

"You recall the outcome of our badminton match?" he asked. "We beat you both times."

"Congratulations?"

"Thank you. And losers agreed to take a swim."

"I'm not a loser, and I'm not swimming."

"Yeah, I think you are."

"A loser?"

John laughed. "No, but you are swimming."

"What about Blake and Frank?"

"Blake already went in, and Frank left."

"What about Becky?" Maddy was getting desperate. "Why don't you toss *her* in?"

Becky squealed in delighted distress, but John shook his head and continued to close the distance between them.

Maddy started walking backward. "I'm *not* going swimming. It's freezing! Burt, protect me!" Her dog was now the only thing that separated her from her contractor. Maddy tried to keep her eyes on John's face and off of the rest of him. He smiled wickedly and pet Burt.

Otis had wisely stepped away from the confrontation, and Maddy tried to look defiantly at John. "Burt will kill you if you chase me." Her dog wagged his tail and looked adoringly up at them.

"Who said anything about chasing?"

"You wouldn't," she breathed, taking another step back.

"Oh, I would," John assured her, matching her step.

Maddy quickly considered her options. "Let's negotiate."

"Excuse me?"

"If I go willingly, will you promise not to pick me up and throw me?"

"Well, I wasn't really going to throw you. Maybe just drop you," John offered kindly.

"How thoughtful. I think I'd rather go in on my own."

Maddy stepped carefully around him and walked slowly toward the water. John followed her, and the boys began cheering her on. She stopped when her feet hit the cold, and John came right up behind her. Normally his proximity had a more thrilling affect on her senses. At the moment, she would have been okay with him backing off a bit.

"Need help?" His voice was low and alarmingly close.

"Not your kind."

"I'll be right here if you need me."

"I need you to go away."

John chuckled, but didn't move.

Maddy thought of a new tactic. "You know, I don't want to get my clothes wet. How about if I go and put my suit on?"

"I think you already have your suit on." The tell-tale straps crossed her shoulders under her tank top. He gave her a little nudge in the small of her back, and she stepped unwillingly forward. She was up to her shins in icy water. "Well?" he prodded.

"Okay, how about this," she turned to make one more offer, and John simply picked her up and began walking out into the surf.

Maddy's natural instinct was to try to break free, but when John responded by loosening his grip, she quickly reconsidered. Breaking free meant immediate cold, and there was still time to bargain. She stopped thrashing and took the only reasonable step for self-preservation. She threw her arms around his neck and hung on. He responded by cradling her quite nicely.

"You know I'm never inviting you to another party," she threatened, trying to look upset, but feeling a little giddy.

"Then I'd better make the most of this opportunity."

He continued walking into the water until he was almost waist-deep, and her backside was introduced to the cold. She gasped.

"Any last words?" he asked.

She tightened her grip. "You're coming with me."

"I was planning on it."

Maddy shuddered and John answered her look of thrilled terror with a smile as he began to fall forward. She tried not to squeal as the water hit her back, and instinctively pulled closer to him as if she could still somehow escape the inevitable icy submersion. The next moment she was immobilized with cold, still in his arms, and he was kissing her.

It happened so quickly that when he released her and she came up for air, she wasn't sure if she'd imagined it. She found herself standing drenched and frozen, with John about a foot away, waving at the crowd in victory. He turned to her, his wet hair wild around his face, and took her hand.

"I'm sorry I had to do that," he said, clearly not sorry at all. "Wanna take another dip?" He grinned and looked deep into her eyes.

Oh, yeah, he kissed me.

"You wish," she said, her teeth and nerves chattering. *What kind of first kiss was that?*

Exquisite. Unforgettable. She was frozen outside and on fire within. Responding with all the maturity she could muster, she sent a spray of water into his face and ran toward the shore. John followed, smiling broadly. As they neared the others, Blake grabbed one of their well-used towels and offered it to Maddy. She took it gratefully, ignoring the sand that covered her as she wrapped it around herself.

"Thank you so much, Blake," she shivered.

"You're welcome," he grinned.

"Here, Dad! Here's mine!" Parker yelled, picking up his towel and sending sand everywhere as he tried to shake it out.

"Thanks, buddy," John said.

"My dad threw you in the water!" Parker giggled to Maddy. "That was so funny!"

"You think so, huh?" Maddy chattered with a grin.

"Oh, yeah!"

"I'm going to walk Miss Maddy back to the house," John told

his sons. "I'll be right back. Stay with Aunt Karen – don't go in the water."

"I can find my way," Maddy assured him. "You've helped me quite enough."

He grinned. "It will be my pleasure." He fell in beside her, and Maddy looked at him warily

"So, I probably should have asked," John began when they were out of earshot of the others, leaning into her shoulder as they walked.

"Asked me what?" Maddy shivered for any number of reasons.

"Asked if I could kiss you."

Who asks for permission? "Kiss me? You kissed me? When?"

The surprise on John's face was priceless, but it didn't last long. His momentary confusion became a grin, which became 'the look,' except that he no longer looked into her eyes. He focused on her lips. Maddy almost dissolved into the sand.

"How could I have missed?" He slowly brought his eyes back to hers.

The door *banged!* and Becky, who had gone inside and covered up again, walked out onto the porch. "What happened to you, Maddy? You look awful."

Pulling her eyes away from John's, Maddy looked up at her sister. "You can thank him for that," she said as she hurried up the steps.

"Wow, you smell like fish," Becky wrinkled her nose as Maddy walked past, and then turned her best smile on John.

"I'm going to get my guys rinsed off in your shower out here," he called to Maddy.

"Help yourself. I'm going to get some dry clothes on."

John grinned and Maddy went inside. She had to get out of her wet clothes before she could get ready for the evening, or make any sense out of the afternoon.

After dinner, the group agreed to take a walk down the beach. Otis declined, claiming that he hadn't eaten enough of Blake's cookies yet. They had been a big hit, as had the rest of the dinner. The steaks and burgers were made to order, and Maddy continued to marvel as she watched people enjoying a meal in her new home. The watermelon fruit bowl definitely won "the most original" award. She wondered if it would be possible to feed her paying guests potluck style. It would certainly be an interesting marketing technique.

With dinner cleaned up the group set off, Otis waving from the swing. The kids ran on ahead, chasing seagulls in and out of the waves. Maddy walked Burt and talked with Karen about her job at a small manufacturing company in town. John, happy that Maddy and Karen were connecting, walked over to Becky, who brightened up immediately. They talked about her art show in Boston and her teaching position in Lexington. John found that when she didn't try to flirt, she could be interesting company.

They made it down to the public beach, which was very crowded; another new experience for Maddy. Vendors wandered through the crowd, selling cotton candy and popcorn, sparklers and small toys. Karen bought each of the kids a glow necklace, figuring it might be smart to have part of them lit up when the beach started to get dark. Burt was a big hit. Most people assumed that he was friendly, and reached out to pet him as Maddy's group walked by.

By the time they got back to the house, Frank and his family had returned. It didn't take long to set up the fire pit and get a blaze going. The kids searched for sticks to roast marshmallows, and Maddy and Karen moved chairs over from the badminton area. The adults got comfortable around the fire, watched the children and talked. The subject of the work done on Maddy's house predominated.

"So, how much more is there to do?" Karen asked.

Maddy looked at John, who launched into the update. "Most of the plumbing and electrical issues have been dealt with throughout the house. The bedrooms upstairs are in good shape, though the floors need to be finished. Both bathrooms upstairs need some work, but the big pieces are in. Then there's the lower level...

"The walls need painting and the floors will be refinished. There's a lot of woodwork that needs attention, and wainscoting to be installed. Of course, furnishing and decorating will follow all of that."

"Another big project is the kitchen," Frank added. "Maddy needs to decide how she wants it updated. A lot of people are having elaborate gourmet kitchens installed, which I generally think is a waste, unless you're opening an inn like this, of course."

"Isn't that terribly expensive?" Linda asked.

"Oh, yeah," sighed Maddy. "They're beautiful and functional I'm sure, but I'm not sure if that's where I want to invest right now." She sat back, pushing her toes into the sand in front of her. "The kitchen isn't really my favorite spot," she confessed. "I'd rather put my money elsewhere."

No one was bold enough to point out that a B&B needed a fairly decent kitchen to provide for the second "B." John was ready with another project, anyway.

"The roof will be just the thing," he grinned. "We'll do that in August. After that, Maddy will need to decide whether she wants to paint, or re-side the house with vinyl." He added this last option with less enthusiasm. As practical as it was, vinyl siding wouldn't be in keeping with the historical character of the home, an important element for a quaint B&B.

"I think we should keep the shaker shingles," Maddy mused. "I'm sure it must be hard to paint them, though."

"The shingles are in good shape, and definitely worth keeping. It is a little time-consuming to paint them, but definitely worth the trouble." John smiled at Maddy, who turned away with a grin.

Frank glanced at each of them and grinned, himself. "Maddy bought some nice antiques for the bedrooms upstairs. It will be interesting to see those rooms start to come together."

The conversation then turned to the other two B&Bs in town and the kind of business they had been doing. A short time later, the first of the fireworks erupted, and the group moved their chairs to watch the display.

Maddy had as much fun watching her guests enjoy the show as she did herself. The finale finally showered above them; a spectacular ending to a wonderful day.

Otis was the first to head home, and the others followed shortly afterward. Maddy saw her guests off with mixed feelings; she hated to see the day end.

John pulled his boys' things together and sent them outside for their flip-flops. For a brief moment, he and Maddy were alone in the kitchen.

"My sister offered to take the boys home with her." John paused and raised an eyebrow. "Okay if I stay a little longer?"

"Oh, I guess," Maddy answered, her mind racing with mixed delight and panic. "I could use some help cleaning up."

She smiled sweetly and turned as Blake and Parker entered the kitchen. "I'm so glad you guys were here to help me celebrate the Fourth of July," she said to them. "I'll see you on Sunday, okay?"

Half an hour later, Maddy found herself watching from the porch as John doused the fire. They had just put her inebriated sister to bed, and the happy prospect of spending a few minutes alone with John was tempered significantly by the fact that Maddy could barely keep her eyes open. She closed them and let the evening breeze revive her.

Her nerves began to dance a little as John walked up the steps. So maybe she wouldn't fall asleep before they had a chance to say goodnight properly. He fell in beside her, leaning his elbows on the railing and looking out over the water. Maddy relaxed a little and did the same.

The moon's reflection shimmered on the waves, which gently lapped the shore. The scene was impossibly romantic, and Maddy found herself contemplating what it would be like to kiss John without being submerged in icy water. This speculation brought a little smile to her face.

"What are you thinking about?"

Maddy turned, hoping the shadows hid her blush. "Oh, I was thinking about that volley in badminton that ended with you flat on your back."

"When Frank dove under the net and tackled me?"

"Hmmm… I thought you just fell over."

John chuckled. "It was a good match. You weren't bad."

Maddy raised an eyebrow. "Thanks."

"Of course, you weren't good enough to beat us, but you made a decent effort."

"Oh, please. We were interrupted…"

John reached over and pushed a wisp of her hair behind her ear, leaving the whole side of her face tingling. "Interrupted?"

She stopped breathing. "Yes."

"And?"

"And we shouldn't have lost."

"I see. Maddy, would you go out with me?"

She drew a breath. "I've already been out with you, John. We've been out for pizza and ice cream, *and* I've been to your house for dinner." She managed an ingenuous smile.

He pushed another strand of hair out of her face. The wind continued to blow it gently. "I want to go out with you *alone*."

"Oh," Maddy replied. "Without Blake and Parker?"

John nodded gravely.

"I'll have to think about that."

John's hand moved to her lips and slowly traced them. Maddy closed her eyes and leaned against the railing. Not sure that her lips would even work, she attempted to speak.

"You shouldn't touch my lips like that," she whispered.

"Well, if I can't touch your lips, would it be okay if I kissed you," he paused and gently turned her head, "here?"

He leaned down and Maddy hesitated only briefly before putting an end to the kiss on her cheek. The kiss, itself, continued, her daring move only slightly surprising her contractor. He readily adjusted, and moved his hands from her face to her shoulders, then gently down her arms until he held her hands. For several wonderful, nerve-wracking moments, Maddy lost herself in his extraordinarily gentle touch.

He finally pulled back and looked at her, and Maddy returned his gaze, feeling a grin tug at her lips.

"Would it ruin my enigmatic persona to say that I wondered what that would be like?"

John laughed. "Enigmatic persona? No, Maddy, no revelation of yours could make you any less mysterious to me."

"Well, that's a relief."

"Anyway, I think I'm more interested in your opinion on this side of the, hmmm, event."

"Event?" It was Maddy's turn to laugh. "That sounds a little grand, but I guess you could call it that."

"And?"

"Well, John, if you're wondering how your kiss measures up ..."

"Maddy."

Something in the way he said her name turned her insides to jelly. She met his gaze. "John?"

He took her face in his hands. "Can I kiss you?"

"You already kissed me," she felt compelled to argue.

"No, Maddy, you kissed me."

"Oh, well, and if I say 'no'?"

John drew back a little, his eyes narrowed. He took in her whole face and then focused on her lips. Maddy was sure her heart had stopped again.

He didn't speak, so she continued. "Well, I didn't want to swim this afternoon, and we know how that ended."

John smiled, but remained focused as he gently stroked her cheeks with his thumbs.

"Yes," Maddy stopped arguing.

It was unlike any kiss Maddy had ever experienced, except, of course, for the one a minute or two prior to it. Part of the difference was the distance John subtly kept between them. While their lips met with considerable feeling, his hands gently held her face or her hands, effectively keeping them from otherwise touching.

This time Maddy pulled back to catch her breath. "Okay, well, in my enigmatic opinion," she paused and looked up at him, "that was very nice."

John smiled in agreement. "So, you'll go out with me?"

"What, because you're a good kisser?"

He leveled his 'look' at her; she could easily discern it in the darkness. "Do you have to argue about everything?" he asked, linking his fingers through hers.

Maddy smiled. Being difficult seemed to be the only way she

could maintain any kind of control, but she could hardly admit that to John.

He lifted one of her hands, and Maddy watched as his lips brushed her knuckles. He dropped her hand and raised an eyebrow. Maddy momentarily forgot the question, but just as she was about to concede that yes, she usually argued, or that sure, a date might be nice, the opportunity for speaking had passed. It was several more well-spent moments before Maddy had a chance to answer in the affirmative. She went with the date question.

"Friday night okay?" John asked, close enough to persuade her, in case she had any other objections.

"Okay," she said.

"I'll pick you up at seven."

twelve

Over coffee the next morning, Becky and Maddy mapped out their day. They would visit the art gallery in town and then drive up the coast to see what other area artists had to offer. Maddy hoped to use local pieces as much as possible to decorate her house, and Becky could certainly help her identify quality work.

"Is there anything else you'd like to see while you're here?" Maddy asked.

"Not really," Becky yawned. "Let's check out the artwork and then see what's happening with the night life."

"Not much," Maddy answered, and then realized that she really didn't have any point of reference. The only nightlife she'd experienced so far was doing research at the library, having pizza with the Fordhams and going to a cookout at their house. She smiled at how thoroughly her life had changed. Reluctantly, she brought herself back to her porch.

"So, how did I get into bed last night?"

Maddy knew this would come up. "John had to carry you."

Becky smiled dreamily. "I wish I could remember."

"Yeah, it was like a fairy tale."

"I think he must have a girlfriend," Becky said thoughtfully. "I tried everything yesterday, and I just couldn't get his attention."

That is just wrong on so many levels. "Yes, you did."

"Got his attention?"

"Tried everything."

"Oh," her sister slumped back in her chair. "I still think he might be interested in you."

"Really?"

"I don't know, but he's definitely got someone on his mind, and I couldn't get him to change it."

"You can't say you didn't try."

"Lighten up. When are *you* ever going to think about dating again? Phil was a moron. It's way past time you figured that out."

"I got that, actually."

"So why don't you go out with John?"

"Maybe I will."

"So, there *is* something between you?"

"Becky, where *were* you last night?"

"You said there wasn't anything going on."

"Doesn't mean I wasn't interested."

"You should have told me."

"I wasn't ready to."

"So, what happened last night that I missed?"

"He kissed me."

"Really?"

"Oh, yeah." She sounded like Parker.

Becky stopped and contemplated this. It was one of her favorite subjects. "What was it like?"

"So nice."

"What else happened?"

"What do you mean, 'what else?' "

"Come on..."

"Nothing else happened. Nothing else should have happened. It was perfect."

"Fine, don't tell me."

"What makes you think there's anything else to tell?"

"In my experience, there usually is."

"Maybe our experiences are different."

"Yeah, too bad for you," Becky smirked.

Maddy held her tongue.

"Come on, guys are guys."

"John's different, I think. I hope."

Becky got up from the table. "You just go ahead and believe that."

"I do," Maddy said with conviction that surprised her. "I'm going to give Burt a quick walk," she said. "How about if we leave in half an hour?"

The restaurant was crowded by the time they arrived, and the girls had to wait a few minutes for a table. Wally's Watershed definitely had the feel of Maine, with lobster cages stacked in the corners and buoys on ropes draped throughout the bar room. Even the curtains were made from fishing nets.

The hostess showed them to a table fairly close to the band. Maddy ordered a glass of merlot, and Becky ordered some strange beverage, the name of which Maddy didn't recognize.

"Thanks for all of your help today," Maddy said. "Those paintings will look great in the living room, or parlor, I should say, and I like your ideas for the room color."

"No problem. I had fun," Becky said with a wave of her hand. "I like those etched lamps we found. I think I want one for my apartment."

Maddy nodded. "We can go back tomorrow."

"So, do you know anyone here?" Becky asked, scanning the room for a handsome face. "Do you think your John will be here?"

"My John," Maddy smiled at the thought, "probably won't. He's got kids, so I'm guessing he doesn't do the bar scene very often."

"Oh, that's right. They're *so* adorable. What a handful that would be," Becky shuddered.

"I wonder what kind of music these guys play?" The band started to set up, and the drummer was busy arranging an enormous drum set that took up half of the stage.

After the waitress took their order, they turned their chairs to watch the band. Maddy looked around the room at her new neighbors, so to speak. She didn't recognize anyone.

"Hey, Maddy."

She jumped at Tom's greeting. He had come up from behind and put his hand on her shoulder.

"Oh, hi..." Maddy answered slowly. "Tom, this is my sister, Becky. Becky, this is Tom, one of John's crew."

Tom drank from his beer and nodded at Becky. "You two look alike," he observed, which surprised Maddy. She didn't hear that very often.

"It's nice to meet you," Becky said, eyeing Tom with interest.

Maddy, uncomfortable with what was brewing, interjected, "So, Tom, do you know anything about the band?"

He looked back at her, took in what she was wearing, and then answered, "Yeah, they're pretty good. They play mostly rock, some blues, not too much." He looked back at Becky. "Where are you from?"

"Boston area," she answered in her sultry voice.

"How long are you in town?"

Becky sighed, "Just until tomorrow. Tonight's my last night." She looked at him meaningfully.

Tom nodded. "I gotta get back to my friends. Maybe I'll see you later?"

"Hope so," Becky replied. Tom sauntered away, and her eyes followed him. "He's cute."

"I wouldn't go there," Maddy warned her.

"Why? What's wrong with him?"

"I don't know him that well, but he asked me out a couple of weeks ago. He got really pushy; John ended up getting involved."

"What did John do?" Becky asked, wide-eyed.

"I'm not sure that he did anything so much as strongly imply that Tom should leave the homeowner alone," Maddy guessed.

"But he doesn't take his own advice."

"It's different with John…"

"Here we go again."

The waitress dropped off their dinners, and the band began to play. They gave up talking while they ate, which was just as well. As they were finishing their meal, Tom returned with a friend who was taller, stockier and, Maddy thought, even more menacing-looking. *This is going to be a treat.*

The girls shifted, and the guys squeezed in at the table. Tom maneuvered in next to Becky, and left his friend, whom he introduced as Brad, to sit on the other side of Maddy. Tom and Becky immediately struck up a conversation, but Brad just sat brooding and drinking his beer. Maddy wanted very much to go home.

A few minutes later, she made an attempt at small talk, which was largely unsuccessful. People started to dance, so they moved their chairs to make more room on the crowded floor.

"You wanna dance?" Brad asked.

Maddy hesitated, turning to Becky, who was getting up to dance with Tom. The song, slow and suggestive, was not one that she wanted to share with this stranger.

"Not right now, thanks."

He pushed his chair back and abruptly left. Maddy felt relieved, but a little conspicuous, alone at her table. She got up to find the restroom, and then walked outside for some air. A few minutes later, she came back in and searched the room for Becky. She was still dancing with Tom.

"Dance with me." A very striking man, tall and blond, had approached her.

Maddy smiled and shook her head. "I don't think so, thanks." It was getting easier.

"You don't think so or you don't know so?" He put his beer on the ledge and took her hand. Apparently he wasn't accustomed to rejection.

She pulled free. "I don't know so."

"That doesn't sound very decisive," he challenged, taking a step toward her. He looked beyond her and then changed his mind, picked up his beer, and walked away. Maddy heaved a sigh of relief.

"You okay, Maddy?"

Maddy whirled around. "Travis!" She could have hugged him.

"Hope you don't mind my glowering at your little friend," he said, pulling her out of the way of a man stumbling past.

"I could kiss you for it," she exclaimed.

"Well, okay," he grinned.

"Seriously, that's the second time someone asked me to dance. It's creepy," she shuddered.

"It's not so creepy, really," he pointed out. "This is a bar, and there's a band and a dance floor, and you're a very pretty lady standing alone."

"Thanks," she smiled at him. "I guess it's been a while since

I've been to a place like this."

"You're not here by yourself?"

"Oh, no. My sister Becky is with me." She pointed across the dance floor. "She and Tom are bonding."

Travis gave a low whistle. "She's a knock-out. Too bad Tom found you first," he grinned.

"To be honest, I would much rather have her dancing with you. Tom makes me a little nervous."

"Oh, Tom's okay. I wouldn't worry about him."

Maddy paused. "Do you want me to introduce you?"

"I'll stop by a little later," he promised. "I don't want to interrupt them."

"Okay. Thanks again, Travis."

"No problem."

Despite the late night, Maddy was up early Sunday morning. Sometime in the middle of the night, she'd heard her sister come in, but hadn't spoken with her. She'd been worried since Becky had agreed to take a ride home with Tom. Maddy was anxious to find out what happened, and somehow got Becky out of bed in time to get ready for church. By nine-thirty, they were sitting on the porch with their coffee.

"So," Maddy began, "how did it go last night?"

"It was okay," Becky replied. "It wasn't as bad as you're thinking."

"I'm not thinking anything," Maddy lied.

"Well, I should have listened to you about Tom," Becky conceded. "I'm usually pretty cool, and I know you don't like this, I'm pretty loose about things, but that guy even made me nervous." She shook her head and Maddy held her breath.

"Anyway, he got a little pushy, just as we were leaving. He wanted to go over to his place, and I just wanted to come back here. Surprised, right?" Becky half-smiled at her sister, who still wasn't breathing. "So, I decided this is bull, well, whatever, I wasn't going anywhere with him, and then Travis came over."

Maddy's momentary relief gave way to new concern. "What

happened then?"

"Those two kind of got into it."

Becky was fairly nonchalant, which really irritated Maddy.

"Got into it? What happened?"

"I just grabbed Travis' arm, and told Tom to, well, whatever, and then, for some reason, he finally backed off."

"And Travis brought you home?"

"Yeah, that was really great of him. He's cute."

Maddy sat back and shook her head. Becky was hopeless. "I'm glad no one got hurt." She looked hard at her sister. "No one got hurt, right?"

"No one got hurt, Maddy."

Half the people in the church looked on with interest as Otis entered with his unusual entourage. Becky, tall, blonde and striking in black slacks and blouse, followed Maddy, who held her own in a casual cream-colored suit. Otis in his predictable church clothes – black pants, white shirt, and blue tie – brought up the rear.

As they passed the Fordham's row, Parker whisper-yelled, "Miss Maddy! Sit with us!"

Maddy turned and smiled at Parker, then Blake, and then John, locking eyes with him. She'd anticipated that moment all morning, and inwardly bemoaned the fact that half a church pew separated them. Leaning down, she said, "We'll see you after church, okay Parker?" She patted his shoulder and continued to a pew several rows up.

Maddy showed Becky where to follow along in the service folder, finding it interesting that she had been in Becky's place, more or less, just a few weeks earlier. She looked up as Pastor Rob walked in front to welcome everyone. She hoped Becky would like him.

"Today we're going to talk about how to be a perfect Christian," he said, introducing the theme for the sermon, as was his habit. "Of course, those of you who are already are free to head down to the fellowship hall and get a cup of coffee. The rest of us will join you in about an hour."

Maddy and Becky exchanged glances.

"No takers? I didn't think so. You'll notice I didn't leave, either." There were a few chuckles throughout the church. "Obviously, there's no such thing as a perfect Christian. What brings us together today is the fact that we're all sinners, and we know where to go for forgiveness.

"What we'll learn from Romans, Chapter Twelve, are some good tools for living out our Christian walk. My prayer for you today is that you really hear God's life-changing Word and let it transform you."

He went on to make a few other announcements, and Maddy considered what he'd said. Did he come across so strongly the last time she attended, or was she just more ready to hear it? Was Becky transformable? *Am I?*

John certainly seemed to be. He took his faith seriously; she knew that. She wasn't sure why that was obvious to her. He didn't talk about it a lot, but she could tell it was a driving force in his life. She looked down at the service folder, and found herself curious about what the pastor had to say.

Halfway into the service, the pastor called the children forward for their message. About a dozen kids came from all corners of the church, and Maddy smiled as Parker skipped up the center aisle, with Blake following at a more respectable pace. The pastor waited until they were all seated on the floor around him and then greeted them.

"Who likes Dr. Seuss?" he began.

Maddy and Becky exchanged glances again. They never talked about Dr. Seuss in church when they were young.

A chorus of approval met his question, and he asked them to name some of their favorite stories. After listening to their animated responses, he continued.

"I like how he rhymes," he said. "I have many of his stories memorized, simply because of his wonderful ability to make them rhyme. I like things that rhyme so much, that I took today's Bible lesson and made it rhyme, so it would be easier to remember.

Would you like to hear it?"

Of course, the kids were thrilled with the idea of the Bible rhyming, and so were most of the adults in the room.

"Okay, I'll need your help," said the pastor. "I'm going to read part of my rhyme, and I want you to finish it. Now some of these words are pretty big, so I want you to listen closely and see if you can figure it out. For example, if I say, *Let love not be false, but sincere, as it should. Hate what is evil and cling to the* blank. How would you fill that in?'

After a moment, Blake called out, "GOOD!"

"Exactly! Good job, Blake," the pastor commended him, repeating the whole verse with the missing word filled in.

Maddy turned to look at John. He was focused on the front of the church with a bit of a grin on his face. He nodded at someone across the aisle, and Maddy reminded herself that he was very much established with this group of people; folks who probably knew him better than she did. She turned casually back to the front of the church. She was pretty sure she was the only one that he kissed on the Fourth of July, and she let that little bit of knowledge warm her right through as she focused again on the children's message. Someone was saying "Other!" and the pastor congratulated her.

"Good for you. *Be kind and affectionate; lift up your brother. In honor, give preference always to the other.'* Here's the next one," he said. " *Be faithful and diligent, not for reward. Be fervent in spirit, keep serving the ...*"

"LORD!" a little girl shrieked, and the adults in the congregation laughed.

"That's it!" Pastor Rob smiled at her energetic response. "We'll do one more, and then I'll have to stop, or I'll give the whole sermon away."

The kids were definitely engaged, as were most of the people in the room. Maddy noticed that even Becky leaned forward a little, waiting for the next verse.

" *Rejoice in the hope that we happily share, be patient in trouble, and steadfast in...*"

"CHAIR!" Parker hollered, and the congregation laughed

again. Maddy was dying to see John's response to this, but decided to behave and keep her attention on the front of the church.

"That's a good guess, Parker," the pastor responded. "The word I'm thinking of rhymes with 'share' and 'chair.' What other word sounds the same?" He folded his hands in front of him.

"PRAY!" Parker answered enthusiastically.

"That's almost it," said the pastor. "Who can help Parker finish that word?"

"Prayer," Blake came to the rescue. The pastor closed his message with the same, and the kids returned to their seats, Parker waving openly to Maddy as they passed by her pew.

After the service, Pastor Rob made a point to introduce himself to Otis and his friends. When he shook Maddy's hand, he said, "I've seen you here before. I'm sorry we haven't had a chance to meet."

"I'm Madeline Jacobs," she answered. "I've enjoyed coming to worship." Today she meant it.

"Well, we hope you'll keep coming back," he said, at which point Parker dashed up between them.

"This is my friend, Miss Maddy. She calls me Parkerpants."

"Oh, she does, does she?"

"Yeah, and this is her sister, Betty."

The pastor held out his hand to Becky, who corrected the mistake. "I'm Becky, actually."

"Welcome, Becky. It's nice to meet you."

"Thank you," she said, disengaging quickly.

John came up behind the group and claimed his son. "Good morning, Pastor," he said, shaking his hand.

"Good morning, John," Rob replied with a big smile on his face. "Are you coming down for coffee?"

"No coffee hour for us today. We're heading over to The Market for brunch."

"Sounds fun. Save me some of that apple strudel. We may stop over there later."

⋘⋙

"So, what do you recommend?"

The tempting array of food was the last thing on her mind as Maddy stood next to John at the buffet.

"You have to try those strawberry crepes."

"I may not wear them as well as you do," she said hesitantly.

He leaned down and whispered, "They'll look great on you – try them."

Maddy complied, wondering why crepe talk made her heart pound. She helped herself to some eggs and fruit, hoping that John wouldn't hassle her about the sausage patties.

He excused himself to help Parker untangle the bacon, and Maddy went back to the table where Becky sat with her bowl of fruit and yogurt. Maddy took advantage of their moment alone to ask her what she thought about church.

"It was nice, I guess," Becky said ambivalently. "I don't need to tell you that it's been a while."

"It had been for me, too, until I moved here."

Becky looked up. "I thought you always went to church."

"I guess I got distracted when I moved to Seattle. It's been a few years."

"Oh," Becky considered this. "What do *you* think of it?"

"At first I was uncomfortable, but I've started to feel more connected. I like the pastor; he seems very down to earth."

"I hope you like him a lot, because he's coming over here."

Maddy looked up, surprised to see Pastor Rob and his wife, she assumed, walking over to their table.

"Hello again, ladies. I'd like you to meet my wife, Rachel."

Maddy and her sister greeted the pastor's wife, a pleasant, pretty woman, with short dark hair and a ready smile. She was also very pregnant. Maddy admired her ability to wear the extra weight so well and wondered why she hadn't noticed her in church before.

John walked up from behind and greeted them. "Hi Pastor, Rachel. Would you join us? We've got plenty of room."

They accepted the invitation and went to get their food, returning a few minutes later. After they were seated, Otis made an observation about the sermon.

"Oh, please, do we have to talk shop?" Rob complained good-naturedly.

Maddy looked up, surprised, and Becky dropped a piece of cantaloupe.

"Honey..." his wife interjected.

"Sorry," he said. "I'm kidding, of course. I'm glad you enjoyed the message, Otis. Romans Twelve has always been one of my favorite passages."

"The children's message was wonderful," Maddy added. "Did you really rewrite the whole chapter to rhyme?"

"I sure did, and memorized it, too. I almost printed it for the bulletin. Maybe I will next week."

"I wish you would. I thought that was clever," Maddy responded.

"Thank you. I'll be sure to do it," Rob beamed.

John watched the exchange with a smile, then added, "It's been a while since we've read Dr. Seuss in our house. We'll have to go to the library and check some of those books out."

"The 'Sleep Book' is the best," Maddy commented with authority, as she dug into the crepes. "If you don't have a copy, I'll buy one for you."

This time, it was Rob's turn to look approvingly at Maddy. "I can see that we're going to get along very well."

On their way to the airport several hours later, Maddy had mixed feelings about seeing her sister go. Her time with Becky was definitely limited, and as much as she sometimes struggled with their relationship, Maddy knew that she would miss her, too.

"So, what are you up to next?" Maddy asked, knowing that Becky's summers were often unpredictable.

"I was thinking of spending a few days in Rockport," Becky answered. "It's such a beautiful coastal town. I'd love to paint the harbor in the middle of summer." She paused. "I have a meeting in Boston tomorrow, and then I really don't have any commitments until I meet some friends in Baltimore in a couple of weeks. Then I'm teaching at my community center in August."

"You're welcome to come up here and paint any time," Maddy

reminded her. "The Maine coast is very picturesque, I think."

"Thanks. I'll keep that in mind," Becky said. "I'll try to stay better in touch," she added thoughtfully.

"That would be great."

"So, what's going to happen with you and John?" Becky asked with a glint in her eye.

"I have no idea," Maddy smiled. "It's definitely going to be interesting trying to work together."

"Good luck getting anything done."

"Looking for furniture will take me out of the house more often. That will probably be a good thing."

Becky nodded. "When do you think you'll be open?"

"My goal is Labor Day. I guess there's nice potential for the foliage season." She paused. "Anyway, my money will probably run out by then, so I'll have to do something if I don't have paying guests."

"What are you doing for insurance?" Becky inquired.

"Good question," Maddy answered. "I can hold on to my current insurance until next spring, then I'll have to find a replacement."

"One of the reasons I teach is for the insurance," Becky confessed. "That's probably not the noblest motivation." She looked out the window.

"It's certainly an important one."

"I guess."

"So, you know that Mom's coming out later this month?" Maddy asked. "She's going to help me with decorating."

"That sounds like fun."

"I think it will be. I'm hoping to have the bedrooms mostly furnished by then, so we can concentrate on the accents. That's never been my specialty," Maddy admitted with a grin.

"Mom will be great at that," Becky concurred.

Maddy sensed a note of sadness in her voice. "She would love to see you, Becky. She'd come to your place if you invited her."

"I don't know about that. Mom's not crazy about how I live." Becky continued to look out the window.

"She's just concerned about you. You know she loves you and

wants you to be happy."

They arrived at the airport and Maddy wished they had more time to talk.

"We have different ideas about what constitutes happiness," Becky pointed out. "I could never be like Mom."

"I don't think you're supposed to be," Maddy answered thoughtfully. "But Mom still has a lot of wisdom. They've lived a while, you know. They've figured a few things out."

"Yeah, well, I just get mad when she tries to push her morals on me," Becky bristled. "It makes me want to run out and do bad things."

Maddy laughed, then realized that Becky probably hadn't intended to be funny. "I haven't always agreed with Mom and Dad, either," she replied. "In the end, I think they're only trying to protect us."

She pulled into the departure lane and up to the curb in front of Becky's airline. She parked and leaned over to hug her sister. "I'm so glad you came," she said sincerely. "Don't wait too long before you come back."

thirteen

Maddy was pouring coffee when John arrived the next morning. He tapped on the kitchen door as he entered.

"Morning, Maddy."

"Morning, John." She handed him his coffee and admired his predictable work clothes: dark T-shirt, faded jeans, boots; no tool belt, yet.

"Thank you," he said, taking the mug. "Not much of a sunrise this morning, huh?"

"No, I slept right through it. It's supposed to rain later today, but it should be nice for the rest of the week."

They walked out to the porch, the weather not really weighing heavily on their minds.

"Did your sister get off okay?"

Maddy nodded. "We had a nice trip to the airport; had one of the best conversations we've had in a long time."

They stood at their favorite spot by the railing.

"When will you see her again?"

"With Becky, you never know. I'd love it if she'd come back when my mom visits, but I don't think that's too likely."

"When is your mom coming?"

"She's planning to visit at the end of the month. I hope to be ready with the bedrooms for her decorating touch."

"They'll be ready," John replied, switching to work-mode. "We're putting the polyurethane on the floors next week, then the rooms are all yours."

"How long do you think the bathrooms will take?" Maddy asked.

"Willy's still working on checking the fittings and pipes, and getting the shower functioning in that second bath. The problem in your bathroom is a little more complicated. He has to replace some of the pipes in the ceiling, and we're having trouble matching what's there. Once that's repaired, we have to patch, prime and paint the ceilings and walls. We'll lay the new tile when all of that's done."

Maddy nodded with satisfaction, her mind spinning with decorating possibilities.

"So what do you have planned for the day?" John asked.

"Oh, I don't know. I thought I'd sit on the beach and get some sun."

John raised an eyebrow.

"Kidding... I'm not going to sit around while you work." She leaned into him.

"You'd be surprised what some people do; women, specifically."

"What do women do, John?"

"Some of the homeowners make it a point to sunbathe while we're working. It can be distracting."

"No kidding."

"I can't imagine what goes through their heads."

Maddy could. "Well, I'm going to go put my swimsuit on."

John turned to her and grinned. "You're going to make this difficult, aren't you?"

"I'm trying to make it easy," she countered, tipping her head to the side.

John set his mug on the table and then rested his hands on the railing on either side of her. He leaned toward her and stopped. "It's your loss if I'm not productive in my work."

"That would depend on what I want to get accomplished." Maddy reached up and put her hands on his shoulders.

John laughed quietly. "You know I can't kiss you on the job." He delayed the inevitable with a slow smile. "I think that would be considered some sort of harassment."

"No, I think that's only if I kiss you," Maddy clarified, now linking her fingers around his neck.

"So you won't fire me if…" and Maddy reached up and kissed him before he could say another word.

"Sue me," she whispered, pulling back to gauge his response.

His response was very agreeable. They heard Burt whine, indicating that someone was in the house. Maddy ducked under John's arm with a grin and went to pour coffee.

"You'll be hearing from my lawyer," he called after her.

Maddy spent the day in Augusta, doing errands and looking for furniture. She purchased several new pieces for the bedrooms, including a small dresser that she barely fit into her vehicle, an end table and a mirror. She picked up some hardware supplies for John as well, and then visited two fabric stores to get some ideas for curtains.

When she arrived home, the crew had gone for the day, but John left a note. He informed her that Tom had quit, but didn't leave any other details. Maddy wasn't disappointed. She wondered how it had all come about, but figured she'd find out soon enough.

Tuesday morning commenced with the financial discussion that they missed Monday afternoon. Once again, John showed up a little early, and he and Maddy sat at the kitchen counter together while it rained lightly outside. John pointed out how projected figures matched up with the actual numbers.

"We went over on projected plumbing costs," he said, "but, so far, the electrical hasn't needed as much overhauling as we originally thought."

Maddy nodded and grinned in response. John looked up and caught her staring, not at the paper but at him. He leaned back and looked at her.

"Have you been listening to anything I've said?" He tried to look stern.

"Absolutely!" she answered. "Plumbing's over, electric's under. Got it." She smiled brightly at him and then looked down at the paper. "What else?"

John shook his head and bent back over his pad. Maddy's hair smelled really nice. "Okay, you're going to have to back up so I can think," he said, pushing her shoulder with his.

"It's my money," she said, pushing back. "I have to see where it's going." They turned to face each other, too close to ignore an alternate method of occupying themselves for the moment.

John finally pulled away. "This is getting... challenging. I really do need to go over this with you." He stood and circled to the other side of the counter, taking his pad and his stool with him. He poured himself more coffee, warmed up Maddy's, and then sat down again.

"Behave," he warned her.

They discussed the expenditures to date, and talked about upcoming costs. John outlined the work remaining to be done, which sobered them both up a bit, but concluded that it was all still possible before Labor Day.

"I need you to give some thought as to how you want us to handle your room," he continued. "We have to get at the floors and the walls, and it'll be easier, obviously, if everything's out. Well, except for the bed." Here he looked at her with some concern. "I don't know if you're ready to leave it yet, but if you are, then we should get your space down here ready so you can just move in."

Maddy nodded; she knew this time would come. "I guess it makes sense to move," she agreed, a hint of sadness in her voice. "Do you think you could add some shelves to my closet down here?"

"I think we can," John smiled. He reached over and covered her hand with his. "It's what we do."

During the following mornings, as Maddy watched the sunrise from her balcony, she imagined what it would be like for her future guests. Although she was sad to see her little season in that room come to an end, it was fun to imagine the memories that would be made by the people who would soon be spending vacations there.

The sunrises weren't the only lure that this romantic location had for her. Maddy spent the next few days finishing the job she started by priming and painting the rails and deck area. By the end of the week, she'd had more than enough time to bond with her balcony.

The rest of the house was full of activity as well. While Willie worked on the bathrooms, John and his crew stormed the bedroom downstairs, patching and painting the walls and refinishing the floor. From Wednesday on, Maddy wasn't allowed in the room, so she kept her computer in the kitchen. She was curious, but she stayed away, even in the evenings when she had the house to herself.

When John led her into her new bedroom late Friday morning, she was stunned. It was the first room in her house that was almost completely finished, and it was beautiful. Maddy was amazed at the quality of the wood floor that had been covered with beige carpeting. John said that they would still give it a coat of polyurethane, but he was pleased with how nicely it had cleaned up, even without that final step. The molding had been stripped and stained, contrasting nicely with the walls, which were painted a soft yellow color.

The room had undergone a significant transformation, but Maddy was completely surprised by its furnishings. There was an antique twin bed and nightstand in a rich maple that complimented the molding. A matching dresser lined the wall, and her antique computer desk now had a chair. Maddy was dumbfounded.

"I don't know what to say," she finally spoke. "Where did you get this beautiful furniture? It's perfect! You even found a chair for my desk."

John explained that the set was from a previous job. The owners were updating, so he got a good deal, and kept it in storage with some other pieces he'd collected along the way.

"I'm glad you like it," he continued. "Of course, you don't have to keep it if you find something you like better. You might want a bigger bed," he said, considering what she'd left upstairs.

"No, it's wonderful," she answered, running her hand along the top of the dresser. "I can't imagine anything better." She turned to him. "Of course, I'll see this expense listed on the next financial report."

"I'll show you the figures."

Maddy wasn't sure that this satisfied her request. "John, this is so beautiful, and I'm thrilled that you went to all of this trouble. But you can't just give it to me. I'm sure you couldn't have been thinking of doing that." She looked back at him, and he shrugged.

"You bought me a coffee mug."

She laughed. "John, I can't accept this."

"We'll talk about it on Monday, okay? Come and see if these shelves are what you had in mind." He took her hand and led her into the closet. "What do you think?"

Maddy looked around, delighted. Shelves lined an entire wall, and several columns of cubby holes were built into the unit. "It's perfect."

"Check this out." John went to the back of the closet, and Maddy followed, watching as he slid back a panel door, revealing one of the first floor bathrooms.

Maddy gasped. "When did you do this?"

"It's been an interesting week." He pointed to the side of the bathroom. "We'll take out that wall and put in a shower, essentially in what is now the hall closet. We'll talk more about fixtures later. It won't go in for a while, but at least now you'll have easier access to the bathroom."

"This is so cool!"

"It is, isn't it?" John pulled her back through the closet into her room, and gestured at the bed. "You'll want to replace that mattress eventually, but it will do for now. I can recommend a few places where you'll have a decent selection and get a reasonable price."

Maddy nodded. "I'm going to need four, maybe five more sets upstairs. I'll definitely be looking for a deal."

"We can look into that next week," John offered. He paused, looking around. "I don't know if you have sheets and bedding for a single bed. I didn't get that far when I set things up in here," he grinned.

"Good thing. You'd probably pick out a bedspread with pictures of fish hooks and other... man things," she said, wrinkling her nose.

John laughed. "I guess you won't be asking for my help with decorating."

Maddy shook her head. "How soon do you want to start on my room upstairs?"

"There's no hurry," John said. "We won't get in there before Monday. Enjoy the weekend."

Maddy smiled up at him. "I intend to."

John pulled into Maddy's driveway shortly before seven that evening. He caught himself as he reached for the door, rang the bell, and waited. He thought of the first time he rang that bell, early in the morning just after they'd met, and Maddy had come to the door in her bathrobe and tousled hair.

This time, Burt's large, drooling face greeted him at the screen.

John cleared his throat. "Well, darling, you look lovely. Are you ready to go?"

Maddy laughed as she came to the door. She was wearing a sleek beige dress, straight-cut and sleeveless, with subtle floral designs throughout the material. She carried a white sweater and a small handbag.

"He's ready, but he's not going. You'll have to settle for me," she said, pushing her dog back as she stepped through. "Bye, Burt," she whispered, and then locked the door and turned to face John. Her eyes were bright, her smile a bit nervous.

John thought she looked amazing. He'd seen her dress up for church, but this was different. This was for him. "Well, darling, you look lovely, too."

He held her hand as they walked to the truck. Maddy smiled as she walked next to him, enjoying the formality of his opening the door and handing her in. Once they were inside, however, a silly wave of nervousness swept over her. She glanced at John behind the wheel. He looked very handsome in his all-black ensemble, maybe even a little dangerous. She smiled to herself at the thought; he didn't seem the type to want to create that impression.

"The Landing is a restaurant about ten miles south of here. It's out in the middle of nowhere, but the food is great. Sound good?"

"Sounds fine." Maddy folded her hands in her lap and tried to relax.

The awkward and unusual silence continued as they drove along, Maddy unwilling to look at John, and both of them acutely aware of the fact that they were on a date. When they did speak, their conversation was stilted, as though it had been a week since they'd seen each other, and not just a few hours. After a while, Maddy asked about refinishing the floors, and they eventually fell into easy conversation over house repair.

The restaurant, built on a large dock over the water, was a gray, boxy building, which looked rather unremarkable from the outside. Maddy felt a little twinge of disappointment as they walked through the gravel parking lot. Was she overdressed? She had envisioned something a little nicer for their first real date.

John opened the door to the restaurant, and they walked into a different world, both elegant and inviting. The host led them to a cozy table in the corner, where John pulled Maddy's chair out for her. He smiled as he sat down across from her.

"This is wonderful!" Maddy exclaimed. "It looks… a little different inside."

"It is deceiving," John admitted. "I've often wondered why they don't work on their curb appeal. The food is delicious, and the atmosphere, once you get inside, is very nice." He shrugged. "I suppose it's kind of like a little secret for the folks who live around here."

"Thanks for letting me in on it."

"You're welcome."

She sighed happily. "So, how was work today?"

John laughed. "Brutal. You should see the place I'm trying to restore. And the owner," he rolled his eyes, Maddy-style.

She laughed. "A real piece of work, huh?"

"Yeah," he said affectionately.

The server came to their table and John ordered wine and a stuffed mushroom appetizer.

"I thought you didn't like mushrooms," Maddy reminded him. "In fact, I recall it causing considerable conflict when I requested them on my pizza."

"These are different – they're stuffed with seafood. It's about the only way I can take them. Some things you just don't put on pizza," he finished with feeling.

"I got that message loud and clear."

"My boys take good care of me."

"You're a lucky man."

"Yes, I am."

Maddy looked across the room at the dimly lit bar where the server picked up their wine. Images of her former life flashed before her, exclusive bars and lounges... She found that she didn't miss that part of her life at all. She came out of her reverie as the server approached, set their glasses on the table, and quietly left.

Maddy took a deep breath and tasted her wine. "This is nice." She looked around the room again. "So, how did you find this place?"

"Frank told me about it," John answered, taking in the room himself. "I'm not sure where he heard about it. I've been out here a few times over the last couple of years, and it's always been good."

The waiter came by and left some rolls and butter on the table, promising to be back with their appetizer.

"It seems like you're a little more careful about what you drink than your sister is," John observed.

"I'm not sure that's saying much," said Maddy, taking another sip of her wine and wondering if she was disproving his theory. She was thirsty. "I enjoy a glass of wine, but I don't like losing my sense of control."

"That's probably smart."

Maddy began to relax a little. "I think it's especially important in dating situations."

"Yeah?"

"Somebody's got to keep things under control."

"And that job falls to you?"

"It always has." Another sip.

"I see."

John thought Maddy seemed more carefree tonight; maybe the wine was helping. He watched her lightly butter a roll and then put it back on her plate. She sipped her wine again.

"I don't know what I'm going to do with you now," she continued, sitting back and swirling her wine gently in her glass.

"Why is that?"

"Well, you kissed me," she reminded him, smiling.

"Yes, I did," he smiled back.

She leaned forward in her chair. "And you're really good at it."

He grinned. She was definitely unwinding; he'd have to get her to eat something. "Thanks – so are you."

"Well, it makes me a little nervous."

"Does it?"

"It's new territory for us."

John liked the new territory. "And?"

She leaned back again and ran her finger around the edge of her glass. It started to ring. "So, who keeps things under control?"

John considered the question. "We both do."

Maddy looked at him doubtfully. "You're going to help?"

"Of course."

"That's not the model I'm familiar with." Another sip.

"Which is…"

"We spar, you advance, I retreat…"

"Why do you retreat?"

Her eyes sparkled. "Why do you advance?"

John smiled and sipped his own wine. He could think of a few reasons. "I won't."

Once again, Maddy looked doubtful.

"Not too much," John qualified.

"How do you know?"

"I've already decided."

"You have?" She looked surprised. "When?"

"A long time ago."

She smiled demurely. "We haven't known each other that long, John."

He grinned back, enjoying the sound of his name on her lips. "Well, Maddy, I made the decision before I met you."

Sitting back in her chair, she regarded him. "What, exactly, did you decide? Or shouldn't I ask?" A look of hesitation crossed her face. "Maybe this isn't first-date conversation."

John smiled. "I don't think this is a typical first date."

"No, I don't suppose so."

"I decided," he paused, "to proceed carefully in relationships."

"Was that a plural?"

He smiled. "In the general sense. It's singular right now."

"That's good news."

"I'm glad you think so."

She thought for a moment. "Have you always been this way?"

"Which way is that?"

"Hmmm," she sipped her wine for courage. This was touchy territory. "So controlled. I mean, I know you're controll*ing*. I've seen you boss everyone around my house," she rolled her eyes, and then leaned forward again. "I mean, have you always been able to control yourself so well?"

"I think it's important to be controlled in certain areas."

"So, in this particular case," Maddy couldn't believe she was pushing this. "In the area of… intimacy," she continued delicately, "you *didn't*…?"

He looked at her thoughtfully, waiting, and then finally saved her. "No."

She sat back. "Until, of course…"

"Obviously."

"And then," here she had the decency to turn a lovely shade of pink. "Not… anymore?"

He sat back and sipped his wine. "Not anymore."

"Wow."

You are beautiful. "It really isn't supposed to be so shocking."

"Well, it kind of is. The pressure out there is pretty over-whelming."

"No doubt," he agreed.

"You're making it very difficult for me to assign you a typical male stereotype."

"Thanks?"

"It's just that nobody thinks that way, anymore."

"Do you?" his tone was slightly earnest.

"Basically."

"Basically?"

She was a little uncomfortable when the spotlight turned on her. "I do," she answered softly, "but no one else does."

"I think there are plenty of us who still do."

"That's comforting, I guess. I've always felt alone."

"Well, you're not." That much he knew.

"So you're not worried about us?"

"Not at all." This was actually not true.

"You're sure we'll behave?"

"Absolutely." That was way more confident than he felt.

She sat back in her chair and tilted her head. "You're not even tempted a little?"

"I'm tempted a lot. Please don't look at me that way."

She laughed quietly and leaned forward. "What if I'm not sure . . ."

"Not sure of what?"

"If I'll behave?" She gave him a beguiling smile.

John sipped his wine, thinking that he should probably take a nice long walk on the beach – alone. Maybe throw himself in the water. "Maybe you've had too much wine."

"I've had half a glass," she protested. She looked down. "Okay, maybe a little more. Anyway, it's not the wine. It's you."

John shifted. "I told you I'd do my part."

She smiled. "I hope I can do mine."

"I hope so, too." John leaned back in his chair, regarding her with a half-smile.

"I don't know," she said slowly. "I might let my guard down." There was that smile, again.

"I think it would be a really good idea if you didn't."

Her smile became playful. "Maybe you're not so tough as you think?"

"I'm not as tough as I was five minutes ago. I think we should talk about something else. Do you like to fish?"

Dinner at the Landing was as delicious as the setting was unusual. John and Maddy took advantage of the opportunity to get to know more about each other as they enjoyed their meal. They talked about their families, their parents and siblings, over a bowl of lobster bisque. Spinach salad with cranberries and a light vinaigrette brought them through their college experiences, and shrimp scampi gave them the chance to discuss the various places they had traveled. Their professional pursuits were highlighted over tiramisu and cappuccino. By the end of the meal, they'd covered some significant territory. They were also ready for a walk.

The beach around the Landing wasn't ideal for a stroll, so they decided to head back into Clairmont. They walked slowly through the parking lot, hand in hand, enjoying the clear, warm night, until the heel of Maddy's shoe caught in the stones. She lost her balance, but John caught her against his side, and Maddy, feeling a little silly but grateful to be upright, thanked him.

"Once again, your reflexes are amazing," she observed. "Thank you for keeping me out of the gravel."

"You're welcome," John answered, happy to keep a firm hold on her as they neared his truck. When Maddy reached for the door handle, John covered her hand with his. She looked up at him.

"I can open the door, John, really I can. I may not be able to walk, but I can open a door."

"Really?" he replied, pulling her fingers from the handle. He lifted her hand to his lips and kissed it.

"John, should you be kissing my hand?"

"You've got a better idea?"

"What about the ban?" she persisted playfully. "Didn't you ban kissing during our meeting Tuesday morning?"

John looked down at her and shook his head with a smile. "What ban?" he asked, clearly ignoring any such restriction, and keeping her from asking any more questions about it.

Other patrons leaving the restaurant had the unhappy effect of reminding them that they weren't alone, and John reluctantly pulled away to open Maddy's door. Once inside the truck, he turned to her with a smile, resting his arm along the back of the seat.

"So," she reminded him as he drew close. "About that ban... When does it apply, exactly?"

John thought for a moment, enjoying their proximity. "Definitely during the work day. I won't get anything done if I know that, at any moment, I can take a break and track you down, and ..." It wasn't necessary to explain further.

"That's probably smart," Maddy eventually agreed. She ran her fingers through the hair above his ear. "Can I do this?"

John cleared his throat. "I don't think that was part of the ban."

She smiled. "I've always wanted to touch these curls."

"Always?"

"Well, not *always*. Maybe since you said, 'My name is John, and I like your dog.'"

"Wow, that's a long time," he grinned at her.

Maddy sat back. "I'm being way too transparent here. I need to get back to being my mysterious self."

John drew back and put the truck into gear. "I find your transparency very refreshing."

The drive home seemed much shorter than the drive to the restaurant. With so much new ground covered over dinner, they had plenty of follow-up questions for each other: friends, hobbies, favorite books. The only subject they mutually avoided was their difficult past relationships.

John pulled onto Fremont Avenue in Clairmont and parked. They got out and walked, hand in hand, passing Checker's ice cream place, now closed for the night. They continued down the street, and Maddy asked John about her furniture. How had he gotten it into her room? He told her he'd driven right up to the house with it that morning, while she'd been busy on her computer. Maddy thought the whole business was very sweet. They'd fight over how she'd pay for it, later.

Turning down another street, they passed one of the town's other Bed & Breakfasts, Maplewood Inn. John asked Maddy if she had a name for her B&B yet.

"I'm not sure. Maybe I'll call it 'Maddy's Inn,' unless I'm out, of course," she said with a smile.

They talked for a while about the house and upcoming projects, and eventually passed a small Baptist church. Maddy commented on the stained glass, and John talked a bit about the history of the building and the community. This conversation led to the subject of their own church, which was the oldest in town, and John asked how Maddy ended up attending.

She paused at his question; she didn't really want to share her less-than-honorable motives, but what could she say?

"To be honest, I hadn't been to church for a long time before I came to Clairmont." She let that unsettling truth sink in before continuing. John nodded, waiting to hear more.

"I was just trying to develop some community contacts," she confessed. She looked up at John. His grip on her hand hadn't changed, but his expression was unreadable as they walked along the dark street. "I guess God had other reasons for getting me into the church, and I'm really glad," she squeezed his hand.

They walked for a few minutes in silence, and then John said, "He always knows what He's doing, doesn't He?"

They walked up the steps to her porch, and they could hear Burt whining inside. Maddy opened the door and greeted her dog, who seemed equally anxious to see John. They managed to step inside, and John took Maddy's hands.

"I had a great time."

"So did I," she answered.

He leaned down to kiss her, and Burt began to whine again. John stopped. "Do you think he's protecting you?" he asked, wondering if that might become a problem.

"Honestly, I think he's pro*testing* me," Maddy said. "I think *he* wants your attention." She looked up at John. "I guess you'll have to choose."

John looked at Burt, and then at Maddy.

"Take your time," Maddy said, crossing her arms.

John took her face in his hands. He kissed her, moving his hands through her hair and around her ears, gently touching her earrings. "I like your ears better," he said against her lips.

Maddy sighed and smiled. "You'd better go home before you get in any more trouble."

"I'm in trouble?" John asked, sounding a lot like Parker.

"More than you know. Burt, you're not going with him." Maddy held her dog's collar as John started back to the door.

John looked regretfully at Maddy. The evening was over, and her huge dog stood between them.

"So, when will I see you again?" They both knew it was a silly question.

"I don't know," Maddy replied. "I'm going shopping with Linda tomorrow."

"That sounds like fun," John sort of lied.

"It really should be. I've got a lot of rooms to fill," Maddy looked around her bare entryway.

"Right, well," John hesitated, then turned to leave. "I'll see you soon."

fourteen

Linda showed up early Saturday morning for their shopping date. They got down to business, walking through the house, discussing possible furniture formations and decorating ideas. Maddy was thrilled to find that Linda had many similar visions for her home. She wasn't sure how she would have handled it if her new friend's taste was vastly different from her own.

After discussing the kitchen, Linda walked into the fireplace room. "You're going to want some sturdy, but comfortable furniture in here," she thought aloud. "Maybe a couch right down the side here, so you can see both the fireplace and the windows, with big, overstuffed chairs by those windows facing the couch."

Maddy nodded. It was a good solution for the problem inherent in having a fireplace on one side of the room and an incredible view on the other. "We could build some bookcases in that corner," she pointed, "and keep books, puzzles and games there."

"Great idea," Linda agreed.

Maddy couldn't wait to get started. "Did you happen to bring a newspaper?"

"It's in the car."

By late morning, the women had conquered every yard sale in the area, and had a truckload of treasures to prove it. Maddy was especially delighted with a headboard that she'd found, with a tall, graceful dresser to match. Linda's most exciting find was an elegant étagère, and Maddy made note of the proper name for what was essentially a corner display cabinet. The price was a little high, but

Linda convinced her that the piece was unique and would be perfect for the parlor. They picked up several end tables and a blue leather recliner for the fireplace room, and three mismatched but interesting wooden chairs. *Eclectic*, Maddy reminded herself. *It's part of the charm.*

They ate lunch at Theo's, and contemplated unloading their purchases so they'd have an empty truck for the next stop. Their successes thus far had fed their shopping fervor, and they were ready to keep going.

"We should probably head out if we're going to get to that estate sale before it closes." Linda got up from the table and picked up her tray.

Maddy followed her. "I hate to take up your whole day. Are you sure you're up for more?"

Linda smiled. "You couldn't stop me if you tried. The only other thing I have going today is Frank's game." She paused. "Did you know Frank and John play on a softball team together?"

"He didn't say anything about it."

"The season's almost over," Linda replied. "The competition gets pretty intense around here, and the games are fun to watch. Maybe we'll finish in time to catch some of the action."

The estate sale was as productive as they hoped. Maddy found a suite worthy of the bed in the master bedroom, and the headboard that came with it would fit nicely in the hole-room. Another significant purchase was a comfortable couch for the fireplace room.

Linda had a great time spending her new friend's money. She picked up an armload of games and puzzles and picked through a box of books, pulling out some of the more popular authors for Maddy's bookshelves. Maddy enjoyed spending the afternoon with someone who embraced the challenge she faced, and clearly enjoyed shopping with her. Tired, but happy, the girls pulled into Clairmont late in the afternoon.

"They're probably about half-way through," Linda guessed, looking at her watch. "If we drive straight there, we could catch some of the game. What do you think?"

"That sounds fun," Maddy answered carefully.

"Okay," Linda said with a grin. "Then you're going to take a left up here."

Maddy followed her directions through town, ending up in a parking lot next to a ballfield complex.

"So, I guess our stuff will be safe here?" she asked, getting out of the truck and eyeing their load of furniture.

"If I see anyone walking around with a headboard, I'll chase them down," Linda promised.

Maddy laughed as they walked toward one of the diamonds. She scanned the players in the field. There was no mistaking the first baseman; he was tall and broad-shouldered.

"John plays first," Linda pointed out unnecessarily. "Frank's over at shortstop."

They walked over to the bleachers, where they found Kelsey, Blake and Parker in the stands with Karen and Annie. They said their hellos, and Maddy's attention was drawn back to the field. The ball was in play, and John made the out at first.

The inning ended and the men ran off the field. John had a short trip to the dugout, and he didn't look into the stands as he jogged in. Maddy wondered when he would be up to bat. What kind of hitter was he? He looked like an athlete, and he was good at badminton, but that was about as much as she knew.

Linda started cheering and offering advice to the batters, and Parker decided to explain to the crowd where Maddy had been the night before.

"We had fun at my Aunt Karen's while you went on a date with my dad!"

A few heads turned, as did the color in Maddy's cheeks.

"I'm glad you had fun, Parker," she answered quietly.

"Did you have fun with Dad?" he asked. Blake tuned in, no doubt taking advantage of his brother's curiosity.

"Yes, I did," Maddy answered, trying to keep her voice low.

"We got to sleep over at Aunt Karen's since you were gone so long."

Karen and Linda both laughed, and Maddy's color took on a deeper hue. Linda made an effort to rescue her new friend. "They went to a restaurant that was far away, Parker, and it took a long time to get there."

"One time we went to a restaurant with Miss Maddy and we had pizza. Miss Maddy likes mushrooms," Parker further explained, certain that his listeners would be scandalized. Maddy smiled and poked him in the ribs.

Parker giggled and yelled, "Hey Dad! Look! Miss Maddy and Aunt Linda are here!"

John stepped out of the dugout, sporting a helmet and holding his bat. He turned at Parker's call and searched the crowd. A slow smile spread over his game face when he saw Maddy.

"No pressure, John!" Linda called out. "Give it a ride!"

The batter hit a line drive single to right field, and John stepped up to the plate, swinging his bat. He let the first pitch pass, and fouled the next two pitches just over the left field line. The next pitch spun unpredictably and John swung hard but missed. Shaking his head, he walked back to the dugout, looking up into the crowd as he passed.

"You made me nervous," he called out to Maddy.

She shrugged apologetically, and Linda elbowed her. "I've never seen him smile at anyone like he smiles at you."

The next two innings passed quickly. John redeemed himself with an impressive double, and soon after, the game was over. The crowd slowly dispersed as families and girlfriends collected their players and began to leave.

Linda went over to talk to some friends, and Maddy stood near the fence, watching Blake and Parker. They were now free to run under and over the bleachers, and did so while their Aunt Karen talked with another player's family.

Maddy jumped when she felt someone touch her shoulder, and turned to see John looking down at her through the wire fence.

"Oh, hi!" she said. "Nice hat." She liked the way his hair curled around the edges.

"Thanks," John said, holding onto the fence. "I'm glad you came."

"So am I. We just got here a little while ago, but it was fun to catch the end of the game. You're good," she added with a smile.

He grinned. "Sometimes."

Maddy wanted to put her hands on top of his fingers where they stuck through the fence; wanted to make contact of some kind. John was about ready to scale the fence to be closer to her.

"I need to get my gear," he said. "I'll meet you around?"

"Sure," Maddy agreed, and walked over to wait with Karen.

John came out of the dugout, grabbing Parker as he ran up for a hug. Blake fell in with them, and the three joined the women, John's cleats noisy on the pavement.

"Thanks for watching the boys," John said to his sister. "Do you and Annie want to come over for supper?"

"Thanks, no," Karen answered. "We've got some errands to run." She turned to Maddy. "It was nice to see you again, Maddy."

"You, too. Take care."

John put his glove on Parker's head, and grabbed his hand and Blake's as they began to walk. "So what did you two buy today?"

"Check it out," Maddy said, nodding toward the parking lot and Otis' loaded truck.

John followed her gaze and whistled. "You were busy."

Linda, Frank and Kelsey joined them from behind. "Looks like Linda spent all of your money," Frank observed.

"We were a good team," Maddy replied.

"We already dropped off the first load at Maddy's house," Linda offered proudly.

"I guess you're looking for manual labor, now that we've worn ourselves out playing ball?" Frank complained good-naturedly.

"Oh, no," Maddy assured him. "You can't work on another Saturday."

"Sure they can," answered Linda. "It'll be fun."

The group reconvened at Maddy's house, and they made quick business of unloading everything into the shed, where Maddy was keeping the furniture she'd purchased. There were generally favorable remarks until it came time to move the couch.

Frank made a pained face as they shifted this last piece off the truck. "How were you planning to move this without us?"

"We weren't," Linda readily admitted. "Thank you for being so big and strong and brave," she cooed.

Maddy had picked up sandwiches at Theo's, and encouraged everyone to stay for dinner. It was a simple, but satisfying affair, and they enjoyed the evening breeze as it began to blow in. Maddy and Linda reviewed the days' shopping with the men, who listened politely, while the kids wandered down to the beach to build a sand castle.

"Don't get too involved, Kelsey," her mother called out. "We need to get going soon."

"So, I hate to bring up work," Frank began, "but have you thought about what you want us to do while you're in New Hampshire?"

Maddy looked up, surprised. She'd forgotten about John's upcoming vacation with his boys.

"Well," John replied, "hopefully the floors will be done and dry upstairs, and ready to have the furniture moved in. Then you can start the lower level. Maddy has the paint picked out, I think, for every room but the kitchen." Maddy nodded. "I'll be happy if you get the carpet out and the molding done. I'll be thrilled if you get the walls started."

"Are you going to replace Tom?"

"I have someone stopping by on Wednesday afternoon," John answered. "He has some experience in laying tile, which will come in handy. He's a teacher, so he's just looking for summer work."

"Sounds good," Frank said.

"We should get going," Linda reminded her husband. "Especially if we have another stop to make on the way."

"Oh, yeah," Frank replied. "We were wondering if your boys might want to go out for ice cream with us."

"I'm sure they'd love it," John answered. "Should I call them in?"

"Let me do it." Frank was determined to make a display of the matter. "Hey, Kelsey, Blake and Parker," he yelled out. "Let's go out and get some ice cream!"

The kids' heads turned immediately and they all came running back to the house, cheering.

"Miss Maddy doesn't have any ice cream, can you believe it? We'll have to go down to Checker's, and see if they have any left."

"They have lots of ice cream, Uncle Frank," Blake assured him.

"They have huge buckets!" Parker added, jumping into his dad's lap to hug him.

"You guys be good for Uncle Frank and Aunt Linda, okay?" John reminded them.

"Yes, Dad," they said in unison.

"We'll take them over to our house afterward," Linda said. "You can pick them up any time."

"Yeah, but don't rush us," Frank warned. "We like to take our time with our ice cream."

"We'll do our best to give you the time you need," John assured his friend.

Burt tugged on the leash as John and Maddy attempted a leisurely stroll down the beach.

"Good thing you're holding him," Maddy said, content to hold John's other hand.

"I can't believe I'm doing this. A month ago, I was pretty sure I didn't want to get to know your dog any better."

Maddy laughed. "You've been very brave."

"Yes, I have."

"So, when do you guys leave for New Hampshire?"

"Next Saturday. We have a cabin over in Conway." John let Burt's leash out a bit. "Bad timing, huh?" He squeezed her hand.

"I'm sure you'll have a great time," she answered, trying to sound cheerful. "When will you get back?"

"The following Saturday, probably late. We'll be in church on Sunday."

"My mom is coming that following Monday," Maddy said.

"That'll be nice," John answered, mentally reviewing the upcoming week's obligations. How much time could they reasonably spend together?

"She'll be a big help with decorating. I'm looking forward to her input."

"Well, since you don't want mine."

Maddy laughed. They had walked south toward the public beach, and the early evening sun was still bright on the water. Coming to a particularly rocky area, they waited as Burt stopped to investigate something in the sand. There were surprisingly few boats out.

"Do you ever go out on the ocean?" Maddy asked.

"I go fishing when I can," John answered. "I love the water."

"I think I'd enjoy sailing," Maddy mused, "but I'm actually kind of afraid of being out in a boat."

"Really? You bought a house on the ocean, and you're afraid of it?"

"Yeah, I definitely prefer the water from this angle."

"We'll have to get you out there sometime, and see if we can change your mind," John said, slipping his arm around her as they continued to take in the view.

"Good luck with that," Maddy answered, leaning into his side.

Burt picked that moment to take off after some little creature, and John laughed as he was suddenly yanked away from Maddy. He called to Burt and reined him in. When the "boys" turned back, the look on John's face changed dramatically.

"What's wrong?"

Maddy slowly turned to look behind her, even as John grabbed her hand and took off running up the beach.

She could barely keep up with him, but concentrating on running was better than focusing on the line of black clouds that had rolled in from the northwest. The storm front was terrifyingly vivid, and they ran straight toward it, hoping to make it back before the heavens opened. The lightning flashed in the clouds, and Burt, fully aware of the coming storm, strained to get home. John did his best to grip the leash and keep hold of Maddy's hand. Although she was quick, she couldn't match his stride.

A rush of howling wind broke the stillness, and stinging drops of rain became a downpour, which seemed to blow horizontally against them.

"Let him go!" Maddy yelled. "He'll find his way!"

John dropped Burt's leash and turned back toward Maddy. His cellphone rang, and he grabbed it off his belt and shoved it deep into his pocket.

Maddy had never seen anything like the frightening sky above her head. She refused to look up as she stumbled forward, trying to breathe through the cramp in her side. The sand was slippery and her legs grew sluggish; she seemed to find every rock with her bare feet.

John tightened his grip on her hand, and they ran the last twenty yards up to the porch. He left her there while he went back out to collect the table and umbrella. The chairs had already blown down the beach.

Maddy sat on the steps, trying to catch her breath. Burt stood over her, occasionally licking her cheek, until she eventually pulled herself up and let him into the house. She began moving the porch furniture together, taking care to avoid the heavy swing that was blowing maniacally in the wind. She carried what she could into the kitchen as John pushed the grill into the fenced shower area where he'd put the other items he'd retrieved. Maddy limped back out to the porch, calling out to him as he disappeared around the side of the house.

She moved back toward the door and braced herself there. Looking out over the water, she was astonished at the transformation from the serene beach they had been enjoying only moments before. The storm front seemed to swallow up the remainder of the bright summer sky as it thundered down the coast. The black waves crashed wildly on the surf; they were higher by far than any she'd yet seen. The wind howled and the lightning flashed and the thunder seemed to shake the house to its foundation. She looked toward the side of the house and watched anxiously for John to return.

She felt a tug on her arm, and her heart gave another terrified leap before she realized that John had come through the house and was pulling her inside. Maddy tumbled into the kitchen as John went back out to take the swing down. A few minutes later, he came inside, shutting and locking the door behind him. He took

Maddy's hand and pulled her toward the fireplace and away from the windows. They fell exhausted onto the hearth, and Burt plopped his heavy, sodden body right next to them.

When Maddy regained her breath, she looked up at John with wide eyes. "The boys?"

He already had his cellphone out, but it was wet and had powered off. "I'll need yours," he said, pushing to his feet.

Maddy jumped up to search her purse, and John followed her into the kitchen. He lifted the receiver from the unit on the wall. It was dead, as he expected.

"Got it." Pulling her phone out, Maddy hit the power button. She watched John's apprehensive face as he waited and prayed for Frank to pick up. Miraculously, there was a connection.

"Frank?" John yelled hopefully.

Maddy waited for a sign of good news. John finally exhaled and smiled. She felt a rush of relief.

"Thanks, Frank, I'll..." He stopped and waited, then hung up and handed the phone back to her. The thunder shook the walls and the lightning flashed incessantly, but it didn't seem to matter. John was smiling; his boys were safe.

"We were cut off, but everyone's fine," he assured Maddy, still trying to catch his breath. "They saw the clouds on their way into town, and drove straight to Frank's house. He said they were making an adventure of it, and not to worry." John ran his hand through his wet hair. "As if that's possible."

"I'm so glad they're okay."

"We had a tornado go through about six years ago. It just missed town, but tore up the woods north of here. It almost never happens, but when it does..."

Maddy shuddered and went to the closet in her laundry room to get blankets. She handed one to John, and then grabbed a couple of candles from the counter and matches from the drawer. "Here's a flashlight," she said. "We'll probably need that soon."

It was already fairly dark when they returned to the relative safety of the fireplace area. Maddy lit the candles and set them in the hearth, then sat down next to John, pulling the blanket around her shoulders. Soaked through and exhausted, they huddled on the floor, John pulling Maddy under his own blanket. She snuggled in, grateful for a place to rest her head. John's shirt was wet, but it didn't matter. She listened to his heart beating, and willed her own to slow down. She still wasn't sure whether the house was going to blow over, but for the moment she felt safe.

John looked down at her. "I wonder if we should move into the cellar."

Maddy hated her cellar more than thunderstorms. "I think I'd rather sit on the porch."

John managed a laugh. "We'll give it a few minutes, but if it gets worse…"

Maddy rolled her eyes and adjusted her position. She was glad to have John to lean against, but he had nothing but the hard, stone fireplace. "I'm sorry I don't have any furniture," her voice was barely audible. "This is probably a bad time to ask you to help me move that couch in?"

John covered her face with one of the blankets.

"So, 'no'?" came the muffled reply.

Burt, lying in a wet heap nearby, began to whine. John pulled the blanket off Maddy's head, and she looked up at him with a grin as he pushed the hair out of her face.

"You're a mess," he said affectionately, pulling her close.

The storm raged around them, and the room was now dark, except for the candles that Maddy had lit. The setting was not terribly comfortable, but decidedly intimate. After a few minutes, John reluctantly pulled away and looked down at Maddy, bundled like a little cocoon next to him.

"I'm going to check the windows upstairs," he said, sliding the blanket off and tucking it in around her. "I'll be right back."

"I'm going with you," Maddy scrambled up after him, half in concern for her house, and half in determination not to be left alone. She grabbed a candle as she got to her feet.

John took the flashlight in one hand and her hand in the other. They walked slowly up the kitchen staircase, Maddy limping and favoring her left foot. John stopped and looked back at her.

"Are you okay?"

"I'm fine. My feet are a little sore," she replied. "I think I'll go rinse them off in the bathroom."

"Good idea," he said, walking with her into her room.

The lightning flashed, and the windows gave them a panoramic view of the storm. Maddy hurried into the bathroom, and John followed, setting the flashlight down and starting the water for her.

Maddy laughed nervously. "I think I can handle it from here. Why don't you go do the dangerous thing, and check the windows?" She climbed onto the edge of the tub and let her feet run under the warm water while John picked up the flashlight and left the room.

"I'll be right back," he promised.

Maddy quickly finished her task; something about running the water during the storm made her nervous. Pulling a towel from the rack, she dried off her body as well as she could, and then took the towel to her head. Her curls generally did not respond well to such treatment, and she stepped gingerly out of the tub to get her brush.

She winced when she put pressure on her foot; she definitely had a nasty cut. Opening the medicine cabinet, she pulled out the first aid ointment and some bandages, just as John came back into the room.

"You didn't have to do that for me," he grinned.

"What?"

Maddy looked in the mirror, literally jumping back in surprise at the wild mess she'd made of her hair. "Oh, wow, sorry," she said, trying unsuccessfully to push it down. "I was getting my brush when I realized my foot was cut."

"Is it bad?"

"Just a few small cuts, nothing serious," she assured him. She grabbed her brush and tried to deal with her hair. "Do you want to rinse off or anything?"

John considered the offer. "Maybe I'll wash up quickly."

"Help yourself to the soap and towels," Maddy said, hesitating at the door. "Do you mind if I put some dry clothes on?"

"Why would I mind?"

"I don't know. It doesn't seem fair."

"You might as well get dry if you can."

"I don't think I have anything big enough for you."

John smiled. "I hope not."

Maddy hobbled over to her closet, averting her eyes from the wall of windows showcasing the storm. She looked for the warmest sweats she could find, and was soon transformed from head to foot into warm, dry clothing. She stepped out of the closet with her bundle of wet clothes.

"You okay?" she called.

"I'll be right out," John answered.

He stepped out of her bathroom a moment later, his beaming flashlight turning him into little more than a shadow. "I don't suppose you have a big T-shirt lying around?" he asked between thunder claps, rubbing his head dry with one of her towels.

"I have some T-shirts that I sleep in; they're pretty big."

John considered this. "Pink? Flowery? Little puppies?"

Maddy laughed. "No, nothing like that. Well," she reconsidered, "nothing that I'd let *you* wear." She walked back into her closet and rummaged through a drawer. "Here's an Indiana University football shirt." She returned and tossed it to John. "One hundred percent manly."

Back in the kitchen with the storm pounding the windows, John tried to help Maddy bandage her foot but she wouldn't let him near it.

"I'm ticklish," she insisted, as she turned away from him and tended to her wound. John was worried about one of the cuts, which looked like it might need a few stitches, but Maddy wouldn't let him get close enough to see it clearly. He continued to hover, and Maddy threw threatening looks his way as she finished her doctoring.

When her cellphone rang, John picked it up and talked with Frank. He smiled as he hung up a few minutes later. "Parker's playing Yahtzee with Kelsey and Blake by candlelight. He's too busy to talk to me."

Maddy laughed. "Sounds like they're doing okay."

"I guess so." He came over and took her hand. Now accustomed to the howling storm, they walked back over toward the fireplace and stood looking out at what they could see of the beach through the darkness.

"I've always hated thunderstorms," Maddy said, tucking into his side.

"I've always kind of enjoyed them," John replied, holding her close.

"Well, I've kind of enjoyed this one," Maddy said, linking her arms around John's neck.

He smiled and leaned toward her. Their lips were just about to touch when Maddy cried out, "Otis!"

John drew back in surprise. He looked around, half expecting to see Maddy's neighbor standing behind him.

Maddy ran over to the windows that overlooked Otis' house. "I can't believe I haven't even given him a thought!" she moaned in self-reproach. "I feel terrible. I hate the idea of him being alone through all of this."

"He's probably been through a few storms," John said. "I'm sure he's fine."

"I hope so," Maddy replied, holding her candle by the window. "I wish he had a cellphone."

"Do you want me to go over and check on him?"

"No, of course, not. I'm sure you're right. He'll be okay." Maddy left the candle near the window, hoping that Otis would see it and respond in kind. She turned with a sigh and then smiled apologetically at John. "Sorry about that."

He grinned and walked back to the hearth, pulling her down beside him.

Maddy nestled in and put her head on his chest. "So, what do you want to do now?"

John wrapped an arm around her. "What do *you* want to do?" He had only one really good idea, but when he tried it, she yelled out the name of her elderly neighbor.

"Well," she thought for a moment. "Let's talk."

John smiled and leaned his head against the stony wall. Talking was probably wiser under the circumstances.

"I've been wondering," Maddy continued. "How does a litera-ture major become a home renovator?"

"I guess I didn't explain that particular link, did I?"

"No, I think we went from education to travels, and skipped back to work."

"Well," John began, "I taught high school literature and English for a couple of years before I started my business."

"Really?"

"Yeah. I'd always planned to teach, and while I enjoyed it, I found that I really loved working with my hands. I worked in construction during college and grad school summer breaks, and even after I started teaching. I finally decided that construction was what I wanted to do, so I got with Frank, and we started FDR."

"Where did you meet Frank?" Maddy asked.

"Long story."

"Look!" Maddy cried suddenly, pointing toward her neighbor's house. "Otis put a candle in his window. He's okay." She smiled happily back at John. "So, speaking of Frank, Linda and I had a great time today. She had some good ideas."

Maddy mentioned the bookshelves that she was envisioning for the corner of the room, and they talked about what else could be done to make the area inviting. Their conversation drifted to the next room, and what Maddy might do in her kitchen. She decided to tell him what she might *not* do.

"I have a confession," she began. "I can't cook."

He raised an eyebrow. "You can't or you won't?"

"A little of both," she conceded.

"So, what are you going to do for breakfast?"

"Tomorrow?"

"No," John laughed. "For your future guests."

"Oh. I haven't quite figured that out."

"This would explain your reticence with regard to updating the kitchen."

"You noticed?"

"You have a decided propensity to avoid the subject," he observed.

She smiled, "There's my English major."

"It wouldn't have to be complicated. You could start simple, and learn as you go."

"Yeah, I could just serve…biscuits," Maddy decided. "I'll open a Bed and Biscuit," she laughed.

John grinned. "Why bake at all? Just serve bagels or… bananas," he suggested.

Maddy giggled. "Oh, that's good. But I think it needs to be a two-syllable word. I *can* fry bacon."

"Excellent," John said. "Maddy's Bed and Bacon."

"I really shouldn't have to limit myself. I can use any letter I want."

"Absolutely," John agreed.

"I could have a B&C and serve croissants," she suggested.

"Cantaloupe's too many syllables…"

"What's with you and the fruit?"

"I like fruit."

"Well, pick a two-syllable one."

"Apple."

"Won't work, I can't have a B&A."

"Kumquat."

"Wow – what's that, a C or a K or a Q?"

"Really, Maddy. It's a K."

"B&K. Sounds like fast food. I don't think I like it."

John pulled her close. "Well, you make great coffee."

"Yes, I do."

"So, open a Bed and a Cup of Joe."

"That just might work."

fifteen

Maddy was relieved that Otis had survived the storm without her, and was reminded by her neighbor that he'd effectively done so for about eighty years; more than fifty, he was sure, before she was born. Maddy smiled at his gentle remonstration, but didn't regret her concern for him.

Both were grateful that neither home had sustained serious damage. Maddy had lost a few shingles and some beach chairs, and Otis needed some gutters and drain pipes re-attached, but that seemed to be the worst of it. As they surveyed the neighborhood on the slow drive to church the next morning, they noticed branches down and debris blown about, but most of the buildings and property seemed intact.

When they pulled in to the church, only one other vehicle occupied the lot. Maddy was relieved to see John's truck in the corner near a small outbuilding. She parked her car carefully nearby.

"Good thing we dressed casually," Otis said. "It looks like we'll be doing more cleaning than worshiping this morning."

"They would do that?"

" 'They' is us," he reminded her with a smile. "If there are folks with pressing needs, Pastor will have us see to them first. I don't imagine God will mind terribly if we delay our worship for a few hours," he speculated.

"Guess not," Maddy answered, walking toward the shed.

"Miss Maddy!" Parker shrieked, racing out of the building. "Miss Rachel had her baby!" He slammed into Maddy with an energetic hug, and she did her best to catch him and keep him from falling onto the pavement.

"Who had a baby?" she asked. Baby talk was not the first thing she expected to hear. Then it dawned on her.

"The pastor's wife," Otis supplied. "I hope she's okay."

John and Blake came out of the shed with matching grins of greeting. Maddy was taken back by how much they looked alike. She'd always thought Parker looked more like his dad, but this morning, Blake took that honor. She smiled in return, curious about their news.

"Hi, Mr. Otis. Hi, Miss Maddy," Blake said politely. "How's your house?"

"It's fine, Blake," she answered. "I just lost a few shingles. How's your house?"

He launched into the dramatic details of the limited damage, especially to their fort. Maddy smiled at John and turned her attention back to Blake.

"...but Dad can put the swings back on. He says maybe we can paint it, too!"

"That would be fun. You could paint the outside walls in camouflage colors, and then, you know what I'd do? I'd paint a map on the wall inside, where you could keep track of your adventures." She lowered her voice appropriately. "You could use chalk and draw right on the map."

Otis smiled at the exchange. Apparently he'd have to be the one to inquire about the baby. "Did Rachel really have her baby? Is everyone alright?"

John pulled his gaze away from his son and his... Maddy. "Yes, they're all fine. She went into labor in the middle of the storm, and they didn't want to drive up to Augusta. A neighbor came over to help, and Rachel had a baby boy early this morning. Name's Jonathan," he said with a grin.

"Well, well, well," Otis replied with a smile. "That's quite an honor, I'd say!"

"Yeah," said John. "It might have something to do with the fact that Rachel's father's name is Jonathan."

"Oh," said Otis.

"And it's Rob's dad's middle name."

Otis chuckled. "And the neighbor who delivered the baby?"

John laughed. "Probably. Although I think it was a woman."

Maddy got up to join them. "So, did I hear you have a name-sake?"

"Not exactly," John answered. He filled her in on the news, and told them that worship was canceled for the day.

"Pastor asked me to swing by and put a note on the door, but I figured I'd hang out and see if we could put together a bit of a cleanup party. You up for joining us?"

"Absolutely," Otis agreed. "We can start right here in the lot."

Maddy was definitely up for helping, although she wished she'd dressed more appropriately. She looked down at her white slacks; at least she hadn't worn a skirt.

"You won't want to get that blouse dirty." John followed her gaze much more appreciatively.

"You have a work shirt in the car, Dad," Blake suggested. "Miss Maddy could wear that."

"Yeah!" Parker circled around in time to join the conversation. "Just like you wore her shirt last night!"

John looked down at his son with a sigh. "You're right, Parker, my shirt got very wet in the storm, and Miss Maddy was nice enough to give me a dry shirt to wear over to Uncle Frank's to pick you up." He probably didn't need to cover all those bases, but he did anyway. Maddy seemed a little relieved, and Otis nodded politely.

"So, how about that shirt?" Maddy asked. "Can I change in the church?"

"Sure," John answered, heading over to his truck. Pulling the shirt out of the back seat, he said, "It's clean, but it's been in here a while." He handed it hesitantly to Maddy, who had followed him.

It was one of his grey tees, and she took hold of it, careful not to bury her face in the fabric while he was watching. "This will be fine. I'd just as soon not trash my blouse."

"Oh, but you're okay with trashing my nice T-shirt?" John asked, not yet letting go of it. He adjusted his grip so that his hand held Maddy's somewhere inside the cloth.

Maddy looked up at him with a smile. "I'll be careful, but I can't make any promises."

"I guess I'll take my chances." He stroked her thumb with his. What kind of bans would be in place while they were working at the church?

"Are you okay?" Maddy asked him.

"I'm fine. You'd better go change." He let the shirt and her hand go.

Maddy reached up to touch his shoulder. "I'm glad you made it home okay last night."

John took her hand and kissed it. "I'm glad I got to spend the storm with you," he said quietly.

"Me, too." She lingered, not wanting their brief, private moment to end. The look in John's eyes seemed surprisingly intense. She decided she'd better leave before she threw herself into his arms and really made a scene.

"I'll be back in a minute," she said, backing away slowly.

"Okay," John answered, watching her retreat.

"I don't suppose you have any jeans in there?" she asked, effectively breaking the spell.

John laughed. "I think you'd have better luck with a pair of Blake's," he answered. "You can check the 'Lost and Found' box in the office. You might find something in there."

"Okay," Maddy answered, turning with determination. Why couldn't she seem to tear herself away? She walked to the church and a much heavier thought hit her. How would she survive a week without him when he and his family went to New Hampshire?

A few minutes later, Maddy emerged with her blouse and slacks neatly folded. She put them in her car, and then joined the boys behind the shed. John greeted her with a whistle of appreciation, and the others also acknowledged how nicely her lime-green sweat pants matched John's shirt and her sandals. She spun around to model her ensemble.

"I'm not sure why someone left their pants at church, but I'm taking advantage," she announced. She finished twirling and looked down. "They seemed clean." She looked up with a grin and a shrug, and walked into the shed.

"I'll need a rake!" she called out to no one in particular.

John answered her call, following her into the small building. "Here's the rake," he began, reaching behind her.

"Here he is, indeed," Maddy grinned back slyly.

John hovered over her, the temptation to behave in a rakish way fairly compelling, the lime-green pants aside. He listened for the sound of young feet having followed, but it remained quiet. He then pulled a startled Maddy into his arms and kissed her more completely than he had, as yet, done.

Maddy didn't hesitate long before returning his greeting with equal fervor. She hadn't been in his arms like that; it was unnerving and wonderful and very short-lived.

He pulled away, looking intently into her eyes. No one had joined them yet, and Maddy's heart pounded as she looked up at him.

John backed up. "I'm sorry."

Maddy could hardly articulate a response. She looked from John to the door, expecting company at any moment.

"They're pretty intent on a rabbit hole they found behind the shed," he explained. "That's why I... I'm sorry, Maddy."

"Why are you sorry?" She finally found her voice. "It was fun! Surprising, but definitely fun."

John just shook his head.

"Were you happy that I wanted to rake?" Maddy reached up to touch his curls.

John smiled, but pulled her hand away. "I'm sorry. We can't do this right now."

Maddy looked up at him, putting her hands instead on her ve-lour-clad hips. "Oh, you can kiss me like you're... like we're..." she hesitated. What *was* that kiss? "But I can't even touch your hair? Who's making the rules here?" She kept her voice low. Rabbit holes could only be interesting for so long.

"I don't know," John said, again backing away. Maddy looked hurt, but he didn't trust himself to touch her.

"You didn't mean it?" she asked. *What kind of question is that?*

"Oh, I meant it," John assured her, shoving his hands in his pockets. "You waltzed out there in my shirt, and every bit of control I've been trying to exercise over the past few weeks just evaporated." He looked at her helplessly. "I'd better go see what the boys are doing."

Bewildered and a little steamed, Maddy watched him disappear through the door. With a sigh, she looked around the orderly shed. Pulling the rake off its hook, she marched out of the door and ran right into her contractor. Luckily, she didn't smack him with the rake, accidentally or otherwise.

"Maddy, I'm sorry," John said, holding her gently by the shoulders, but keeping a distance. "I shouldn't have walked out on you."

She agreed, but didn't immediately respond. He dropped his hands. "Okay," she answered. "I have work to do."

She walked past him into the yard and began raking earnestly. Blake and Parker soon joined her, picking up the larger sticks and piling them near the campfire pit. John helped Otis clean up the parking lot, enlisting the help of other worshipers as they arrived.

Before long, a group of about a dozen people gathered, and restored the church to its pre-storm beauty. The church itself had sustained little damage. The work was largely cosmetic, combing through the gardens and sweeping up debris. A general air of celebration prevailed, as people shared their stories of making it through the storm, and especially as they found out that Rachel's baby had been born.

The church grounds were in good shape by noon, and most of the group agreed to have lunch together at Theo's, if the store was open. Maddy declined, claiming that her feet were hurting, and bid a quick farewell while John was busy. Blake and Parker waved her off, promising to take good care of Otis.

Once home, it didn't take long to unload the unattractive legwear, and especially the sandals. She took off her bandages and washed out her cuts. Maddy hesitated, but only briefly, when it came to removing John's shirt. She was pretty sure she was irritated with him, and she wasn't going to get distracted by the smell and feel of his shirt against her skin.

She donned her own shorts and tank top, and threw his shirt in with a load of laundry. Before she could brood on her porch, however, she had to move the furniture back out from the kitchen, which only added to her sense of frustration. Finally sitting in her "happy place," Maddy scowled as she ate her lunch in silence, Burt lying quietly at her feet.

After her meal, she took another limp around the property. She found that one of the windows in the shed had been broken, so she put up a make-shift covering until one of John's crew could replace it. She picked up the branches in the yard and then decided to rest her feet. She wasn't sure what one did to clean the beach, anyway. The storm had washed up quite a bit of interesting debris, but she figured she'd wait until the boys had a chance to look through the intriguing mess.

Some time later she pulled John's shirt out of the dryer and folded it carefully. She looked at it a moment, and then pressed it to her face, her mind going back to his kiss. It was the kind of kiss she imagined might have happened in the midst of the thrill of the storm as they huddled by her fireplace. Instead, John had been very careful while they were alone together for hours. Then this morning, *in the church shed*, he kissed her with a fire that still took her breath away.

Maddy put another load in the dryer. John seemed mortified that he'd kissed her like that, and really seemed to regret it. She went to her room and sat down at her computer. She knew she'd fallen fast for John. She'd been pretty reckless for someone determined to protect herself.

Once again, she resolved to rein things in a bit. It was time to insist on a few bans of her own.

The website was shaping up nicely, and Maddy looked forward to plugging in the details of the rooms, once she got them decorated. When she disciplined her mind, she found that she had plenty to keep her occupied and challenged.

After wrapping up her computer work, she gave Burt a short walk and made a salad. She took her furniture list to the porch while she ate, and evaluated what was left to buy. She considered the mattresses she had yet to purchase. It would probably be worth driving up to Augusta to some sort of outlet store.

"Maddy?"

She jumped at the sound of John's voice. He walked up the steps, and Maddy's newly focused and disciplined heart began to race.

"Hey, John," she said, cool and casual.

"Mind if I join you?"

"Of course not. Sit down."

John pulled out a chair. "What are you working on?"

"My furniture list."

"I see."

"I need to get those mattresses."

"There are some decent stores in Augusta."

"That's what I figured. I'll probably go this week sometime."

"I'm going up on Tuesday, and my business shouldn't take more than a couple of hours. If you want to come with me, I could show you some places that might give you a good deal."

That's all I need, Maddy thought, *mattress shopping with John.* "Sure," she found herself saying. "I'd appreciate the help."

Burt was fairly insistent on John's attention, and he allowed his focus to remain on the wolfhound. Maddy seemed a little withdrawn as she looked at her list on the table. She appeared deep in thought, serious and focused. She was also still wearing his shirt.

"The yard looks good; you must have worked hard around here today," he observed.

"Yeah, I got the big pieces picked up. Oh," she looked up. "There's a window in the shed that's broken. I covered it, but it's going to need a more permanent fix."

"I'll take care of it tomorrow."

"Thanks."

The dryer buzzer sounded and Maddy said, "Oh, I washed your shirt. Oh!" she looked down. She forgot that she'd slipped it back on.

She looked up, ready to scowl in response to whatever John was doing. He simply leaned back in his chair with his arms crossed, one hand casually stroking his chin and covering his mouth which had an unmistakable grin. His eyes were crinkling on the sides. She loved that part of his smile, usually. Right now she didn't like it so much.

She began to take the shirt off, which effectively changed John's smug little smile. That much was satisfying, she thought as she pulled it over her head, revealing her tank top underneath.

"I was just trying to remember to give it back to you," she muttered.

John had regained his smile as she handed him the newly folded shirt. "So, did you know I was coming, or were you were going to wear it until tomorrow morning?"

Maddy gave him a sour look. "No. Maybe. Where are the boys?"

"They went to a movie with the neighbors," John answered. "I thought I'd come over and see what you were up to."

"You might have called first."

"I probably should have," John acknowledged. "But neither of my phones work, and I really didn't want to give you the opportunity to say no."

Maddy smiled a little. Deep down, she was happy that he was sitting on her porch. "Can I get you something to drink?"

John followed her into the kitchen, and Maddy poured lemonade. They sat down at the counter and sipped their drinks, uncertain how to begin to sort out the strangeness of the morning.

"Maddy," John began.

"If you apologize again for kissing me, I'll…"

John sat back. "You'll what?"

"I don't know," Maddy blew some hair out of her eyes. "What were you going to say?"

"I was going to ask why you didn't come to lunch with us."

Maddy played with her glass, watching the ice cubes swirl around. "I guess I was still upset with you."

"Okay." John waited for more.

"It's just that you were irrational, and it scared me."

John grimaced. It was a fair observation. "I know. It scared me, too."

Maddy looked up at him. "But which part do you think was irrational? Kissing me or shutting me out afterward?"

Ouch. "Both, I think."

"If you think kissing me was irrational..."

"Maddy, I don't regret kissing you." He looked at her earnestly. "It just scared me; the lack of control I felt. If I can't control myself in the church shed, with my boys around the corner, then what will I do when I'm alone with you?"

Maddy looked around. *Like right now?* There was a part of her that really wanted to find out. Another part of her had the good sense to acknowledge his struggle.

"Well, we decided that we're in this together, both 'doing our part,' so to speak," she said.

John nodded. "And you did your part to stop my rather sudden advances this morning?"

She inhaled, stopped. What could she say?

"Nothing was going to happen in the church shed," she finally answered. *Was it?*

John grinned. "No thanks to you."

"You have to trust yourself more."

"I'll try."

"And me, too."

"I will."

"And if we make a mistake or cross a line, we have to work it out together," she said with feeling. "Nobody leaves the shed."

"I won't walk away again."

"Thank you," she said, looking away. *I really need to be able to trust you, John.*

He picked up one of her hands. "Maybe this would be a good time to tell me what happened in Seattle."

She looked at him, aggravated with herself for the inevitable tears that were now too big to keep from spilling over onto her cheeks. John wiped them gently with his calloused thumb.

She gave him a small smile. "The whole story?"

"As much as you feel like telling me."

Maddy took a deep breath. "I met Phil at work. He'd been at the firm a couple of years when I started, and he kind of took me under his wing. We would kid around about starting our own business, becoming our own bosses and all of that. We eventually came up with a plan, and with some help we launched our own consulting firm. Since it was mostly service-oriented, the initial investment was minimal.

"Well, it really took off." She stopped and thought for a minute, a smile tugging at her lips. There were some good memories in with the bad. "Anyway, we spent a lot of time together, all of us, but especially Phil and me. It just seemed natural that we thought we belonged together." The smile left her face as she looked past John and out of the window.

"Of course, it was exciting for a while. I did love him, or at least the idea of him," she acknowledged, "but I guess he wasn't really invested. I know he was frustrated that I," Maddy paused, trying to recall the phrase, "that I chose 'to proceed very carefully in our relationship.' " She smiled a little at John. "Phil felt strongly that we were moving too slowly. It was a constant battle. I wish I could tell you that I held out for more lofty reasons, but the truth is, I didn't like him controlling me." She sighed. "So there's another confession for you. I don't seem to be a terribly committed person, do I?"

John took her hand, again. "You're honest, and that's what matters to me. And I think you're more committed than you give yourself credit for."

Maddy took another deep breath. "Anyway, we got engaged, started planning a big wedding. It was exciting, like I said, but I was never completely at peace with it all. I kept thinking that we'd be happy once the business got established, once we were married, once we had children. I knew I was *supposed* to be happy… and I really did think I was in love." Maddy stopped again.

Then she recalled the details of her break-up with Phil, such as it was, and John listened quietly, holding her hand. The tears rolled quietly down Maddy's cheeks as she spoke. When she was done, John wiped them away again.

"I'm so sorry," he said.

She gave a little smile in return. "It doesn't hurt so much anymore," she acknowledged. "It just makes me mad."

John nodded; he definitely understood. "Have you seen him since then?" he asked, resting his hands on hers.

"No," Maddy answered, distracted by how her hands seemed to disappear under John's. "A couple weeks later, he left a box with a few of my things – pictures, that kind of thing – on my desk, with a note." She shrugged.

John's observations about Phil's character probably wouldn't help Maddy at the moment. "How long ago was that?"

"It happened in December, so it's been a year and a half. It took me a year to figure out that I needed to move on with my life. Of course, that time was also spent helping with the transition at work." Maddy pulled her hands out from under John's, and ran her fingers along his knuckles, inadvertently tracing the occasional scars that marked them. "I started looking for property the following Christmas, and then found myself checking this place out in February." She looked around the room, her smile returning. "I really can't believe I'm here."

"Thanks for trusting me, for telling me all of this."

"Thanks for listening."

John's face grew serious. "I'm sorry for what you've been through, but I can't help but be happy that it brought you here."

Maddy smiled softly. "Me, too."

They were both quiet, lost in thought, and then Maddy asked, "So, do you want to tell me about..." she hesitated.

"Jennifer." Their conversation had obviously stirred some memories. "She left a little over two years ago." He stopped to consider this. "In one sense, the time seems to have flown by, but it also seems like a long time since she was in our lives." He looked beyond Maddy at nothing in particular. "Time is a funny thing."

"How long were you married?"

"Six years."

Six years. It was strange to think of John having a significant past with someone else. "Where did you meet?"

"We met in college, and ended up going to grad school together." John replied. "We got married after we got our masters', and she began her doctorate study that summer. I started teaching here in Clairmont the following fall. Our lives seemed to go in separate directions, almost from the start."

"What was she studying?"

"History. It was really her passion." He shifted in his chair. "Apparently she never wanted to have kids, and when she got pregnant with Blake," he stopped, and his look became grim, "that was my first clue that I really didn't know her."

Maddy listened quietly, stroking John's hand.

"I was a little overwhelmed, but excited about being a father. She just said she wasn't ready. It was an awful time for both of us." John rubbed his eyes. "We both panicked. She was afraid of having a child and giving up her career. I was afraid that she'd have an abortion." John looked at Maddy. "That's when I got reacquainted with God and really started to pray.

"We got through that, and we were okay for a while once Blake was born. I started my business when he was a year old, and things got a little crazy because we were both so busy." He stopped, lost in thought. "I feel like I missed out on the first years of Blake's life, and I know Jen did. When Parker came along, she just kind of snapped. She felt trapped by motherhood and only saw me as someone trying to hold her back. By then, my business was up and running, and I took more time with the boys. Frank was great." John smiled for the first time in his narrative. "He just took over and let me take care of my kids."

"Frank's a great guy."

"Without a doubt," John agreed. "Anyway, Jen had been talking about studying abroad; said she needed some space and time for herself. Somehow, I knew it was the end. A mother doesn't just leave her young children to study overseas for six months. Blake was devastated."

John stopped for a moment, and Maddy ached to see the pain in his eyes. "I could deal with her leaving me. Our marriage wasn't the same once she got pregnant with Blake. But the kids…

"Parker was too young to know what was going on, but I told Blake from the beginning that his mother wasn't coming back. It sounded so cruel," his voice caught, "but I knew it was the truth.

When she wrote after three months and confirmed it, we were more or less ready. She asked for nothing in the divorce – her parents had left her money – but the fact that she willingly gave up all rights with the kids blew me away. She just wanted to be released from the family."

Maddy's mind reeled. "And you haven't seen her since?"

"No. As far as I know, she's still in Europe."

"And she hasn't seen the children?"

"No," John replied. "I have reason to believe that she has other distractions over there."

"And her clothes and other things?"

"Her sister came and packed up her stuff. It was surreal. We hardly spoke during the two days she spent going through the house. I know she felt bad; didn't like what she had to do."

"Do the boys ever see her?"

"Jen's sister? No, she lives in L.A. And Jen's parents died before we met, so the boys have no grandparents on her side."

Maddy didn't know what to say. She came around the counter and put her arms around John. He stood and held her.

"I'm so sorry," she said.

"It's okay now. It took a while." He shook his head. "I had to figure out what forgiveness really meant. It basically amounted to dropping the whole thing in God's lap." He smiled a little." That's how Blake and I talked about it, anyway."

"Well, you've done a wonderful job raising the boys," Maddy said.

"Thanks," he said. "And you were pretty brave to move across the country and take this on." He looked around the room.

"Yes, I was, wasn't I?" She grinned up at him. "I've had good help."

"Yes, you have," John agreed, kissing her forehead.

Maddy put her arms around his neck. The last time she'd faced her break-up with Phil, she'd spent the night crying with her dog. The healing process had definitely taken a pleasant turn.

sixteen

The storm damage response required only a few hours' work for the crew Monday morning, and that included making the minor repairs to Otis' house. At noon, Maddy and Otis picked up sandwiches downtown, and everyone convened on her porch for lunch.

Otis finished fairly quickly, and after thanking everyone again, made his way home for his afternoon nap. John started outlining the week for the rest of the crew, mentioning that he'd be out of town Tuesday, and that the new guy, Bill, would be joining them Wednesday. They talked through the week's projects and were wrapping up when the topic of John's trip to Augusta came up again. Frank wanted to confirm the paint choices for various rooms in the house, but then acknowledged that Maddy would be around if he had any questions.

"No, Maddy's coming to Augusta with me," John replied.

The grin that spread across Frank's face caused Travis and Willie to reconsider what had, at first, been rather mundane news.

"You putting her to work on the Augusta job?" Frank asked, biting into his sandwich.

John looked hard at his friend. "No, Frank. I'm giving Maddy a ride so she can look for mattresses."

Too much information, thought Maddy, as the grin on Frank's face grew wider. Travis and Willie began looking from Frank, to John, and then to Maddy, and back to Frank, again. The latter's smile was especially entertaining.

"I'm going to need to buy at least four mattress sets. I figure I might get a better deal up there," Maddy explained.

"No doubt," Frank agreed, chewing and grinning, and looking back and forth between John and Maddy. She decided it would be a good time to clean up from lunch.

"We're going to start on your room upstairs, Maddy," John reminded her. "I think we'll move the furniture, except the bed, in-to the hole-room, so if you could finish moving your personal things down here, that would be great." His efforts to sound de-tached and businesslike were pretty much in vain. Travis and Willie now wore smiles that matched Frank's as they brought in their lunch dishes. Wisely holding their tongues, they left John and Maddy to finish their conversation with forced disinterest.

By the end of the afternoon the master bedroom was primed and the molding stripped. The bookshelves had long since been finished and the end result should have pleased Maddy a great deal. Instead, the room looked empty and sad to her when she looked in at the end of the day. The bed, which had been partially disassem-bled, stood in the middle of the room; the mattress and box spring propped against the frame. She heard John's footsteps and a mo-ment later he joined her in the doorway.

"Looks different, doesn't it?" he asked.

"It looks good," Maddy nodded. "I'm going to miss this room, but I like what you've done to it."

"It's not like you can't stay in here when you don't have guests," he reminded her.

"Yeah, but it won't be the same," she answered. "It's not really my room, anymore. My room is downstairs," she said with more conviction. "It will be fun to shop for bedding and make it cozy." Her enthusiasm started to become real. "I'll do that while you're doing your thing in Augusta."

John leaned down to get a closer look at her smile, but Maddy met his lips with her finger. "Work day," she reminded him, slip-ping past him down the hall. She turned with a grin at the top of the steps. "Your rules, not mine."

While the men started painting the walls and lacquering the trim in the master bedroom the following morning, Maddy and John got on the road for the trip to John's other work site. Travel coffee mugs in hand, they talked about the day ahead, and Maddy asked John about the house he was working on. He filled her in on some of the renovations they had done, explaining that the house was large and relatively new to begin with, so they were basically installing a lot of expensive new fixtures. It wasn't his favorite kind of work.

"I really prefer bringing an older home back to life," he smiled at Maddy. "It's more challenging, but definitely more satisfying."

"So how did you get involved in this job?"

"It was a contact through my sister," John answered. "She went to school with Dave Perkins, though his wife is making most of the decisions about the house. He's never around."

Really? "What's Mrs. Perkins like*?" Is she young? Old? Is she pretty?* John glanced at Maddy. "What do you mean?"

"Does she know her stuff? Is she easy to work with?" *Is she pretty?*

"Well," John considered the questions. "She has very expensive taste, and has plenty of money to burn, so it's really a matter of helping her make good decisions. She definitely appreciates the input."

I'll bet she does. "So, how old is she?" Maddy thought she'd make small talk.

John gave Maddy a sidelong glance. "Probably early forties."

Ouch; not old enough. Might as well dig. "Is she pretty?" Maddy continued to look at the countryside, and when John didn't answer immediately, she looked over at him, innocent curiosity carefully displayed on her face. It gave way to a sheepish grin when she beheld the look on John's. "I just thought I'd ask."

"She could be considered pretty, if you like her kind of style."

"Do you?" The question came out before Maddy could stop it.

"Maddy…" John said her name with a slight hint of exasperation.

"Was that your scolding voice, John?"

"No, that's my 'you're getting too nosy' voice."

"Well!" Maddy crossed her arms and looked out the window. Convicted, but unrepentant, she turned on him again. "Is she a sunbather?" The possibility dawned on Maddy with some alarm. She looked hard at John and saw his face color a little. "She *is* a sunbather!" Maddy gasped. "I'm coming with you."

"You can't come with me," he said, pulling off the interstate. "We're at the mall, and I'm dropping you off here. I'll call you when I get back."

Maddy looked at him defiantly. "Fine."

John pulled into the parking lot. "Maddy, I don't want to leave you like this, but you can't come. You'd be bored, anyway."

"I don't really want to come," she assured him, getting out of the truck. "I'll see you later." She turned and left without another word.

"I'll be about two hours," he called after her.

She waved dismissively and pulled out her lists. She refused to think about John working with rich, beautiful, sunbathing women. It was time to do some shopping.

Two very long hours later, with John's work complete and Maddy's shopping unfruitful, they drove in silence to the first mattress store.

"Want to stop for lunch?" John glanced over at Maddy, unsure which mood might color the next phase of their day.

"Let's check out one of the stores, first," Maddy suggested. "I'd like to get an idea of what I'm in for, if you don't mind waiting to eat."

"Fine with me," John answered. "Conrad's Furniture is only about five minutes away."

"Okay," she replied. She looked out the window, brooding for a few minutes, and finally said, "I'm sorry for asking so many questions before. It was none of my business."

"It's okay." John paused. "I might have had a few of my own if you were meeting with another contractor."

Maddy smiled a little. "So far I'm satisfied with the one I have; not that it couldn't change."

John grinned. "Threat duly noted."

Maddy was still a little curious about how John had spent the last two hours, but since she'd just apologized for being nosy, she could hardly ask him outright. She contemplated how to get him to be more forthcoming about his recent renovating experience. He seemed content to drive along in silence. She had to bait him somehow.

"So, how many lovesick homeowners are there?"

"How many *what*?"

"Lovesick homeowners, you know, like Mrs. Perkins?" Maddy was trying to sound casual, even flippant, but she really did want to know.

"Maddy," he began.

She looked at him innocently. "You're the one who told me about the women who sunbathe while you work. I just wondered how many of us there are?"

"Women who sunbathe while I work?"

"No, John, lovesick homeowners. You know what I mean."

"Honestly, I don't," John answered, beginning to enjoy watching Maddy trap herself.

"Oh, please."

"Well, I can think of *one*." He hesitated long enough to make her almost ask for details. "I don't know if you'd call her lovesick, but I'm pretty sure she's interested."

Maddy cringed and looked out the window.

"She's younger than Mrs. Perkins – I don't know how much – I haven't figured that out, yet. And she's very pretty, if you like her kind of style."

Maddy shifted, trying to be aloof, but wanting very much to hear more.

"She's got great…" he hesitated, could sense Maddy's curiosity, "well, I probably shouldn't be mentioning that." He was quiet for a moment, and Maddy turned to look at him. He grinned as he drove along, and she found his profile both adorable and infuriating.

"She's difficult to work with," he continued as he pulled into the lot of the furniture store. "She's strong-willed and irritable…"

Maddy inhaled sharply.

"Until she's had her coffee," John explained. "And I might not have the patience to work with her at all, if she didn't have such a cool dog." He parked his truck and looked at her. "Know anyone like that?"

Maddy's face revealed an entertaining mix of emotions. John enjoyed seeing her at a loss for words.

"I know someone who might be *moderately* interested, who's *way* younger than Mrs. Perkins," she replied. "In fact," she continued, opening her door, "she's probably way younger than you, too, so it would never work."

She exited his truck with a flourish, and she heard John's laugh as she closed the door. At the store entrance, he held the door for her, still grinning as she walked through it. Maddy maintained her attitude of hauteur as she marched ahead to the mattress department.

"I'm going to look at these bunk beds," John called after her. "I'll join you in a minute."

"Take your time," Maddy threw over her shoulder.

She found her way to the mattresses, and a pretty young saleswoman walked up to greet her. *Figures*, Maddy thought.

"Hello, ma'am, how are you today?" She smiled pleasantly at Maddy, who cringed at the 'ma'am.'

"Fabulous," she answered, somewhat curtly.

"Can I help you find something?"

"I'd like to see some mattresses," Maddy began.

"What size are you interested in?"

"You name it."

The clerk returned a puzzled smile. "Well, we have everything from twin to king-size. Some are pillow-topped, and some are extra long. It depends on what you're looking for, and what you want to spend."

Maddy wasn't sure where to begin, but was fairly certain that John was coming up behind her, based on the increased animation of the pretty mattress clerk.

"My guess is you'll need one of our longer mattresses," the girl continued, smiling and waiting to be introduced to Maddy's shopping partner.

Maddy found herself blushing right along with the clerk. "Not necessarily," she replied through her teeth.

"Oh," the girl squeaked, not altogether disappointed. "Sorry, I just assumed." She stared up, wide-eyed, at John as he joined them.

"Assumed what?" John asked, casually putting his arm around Maddy's shoulders.

"She assumed that we were mattress shopping together," Maddy explained, hoping to include him in her embarrassment.

"Oh, well, we are, aren't we?" He looked at Maddy, then at the clerk. "Hi, I'm John," he said, extending his hand.

She shook it, the silly smile still spread across her face. "I'm Darlene."

"Of course we're together," Maddy interrupted them, irritated that John remained so composed and oblivious. "But we're not buying a mattress *together*. You're just helping me."

"Oh, right," John replied.

"Let's start with the queen," Maddy said, trying unsuccessfully to catch his eye so she could scowl at him.

Darlene began explaining their options and walked them over to the queen-size mattresses, inviting them to lie down and test them. Maddy declined, but John stretched out readily on the first bed. Linking his hands behind his head on the pillow, he grinned at Maddy.

"It's nice. You should try it."

She looked hard at him. "I'll take your word for it."

"You really should try it," the clerk encouraged Maddy. "It's the only way you'll know if you like it."

Maddy looked at Darlene, and then at John, who continued to grin at her. "No thanks, I'll try this one." Maddy turned to the next bed and lay down on it. The pillow top made it very comfortable.

"How do you like that one?" John asked her. "Should I try it?"

"Not necessary." Maddy slid off the bed before John could move to join her. The clerk, puzzled, looked back and forth between her customers.

John sat up on his bed and looked around. "What's the difference between this one and that one over there?" he gestured to another bed close by.

Darlene launched into mattress descriptions, which John attended to very seriously. Maddy watched as he tried out another bed, and talked animatedly with his new friend. She was tempted to wander off and look at foot stools and let him have his fun. Instead, she walked over and lay down on the bed that John was testing.

Surprised, he turned his head. "What do you think?"

"It's nice. A little firmer than the other one I tried. I definitely like the pillow top."

Darlene watched them a little wistfully. "Would you like me to price it for you?"

Maddy sat up. "Well, I'm going to need one queen and three double sets. Can you offer a price break with a larger purchase?"

Darlene was a little overwhelmed. "I'll go check with my manager."

"Thanks," Maddy said. "We'll wait here."

Mega-Mattress was located in a large strip mall, and it looked like it had been around for years. Maddy hoped that the stark walls and cold, cavernous space were evidence that the owners passed along the savings on decorating to the customers. A middle-aged gentleman came up to greet them.

"Good afternoon, folks. My name is Steven. How can I help you today?"

"Hi, Steven. My name is Maddy, and I would like to look at your mattresses."

Steven grinned, and Maddy rolled her eyes. It was a mattress store – of course she would like to look at mattresses. "Queen-size," she quickly qualified, ignoring John.

Steven didn't. "And who's this fine-looking gentleman with you, Maddy?"

"He's my… John," she finished, confirming her inability to communicate.

John reached out to shake hands. "Nice to meet you, Steven."

"Same here, I'm sure. Now, what are you two looking for?"

"A medium-firm pillow top," Maddy answered decisively. Then, anticipating John's interference, added, "He'll tell you he likes a firm mattress, but don't listen to him."

"Well, well," chuckled Steven. "I've got quite a variety, but I don't think I can accommodate those two options in the same bed. Are you two sure you want to sleep together?"

Steven couldn't have anticipated how long he would have to wait for an answer to his question, which was fine with him, because as far as he was concerned, it was rhetorical. He strolled up the aisle, leaving one discomfited and one thoughtful customer to follow.

Maddy was the first to move, glad to have a reason not to look at John. She just knew he was grinning; she could feel his gaze on her back as they walked.

"Now, here's a fine mattress with a smaller pillow top. Might suit you both," Steven was saying.

"Probably not," Maddy found her voice. "John's pretty fussy about these things. We should probably just buy separate mattresses, shouldn't we, dear?"

"Now, that will never do," Steven answered for him. "I'm sure we can find something that will work for both of you." He maneuvered around the beds and gestured for them to follow. "This one over here has no pillow top, but it's surprisingly comfortable for a firm mattress. Why don't you give it a try, Maddy?"

"Maddy really likes her pillow top," John joined in. "Let's look at these over here."

Steven seemed a little flustered, and Maddy felt bad that he was caught in the middle of their silly game. She decided to test and fall in love with the first thing she tried. It wasn't difficult. The first mattress she lay down on, and she was careful to pick one that was on sale, felt more comfortable than any she'd tried at the other store.

"I do like this, Steven. What kind is it?"

Steven's face lit up at her interest, and he immediately explained all the wonders of the mattress she had chosen. John sat on the edge of the bed and listened politely, and Steven sauntered over to him as he talked.

"Now you just give this a try, John. Your little lady likes it." He nudged John on the shoulder, and he fell back onto the bed next to Maddy.

Maddy looked over at him. "What do you think, honey?"

"I think it's great, darling." He smiled at her and looked back at the clerk. "Do you think it will help with Maddy's snoring?"

Maddy punched John's arm, as Steven looked on with a kindly smile.

"Well, a good mattress has a lot of benefits, and if you're sleeping better, there's a good chance you'll snore less. Or at least," he added, his smile widening, "You'll sleep right through it, John."

"I sure hope so," John answered with feeling. He was rewarded with another punch.

"Ouch! Maybe we *should* get separate mattresses." John faked a yawn and stretched, effectively clothes-lining Maddy. Steven found the whole display very entertaining.

Maddy twisted out from under John's arm and slid off the bed. "This is great, and it's on sale, right? How much for one of these and three double sets?"

Steven was dismayed. "You really want separate mattresses?"

"I'm opening an inn down in Clairmont," Maddy replied. "And I need to buy at least four mattress sets from you. I was hoping you could give me a deal."

"But you're not," he sputtered, looking at John and back at Maddy.

"No, we're not," Maddy told him. "But I really do like your mattresses," she added, noting the look of disappointment on his face.

"I just thought you made the nicest couple," Steven said, feeling let down for all the wrong reasons. "I'll go see what I can find out for you." He walked away, muttering about snoring and pillow tops.

Maddy put her hands on her hips and looked at John. "You've been nothing but trouble today. Did you see how sad you made Steven?"

John laughed. "*I* made him?"

Maddy shook her head with a grin. Steven returned with his figures, and Maddy was pleased with the deal that he offered. She signed for the purchase, further delighted that Steven promised to throw in half a dozen pillows for free. When he assured her that they would be delivered within the week, Maddy felt her first twinge of disappointment. She didn't know how long she thought it might take. She supposed she hoped Steven would follow her home in his big Mega-Mattress truck.

John and Maddy made it back to Clairmont just before six. He dropped her off with a disappointingly quick kiss, which did not do justice to a couple who pretended to be married for the afternoon. Maddy waved him off with a sigh and went in to update her lists.

seventeen

It was business as usual on Wednesday, and Maddy reminded herself not to be surprised at John's distance when he was in "work mode." It was just such a contrast from the day before, that she found herself a little concerned. She brooded over this as she arranged her things in her new room, gradually cheering as she put things away.

The men coated the bedroom floors with polyurethane, which filled the house with an interesting and decidedly unpleasant smell. Maddy walked Burt and then decided to shop for bedding. She needed to think about something other than her contractor. Being in the same house with him while he was so focused on anything but her was driving her crazy.

Shopping fulfilled its purpose on several levels. She found bedding, sheets and window treatments, and was happily distracted in the process. Armed with her purchases, she began the drive home, her mind now full of decorating ideas. Finishing the bedrooms was within sight, and outfitting the parlor, dining room and sitting room was around the corner. *Then the kitchen...* She sighed, wishing she felt more excited about that project. She'd have to take another look at her finances and see where she stood.

When she finally pulled into her driveway, only one truck remained, and Maddy smiled. It seemed natural to come home to John, and as she maneuvered her armload of packages through the house, her mind skipped ahead to the not-so-distant-future when his work on her house would be done. She pushed the door open into the kitchen, where he was bent over some paperwork at the counter. She smiled at his profile; his left hand braced his chin, his fingers rifling through the hair above his ear, as was his habit.

He finished writing and turned to her, his look of concentration replaced with a smile.

"Hey – you're back."

She set her bags down on the ground and tossed her keys on the countertop. "What are you working on?"

"We never had our financial update this week, and we need to do it before I leave on Saturday."

Maddy frowned at the reminder. "I was thinking along those lines on the way home. How does it look?"

"I'll need a few more minutes, and then I'll let you know."

Maddy disappeared into her room, and John smiled, listening to her hum while she put her things away. He was tallying another column of numbers when she re-entered the kitchen.

"Do you want something to drink?" she asked.

"I'm good."

Maddy poured herself some iced tea, leaned against the counter and watched him. He felt her eyes and looked up.

"You okay?"

Maddy smiled. "Oh, I'm fine. I just like watching you work."

"It's a little distracting."

Maddy circled around the counter and leaned into him while looking over his shoulder. John stopped and looked up into her mischievous face.

"Maddy, go away."

He elbowed her and she giggled and went outside. She sat down on the rocker, taking in the view. She didn't last long, and soon came back in with a *bang!*

John tried to give Maddy one of his 'looks,' but she was oblivious, marching past him to the pantry to get some pretzels.

"Oh – the new guy! Did he show up today? What's he like?"

John put his pencil down. "He talks more than Travis."

"Get out."

"But not more than you."

Maddy drew breath to argue, looked hard at him, and then walked up behind him and wrapped her arms around his shoulders.

He turned toward her. "What's gotten into you today?"

Maddy grinned. "Well, you ignored me all morning, and I need some attention."

"I ignored you so that I could concentrate on fixing up your house."

Maddy grinned some more and rubbed her nose on his.

"I should be ignoring you now, so I can finish this, but you're making it impossible."

"Am I?"

"Don't make me break a ban."

"John, you wouldn't!" Putting her hands on either side of his head, Maddy turned him to face his work. Her hands lingered as she smoothed the hair behind his ears. "Is that better?"

"Absolutely not. I have no idea what any of these numbers mean."

Maddy laughed and dropped her hands. "I'll leave you alone, now. I'm going to go make up my bed. I have a new bedspread," she boasted, trotting off to her room.

John smiled, wondering how long it would be before she re-emerged. Although she didn't actually leave her room, Maddy's efforts at sabotaging his work were complete a few minutes later when she blasted her radio. He stacked his papers in a pile and pushed away from the counter. The work day was over. It was time to greet Maddy properly.

John leaned against the doorframe and watched Maddy at work. She balanced somewhat precariously between a chair and the window ledge in an attempt to remove the curtain rod. For a moment he thought she was going to fall, but she caught herself and continued to wrestle with the stubborn rod. She looked over at him.

"John! Hi! Did you finish your work?"

"No, Maddy, I had to give up."

"I'm so sorry. Would you give me a hand here?"

John didn't move. "You're not sorry at all." Maddy grinned in response. "But," he continued, "I am. I'm done for the day, so *I'm sorry*, I can't help you."

Maddy was rather shocked. "You really won't?"

"Nope," he said, walking over to her.

She stood on her perch, looking down at him. "Fine, I'll do it without you." She turned back to the window and gave the curtain rod one more yank. When it came loose, Maddy lost her balance, and John reached up to steady her. His hands around her waist, he waited for her to find her footing.

"Thanks," she grinned. "I thought you weren't going to help."

"I wasn't going to watch you fall through the window."

"Well, you're my hero," she replied matter-of-factly, returning to her work of threading the curtain rod through the curtain.

John watched her for a moment. "You don't have to do that up there, you know."

Maddy smiled sweetly and kept working. In the next instant she was up in the air as John pulled her off her perch and brought her down to the floor. She stood very close, looking up at him.

"You can't just pick me up and put me places," she scolded.

"Actually, I can," he countered, still holding her.

"Well, would you put me back when I'm done?" Maddy made an effort to finish attaching the curtain. It wasn't easy; she didn't have a lot of space to maneuver.

"Maddy, I told you, I'm done with work."

"Then why did you bring me down here?"

John took the curtain rod and set it on the bed, and Maddy very quickly forgot about her window dressing.

Maddy's mood went south with John's departure later that afternoon. She was in no mood for socializing when Otis showed up and reminded her of their dinner date with the neighbors. She all but scowled at her elderly neighbor, whom she had hardly seen all week.

"I'm sorry, Otis, I'm just not in the mood to be nice to people I hardly know. Any way we can reschedule?"

"Maddy, we've had this planned all week. They were kind enough to invite us, and you can't cancel last minute."

"Well, I'm not feeling that great," Maddy replied lamely. She ventured a look at Otis. He wasn't buying.

"What's wrong, Maddy?"

"John's leaving for vacation on Saturday."

Otis lifted an eyebrow.

Maddy scowled. "And I'm going to miss him."

"It won't be so bad."

Maddy checked the evil look she wanted to give him. "Yes, Otis, it will. It will be very bad."

"Well, they haven't left, yet," he challenged her, "and it would be a shame to ruin the time you have remaining by complaining about it."

Maddy grudgingly conceded his point.

"Let's get over to the Browns'. I'm sure they have a nice dinner planned," Otis suggested.

Maddy pushed her chair back. "Was I supposed to bring something?" It suddenly occurred to her that she may have forgotten more than just the invitation.

"No, they said they had it all covered. Now cheer up, and let's go and be neighborly."

They started across the beach, and the girls next door called out from their deck in welcome. Maddy smiled reluctantly. They were sweet kids, and it wouldn't kill her to be civil for an hour or so. After that, she wasn't making any promises.

Thursday morning's overcast skies aptly mirrored Maddy's outlook as she stomped around the house, getting ready for the day. She made the coffee extra strong, then sat, tapping her fingers on the counter, waiting for the pot to brew. It took an unusually long time, and Maddy was good and irritated by the time it was ready.

She thought briefly about her conversation with Otis the night before, and acknowledged that while his advice was sound, she didn't have the wherewithal to take it. She'd spent the last bit of her happy energy pretending to be nice to the neighbors. The evening had passed pleasantly enough, but Maddy simply couldn't relate to the rich and rather snobby outlook of her affluent hosts. After the fourth reference to their much larger home in the city, she almost jumped off the second-story deck. Otis kept her in line with his fatherly looks and she grudgingly behaved.

The morning did not bring with it a sense of new beginnings, as mornings were supposed to do. Instead, Maddy only felt the Fordham's impending departure more keenly. As the clock ticked away the endless minutes until eight a.m., Maddy knew that there was only one solution. She had to pick a fight with John.

After slamming her finger in the cupboard in the laundry room, she was more determined than ever to be uncivil. By the time Frank and John arrived, the tension in the kitchen was acute.

"Hey, Maddy," Frank greeted her cheerfully, almost immediately sensing that his enthusiasm would not be met.

"Hi Frank, John." Maddy nodded at them and looked back down at her list. "Coffee's on, but look out; it's pretty strong."

Frank raised an eyebrow at John, who shrugged. "Linda said you can call her any time next week to shop," he said, hoping to inject some good news into the morning.

"I'll be sure to do that. Thanks."

Frank poured his coffee and hurried upstairs.

John walked over and sat down. "Maddy? You okay?"

"No, John, I'm not," she answered crossly.

"You want to talk about it?" he asked gently.

She looked at him and didn't know whether to punch him or throw herself into his arms. She decided instead to complain about her bathroom.

"I don't know why I ever agreed to having just a shower in my bathroom down here. I need a bathtub."

"Well," John replied evenly. "We decided a shower would be better because of the space issue. You'll have almost no closet left if we extend that bathroom wall any further."

"It's just the hall closet," Maddy practically growled.

John cleared his throat. "I'll look into it with Willy and see what he thinks," he answered. "Maybe there's a way to use the space more efficiently."

"Are you just giving in to me because I'm being difficult?"

Good ol' direct Maddy. "No, I'm looking into it because you're the homeowner, and what you want is most important."

"So, now I'm just the homeowner?" She warmed to the pointless argument.

"No, Maddy, you're not just the homeowner, you're my…"

She pushed back from the counter. "Don't bother trying to define us; it's impossible," she stormed.

John followed her. "Maddy."

She looked up at him and tried unsuccessfully to hold onto her pointless anger. Her scowl softened, and tears started to form in her eyes. That made her mad again, and she tried to push past him, but he gently blocked her retreat. She looked up at him defiantly, and then sighed and leaned her head against his chest. "I'm sorry."

John wrapped his arms around her and held her, and she took another deep breath. The tears retreated, and she finally looked up at him.

"I don't know why I can't handle it that you and the boys are going away. I should be happy for you, but…" She tucked her head back into his chest.

Burt was getting restless, and John knew they only had a minute more alone. "I'm going to miss you, too," he said quietly.

"Even after this?" came the muffled reply.

John heard the guys walking in the front door. He continued to hold her. "You can't get rid of me that easily."

Maddy looked up with a small smile. With her head no longer buried, she heard the footsteps as the rest of the crew made their way toward the kitchen. She ducked under John's arm and dashed over to the coffee maker, just as the kitchen door opened.

"I'm glad to hear it," she answered. "Morning, Travis, Willy. You must be Bill," she said, extending her hand to the newest member of the crew.

John smiled at the transformation, marveling at how quickly Maddy could turn on the charm. The new guy was already stammering, although that wouldn't last. He was far too good at incessant conversation to get hung up for long by a pretty face.

John made eye contact with Maddy while the others were getting their coffee. She grinned sheepishly, and he smiled back.

"I'll check in with you later," he said, and headed up the steps.

The others followed shortly afterward, and Maddy was left to make sense of her strange and shifting moods. She was relieved that, as hard as she'd tried, she hadn't scared John too much. She grimaced as she thought about her ravings, and then wondered if she'd get a bathtub out of the deal after all.

All of the bedroom floors were finished by Friday afternoon, which meant that furniture could be moved in first thing Monday morning. Maddy was thrilled at the prospect. Renovations had also been completed on both upstairs bathrooms, including the replacement of the elusive pipes in the master bath. Bill had laid the flooring and Maddy was very pleased. He seemed to fit in well with the others and there was a general sense of relief as everyone adjusted to the "new guy."

John had invited Maddy over for dinner and she offered to cook. The menu included a hamburger casserole that her mother used to make, homemade biscuits and a tossed salad. Brownies were an inevitable conclusion to the meal, and the men teased Maddy about smelling up the house while they worked.

John joined her late Friday afternoon, smiling as he watched her maneuver around the kitchen. "Smells good. Who's cooking?"

Maddy threw an oven mitt at him, and he caught it, walking over and returning it with a rather compelling kiss. Maddy leaned back against the counter, surprised. "Was that allowed?"

"I'm not thinking clearly, the way this kitchen smells."

"What if one of the guys had walked in just now?"

John looked back at the closed door to the stairway and shrugged. "I would have heard them."

"And I thought I was safe." She walked over to check her brownies, just as footsteps rumbled down the steps. John walked casually over to the sink as the door opened and the rest of the crew joined them. Maddy finished pulling her meal together, leaving a few brownies out for the men. Saying her good-byes, she went to her room to get ready for her date with the Fordhams.

Blake answered the door when she arrived, and invited her in very properly. Parker came around the corner and hugged her, almost knocking the brownies out of her hands.

"Easy there, buddy," John said, coming up and taking the plate from Maddy. He looked at her and smiled. She'd taken the time to dress up a little, and she looked great. He leaned down to kiss her cheek. "Hey, Maddy."

"Dad, how come you kissed Miss Maddy's cheek?" Parker asked with a giggle.

"Well, Parker, I aimed for her nose, but she moved." John winked at Blake, and Parker laughed.

"Dad! Don't you want to kiss her lips?"

Blake shook his head and smiled, and Maddy turned an inquiring eye on John. He looked at Parker, then Blake, then back at her.

"You mean like this?" he asked. He put the brownies down and carefully cupped Maddy's face with his hands, kissing her gently on the lips. The kiss was very brief, and Parker shrieked happily.

"Now, enough kissing," John said. "Let's see what Miss Maddy brought."

A few minutes later they were sitting on the deck, and after Blake said a prayer, they began to eat. The boys poured out stories of past vacations, accounts sadly devoid of a mother figure. Maddy was touched by their excitement about the coming week with their dad. John seemed to catch their enthusiasm, and Maddy drew some comfort from the fact that they would at least be away having fun together.

The evening passed far too quickly, and Maddy eventually acknowledged that it was time to go.

John reluctantly agreed. "We'd better finish our packing."

The boys carried their dishes into the kitchen, talking excitedly about which toys they were going to take. They disappeared down the hall while John and Maddy cleaned up. A few minutes later Parker marched back into the kitchen with an overflowing backpack.

"Parker, you can't take all of those toys. We're going to have to go through your things together."

"Oh, man!" Parker responded, disappointed. He let his backpack drop into a chair and looked up at his dad expectantly

Maddy took the hint. "I'll get out of your way so you can pack."

"I'm going to walk Miss Maddy to her car," John said. "Why don't you go pull out your clothes, and I'll be right down to help?"

Maddy smiled ruefully up at John. "You don't have to come out to the car with me," she said.

"You're not going to talk me out of my last minute alone with you for a week," he said quietly, falling in next to her as they walked outside to say good-bye.

eighteen

If Thursday morning's overcast skies reflected Maddy's mood two days earlier, she could hardly imagine what kind of weather would do justice to her feelings on Saturday. She lay in bed considering the possibilities. A violent storm was out of the question; there was too much emotion in that. A gentle rain was less emotional, but too pleasant. *Maybe a relentless and unforgiving snowstorm*, she decided. Cold, hopeless, desolate.

Of course, none of those things happened Saturday morning. The sun rose with irritating precision, assuming that all was well with the world. Grumbling about nothing in particular, Maddy rolled out of bed and tripped over her dog.

"Burt, what's wrong with you?" she demanded.

He looked up groggily, and put his head back down with a sigh. He wasn't quite ready to start the day.

Maddy put the coffee on and decided to go sheet shopping. Generating a list for the outlet mall, she felt her mood lift. She needed to keep busy during the coming week, and she had plenty of lists to make it happen.

John turned the radio on and tried to tune in something reasonably distracting as they began their trip west. The boys were tucked into the back seat with their books and toys, and the front seat was well supplied with snacks. This was normally a very happy time for the three of them.

Well, at least we're two for three.

John was relieved that the number was up to two after the stressful morning they'd spent preparing to leave. He had been especially impatient with the boys; they didn't move fast enough, their arguments were particularly irritating, and nothing seemed to go right as he tried to close up the house.

John gave up on finding a decent station, and turned the radio off. Parker started humming one of his Sesame Street songs, and before long, began to sing with gusto. Blake giggled, and John smiled at his sons in the rearview mirror.

"Dad, I'm so hungry I could eat a whole box of animal crackers."

"You just had breakfast an hour ago, Parker."

"But I'm just so hungry!"

"I'll break out the snacks in a little bit. Let's try to get out of Clairmont first."

"Okay, Dad. But I'm still hungry."

"Okay, Parker."

Parker continued to sing and seemed to forget about his hunger. Blake got lost in a video game adventure. John sipped his coffee and thought about Maddy as their truck made its way across the state.

Maddy kept herself so busy Saturday that she literally fell asleep in the bathtub after supper. She awoke with a start and a sputter, as her legs relaxed and her face dipped below the water line. The water had cooled considerably, and she hurried out of the tub and quickly prepared for bed.

She jumped when the phone rang. *Is John checking in already?* Grabbing the receiver on the third ring, she answered hopefully, "Hello?"

"Maddy?"

"Oh, hi."

"Well, it's nice to hear your voice, too. Am I interrupting something?" Becky's imagination became fully engaged when Maddy assured her that she was just getting ready for bed.

"Alone?"

"Oh, please."

"Sorry, I couldn't help but ask."

"So, what's up?" Maddy tried to sound a little more upbeat.

"I thought I'd take you up on your offer to come and paint at your place for a while."

"Great. You can start with the parlor."

"Ha ha. I thought I'd just drive up and spend a few days. Does that sound okay?"

Company – Distraction! "You bet. You're welcome any time."

"I don't want to interrupt your time with John, or anything."

"Don't worry, you won't. He's out of town."

"Oh. Is everything okay?"

"Yeah, it's fine. They're just on vacation."

"Well, you'll have to fill me in on *everything*. I want to know all the details."

Maddy was on her way to bed when the phone rang again. *What did Becky forget?*

"Hello?"

"Hey, Maddy."

"John! How are you?"

"I'm fine. Had a good trip. How are you?"

"I'm fine. I shopped all day. How are the boys?"

"They're having a blast. Or had. They're in bed now. We've got an early fishing date for tomorrow."

"Sounds fun."

"Really?"

"No, sorry."

John laughed. "I wish you were here."

Maddy sighed. "Wouldn't that be nice?"

"Oh, yeah."

She smiled. "What's your cabin like?"

"Very rustic; a good 'guy' cottage. Indoor plumbing, though, so we're lucky."

"Sounds dreamy."

Another laugh. "I should probably let you go."

Why? "Yeah, I guess so. Tell the boys I said hello."

"I will."

"Thanks for calling."

"My pleasure. I miss you, Maddy."

"I miss you, too."

Pastor Rob greeted the congregation and assured everyone that Rachel and the baby were doing fine. He thanked them for the meals and gifts. "I don't need to tell you that I have pictures, and I'll be happy to share them at the coffee hour after the service."

There were a few laughs, and then the proud dad gave way to the earnest preacher. "Today we're going to talk about being sufficient in Christ, based on Lamentations, Chapter Three. Now, I know you're thinking, 'Lamentations… that's going to be a bummer,' but wait and see. I think you'll find these verses full of hope and, frankly, good advice."

He concluded his remarks and the service began. Maddy didn't remember a book in the Bible called Lamentations, nor did she ever remember hearing a pastor use the word, "bummer." She smiled, thought about John and the boys, and then settled in for the service.

"It amazes me," Otis observed on their way home from church, "how many of the sermons seem especially tailored to some concern of mine."

Maddy nodded as she drove along. "What hit home for you?"

"Well, sometimes I struggle with being alone," Otis admitted. "I miss my Louisa so much, and sometimes I wonder why the Lord keeps me around."

"Otis, you are important to so many people, and I'm one of them," Maddy protested.

"Thank you, my dear," he said. "You have become so dear to me, too, and I appreciate your kind words. It's just that," he paused, "I have to find my peace with being alone, for the most part, and it was good to be reminded that, 'The Lord is my portion, therefore I hope in Him.'"

Maddy thought about her own loneliness, which was sure to

end in a week, and felt guilty for how hard she was taking it. Otis may have family and friends, but he was essentially alone most of the time. He really seemed comforted by the idea of the Lord being his portion. She wondered if she could want it as much as he did.

"Maddy?"

"Oh, I'm sorry, you just got me thinking, as usual." Turning onto their street, she added, "I'll stop by a little later, okay?"

"After my nap," Otis qualified.

"After your nap," Maddy agreed with a smile.

"A day of rest" was still an elusive concept for Maddy, who had always spent the weekend catching up around the house after a heavy workweek. After a quick lunch, she decided to start dealing with the smaller pieces of furniture that she'd purchased. She wiped them down and separated those that needed repair. Thankfully, the latter group was small, and after she finished cleaning, polishing and tightening knobs on drawers, she began moving things from the shed into the house. The trek to the second floor was significant, and by mid-afternoon she was beat.

Maddy stopped by Otis' house later in the day, and he accompanied her while she took Burt for his walk. Instead of walking along the beach, they strolled through the streets of their neighborhood, and Otis filled her in on where the year-round versus summer residents lived. There was often a story to accompany any given family, and Maddy enjoyed getting to know her neighbors in this borderline subversive way.

After their walk, Otis invited Maddy over for a bowl of clam chowder. They ate together at his kitchen table, and looked at a photo album from his early years of marriage. His mood seemed to lift with the happy memories, and Maddy was relieved for him. An hour later she left, promising she'd see him the next day.

The rest of the evening passed slowly for Maddy. She tried to get lost in her website, but didn't feel terribly creative. The novel on the kitchen counter held her attention for less than half an hour. She finally took a bath and got ready for bed. She knew she'd be up with the sunrise, and it would be a busy day.

CRICO

It took the better part of Monday morning to move the bigger pieces of furniture in and reassemble them, where necessary. Maddy went from room to room, cleaning and polishing each piece as it was brought in. When everything was in place, she couldn't believe the transformation.

The master bedroom was especially grand. She could hardly imagine how the addition of mattresses, bedding, and curtains would further warm the room up. She'd seen a beautiful privacy screen at the antique shop downtown that would be perfect for the corner by the bathroom, and made a note to check if it was still available.

Revisiting the other rooms, Maddy updated the list of furniture that she still needed: a bedside table, another quilt rack, a small desk and chair, one or two more dressers. She pulled out the bags of trinkets and decor that she'd bought on her first road trip down the coast, and started sorting through them. It felt a little like Christmas as she spread them all out, removing price tags and contemplating which room would receive which gifts. She passed the afternoon quite contentedly in this manner, and was surprised when the men called out their good-byes at the end of the day.

While the floors were being prepared on the lower level on Wednesday, Maddy began stripping the molding in the front hall. It was a tedious process, but one she embraced more readily, since she'd had the fun of a more creative project the day before.

Along with the satisfaction of having the mattresses delivered, Maddy had prepared the master bedroom in anticipation of Becky's visit. She'd spread her down comforter on the new sheets, placed new towels in the bathroom and fresh flowers in a vase on the dresser. She marveled at how well the room came together; the bed, dressers, night stand, and even the rocker by the window. The quilt rack would soon hold a quilt that her grandmother had made, and the screen did look perfect in the corner. All in all, the first bedroom was shaping up nicely.

Becky's arrival later in the afternoon spared Maddy further molding work, and after she cleaned up, they went out for seafood. Catching up on each other's lives after only a couple weeks was a welcome change for both of them. Maddy shared the latest on house projects, and, more important, as far as her sister was concerned, her status with John.

Becky was a little disappointed with the lack of information.

"There's not a lot to tell," Maddy defended herself. "We went out; it was great. I went to his ballgame. We got stuck at my house in a storm. He worked on renovations, and I saw them off to New Hampshire." She shrugged and sipped her drink.

"You got stuck in a storm?" Becky's eyes lit up. "What happened?"

Maddy recaptured the experience as well as she could, amping up the storm a little for good measure.

Becky remained unimpressed. "That's it? You talked? Oh, Maddy."

Maddy smiled. "Believe me, it was exciting enough."

Becky rolled her eyes. "So, how does John look in his baseball uniform?"

"Nice."

The simple word spoke volumes with the right inflection. This brought a smile to Becky's face.

"Well, at least you noticed. Sometimes I wonder about you."

Thursday's shopping and art gallery visits exhausted the girls to such a degree that the only reasonable plan for Friday was a day at the spa. They drove all the way to Augusta to find one, but it was well worth the effort.

They started the day with hot-stone massages, and, regrouping an hour later, they shared neighboring chairs while they received pedicures. Talking and laughing and drinking herbal tea, they forgot, for a little while, about the rest of the world. They also forgot about lunch altogether when they went into a third area for manicures. Time in the steam room and sauna concluded their visit.

They left the spa with bags of soaps and body creams to continue the indulgent treatment at home. Loading their treasures and pampered bodies carefully into Maddy's car, they started the trip back to Clairmont.

Becky yawned languidly. "When did we eat last? I'm starving."

"I think it was the biscotti that we had with our cappuccino, whenever that was."

"Well, I need something really caloric, and soon."

"I'm on it."

"Look at all they got done!"

Maddy walked through the rooms, really noting for the first time the week's accomplishments. The front hall, parlor, dining room and sitting room were all painted. The colors she'd selected looked rich and inviting, and she was anxious to see how the artwork that they'd purchased during Becky's first visit would look on the parlor walls. The kitchen, in contrast, looked particularly dull and neglected.

"Do you want a glass of wine?" Becky asked, already going through the cupboards to help herself.

"I think if we relax anymore, we'll probably fall asleep on the kitchen floor."

"You're right. We're supposed to drink lots of water anyway," Becky agreed, digging in the fridge.

Maddy walked out to the front porch, taking in the warm, muggy evening air.

Becky *banged!* out after her. "You should get that fixed."

"No way. I love that sound. John keeps threatening to fix it, and I keep threatening to fire him if he does."

Becky sat down and lifted her water to her sister. "Here's hoping you don't have to fire your contractor."

Maddy tapped her sister's bottle. "I'll drink to that."

They sat for a few minutes, sipping their drinks and enjoying the breeze that had begun to blow in. "I should paint right here," Becky mused, taking in the rocky shoreline and the boats on the water.

"You're more than welcome," Maddy said. "Just leave me a

few prints to sell in my gift shop."

"You're going to have a gift shop?"

"Maybe not right away, but I think I want to have something like that eventually."

"That's a great idea," Becky replied. "You could use the sitting room. It's just off the front hall; it would be perfect."

"That's what I was thinking," Maddy agreed. She didn't quite have the energy to speculate about it at the moment. The day's rigorous activities were starting to take a toll on her senses. Happily relaxed and sleepy, she sat back and considered the possibility of turning in early for the night.

Burt barked, which surprised them both. Maddy, sitting with her painted toes propped on the railing, might have started to doze, but for the interruption. She scowled at her dog as he ambled quickly to the screen door.

"What's up with him?" Becky asked with a yawn.

"I don't know," Maddy answered, slowly getting to her feet. "Someone's probably out front."

"If Travis is back, send him on out here!" Becky drawled.

Maddy smiled and followed her dog through the house.

"Miss Maddy!"

She met Parker's eyes a split second after she heard his greeting. "Parker! You're back!"

She opened the door and knelt down to give him a hug. "Welcome home, Parkerpants!"

Parker returned her hug eagerly, and Maddy smiled as Blake walked up the steps, grinning shyly.

"Hi, Miss Maddy."

"Blake, I'm so happy to see you!"

"Look at Burt! He won't let my dad come over here!" Parker laughed.

Maddy turned to see John for the first time in a week. He stood by his truck; tall and handsome, petting Burt and smiling. He'd gotten a lot of sun, and his teeth glowed from his tan face. Maddy's heart dropped down into her pedicured toes.

"I'd come and say hello, but I don't think I can!" he called out, both hands engaged in scratching Burt's ears. "Can I get you to come over here?"

Maddy thought she could close the distance between them in a matter of seconds, but decided it might not be dignified to test that theory. John's smile was hypnotic, she decided as she neared him, though it was, unfortunately, split between her dog and herself. Burt was fairly demanding.

Maddy came within touching distance, and stood on the other side of her pet. "Welcome home," she said, tilting her head and smiling up at him.

"It's good to be home," he answered. He reached over Burt and touched her cheek.

"You're back early," she observed happily.

"Yeah, we couldn't wait," John answered with a grin. His hand dropped as the boys came up behind her.

"Look! Miss Maddy has red toes!" Parker squealed.

John glanced down at her bare feet. He raised an eyebrow. "Been busy?"

Maddy laughed. "My sister's here, and we went to a spa in Augusta today," she explained, trying to justify her excursion into self-indulgence.

"What's a spa?" Parker asked.

Maddy's answer was lost on John, who was processing some disappointment in the fact that she had company. It explained the red convertible parked in her driveway.

"John?" Maddy took his hand.

His fingers immediately curled around hers. He looked down at her, the concerns of the moment lost as he took in her face. Burt still blocked him from greeting her properly, and the audience didn't help either.

"Let's go sit on the porch and talk about your trip. Can you stay for a few minutes?"

John smiled. "We won't stay long. We still need to go home and unpack."

"Okay, Burt, get out of the way," Maddy said, pushing him so that she could walk next to John. She loved holding his hand, and very much looked forward to expressing her welcome in a more meaningful way. The boys skipped on ahead as they made their way up to the porch.

John squeezed her hand. "I like your toes," he said quietly.

She leaned into him. "I figured you'd give me a hard time."

"Oh, I will," he assured her, "but I still like them." He leaned back into her.

Blake and Parker waited on the porch, and John opened the door, ushering them and then Burt, inside. He let the door shut before Maddy could go in, and she looked up at him with an inquiring smile. John watched his boys head toward the kitchen and then turned back to Maddy, taking her hands.

"I don't really want an audience right now," he said.

Maddy's heart beat happily, erratically, as she looked up at him, and John's smile dissolved into something wonderfully unsettling as he met her gaze.

"Hello, John!"

Maddy was so intent on John's lips at that moment; she was just so sure he was going to say something really important, that she didn't see Otis walking across her yard. John was equally surprised, but managed not to jump as Maddy did.

"Otis, hello."

Otis chuckled as he walked up the steps. "I wasn't interrupting anything, was I?"

"You know you're always welcome," Maddy assured him.

"Thank you, my dear. How was your trip?" Otis shook hands with John.

"It was great, thank you. Caught some nice fish, got ourselves lost in the woods, and ate way too much junk food," John answered with a smile.

"I'm glad to hear it," Otis replied. "The fish part, anyway."

"Would you like to join us on the porch?" Maddy asked.

"Oh no, I'm going to run a quick errand downtown," Otis said. "I just saw John's truck and wanted to come and say hello." He turned and walked back down the steps, waving over his shoulder. "I'll see you at church on Sunday. Say hello to the boys for me!"

"See you Sunday." John opened the door for Maddy. "About those boys…"

Maddy sighed and led the way through her house. John followed, noting the work that had been done. Maddy wasn't surprised to see Parker and Blake on the swing through her kitchen window. Wondering what kind of conversation Becky might be having with them, she pushed the screen door open.

"Becky, you remember Parker and Blake?"

Becky sat sipping her water and regarding them warily. Her expression changed as John followed Maddy onto the porch.

"Of course, I remember them," she said, getting to her feet. "And I remember John," she added, extending her manicured hand to greet him.

John shook her hand and smiled. "It's nice to see you again, Becky."

"Your boys were just telling me what a nice vacation they had," she said.

"Yeah, it was a good time," he agreed.

"Can we get you a drink?"

"Thanks, no," John answered. "We had a long trip today, and I should probably get these guys home."

"You came straight here?" Becky asked, an eyebrow raised as she looked over at Maddy.

John grinned. "Yeah, I guess we're wearing our hearts on our sleeves, aren't we boys?"

This concept was lost on his sons, but not on the sisters.

"I want to see the hideout!" Parker suddenly exclaimed, trying to stop the swing so he could get off. Blake looked hopefully at Maddy.

"It's up to your dad," she said with a laugh.

"I'd like to see how it looks up there," John replied. "This floor looks great, by the way. I like the paint selection, too; the dining room is especially impressive."

"It's really exciting," Maddy agreed. "Wait till you see the bedrooms." She looked at her sister. "You coming, Beck?"

"No, you guys go on ahead," she dismissed them with a wave. "I'm too tired."

The rest of the group moved into the house, the boys racing on ahead. John and Maddy walked slowly up the steps behind them, arm in arm. On the landing, John stopped and pulled Maddy close.

"Dad!" Parker shrieked. "You gotta see this!"

John took a deep breath as they turned to follow Parker's voice. He was duly impressed with how the hole-room looked with its furniture, and Maddy happily lost herself in the hostess role.

"Doesn't it look great?" she asked. "I love how these pieces go together." She chattered on about the floor and the walls, and John didn't know whether to look at the room or just absorb Maddy's delight in it. "Of course, it needs curtains and artwork, and all of the rest," she concluded, looking around the room herself.

"It came together well," John agreed.

The boys had disappeared, and John stepped into the closet to check on them.

"You guys okay?" He knelt down to look into their secret room.

"We're fine, Dad!" Blake called out.

"Tell Miss Maddy to come in!" Parker yelled.

Maddy grinned as she came up behind John. "Go ahead," she nudged his back with her knee. "I'll follow you."

He looked over his shoulder and then slowly stood. Maddy was struck again by his height as he unfolded in front of her.

"You're really tall."

John smiled and picked up her hands, lifting them so that her fingertips faced him.

"You've got fancy fingers, too."

"I know. Look what happens when you leave."

He slowly lifted one hand to his lips. "How are you going to sand with these fingers?" he asked, kissing them gently.

Maddy could hardly stand, much less sand, and wondered if he knew that he was probably holding her up.

"Miss Maddy!" Parker yelled from the hideout.

"Just a minute!" she called back, looking inquiringly at John.

He smiled and pulled her hands around his neck, where she happily linked her fingers.

"I have a secret meeting," she reminded him.

"I know," he said quietly, putting his hands gently at her waist.

His kiss was everything she'd dreamed about all week. Maddy wondered, for one bizarre moment, if their most passionate interludes were destined to be spent in strange and unromantic places.

"Miss Maddy?"

To her surprise, John didn't release her, but she felt his lips form a smile over hers. She was the one who finally broke away, fearful that a curious face might suddenly appear at their feet. She looked at John, touched his rough, unshaven cheek, then quickly ducked down to the floor before she changed her mind.

"Sorry," John heard her say. "I was seized by the enemy, but I got away."

Maddy walked the Fordhams out to John's truck, saying good-bye to the boys as they climbed into the back seat. John kept hold of her hand as they slowly strolled to his door.

"So, when can we go out?" he asked. "Do you want to wait until your sister leaves?"

This thought so obviously distressed him that Maddy had to laugh. "No, we can go any time. She came to paint, so she'll keep herself busy."

"Tomorrow night?" John asked, holding her hands and stroking her fingers.

"Tomorrow night's great."

"I'll pick you up at seven?"

"Sounds good," she answered, then added, "What should I wear?"

"Well, it's a nice place; on the outside, too," he grinned.

"I'll dress up then."

"I'm looking forward to it."

"To my dressing up or to going out?"

John laughed. "To going out. You can wear whatever you want. I'll be happy."

Maddy's mind flickered over the black dress. "Okay," she replied. "We'll see about that."

John leaned down and kissed her lightly, knowing his boys were watching from inside the truck. They heard the giggles to prove it.

"I'll see you tomorrow," Maddy said, backing away.

John climbed into his truck with a wave and a smile. Twenty-four hours seemed like an awfully long time to both of them.

nineteen

John managed to fill the twenty-four hours with the necessary details of returning from vacation: unpacking, laundry, reading the mail and lawn care. By 6:30, when he got out of the shower, he was more ready for a nap than a date. He fed his boys and got their things ready for the night with their aunt and cousin.

The fact that Maddy was her brother's top priority upon his return was not lost on his sister. She kept these thoughts to herself as she welcomed her nephews and waved John off. She liked Maddy well enough, and while she wanted her brother to find a "friend," Maddy had quickly become much more than that. She hoped that John knew what he was doing.

Maddy spent far too much of her twenty-four hours contemplating her evening with John. Becky didn't help, being all too ready to keep the topics of wardrobe and jewelry and hairstyle ever before them. She wondered if it was wise to take Becky's advice, but had to admit that it was fun to have her there to share the day and help pass the time.

By 6:45, Maddy looked ready for a night on the town. Her hair was pinned up in some sort of haphazard twist, which Becky insisted was very stylish, and which had taken her a rather long time to create. Maddy hadn't worn the dress or the shoes that went with it in a long time, and they felt foreign to her. Becky insisted that she looked perfect, though her endorsement made Maddy just a little bit nervous.

Her sister poured them a glass of wine while they waited for

John to arrive, but Maddy took only a sip. When the doorbell rang, she panicked and looked wide-eyed at Becky.

"I can't wear this. I have to go change!"

"Don't you dare," Becky laughed, but managed a threatening look. "Just go get that shawl we bought and come right back downstairs. I'll go let Mr. Contractor in; see if he looks good enough to take you out."

Maddy obeyed, and Becky took her time walking through the house to greet their guest. There was no harm in making him wait a minute or two. At the front door she stopped and stared. John looked very striking in black slacks, a charcoal shirt, and black tie. Becky thought he seemed taller and, for some reason, more formidable.

John waited patiently, then raised an eyebrow. "Hello, Becky."

She opened the door to let him in, wondering if she should have pushed so hard for the black dress.

"Hey, John," she replied. "Maddy's upstairs. Come on in."

John walked into the foyer and waited for Becky to finish her appraisal. She wasn't very discreet.

"Thanks for letting me steal Maddy away," he said.

Becky met his gaze, a hint of wariness in her eyes. "Well, you two will make a pair, that's for sure," she answered, turning to lead John through the house.

Maddy was halfway down the staircase when they entered the hallway, and this time John stopped in his tracks. Becky looked at the two of them as they regarded each other, amused and a little alarmed. It was like seeing two little kids playing with fire; a fire with which she was all too familiar. She slipped quietly out to the porch.

John watched Maddy descend the stairs in her black dress. He'd never seen her so elegant and so... completely dazzling. Her hair was pulled back, but some of it fell in wisps around her face. Her shoulders were mostly bare, except for two narrow straps that disappeared somewhere behind her neck. He finally drew a breath. The dress wasn't low cut or particularly short, but it definitely demanded attention; so did her very nice legs.

He brought his eyes back to her face. She was smiling, but she looked nervous, too. Even so, he felt like an awkward, gawking schoolboy. He cleared his throat.

"You are beautiful," he said, taking her hand. "You look… amazing."

"Thank you. You look great yourself," Maddy's heart hammered so loudly she was sure he could hear it. They stood in the hallway for a moment, uncertain what to do next.

"Guess I'll say good-bye to Becky," she said, and John looked up, surprised to see that her sister had gone.

They walked outside and Becky sighed and smiled.

"I'm going to need a picture of this," she said, heading into the kitchen for her camera.

When she returned, she had them stand with their backs to the water. John draped his arm around Maddy's shoulder and she snuggled into his side. It was a cozy, happy picture; both of their faces reflecting far more composure than either one of them felt.

"Good luck," Becky said, putting her camera away.

"I'm sorry?" John asked, taking Maddy's hand to lead her back through the house.

Becky shrugged. "Have fun – not too much," she qualified.

"Thanks, Becky," Maddy answered. "Help yourself to anything that looks good."

"Oh, you know I will," Becky waved them off.

John put his hand on Maddy's back as they walked out the front door and down the steps. He looked at her spikey black heels.

"How do you walk in those?"

"I used to do it all the time. It's a little weird now."

"Is the dress new?"

"Oh no, it's just something… from the old days. Is it okay? Is it too much?" She had so wanted to look nice for him, to show him a more glamorous side than the paint or mud-stained Maddy to which he was accustomed. Mostly it was Becky's fault.

"No, you look wonderful," John assured her as he opened his truck door. "You don't look like you belong in this vehicle," he observed, helping her in and trying not to focus on her legs as she sat down.

Maddy laughed and waited for him to come around the other

side. "If you want me to go change, I will."

"No, of course not. It's just very…"

"Ugly," she supplied with a serious nod.

"No way, no," John laughed. "I just don't know if I want anyone else seeing you in it. Maybe we can order in?"

Maddy smiled at his protective tone. "I want to go *out* with you," she replied, turning toward him and crossing her legs.

John glanced at her legs and back up into her eyes.

"You'd better behave. If anyone messes with you, I'll probably end up in jail."

A half-hour drive brought them to their destination near a small town up the coast. The trip passed quickly as they forgot their discomfort and talked about John's vacation. Maddy enjoyed the stories about Parker and Blake, and John marveled that anyone who looked the way she did could take such obvious pleasure in his boys and their adventures.

The restaurant was in a large, federal-style house right on the ocean. Maddy was enthralled with the elegant lobby, delighting in the prospect of a quiet, romantic dinner. The setting for that dinner changed, however, when they were told they'd have to wait an hour and a half for a table.

"I tried to make a reservation, but they don't take them anymore," John said as they backed out of the parking lot. "I didn't think it would be that long of a wait."

Maddy settled into her seat, her momentary disappointment replaced by the adventure of being anywhere with John. "We'll find something," she replied. "Do you know what else is around here?"

John began driving slowly toward the little town just north of the restaurant. "I'm not sure," he said, watching for billboards or signs of any kind. "I've only been up here a couple of times."

A ten-minute drive through the little village and most of its side streets revealed very little, except a quaint little drive-in, which didn't really appeal under the circumstances. They began the drive back toward Clairmont.

"There's a lobster place somewhere along here," John offered, and Maddy perked up. "The food is good, but the setting is pretty casual. I'm not sure it's what we're looking for tonight."

While Maddy didn't feel strongly about lobster, she was getting hungry. "How casual?"

They pulled into a crowded parking lot a few minutes later, and she had her answer. People in blue jeans and shorts and even an occasional bathing suit poured in and out of their cars on their way to and from the restaurant. John pulled into the lot, but didn't turn off his engine. They watched the extremely casual commotion for a moment.

"Do you like lobster?" he asked.

"I've had it before," Maddy replied, trying to mask her ambivalence. It seemed ungracious not to be more enthusiastic about this Maine food staple. "I'm not sure I remember how to eat it."

"I can help you with that," John assured her, warming to the idea of a nice fresh lobster, even if they had to eat al fresco with the mosquitoes.

Maddy couldn't help but smile at his enthusiasm. "Okay, if you'll coach me."

They got out of the truck and walked toward the building, receiving their share of double-takes from other customers, who clearly thought they'd overdressed for the occasion. John took Maddy's hand and guided her to the large tanks where they could select their dinner.

Maddy wrinkled her nose. "We pick one while it's swimming around?"

John nodded. "I know, it's brutal. Which one do you want?"

She looked at the mass of clambering crustaceans. "I'll let you pick for me."

John did, and they continued up to the counter to order the rest of their meal. Assured that their number would be called when their food was ready, they walked out and claimed a picnic table with a remarkable view of the driving range next door. They toasted each other with a local brew served in red plastic cups.

"To the most beautiful woman at this lobster stand," John tapped her drink.

Maddy grinned and sipped gingerly from her cup. She wasn't really big on beer, either. "You are so charming."

John grinned back and reached for her hands across the table. They looked happily at each other, oblivious to the noisy crowd around them.

"John," Maddy said in a soft, seductive voice.

"Yeah?" John looked into her eyes. He liked that voice.

"My elbows are stuck to the table."

He laughed and reached for the napkin holder and the bowl of wet naps. "I'm sorry for the rustic setting," he said.

Maddy smiled and wiped down the table in front of her. "I'm just happy to be here with you."

John touched her cheek, and then looked up as their number was called. "My steamers are ready!"

He jumped up, leaving Maddy marveling at his transformation from romantic date to hungry man. He returned a few minutes later with a tray in his hands and a big smile on his face.

"Have you ever had these before?" he asked, setting the platter on the table between them.

"I've had oysters. Is that what those are?"

"These are clams," he corrected her, proceeding to pull one out of its shell.

Maddy was not about to tell him what she thought it looked like. She watched as he dipped the delicacy in the rinse water, and then in the little bowl of liquid butter. She bit her lip as he held it out to her. Apart from how unappetizing it looked, she usually tried to avoid eating anything dipped in straight butter. John grinned, waved it in front of her, and then popped it into his mouth. Apparently, he didn't share her reservation.

Maddy tried to look happy for him. "Yummy, huh?"

John smiled his agreement. "The next one's for you." He began preparing another clam.

Maddy reached for her beer. She took a healthy swallow and then gritted her teeth. "I'm ready."

John held the dripping clam close to her lips. "It would help if you opened your mouth."

Maddy did so, keeping her teeth together.

John laughed. "Maddy…"

She closed her eyes and opened her mouth. She felt the clam touch her tongue, and then felt John's finger on her lips. She forgot about the clam as she opened and locked eyes with John.

"Well? Do you like it?"

After a moment she replied, "I didn't think I would, but I do." She bravely rested her arms on the table again and leaned toward him. "How about another?"

John grinned and slowly prepared the next clam as Maddy watched. When it was ready, he held it between them and she leaned forward. John did too, looking into Maddy's eyes, then at her lips. She sighed and waited. John slowly, deliberately, dropped the clam into his own mouth.

"Greedy," she said, affronted.

"You could get your own."

"No way, I'm not touching them."

"Then you'll just have to wait."

The next few minutes passed in delicious slow motion as Maddy and John shared their plate of steamers. The mood was decidedly broken when their number was called again, and John went to pick up their lobsters. Maddy watched him walk to the ramshackle building, drawing the stares of almost every female he passed.

He came back a few minutes later with two plates piled high with lobsters, cole slaw, and corn on the cob. Maddy considered the food with some trepidation. She could hardly imagine how she'd keep the messy meal off her expensive dress.

John showed her how. He pulled out two plastic bibs with bright red smiling lobsters printed on them. He walked around the table, and ceremoniously tied one around Maddy's neck. She felt impossibly glamorous.

John returned to his side of the table, fastening his own bib as he did so. "You look good," he assured her, sitting down. "I knew I'd find a way to keep the guys from staring at you."

An hour later, it was time to walk off their interesting meal. They drove to a beach nearby, where they parked and found their way over a small sand dune. The moonlit ocean spread out before them, the sparkling waves quietly lapping the shore. John held Maddy's hand tightly as they walked through the sand. He looked down at her feet.

"Seriously, how do you walk in those?"

Maddy smiled, lifting her heel so she could loosen the strap of her sandal. "I don't intend to," she said, sliding her shoe off and putting her bare foot down in the sand. "That feels so good." She leaned against him to lift her other foot, and repeated the process.

"There," she said, satisfied. She held her purse and both sandals with one hand, and took his hand with the other. She smiled up at him. "Ready?"

"I think I just got taller."

Maddy laughed as they walked to the water's edge.

"Are you warm enough?" John asked, dropping Maddy's hand and putting his arm around her.

"Well, my shawl is surprisingly warm," Maddy assured him, "especially since you managed to wind it several times around me."

John patted her shoulder. "Might as well make good use of it."

"It's supposed to be more like a drape, and less like a tourniquet."

John chuckled and Maddy pulled away to walk closer to the water. She seemed determined to walk in the waves, not really behaving like someone in a sleek cocktail dress. Silhouetted against the sparkling water, she walked gingerly around the shells, turning to him with a grin he felt sure was there, but couldn't see clearly in the darkness.

He reached out his hand, which she took again, coming back to his side. *There's the smile.* He pulled her in and took the smile right from her lips onto his own.

John tuned the radio in to a quiet jazz station and they listened for a while in companionable silence, reflecting on a thoroughly wonderful evening, despite the unexpected change in venues.

"I can honestly say that I never thought I'd see you in a bib," Maddy declared.

"Few people are so lucky."

Maddy laughed. "Well, it's a good thing my phone takes great pictures."

"I've long since divested you of that device."

"You didn't!" Maddy replied, checking her purse. "Ha! I still have the evidence."

"Maybe," John replied mysteriously.

"Well, the bib was the least of the show. It was a little terrifying how you cleaned out your poor lobster."

"I was taught not to waste food."

"Obviously. You didn't waste mine, either."

"You looked like you were losing interest."

"I was afraid, John. I didn't want to get in your way."

It was John's turn to laugh. "I'll try to let you eat your own meal next time." He pulled into her driveway. "Should we try again tomorrow?"

"I'm still hungry now. Are there any diners open?"

John parked his truck, and reached out and played with one of her earrings.

"Sorry, Clairmont's closed. How about if I make you a peanut butter and jelly sandwich?"

"What? With my food? You're a thrifty date."

John smiled, stroked her cheek. "I make a great sandwich."

Maddy sighed and forgot about food.

A few minutes later, they thought it might be a good idea to walk on the beach again. The moonlight still sparkled, and they strolled slowly, their fingers intertwined.

"Do you want to come in for a few minutes?" Maddy asked.

"Yeah." John looked down at her in the darkness. "But I should probably leave."

Maddy slowly let out her breath. She really didn't want him to go. "A few minutes on the swing?"

John smiled. "Sure."

They walked up to her porch and sat down. Maddy snuggled in next to him and he put his arm around her.

"This isn't going to get any easier." John rested his chin on her head.

Maddy played with his tie. "So, what do we do?"

John was quiet for a while. "I've got some ideas about what we could do, but I'm not sure you're ready to hear them."

Maddy sat back and looked up at him, confused and a little alarmed. "What do you mean?"

John pushed and the swing gently swayed. Maddy would have been amused at the oversized version of Parker if the mood hadn't become somewhat tense. The breeze was cool and she pulled her wrap around her shoulders, waiting for him to elaborate. For a moment, she entertained the sickening notion that he was wrestling with whether or not they should see each other anymore. If he thought that their relationship had gotten too complicated...

She watched as he got up and began pacing like a caged cat. He looked larger than life in the darkness, his form silhouetted against the moonlit beach. He turned to her and she held her breath.

"Maddy, please tell me that you see us sharing our lives together, at *some* point." He sat down next to her, putting the swing into motion again. Maddy grabbed his arm and the armrest to catch her balance.

Relief swept over her. She let John's arm go, smoothing the sleeve where she'd gripped it. Smiling up at him, she said, "I see us sharing our lives together, at *some* point."

John grimaced briefly, but her answer very quickly brought a smile to his face. "I'm sorry. I shouldn't tell you what to say."

"Yeah, well, we both know you're bossy."

John took her face in his hands and looked into her eyes, then leaned down and kissed her. Maddy finally pulled back and looked at him with a decidedly happy and slightly glazed smile.

"So, about that whole 'sharing our lives together' thing..." John reminded her.

Maddy ran her hands over his tie and held it, absently playing with his tie clip.

"There's really no question that I want to be with you," she looked up at him. "And I love your boys."

"You love my boys?"

"Of course I do. I *think* I do," she said, considering. "Well, I must. I love being with them, and that night of the storm – I've never felt so worried about anyone," she realized aloud. "Yes, I definitely love them." She looked up at John with a smile.

"That's really great." Of course, he wanted to hear that. Of course, he wanted to hear more.

"Yeah, it is," Maddy agreed. She snuggled in happily next to him, pulling his arm around her. It was a little chilly.

"Maddy?"

"Yes?"

"What about *me*?"

"What about you?" Maddy asked, her grin audible.

"Maddy," John said, shifting her back so that she faced him. "I'm not going to give you the answer for this one."

"Oh, well," she thought for a moment. "I *am* awfully fond of you," she decided, tilting her head with an innocent smile.

"I'm glad to hear it," he said, indicating just how glad he was. Then, remaining very close, he whispered, "I love you, Maddy Jacobs."

She felt a delightful, happy warmth spread through her body. "I love you, too, John."

Their ensuing expressions of contentment at this mutual revelation were interrupted by the *bang!* of the screen door.

"I thought I heard someone out here," Becky yawned, walking over to the swing and ignoring their scramble to separate. "Don't worry about me," she waved at them, dropping down into one of the chairs by the table. "How was your dinner?"

Burt had followed her and was helping to make room between John and Maddy as he thrust his head between them and demanded their attention.

"It was great," Maddy answered, trying to switch gears so she could have a lucid conversation with her sister and try to keep Burt from drooling on her dress. She pushed his face over to John, who intercepted Burt's big head with a laugh.

"I'm glad," Becky said, rather abruptly.

Her tone had changed, and Maddy was immediately concerned. "What's wrong?"

Becky regarded her sister. "I'll just tell you later," she decided, pushing her chair back and getting up. "Don't stay up too late," she added, heading back toward the door.

"You can't do this to me," Maddy insisted. "Are Mom and Dad okay? Did something happen?"

"Nothing like that," Becky said.

"What *is* it?" Maddy got up from the swing.

Becky hesitated and turned. Maddy looked at her expectantly.

"Phil called."

Maddy sat down abruptly and John put his arm around her.

"Okay," she said slowly. "What did he want?"

"I think he wants to talk to you."

"Oh," Maddy paused again. "Does he want me to call him back?"

"I don't think that's necessary."

"Why not?"

"Because he's coming here."

twenty

"When?" Maddy's voice sounded distant and lifeless to her ears.

"I think he has business in Boston this week. He mentioned something about driving up, but I'm not sure when. I figured you'd want to know right away."

"Yeah," Maddy sat, immobile, on the swing.

"I told him it was about a seven-hour drive," Becky said, and Maddy looked up in surprise. "Depending, of course, on the traffic … and the moose."

Maddy managed a smile. "Thanks for that, at least."

"Are you okay?" John asked quietly.

The sound of his voice was comforting and confusing at the same time. *Phil…* Just hearing his name made her feel sick. She drew a deep breath.

"I don't know." She stood and walked to the railing. "I guess something like this was bound to happen eventually. We didn't really have much closure." There was a decided edge to her tone.

"So…" Becky interrupted. "I guess I'll head in…"

"Is there anything else I should know?" Maddy asked, the edge joined by a hint of fear.

"No." Becky thought for a minute. "He sounded fine, friendly and everything." She shrugged. "I told him you were on a date."

Maddy stiffened slightly, but said nothing.

"Well," said Becky, backing into the house, "I guess I'll talk to you later. Good night, John." She didn't figure he'd be hanging around for long.

"Good night, Becky."

A few minutes passed. "Maddy?"

She turned slowly to face him, all of the joy of their earlier conversation drained from her face.

"What can I do?" John asked.

She looked at him for a moment, completely unaware that this troubling news was no less so for him.

"There's nothing you can do," she replied. "I just have to figure out how to deal with this."

"I'd like to help."

Maddy managed a stiff laugh. "You want to talk to him?"

"I will."

Maddy looked hard at John. "No, you won't."

He was taken back by the bite in her tone. "Maddy, I would never..."

"Everyone always thinks they have to step in for me and solve my problems. Phil did it too, and he became the biggest one of all."

"I'm not Phil."

"Then just let me take care of myself."

Stung by her dismissal, John stood. "Maybe I should leave."

"Maybe you should."

The whole evening's events and conversations flooded over her, and it was suddenly too much. Maddy panicked. Phil had thought he wanted to marry her, too, and that ended in unbelievable heartbreak. Where were her walls?

"This is just moving too fast, John."

He took a step back. His own protective instinct kicked in, and he walked to the edge of the porch. "Are you going to be okay?"

Maddy didn't really expect him to leave so abruptly, but managed to say, "I'm fine." She was driving him away, but couldn't seem to stop herself.

John started down the steps to the beach. He knew he should go; they were both hurting and needed some space.

"Maddy, if you can't forgive him..." he paused.

"What, John? Is this some sort of threat?"

"Of course, not! I'm only saying..."

"That I have to do this your way."

He looked at her and turned to leave. "Good night, Maddy."

She watched him, feeling angry and confused and alone. John disappeared around the corner, and the tears began rolling down her face.

Maddy sat on the porch with her coffee the next morning, refusing to acknowledge the glory of the sunlight on the water in front of her. She brooded over the last twelve hours' events and especially her handling of them. Why had she treated John so badly? Why did Phil have to reappear in her life? *Why now?*

John told me he loved me… She wanted to believe that it was possible. She sighed and thought about the moments following that particular exchange. *Maybe it was a good thing Becky interrupted us,* she thought with a wry smile. She shook herself; it was no good reliving that moment. Phil was trying to ruin her life again, and she had to decide what to do.

She could just tell him not to come. That seemed reasonable. Why would he bother driving all the way from Boston in the first place? Had his girlfriend left him? Did he get his heart broken, or was he lonely? Maybe he was just curious about what she'd done with her life.

It was unsettling to contemplate that he might still be interested in her. How would it feel to see him again? Maddy's mind darted all around the possibilities, and none of them made her happy. Only when she let her mind return to John did she have any sense of calm, or contentment, or happiness… Maddy marveled at the effect that thinking of John had on her pulse, even after she'd started a fight with him.

"Hey," Becky broke into Maddy's reverie. Burt lifted his head when the door *banged!* and then dropped it back down with a sigh.

"Hi, Beck," Maddy replied absently.

"So, what are you going to do?"

"I have no idea," Maddy admitted. "I really don't think I want to see him, again."

"Aren't you a little bit curious?"

"I guess I am, but not enough to ruin what I've started here."

"Just tell him not to come."

"I've thought about that."

"What do you think he wants?"

"I can't imagine."

"I can. He wants to get back together. Why else would he drive all the way up here?"

Maddy didn't have an answer.

"Are you going to tell him about John?"

Maddy looked up at her. "It depends on what he wants. I'm not going to hide anything."

"What if they get into a fight?" Becky asked, her eyes sparkling.

"Stop it, Becky. That's not going to happen."

"Well, it could. Who do you think would win?"

"Becky!"

"Well, obviously, John's bigger, taller, and with that big strong back," she observed, a little too dreamily, as far as Maddy was concerned. "But then Phil always worked out all the time, and he really seems like the fiercer of the two."

Maddy looked at her sister, hardly knowing how to articulate an answer. "Becky, you're taking this way too far, and really, I don't want you contemplating John's... anything. Fantasize about Phil all you want, but leave John out of it."

Becky had the decency to look a little ashamed. She sipped her coffee. "Shouldn't we be in church?"

Maddy was glad and convicted to hear the plural pronoun. "Yeah, we should. I didn't feel up for it today."

They were still on the porch, making lists and arguing about artwork, when Otis came up the steps from the beach.

"Mind if I join you, ladies?"

Maddy normally enjoyed Otis' company, but she wasn't in the mood to be berated for missing church. To be fair, Otis wasn't much of a berater, but he was a bit of a confronter; an "exhorter," he called himself. Whatever it was, Maddy wasn't interested in being on the receiving end of it.

"Come on up, Otis. How are you?"

"Just fine, thank you. Hello, Miss Becky."

"Hi, Otis." Becky looked at him warily and went back to filing her nails.

"We missed you in church today."

It took less than a minute to cut to the chase. Maddy and Becky exchanged glances, and then Becky looked back down and left her sister to explain.

As Maddy drew breath to do so, Becky suddenly blurted out, "I told her we were missing church!"

Otis and Maddy looked at Becky. She immediately dropped the self-righteous act and gave her nails her full attention.

Maddy turned back to Otis. "I know, Otis. How was it?" Better to admit defeat; it might diffuse the admonition.

"Oh, it was fine; little John was there."

Maddy looked up in surprise. Since when did anyone call him, "Little John"?

"Rachel and Pastor were so proud. He's getting baptized next week," Otis finished.

"That's nice," Maddy answered, feeling a little silly. "I wish I could have seen him."

"Oh, he'll be around," Otis answered with a smile.

"Can I get you some lemonade?"

"That would be nice," he answered, settling into a chair.

"I'll get it," Becky offered. She set off on her good deed, effectively removing herself from the ensuing discipline.

"Thank you," Otis called after her. He sat back and looked out over the ocean. "This is so beautiful."

"Yes, it is," Maddy agreed. The sunlight sparkled and shimmered on the water, and there were numerous boaters out enjoying the day. *I bet they didn't go to church, either,* Maddy thought defensively.

"You know, I used to have the silliest idea that I would miss all of this when I got to Heaven," Otis mused. Becky joined them again, and set the glasses on the table.

"As though the good Lord isn't able to make Heaven just as beautiful as this fine Earth, especially this particular part of it," he added, taking a sip of lemonade. "I guess I always pictured Heaven as lots of clouds with angels and harps…" he paused and chuckled. "I'm not much of a musician, and I was afraid it might be a little boring." His eyes twinkled as he looked at them.

This assessment of Heaven found a fair amount of support between his listeners. Although Maddy's simplistic and unsatisfying version of Heaven was undergoing reevaluation, Becky had no problem relating to Otis. She had a hard time picturing Heaven as a fun place.

"Then one day, it just hit me while I was sitting and looking over the water."

He paused again, and both girls were rapt, waiting to hear what exactly had hit him.

"How could I suppose that Heaven would be any less grand than Earth? How could it be any less beautiful, awe-inspiring, engaging or exciting?" he smiled. "I was much younger then."

Both girls smiled in response and waited for him to continue. Otis was content to simply contemplate these things as he sipped his drink

Maddy finally broke the silence. "Otis, you're not... there's nothing..."

Otis looked at her with a puzzled expression, which immediately gave way to a smile. "Oh no, my dear," he chuckled. "I'm not planning on researching my theories any time soon."

Maddy breathed a sigh of relief.

"I just always think of Heaven when I look out over this particular bit of God's creation," he explained. He took another drink and then pushed his chair back. "That's it for me, today. I'd better go take my nap. Thank you for the lemonade."

"You're welcome, Otis. Enjoy your day of rest," Maddy said.

"You, too, my dear. I hope you do, too." He waved over his shoulder as he walked across the beach to his home.

An hour later, Maddy and her sister were remeasuring the windows in the bedrooms and taking notes for window dressings. Becky was struggling with the measuring tape, fearful that it might snap back on her fingers again, as it had done repeatedly over the past half hour.

"I keep telling you, there's a lock," Maddy said. She set her pad and pen down and walked over to where her sister was trying to latch the end of the tape to the top of the window frame.

"Thank you, little Miss Tool Belt," Becky answered dryly, allowing Maddy to take over the task of measuring.

Maddy couldn't help but smile a little as she fearlessly pulled out the metal tape and noted the measurements. She had learned a thing or two over the summer.

"Impressive," Becky monotoned. "So, what happened with you and John last night?" She was tired of waiting for Maddy to bring up the subject.

"It wasn't good," Maddy answered. "John thinks I just need to forgive Phil; I don't think it's that easy."

Becky sat on the bed and watched her sister work, this time saying nothing in response.

"When he left we were both upset. I don't even know how it ended that way." Maddy shook her head in frustration.

"You guys looked pretty cozy when I came out."

Maddy blushed and smiled in spite of her confusion. "Yeah, we had actually been having a really good talk."

Becky laughed. "That's not what I saw."

Maddy continued to measure. "Well, we talked… beforehand."

"However it ended, I'm sure you guys are going to be okay."

"I hope so. I just need to get through this thing with Phil, and I don't want anyone telling me how to do it. John almost made it sound like…"

"Like what?" Becky prodded.

"I don't know, not really like a threat, but sort of. It's hard to explain. It really upset me."

"I have a hard time imagining John threatening you," Becky said, kind of wanting to slap Maddy.

"I know," Maddy said, frustrated. "It wasn't really like that. It just seemed like if I didn't do it his way, then, I don't know, things wouldn't be the same between us."

"That doesn't sound like John, either."

"I know!" *Who made Becky John's defense attorney?* "Never mind John for a minute. This is about Phil. I honestly don't care about him and I really don't even want to see him. But forgive him? Just say it's okay what he did? He doesn't deserve that."

"Well," Becky considered this for a moment. "If you ask me, this is really about John."

Maddy looked back at her sister. "What?"

"You said you don't care about Phil, so it's really not about him. You do care about John, and he just wants to help you deal with it. Why don't you let him? Why get so defensive?"

Maddy stared at Becky, who was hardly a master at the relationship game, and dropped down on the bed.

"You're right."

It was Becky's turn to look surprised. "I am?"

"Yeah. Crazy, huh?" Maddy grinned.

"You'd better go talk to him." Becky figured she'd better push her advice while Maddy was taking it.

"I'm not sure he'll want to talk to me."

"Just call him and go over there. You can fix this."

Maddy looked at Becky. "You really think so?"

"Absolutely."

"I really pushed him away."

"Well, pull him back in," Becky answered. "Quit whining and call him."

Maddy scowled and left the room.

By the time she reached John's house, Maddy's stomach was in knots. Was it only twenty-four hours ago that she was preparing for her date, happily nervous? This was an entirely different kind of anxiety. She pulled into John's drive and searched the yard for any of the Fordham boys. No one came running to greet her.

She parked and slowly got out of her car. Looking down at her outfit, she wondered again if she'd overdone it. Her shorts were casual, but the sleeveless blouse was... well, it certainly wasn't one of her work shirts. Becky insisted that it set off her tan nicely, and that John needed to be reminded that Maddy was his girl. If Becky had had her way, Maddy would have shown up in the black dress again. She wasn't into taking chances.

Maddy was glad that she'd foregone the formal wear when she

finally saw John approaching from across the street. He was in sneakers, low-riding athletic shorts and a sweat-stained T-shirt. He'd obviously been doing yard work and he never looked so good. Coming within a few feet of Maddy, he stood with his hands on his hips.

"Blake said you called."

No kiss? Not even on the cheek? "I hope you don't mind my stopping by."

"It's fine." He eyed her clothing. "You look nice."

"Thanks," Maddy said, shading her eyes as she looked up at him. "Where are the boys?"

"Back in the fort. They're with some friends."

"I see."

"Can I get you a drink or something?"

Oh, he's being cool. "You look like you could use one. I'll join you."

John nodded and started toward the house.

"Thanks again, John!"

Maddy heard a woman's voice from behind them, and turned to identify the source. A very attractive woman was waving from her porch across the street, and John waved back.

"No problem! See you later," he called out, opening the door for Maddy. She couldn't help but look up at him, wondering what he'd done for his neighbor. John met her gaze, but offered no explanation as he led the way into the house. Maddy found this exchange extremely unsatisfying and scowled as she followed John's broad shoulders into the kitchen.

He poured her some lemonade and grabbed a beer for himself. "I'm sorry, did you want a beer? I assumed you'd prefer lemonade."

Something about his polite but distant demeanor irritated her. She picked up the glass of lemonade. "This is fine, thanks."

"Let's head out back. I need to check on the boys."

Maddy took a deep breath and walked out to the deck. Blake saw her almost immediately, and ran over to greet her. Parker followed a few minutes later, bringing one of his friends with him.

"Hi, Miss Maddy! This is Brandon."

"Hi, Parker. Hi, Brandon. It's nice to meet you."

Brandon smiled shyly, and Parker asked, "Why weren't you in church today?"

"I didn't feel... up for going."

"Oh. I saved you a donut. It's inside on my dresser."

Maddy smiled and touched his cheek. "Thank you, Parker."

He grinned. "Miss Maddy is my dad's girlfriend," he giggled to his buddy as they walked away. He leaned over and whispered something and they both laughed.

Maddy turned to John.

"Have a seat," he said.

She sat down and folded her hands on the table.

John sat back in his chair. "So, what's up?"

Maddy exhaled quietly. "I'm sorry, John. I'm sorry for pushing you away last night. You were just trying to help me." She looked up at him. His expression softened a little, but not much.

"You were upset."

"Yeah, well, it wasn't right to take it out on you."

John nodded and sipped his beer.

"I said I had to do this alone," Maddy said softly, "but I'm beginning to think that I can't do it without you."

"Do what?"

"Deal with Phil."

John stood up and looked at his boys, who were happily distracted in the fort.

"You said this was moving too fast, and I think you're probably right. You need time to work through your thing with Phil, and I think it would be best if we just... if we just played it cool for a while."

Maddy's heart broke and her mind reeled. She could almost feel the walls reassembling around her heart. "Meaning?"

"I'm going to concentrate on fixing your house, and I think that's the relationship we should focus on right now."

Maddy put her hands on the table. "If that's what you want."

Pain filled John's eyes, but Maddy had turned to watch the boys as he said, "It's probably the best thing right now."

Maddy forced a smile and a wave in response to Blake, who'd

caught her eye. "Please tell the boys I said good-bye," she replied. She stood and walked off the deck. Circling the house, she got into her car and pulled out of the drive. For once, no tears came to her eyes. She just felt numb. She didn't remember driving home.

Becky met her in the drive when Maddy pulled in. "Are you okay?" she asked anxiously. Maddy didn't look so good.

"Not particularly. How about you?" Maddy noticed that Becky didn't look so good, either.

Becky was tired of sharing bad news. "Mom called."

"Is everything okay?"

Becky hesitated. "Dad had a fall." She put her hand on Maddy's arm. "He's okay. It happened this morning, and they're already home from the hospital."

"The hospital?" Maddy leaned against the car. "What happened? How badly is he hurt?"

"Apparently, he fell in the barn and broke his ankle. Luckily, Mom was going out to call him for lunch, so she found him soon after it happened."

"Is he in a lot of pain? How did Mom sound? Is she okay?"

"Yeah. She was pretty shaken up, but mostly relieved, I think. Dad's okay. He's just mad that he can't get around for the rest of the summer."

Maddy processed this, catching her breath. "So, she's not coming tomorrow?" There really wasn't a question.

"No, she's going to stay with Dad and make sure he's okay. She said she might be able to come later in the summer, but she'd have to see."

"Of course."

"They're going to be okay, Maddy, and I'll help you get your house ready. I can stay for at least a week before I have to leave." Becky put her arm around Maddy a little awkwardly, new to the role of looking out for someone else.

Maddy leaned her head on Becky's shoulder. "Thanks, Beck. I think I'm going to need you."

"It didn't go well at John's, huh?"

"No."

"I'm so sorry, Maddy. What did he say?"

"He basically said that we're back to being contractor/home-owner." Maddy's voice was hollow.

"You're kidding!" Becky held Maddy's hand with both of hers.

"No. Apparently he's giving me what he thinks I want, which is the space to deal with Phil on my own."

It sounded reasonable to Becky, but she was still angry at John for making Maddy sad.

"Well, we'll make him regret that," she replied with determination, already speculating about the possibilities.

"I'm not going to play games," Maddy sighed.

"You just leave it to me," Becky said consolingly.

Maddy looked at her warily.

"No games," Becky promised, thinking, planning. "But there *will* be interesting beachwear."

"Becky," Maddy protested. "I'm not going there."

"We'll see," Becky answered with a smile. Perhaps this week would be a little fun after all.

twenty-one

Maddy figured that she'd be nervous about seeing John on Monday morning, but she awoke feeling empty and incapable of emotion. Rather than watching the sunrise, she turned over and burrowed her head under her pillow.

Sleep escaped her, however, so she finally got up to make the coffee. Her mind passed over the events of the last day and a half, and she simply didn't have the capacity to deal with them. Filled with her highest and lowest moments with John, the news of her father's injury and her mother's change of plans, and the supremely unwelcome news of Phil's visit, she was drained of the energy to feel anything.

Burt let her know that the men were arriving, and all she could muster was sadness. She let him out, and followed with her coffee and her pad. Looking at her list without seeing it, she listened as the crew made its way into the kitchen.

"Help yourselves to coffee!" she called out, and was met with a chorus of thanks.

"Maddy makes the best coffee," she heard Travis say, and she smiled a little. She looked over at Burt, who was whining and frantic to get inside to say his hellos, especially to John. Apparently her dog didn't understand that things had changed. She looked back at her list, waiting for her first post-dating interaction with her contractor.

The door *banged* gently and she looked up, staying surprisingly cool at the sight of John in his faded jeans and tool belt. She swallowed and nodded at him, "Morning."

"Good morning, Maddy." A momentary warmth gave way to a

vague professional nod.

Maddy went back to her list. There was really no need to alphabetize her groceries, but it kept her focused on her paper. The other men joined them on the porch, bemoaning the start of another work week with relatively good humor. The conversation then centered on John and his vacation, and Maddy excused herself to work in her office.

"So, you know about the roof, Maddy?" Frank asked as she opened the door.

"What about the roof?"

"The weather is supposed to be dry all week," John said. "So we're going to start on that project."

Frank looked at John, who stood at the railing with his coffee. John turned his attention to Burt who had been waiting patiently for some sort of greeting. Frank looked back at Maddy, and she looked down at her list.

Squash should not have come before spaghetti.

"So, is that okay with you?" Frank, puzzled, tried to interject some warmth into the conversation.

"Of course. Do what you need to do," Maddy replied quietly.

"We'll be removing the old shingles all day tomorrow, and probably into Wednesday," he further explained, looking again at John and wondering why he was suddenly the spokesman for the crew. Frank shook his head and looked back at Maddy. "Anyway, they're delivering the dumpster first thing in the morning. It's pretty big; you've probably seen them. It'll go right up next to the house. You'll need to park your cars by the shed for a few days."

"That won't be a problem."

"The shingles will be delivered Wednesday," John added.

Maddy didn't look up. She fit the word "shingles" between salsa and spaghetti. "We'll try to stay out of your way."

Frank, increasingly troubled, looked again at Maddy and then at John. Neither returned his glance.

"I'll let you guys catch up," Maddy said, walking into the kitchen and holding the door so that it wouldn't slam shut.

John cleared his throat and said, "We'll start stripping at the top and dump it tomorrow." The groans were less cheerful with

Maddy out of earshot, and coffee cups were drained as the chairs scraped across the porch.

Becky was sure that the outlet mall would provide a safe haven from falling shingle debris, and especially from the men "stripping on the roof," a concept that Maddy did not find nearly as amusing as she did. Before they started their shopping, Becky insisted that they stop at a nearby coffee shop. Maddy's spirits started to lift as they went through her lists one more time over large cups of vanilla iced coffee.

Thus prepared, they began the significant project of buying accessories for the bedrooms. Maddy got lost in the challenge of outfitting the rooms, zeroing in on themes and searching doggedly until they bought almost everything they needed for every bedroom but the master. There seemed to be an endless supply of bedding, lamps, window dressings and miscellaneous decor to fit the various themes they'd selected. The fact that they hit a number of sales made the day's accomplishments even more satisfying.

After mastering the puzzle of fitting everything into the car, Maddy and Becky stopped for a quick bite on the way home. They arrived back at the house well after the men had left for the day, and unloaded their treasures before stopping to put their feet up. Burt was thrilled to have them home and circled them repeatedly until he eventually relaxed and lay down between them.

"We accomplished a lot today," Maddy observed, sitting back in her chair with her eyes closed. "Thanks for all of your help."

Becky waved her off. "I told you we'd get it done," she said with a tired grin. "I think our last stop was the most productive."

Maddy smiled. "Yeah, I really needed a new swimsuit."

Becky nodded. "Yes, you did, and so did I."

They sat for a few minutes. "Thanks for staying, Beck," Maddy said quietly.

"You're welcome." Becky paused. "I'll just hang out until you get your life back together."

Maddy smiled sadly. "That may take a while."

"Not with that new suit."

80C3

Tuesday's weather was sunny and steamy; a perfect day for the beach, as far as Becky was concerned. She forced herself out of bed early, determined to have her say regarding the day's plans. Maddy had made some ominous references to appliance shopping and Becky was not about to waste her time on that detail. Her expertise could be better applied to making sure that John kept Maddy firmly in the middle of his radar. Yesterday's purchase and strategic sunbathing would do the trick.

"What do you mean we can't sit on the beach?" she demanded of her uptight older sister, who was already steeped in her work.

"Becky, we're not going to sit in the sun while John's crew is working on the roof. With that swimsuit you bought, it would be dangerous." Maddy continued typing.

Becky looked down and grinned, despite her thwarted plans. "We wouldn't be too close to the house," she offered.

Pulling some papers together on her desk, Maddy shook her head. "Your beach chair would probably be facing the house."

Becky shrugged. She'd much rather see Travis and the others working on the roof in all their glory than stare at the water any day. "We could go down to the public beach," she persisted.

Maddy considered this. She was already hot and sticky, and the day had only begun. Cooling off in the water actually sounded pretty good, as long as they were well away from the house. She didn't want to make the list of women who gratuitously sunbathed in front of John's crew.

Becky took advantage of the pause and pressed on. "Come on, Maddy, your new suit is gorgeous! Don't you want to try it out?"

"Okay, fine," she answered. "Let's see if we can get out of here without drawing attention to ourselves."

Becky rolled her eyes. "You really don't get it, do you?"

Maddy watched her sister leave and smiled a little. *Why not have some fun?* She went to her dresser and pulled out her new suit. The bright orange and yellow print normally wouldn't have appealed to her, but Becky insisted that it was just right for Maddy's coloring. She looked at the two-piece with matching sheer cover-up, sighed, and started to change.

Meanwhile, Becky was engaging in a bit of a skirmish with John in the kitchen.

"You can't be anywhere near the house," he warned her.

Becky smiled coquettishly and pulled two water bottles out of the refrigerator. "Really, John, the beach is quite large. Besides," she added, "The tide is out!"

John withheld comment as the sound of the rest of the crew making their way through the house interrupted their conversation. The men poured into the kitchen for a water break, and not one of them had a shirt on. Becky's eyes lit up and she pulled out one of the stools at the counter.

"Come on, you guys," John growled. "Get your shirts on."

"Don't worry about me!" Becky smiled.

Travis grinned and pulled his shirt from wherever it had been tucked behind him. He took his time pulling it over his head, flexing and posing as he did so. The others found their shirts and followed him out to the porch and the cooler. Becky tagged along, determined to enjoy the favorable men-to-woman ratio.

"So, guys, we're going to hang out at the beach today. If you need a break," she began shamelessly.

This invitation was met with a fair amount of enthusiasm, and John scowled, Maddy-like, at his men.

"There won't be any significant break-time today."

"Whatever. I just thought I'd offer."

"It would be best if you didn't stay close to the house," John reminded her, really disliking the idea of his guys being sidetracked while they stripped shingles. He definitely didn't want any of them gawking at Maddy in a bathing suit.

"Fine, we'll go to the public beach," Becky said. "Maddy and I both have fabulous new swimsuits; we can show them off there." She made a point to look wickedly at John, who almost scowled back. "Where *is* she?" Becky asked, determined to keep torturing him. "Wait until you see her; she looks adorable," she said to the rest of the group.

No one made eye contact with John as they shifted in their seats and focused on their water bottles.

"Well, you guys are boring," Becky decided. "Oh," she added with delight, "here she is!"

Maddy backed through the door, focused on punching a number into her cellphone. She put the phone to her ear and turned, surprised to find that the quiet porch was full of people. A predictable blush covered her face, and she glared at her sister, closing the phone before the call went through. All eyes were on her after Becky's introduction; they could hardly help it.

"Where is your cover-up?" Becky asked, disappointed. "That's the best part of the suit!"

"It didn't cover *anything*," Maddy muttered, supremely relieved that she hadn't been reckless enough to wear the pointless piece of clothing. She looked briefly at the men and nodded. "Hi guys. How's your work going on the roof?"

It was the first time John had talked to her all morning, and he was both relieved and a little disappointed to see her in swim shorts and a T-shirt.

"We've got half of the roof stripped," he answered. "We're going to eat an early lunch and then get back at it. They're delivering the shingles tomorrow afternoon."

"How will you get them on the roof?"

John's eyes softened a little at the concern on her face. "They have a crane that lifts them up there."

Maddy nodded, relieved, and turned to the others. "Well, we're heading down to the beach. Sorry to leave you with all the work," she added, smiling sheepishly.

Frank was glad to see her smile at all. Her grin had been noticeably absent; a fact that had him really baffled.

A day at the beach turned out to be a good diversion for Maddy. It wasn't so bad to get a little attention from some college boys playing volleyball and harassing nearby sunbathers. The girls talked and laughed and soaked up the sun and even ventured into the waves a few times. Maddy felt like she was back in high school, carefree and indulgent, and the weight of the week's problems seemed to lift for a few welcome hours.

They finally packed up their beach gear and headed home in the middle of the afternoon. Maddy stopped several houses short of her own to pull her T-shirt on over her suit.

"Really, Maddy. Would it be so bad for John to see some skin?" Becky tossed her head and kept walking, determined to let at least Travis catch a glimpse of her own new suit without its cover as they approached the house.

Maddy didn't answer, her eyes drawn to the roof as they got closer. There was no sign of work being done. *Maybe they're inside?* The girls climbed the steps to the porch and heard nothing from indoors. Curious, they dropped their things in the kitchen and greeted the dog.

Even Becky started to feel a little silly, wearing only her skimpy bikini in the kitchen. "Is it okay if I go shower?" she asked, looking out the windows one last time.

"Go ahead. I'll clean up when you're done."

Becky disappeared up the steps and Maddy stepped into her room, anxious to get out of her sandy beachwear. She made a mental note to talk to John, or somebody, about the fact that only one hot shower or bath could be taken at a time. Willy had hoped to resolve that problem, but Becky's visit proved that it was still an issue.

Maddy took off her T-shirt and shorts, and tried on the filmy little beach dress that went with the suit. She looked at herself in the mirror. It was worse than no cover-up at all. At least without one, people expected to see a swimming suit. With the cover-up on, she felt like she was in a see-through dress and the world could see her underwear. She didn't know why she let Becky talk her into buying it. It wasn't her style at all.

She tempted fate by walking out into the kitchen and refilling her drink.

"Hello, Miss Maddy!"

Maddy spun around to see Otis standing at her kitchen door. "Otis, come in!" she answered, relieved and a little embarrassed. She stood behind the counter as he walked into the room.

"Those boys gone for the day?"

"I'm pretty sure," Maddy said. "We haven't seen or heard anything since we got back about twenty minutes ago."

"They're working hard on that roof," Otis observed. "They probably wrapped it up early."

"Probably so," Maddy agreed. "Can I get you something to drink?"

"Oh, I'm alright," Otis answered. "I've been drinking lots of water all day. I just wanted to get this to you." He dropped a piece of mail on the counter. "It got delivered to my house by mistake."

"Thanks," Maddy replied, glancing at the letter.

"Are you okay?" Otis asked gently, standing at the door.

Maddy looked at him warily. "I'm fine."

"How's John?"

"Keeping busy with the roof."

Otis nodded. "Has your mother arrived yet?"

"Oh, you didn't hear." Maddy told him about her dad's accident and her mom's change of plans.

"I'm so sorry," he said. "I know how much you were looking forward to her coming."

"I really was," Maddy replied. "Well, Otis, I don't mean to run you out, but I think I'll go see if it's my turn for the shower."

"I won't hold you up." He looked at her meaningfully. "You take care."

Maddy watched him walk slowly past the kitchen window, touched and a little troubled by his concern. The last thing she needed was sympathy. She'd moved over three thousand miles to escape it before; there wasn't much further she could go. She turned with a sigh and almost ran into John, who had entered through the dining room door. How had she not heard his boots?

She stopped and stared at him, and then looked down at her see-through dress. She quickly backed around the counter.

"You're still here? I thought you'd left for the day."

John tried not to stare at Maddy's see-through dress, though the fact that she was trying to hide made him absurdly determined to see it. She looked wonderfully sun-drenched and smelled like some sort of tropical oil. John's unprepared senses overloaded.

"We finished early," he explained. "The sun was pretty brutal, so I sent the guys home."

He wanted to follow her around the counter and tease her about her silly "cover-up," take her in his arms and break all the bans they'd needlessly made. He tore his eyes away from her and focused on the countertop.

"Tomorrow's supposed to be even hotter, so we'll probably only spend the morning on the roof." He paused and looked out the window before turning back to her. "Willie will be back to work on your bathroom down here, so we need to know whether you want a tub or a shower."

"Oh, that reminds me. You can't have two in the shower at once."

John raised an eyebrow, and Maddy almost choked.

"I mean, only one person can shower at a time."

John continued to regard her. "Really."

"I mean," Maddy repeated, exasperated, "Becky's showering right now, and I have to wait, because there's not enough hot water for two showers to run at once." She blew her hair out of her eyes. "It doesn't really matter now, but later on…"

John nodded. "Right. I'll talk to Willy."

"Thanks."

"What do you want to do about the bathroom down here? Do you still want a tub?"

"I guess I can do without one," Maddy decided. "There really isn't enough room, and I can always use the one upstairs when I don't have guests." She continued with more resolve. "Just have him put in the shower we discussed. That will be fine."

John nodded, wishing she'd fight with him and insist on a bathtub the way she had the day before he left for New Hampshire. He walked around the counter toward her, and Maddy seemed to freeze, crossing her arms to ineffectively cover her midsection as he approached.

John stopped in front of her, unable to keep himself from taking in the full effect of her ensemble. It was more of Maddy than he'd ever seen, and he willed himself to remember that she was absolutely off-limits to him.

Maddy couldn't breathe or form a coherent thought. Feeling vulnerable and frustrated, she placed her hands on her hips, and demanded, "Do you stand this close to all of your sunbathers?"

John rocked back in disbelief. "I'm sorry you felt so threatened. I just need my pad; it's on the counter behind you."

Maddy quickly moved around the counter, embarrassed but ready to fight. "I'd hardly feel threatened by you, John." The words were harmless enough, but the delivery was clearly not complimentary.

John picked up his pad and slowly turned to her. "Meaning?"

Maddy shrugged and looked at him petulantly.

"Maybe you were hoping someone more interesting was going to walk in just now? Someone who might act with a little more resolve when he saw you in next to nothing?"

Maddy wasn't ready for that. "You think I'm hoping Phil will show up?" She looked at him, incredulous. "That's what you think of me?"

John passed up the opportunity to retract the damaging remark. Maddy, having given him plenty of time to do so, walked into her room and locked the door.

twenty-two

Maddy's sunburn had a deleterious affect on her mobility the following day. She had been looking forward to getting the bedrooms put together, but she could hardly lift her coffee mug to her lips. She groaned and wondered why she'd been so stupid. Feeling silly and irresponsible and sore, she moved slowly back into her bedroom, thinking she could work on her computer. With a sigh, she remembered that Willy would be starting her bathroom.

Burt began to whine in the kitchen, and she mustered the energy to greet the men and pretend that she didn't feel like burned toast.

There was no need to feign bravado. Everyone else was sunburned, too. Maddy commiserated with the less than cheery crew as they moaned their way into the kitchen. She wished that she shared their fate for a more noble reason.

John, the responsible one, seemed to be the worst off. Although she was more than a little angry, and had been ready to continue their fight at the least provocation, Maddy still felt worried as her contractor slumped onto the bar stool with his coffee.

She looked up at the rest of the men. "I feel so bad for you all," she said. "Can you do something besides the roof today?"

The guys looked hopefully at John, who shook his head, and winced. "We've got to finish stripping this morning before it gets too hot." He continued, a little louder, over the groans. "We'll work inside framing the shower this afternoon."

Maddy left them to their unpleasant task and went upstairs. She spent the next hour unloading her recent purchases and making sure all the room accessories matched up. She heard the crew on the roof and was relieved that the sky had become overcast. Venturing back downstairs mid-morning, Maddy walked into her room and was blessedly overwhelmed by a rush of cool air. Someone had installed an AC unit. Travis? Frank? She didn't imagine John was kindly disposed toward her this morning.

She sat down at her computer and her phone rang.

"Hello?"

"Maddy?"

Her heart began to pound, but it wasn't a pleasant sensation.

"It's Phil."

"I know."

"You don't sound too happy."

"A pretty fair assessment." Maddy stood and began pacing.

"Ouch. Well, you been okay?"

"I'm great."

"It's been a long time."

"Yes, it has."

"I was hoping that we could talk."

Maddy returned to stand in front of her computer screen. "Go right ahead."

"Maddy…"

"What, Phil?"

"I want to see you."

She paused, confused and angry and overwhelmed. One thing she knew; she didn't want him near her house, to see where she lived or have any part in her new life.

If he wants to see me, then, "I can arrange to meet you." If he was in Boston, then she'd meet him in Portsmouth, or somewhere far from her home.

"Well, you won't have to come far."

Maddy's heart stopped. "Where *are* you?"

"In your driveway; at least I think I am. Do you have a bunch of guys on your roof?"

Maddy sat down heavily in her chair. She had no time to collect her thoughts or prepare to see him for the first time in a year and a half. Leave it to Phil to keep her as defenseless as possible.

"Maddy?"

"I'll be right out."

"Can't I just come in?"

Maddy didn't want him in her house, although his necessary path through falling roof debris gave her uncharitable pause.

"I said I'd be out. Give me a minute."

She hung up abruptly and considered cleaning up and changing her clothes. Looking in the mirror, however, she decided that she felt good about the woman looking back at her. Her hair was longer than she normally wore it, and she had on very little makeup. Still, she liked what she saw. She pulled her hair back and put on a little lipstick. Phil wasn't getting any special treatment, but she knew she looked just fine.

Phil lounged against the silver Mercedes he'd rented, his sunglasses covering eyes that took in every detail of his surroundings. Thirty yards away and two stories up, John and Frank looked down at the new arrival.

"Who's that?" Frank asked, leaning on his shovel.

"I'm guessing Maddy's old boyfriend," came the curt reply.

"No!" Frank looked with new interest at the stranger below, his questions about the tension in the house finally answered. He watched as Phil leaned over and checked the passenger's side mirror.

"I don't like him," Frank decided.

John withheld comment, wondering if Maddy even knew that Phil was there. Her voice interrupted his thoughts a moment later.

"John? Frank?" she called. "Is it okay if I come out?"

"Hang on, Maddy," John replied, calling to Bill and Travis to stop their work. "Okay," he yelled back down. "It's safe."

She turned at the bottom of the steps and gave them a small wave. John raised his hand, feeling helpless as she walked away from him. When she reached Phil, he didn't have the heart to watch them.

Frank did. "Maddy doesn't look too happy," he said, unashamedly observing the reunion in the driveway. "I wish I could hear them." He eased further toward the edge of the roof.

"Frank…"

"Look at the way he's crossing his arms; he's got biceps the size of my thighs."

John looked over at Phil and then back at Frank. "You okay?"

"Just checking out the competition." he answered, determined to provoke his friend. "Oh look, she's waving!" Frank almost lost his balance as he returned her greeting a little too energetically. "I think he looks like an ape."

"Really, Frank?"

"Sorry. Do you even know why he's here?"

John shook his head.

"Did you know he was coming? You don't seem surprised."

"I found out Saturday night when Maddy did."

"And so you've decided to abandon her now that this jerk has shown up?"

John gave Frank a withering look. "I'm giving her space to figure out what she wants."

"Oh, that's what you call it."

"You think I should be out there standing between them?"

John was starting to get angry, and Frank concluded that Maddy meant more to his buddy than he realized.

"Of course not. It's just that you've been so distant these past few days, and Maddy seems so sad. I didn't know what was going on."

John turned away, his head beginning to pound. Why was Frank making him look like the villain?

"She's coming back. Maybe she told him to get lost!" Frank reported with enthusiasm.

Maddy was walking back to the house, while Phil made a flashy exit in the Mercedes. Maddy shaded her eyes to look up at Frank and John, who waved her onto the porch.

"Think he'll be back?"

"I don't know," John answered, his voice tired. "I hope not."

"He's here? Where? Why didn't you get me?"

Sunburned and irritable, Becky had found her way to the coffee pot and then to the comfort of her sister's room within minutes of Maddy's return.

"He didn't stay long. Sorry I didn't think to let you share the moment."

The sarcasm was ignored. "How'd he look?"

Maddy rolled her eyes at her sister. "I guess he looked good; still working out."

"What was it like to see him?"

"Strange. I was nervous at first."

Maddy lay back on her bed and looked at the ceiling, wondering why she felt so little after this significant meeting. It shouldn't have been surprising, given her numbness over the past few days. Maybe she was incapable of feeling anymore. When she first saw Phil, there had been an initial rush of nerves and a momentary attraction; old habit, she guessed.

"Is it possible for someone to look too good?"

Becky sat down next to her. "Absolutely not."

Maddy sighed. "Phil was always careful about his appearance, but he seems to have taken it to a new level. Not a hair was out of place, and he was driving a convertible. I swear he stopped along the road to get his shirt pressed."

"That's a little much." Becky shrugged. "Maybe he just wanted to impress you."

"Hmmm…"

"So, when is he coming back?"

"Later this afternoon." Maddy pulled a pillow over her head.

"Did John say anything?"

A series of strange, muffled sounds came from under the pillow. Becky pulled it off Maddy's face and threw it in the corner.

"What did you say?"

"If he did, I didn't hear him. He's on the roof."

"Did he see Phil?"

"I guess so. We were just talking in the driveway."

"I wonder what he was thinking," Becky mused.

Maddy suddenly felt very sad. "We have to clear out of here. They're starting work on the bathroom soon." She should have been excited about the prospect, but, predictably, felt nothing.

"Let's go waste time downtown. Maybe there's something new at one of the antique shops."

Becky nodded. "I'll go grab my purse."

When Phil pulled in later that day, Frank and John had just returned to the roof. They watched as he made his way toward the house, giving them a nod on the way. Frank, closer to the edge, waved at him and then walked back up to join John, knocking a small pile of rubble off the roof in the process.

"Hey! Watch it up there!"

"Oops," Frank grinned.

"Classy, Frank."

"So, are you going to go down and meet him?"

"I don't know why I should."

"Aren't you a little curious?"

John looked at his friend. "Whether I am or not, I'm sure Maddy doesn't want me down there."

"I don't know about that. We're done up here anyway." Frank started heading toward the ladder.

"Don't make a scene, Frank."

"Come down and stop me."

Maddy and Phil were standing by the door as John and Frank climbed down the ladder and up the steps. There was an awkward moment as the group converged and then stopped.

Frank broke the silence. He reached his hand out. "Hi, I'm Frank."

Phil extended his hand in return. "Phil. How's it goin'?"

"I'm sorry," Maddy said. "Frank, John, this is Phil. Phil, these guys are restoring my house with me. John is my contractor."

John stepped up onto the porch, and Phil inadvertently took a step back, apparently not interested in looking up to say hello.

John nodded. "Hello, Phil."

Phil crossed his arms. "Looks like you boys are doing a good job."

"It's been interesting." John looked briefly at Maddy. She didn't look particularly happy; something about her haunted expression struck a protective chord. He took a deep breath and looked back at Phil. "We won't keep you."

"Don't worry about us. We're on our way out." Phil ushered Maddy ahead as they walked down the steps to his car.

John watched for a moment, and then turned to walk into the house. Frank followed, for once, not knowing what to say.

"So, you spent two hours together and you didn't talk about why he walked out on you?"

Maddy stuffed a pillow into its new case. "He's coming back on Friday; we'll talk more then."

"Why Friday?"

"He's doing something up in Augusta. He'll be back in time for dinner Friday night."

"So you had a nice little chat this afternoon?"

Maddy shrugged. "For some reason, we just spent the time catching up. It was strange, like no time had passed."

Becky regarded her sister skeptically while she tucked the coral-colored shell spread into place. "Sounds magical."

Maddy scowled. "It's not like I'm going to let it all go so easily; I'm not stupid. He just caught me off guard. Believe me, I was on the defensive – but he just started asking about my business, and then we caught up on each others' families. It was surprisingly comfortable."

"I'm sure that was no mistake."

"Well, he seemed genuinely interested. I've had enough conflict around here this week. It was nice to have a civil conversation."

Becky threw the last of the decorator pillows on the bed. "He broke your heart, Maddy." She fluffed a pillow and rearranged it. "Or more like ripped it out and stomped on it." She turned to her sister. "You're okay with that now?"

"Of course not!" Maddy shot back, obstinately rearranging the pillows. "I'm just trying to stay neutral. He came across the country to see me. I can at least hear him out."

"You owe him nothing."

Maddy looked hard at her sister. She was right, of course. She leaned down to collect the plastic wrappings from the bedding. *Why am I defending Phil?* She seemed to have no framework for figuring out either Phil or John. The one person she didn't need to be arguing with was her sister. Preparing to make this generous observation, she looked up and caught a pillow in the face.

Sputtering with surprise, she hurled it back at her sister. Becky caught it with a grin, and slowly lifted it with both hands. Maddy took a step back and ducked just in time. The pillow flew over her head, and Maddy jumped back up, only to get one of the smaller decorator pillows in the chest. Ammunition wasn't far away, and she quickly armed herself. A full-out pillow fight ensued, covering the entire upper floor, and involving every new pillow and several of the unopened mattress pads.

Burt began to bark, frantic that he couldn't get upstairs to stop the melee. The girls finally fell in a heap on the bed in the master bedroom, laughing and exhausted.

Maddy turned onto her stomach. "I wonder how many of those pillows I'll have to replace?"

Becky looked up at the ceiling. "Probably all of them. Do you have homeowner's insurance?"

Maddy giggled and pulled one of the abused pillows under her chin. "I haven't laughed that hard in a long time."

"Me neither."

"This has been a good week with you, Becky, no matter what happens with Phil or John." Maddy looked over at her sister, who still lay on her back, trying to catch her breath.

She turned over and rolled up next to Maddy. "Well, I have to leave on Saturday," she said a little glumly. She put her chin in her hands. "That gives you less than seventy-two hours to get those boys straightened out."

Maddy sighed. "I'll do my best."

John pulled in next to the Mercedes the next morning and felt physically ill. He put his head down on the steering wheel and tried to breathe. Throughout the whole difficult situation with Maddy, he'd held onto the grain of hope that they would eventually work things out. That grain now seemed to have slipped through his fingers. He forced himself to pull air into his lungs. He wasn't sure he could even move to get out of his truck.

He did, though. Somehow he hauled himself out of his vehicle, strapped on his tool belt, and trudged up the steps to Maddy's porch. He wondered if he should still just walk in, or knock and wait for Maddy to come to the door.

He knocked and then let himself in. He walked slowly to the kitchen, his sadness galvanizing into anger as he agonized over Maddy's betrayal. He pushed the door open, his heart in his throat as he looked at her standing by the coffee maker, filling her mug like his world hadn't just fallen apart.

"Morning, John."

She looked tired. John felt sick about why that might be so.

Maddy was taken aback by the anger in John's eyes. She had never seen that look on his face, at least not directed at her. She sipped her coffee and waited, a feeling of intense unease working its way through her body. The raw silence stretched out between them.

"Are you okay?" she asked.

"No," he choked as he turned to pour his coffee. He took a swallow and then faced her again. "You seem to be just fine."

Maddy, puzzled, replied, "Not really."

"Good company last night?"

Maddy thought about the pillow fight with her sister. How could John possibly know about that? And why would it make him so angry? She smiled a little at the thought, but before she could reply, John set his coffee mug down with a thud.

"I think I have my answer." He started toward the stairwell. "Is it okay if I start my work, or does someone need his rest?"

Maddy's mouth dropped open. "You think Phil spent the night here? *With me?*"

Relief and mortification battled for expression as John realized the depth of his error. "But his car..."

"Has a flat," Maddy bit off the words. "He took mine back to his hotel."

She stood regarding John with a mixture of hurt and contempt that made him reel.

"Maddy, I'm sorry."

"I don't want to hear it." She picked up her purse and keys.

"I shouldn't have assumed…"

"But you did," she snapped. "Just because you're so well-behaved, doesn't mean the rest of us are animals, John."

"Maddy…"

"You know, this week has been very revealing," she observed. "You really have a terrible opinion of me, don't you?"

"No, that's not true." John replied with feeling. "The possibility of his being here just seemed so real and I thought I'd lost you." He stopped, self-conscious about the revelation. "I didn't try to find another explanation."

Maddy swallowed, the stupid tears brimming in her eyes. She turned and walked out the door.

Appliance shopping was more distracting for Maddy and less painful for Becky than either of the girls had hoped.

Admittedly, it took a long walk with Burt and a stop at the library, grocery store and bank before Maddy cooled off enough to focus on outfitting her kitchen. Becky was good company and had surprisingly thoughtful input. They liked the look and practicality of the stainless-steel appliances, and after conferring at length with the saleswoman, Maddy selected her refrigerator, stove, microwave and dishwasher. Becky insisted that they celebrate their success by stopping at the shoe store and buying sandals. It ended up being a very productive morning.

When she grudgingly reported her accomplishment to John at his lunch break, Maddy did not get nearly the positive response she expected. Despite their morning's altercation, she figured he'd be happy that she'd taken interest in the kitchen at all.

What's wrong with him now? she wondered as she watched him drink from his water bottle and process the news. The men had been working hard on the roof, and now John stood in the middle of her kitchen, dirty and sweaty and apparently not very happy.

Maddy crossed her arms.

John put his bottle on the counter. "I'm glad you found some appliances that you like," he began.

"But?"

"But I thought you wanted to paint these cupboards," John said carefully.

Maddy looked around the room at the dark wood. She did want it lightened up, and she was prepared to do it herself.

"I figured I could start that this afternoon," she explained. "I'll prime them today and tomorrow, and paint them on Saturday and Sunday. The appliances won't be delivered until Monday. Won't that be okay?"

John glanced at Frank, who shrugged and attended to his own water bottle. Becky had gone outside to eat lunch with Travis and Bill, so no one else was there to share in Maddy's apparent folly. What was wrong with her plan? She frowned at John, who almost lost his train of thought when he observed her remarkable scowl.

"It'll be great to have your help with the cupboards, and I know you'll do a good job," he began again.

Don't flatter me. "But?" Maddy was getting really irritated with her contractor, and since it was the only emotion she was allowed to feel for him, she indulged it freely.

"But the process is a little more complicated than what you're describing." He walked over to the cabinets nearest her and ran his hand over the surface. "This isn't paint. This is a dark stain, with layers of oil and grease from cooking, and it all needs to be stripped down to the bare wood."

"So we strip and then prime and then paint?" she clarified.

"Yes," John answered slowly. "But even the stripping process is three-fold," and he launched into a brief description of the rather lengthy procedure.

Maddy sat down on the barstool. She looked at him mutely as he continued.

"In order to do that, we need to remove all of these cabinet doors and drawers. We can lay them out in the fireplace room, and strip them in there."

Maddy nodded, and John said, "If you're ready to get started, you can label and remove the hardware. The knobs, hinges and screws can be stored in plastic bags to keep them together. We'll help when we're done with the roof, but anything you can do to get the job started would be great."

She nodded again, feeling silly for underestimating the process. "Should I have them hold on to my appliances?"

"It would probably be a good idea to wait another week. This kind of refinishing is a pretty slow process."

"I'll call them," Maddy said, getting up.

"You can have them delivered and keep them in the shed," Frank offered. "I can install them when we're ready."

Maddy looked hopefully at John, who agreed. "That will definitely save you some money."

"Well, I don't know about that," Frank interjected. "I'll have to charge you my special installation fee, of course." He grinned at Maddy, and was rewarded with a grin in response.

"Thanks, Frank. I'm sure you're worth it."

"You'd better believe it," he agreed, draining his water.

twenty-three

At quitting time, most of the crew beat a hasty exit, except for Travis and John. Travis managed to entice Becky away for a quick walk on the beach. John walked into the fireplace room to find Maddy on all fours, carefully labeling the cupboard panels with small pieces of masking tape. She had removed about a dozen, and laid them out on newspapers in orderly rows. She looked up at him and sort of smiled around the writing utensil between her teeth.

"Hi," she whistled.

"How's it going?" he asked, trying to ignore her tanned limbs and focus on her progress with the cupboards.

"It's slow," she conceded, taking the marker out of her mouth. "But I'm getting there."

John nodded. "I'll pick up those compounds that you'll need for stripping tomorrow. You should have plenty to do until then."

"That's for sure," she answered, turning to sit on the floor. "You heading out?" It was almost a normal conversation.

"Yeah," John began, when his phone rang. "Excuse me," he walked back into the kitchen.

Maddy couldn't help but hear John discussing some scheduling conflict that involved Blake not feeling well. She watched as he stopped to look out over the water while he listened. She stood up and walked over to him, her heart for some reason doing its ridiculous, undisciplined leap when he looked at her.

"I can watch the boys," she mouthed quietly, trying to ignore the way he looked at her lips while he read them.

He nodded at her and said, "Hold on, Karen. I'll call you right back." He turned to Maddy. "My mother's returning from San Diego tonight. Karen was going to pick her up on her way home from the airport, but her plane's delayed in Atlanta. I'd take the boys to meet the train in Augusta, but Blake's been down with a cold."

"You go ahead. I'll stay with Blake and Parker."

John looked at her doubtfully. "You sure you don't mind?"

"Of course not."

Maddy turned away to remove another cupboard door. She waved over her shoulder at his, "Thank you, Maddy," and knelt down to get back to work. This was no time to get emotional; it made sense to help out. Besides, she missed the boys. She'd enjoy an evening with them.

John finished his phone call. "I really appreciate this. I hate to leave Blake, but I think it would be even harder on him to make the trip."

Maddy looked up briefly. "Honestly, it's no big deal."

"I'll go home and feed the boys," John said. "Can you come over around seven-thirty?"

"Sure," Maddy answered, focusing on her cupboard.

She was glad for the distraction when Becky and Travis entered the kitchen. A few minutes later, the men walked out to their trucks, and Becky joined Maddy, a satisfied little smile on her face.

"So, what's up with you?" Maddy asked.

"Well," Becky began slowly, "Travis and I talked about getting some dinner." Her smile became a look of concern. "Of course, I don't need to go if you want me to stay here and..."

"Dismember kitchen cabinets?" Maddy finished with a grin.

"Yes?" Becky tried to sound willing.

"Go have fun with Travis," Maddy replied. "I've got something else I need to do anyway."

"Which is..."

"I'm going to watch John's boys while he picks up his mom at the train station."

"Really?"

"Really."

"Isn't that nice?" Becky smiled. "That's very accommodating of you."

"Blake's sick," Maddy explained, "and John's sister was supposed to pick up their mom, but her flight from Atlanta's been delayed."

"I'm just so sorry," Becky replied.

Maddy ignored the tone. "So, when are you guys leaving?"

"Not until around eight. I told Travis I needed some time to help my sister, but it turns out she's taking off on me."

"Why don't you go see if you can catch him and make it earlier?" Maddy suggested.

Becky thought for a moment. "No, that's okay. That way you can get ready first, and I'll just take my time when you're done."

Maddy looked at her sister, impressed. "Thanks, Beck, that's thoughtful of you."

"I know," she said flippantly. "It's also not a bad idea to keep Travis waiting, don't you think?" She flashed an impish grin as she headed for the stairs.

Becky was dismayed when her sister emerged from the bathroom dressed in a T-shirt and sweats. "Really, Maddy, can't you do better than that?"

Maddy looked down at her Winnie the Pooh T-shirt. "Parker loves Pooh," she answered. "He's the one I have to impress tonight."

Becky shook her head and walked over to Maddy's closet. "Do you have anything even remotely stylish that I can borrow for the evening?"

"My Tigger shirt is clean."

Becky threw a slipper in Maddy's direction. "How about this sweater dress thing? It's gorgeous!" She pulled it out to get a better look. "What's it doing in *your* closet?"

Maddy laughed and left her sister to sort through her mostly unremarkable wardrobe. "Wear whatever you want, and have fun tonight. I have to run."

"Have fun, yourself," Becky replied with a smile.

CRBO

"Miss Maddy, I'm so glad you're here! Blake's sick, but we can still play Uno. I like your shirt!" Parker grabbed her hand and started pulling, then stopped. "Oh, I forgot you have to kiss my dad!"

Maddy and John looked at him as though he'd suggested they throw themselves off the roof. He looked up at them expectantly; completely unaware that anything had changed between his two favorite adults.

Maddy responded first, keeping her eyes firmly on Parker. "But my date is with you tonight, Parker."

"Well, I'm not kissing!" He giggled and ran around the corner.

"Yeah, well, I'm making no promises!" Maddy called after him, hearing another terrified giggle in response.

John smiled, ignoring the tightness in his chest as he led the way into the living room where Blake lay on the couch watching TV. He looked up and waved at Maddy, who walked over and knelt down next to him.

"Not feeling so good, huh?" she asked.

He shook his head.

"His throat's sore, so it hurts to talk," John explained.

Maddy nodded and gently touched Blake's shoulder. "We'll take it easy tonight. We can play more next time."

"Thanks again for doing this," John said as they walked into the kitchen. He pulled out Blake's medicine and outlined the bedtime routine for the boys. "I'm hoping to be home by eleven, but if the train's delayed..."

"Don't worry. We'll be fine."

"Okay," he said, looking at his watch. "I'd better head out."

"As long as Parker doesn't cheat at Uno, we'll be fine," Maddy qualified, catching a glimpse of her adversary's head as he sneaked up behind his dad. Parker shrieked, giggled and ran around the corner again.

"Good luck," John said. He stepped into the hall to intercept Parker's bolting body, told him to slow down, and said good-bye.

Two hours later, Maddy fell onto the couch exhausted, marveling at the energy it took to keep up with just one energetic little boy.

She picked up a magazine and paged through it. Tiring of that, she turned on the TV and started flipping through the channels. Nothing appealed, so she turned it off and rested her head.

Her eyes flew open at the sound of someone crying out. A glance at the clock revealed that almost twenty minutes had passed. She jumped up, wondering who had been crying and for how long. She hurried to the boys' room and found Blake sitting up in bed, visibly shaken.

"Are you alright, Blake?"

She sat down next to him and turned on a small bedside lamp. To her surprise, he lay his head in her lap. Maddy gently stroked his hair, and a few minutes later, Parker began to stir.

"Did Blake have a bad dream?" he asked sleepily.

"I'm not sure, Parker."

"He has lots of bad dreams."

"I'm sorry to hear that." Maddy looked down at Blake with re-newed concern.

"When is Daddy coming home?" Blake sniffled.

Maddy looked at her watch. "It won't be too long," she an-swered vaguely.

"Can I sleep in his bed?" Blake looked up at her hopefully. Maddy had no idea what to say.

"Dad always lets us sleep with him if we're scared or sick," Parker piped in with a yawn.

Lucky John. Maddy scooped Blake into her arms, and her knees buckled a little. She shifted him carefully, and said, "Okay, let's get you to your dad's bed." She maneuvered her sniffling load across the hall.

She felt strange walking into John's room, but dismissed the unsettling thoughts as she laid Blake down on the bed. Pulling back the covers on the other side, she gently rolled Blake over onto the sheets and tucked him in. She started to tip-toe out of the room, when Blake whispered, "Will you stay with me?"

Maddy stopped in her tracks. "Sure. Let me just go check on Parker and turn off the light." She came back a few minutes later, sat on the bed next to Blake, and stroked his back.

Maddy looked around the room, which was neat, but not obsessively so. There was a picture of the boys in a frame on the table next to the bed, along with a devotional book and some change. On the wall there were several more pictures, but it was hard to make out the details. She guessed that one of them was of John's parents, and another of the whole family. Maddy wondered if there was a picture of John's ex-wife anywhere in the house. She didn't recall seeing anything in the boys' room.

Blake sighed a shaky sigh, and Maddy renewed her efforts to rub his back and stroke his hair. Certain that he was finally asleep, she tried to get up and leave a few minutes later.

As she reached the door, he murmured, "Will you come back?"

"Of course," she assured him. She looped slowly through the house, checking on Parker and turning off one of the living room lamps. All was quiet, so she returned to Blake, who watched as she came back into the room.

"Thanks for staying with me," he said softly.

"You're welcome," she answered, feeling a lump in her throat. "Can I get you anything? A drink of water or something?"

"I'm alright," he answered sleepily.

"Okay," she replied as she climbed back onto the bed and sat next to him. She propped the pillows up so that she could sit more comfortably, and tried not to think about where she was. She closed her eyes and started to doze off, but caught herself. She looked at the clock and then closed her eyes again. She'd rest for a few more minutes, and then sneak out into the living room and watch a movie. Five minutes, tops...

"Maddy?"

Her eyes fluttered open and she took in the dark room. Turning, she saw a shadowed form on the edge of the bed. She sat up quickly and tried not to look like she'd been nesting in John's personal space.

For one terrible moment, she feared that Blake had awoken and wandered back to his own room, leaving her there alone, but he was still next to her, sleeping like a baby. She pushed the hair out of her face and looked sheepishly at John.

"Sorry about that."

"About what?"

"About being here, in your... room," she stammered. She couldn't see his expression. She wished he'd move so she could get up without having to climb over his son.

"Nothing to apologize for," he answered quietly. "Thanks for taking care of Blake. Did he have a rough night?"

Maddy recounted the evening, feeling increasingly conspicuous. Still, John made no move to let her up. They talked quietly about the night's events and he told her that his mother had arrived and was safely at home.

"That's nice," Maddy replied, absently stroking Blake's head and wondering if she should just ask John to move. He finally got up and offered his hand. Instead, she slid off the bed, straightening out the pillows and spread.

"Don't worry about that," John said, this time taking her hand.

Maddy looked down at the hand John was holding. He hadn't held her hand in almost a week, and she wasn't sure she wanted him holding it now. Her heart thudded gently in her chest. *Why isn't he moving?*

"Daddy, you're home!"

John turned to his son and Maddy exhaled.

"Hey, Parker, what are you doing up?"

"I beat Miss Maddy at Uno seven times!" Parker tried to keep his voice quiet for Blake, but the news was too important.

John kissed his son's head as he picked him up. "Sounds brutal."

Maddy walked over to Parker. "Thanks for being such good company tonight."

"I had fun," he yawned.

John watched the two of them and said, "Let's get you back to bed," to Parker, while trying unsuccessfully to make eye contact with Maddy.

"'Night, Miss Maddy!" Parker called out as his dad carried him across the hall.

Maddy lost no time in picking up her purse and slipping out the front door, knowing that she wouldn't survive another encounter with John. She hurried out to the car and had her keys in the ignition before the door was closed. She started down the street, refusing to look back. He had no right to change the rules in the middle of the game. As she turned the corner, the tears came, hot and furious. It appeared that all of her emotions were still intact. It wasn't necessarily much comfort.

twenty-four

When John pulled up to Maddy's house Friday morning, he'd never felt so sure about what he wanted and never so uncertain about whether or not he could have it.

He'd told his mother about Maddy, and his mom had asked, "And you're just going to let her go?"

That idea kept haunting him; Frank had alluded to it, too. Had he really just abandoned Maddy when she needed him? Wasn't it right to protect his kids if she wasn't sure what she wanted? And what about a little self-preservation? He'd experienced a fair amount of heartache in his first marriage. Didn't he have the right to protect himself as well?

These thoughts helped him keep his distance from Maddy throughout the week, but it got more difficult as the days went by. He was beginning to feel unraveled around her. Every move she made was sensual, enticing, and as far as he could tell, unintentionally so. When she'd shown up at his house in sweats, he knew she'd made an effort to be anything but alluring. It didn't work. Finding her in his bed when he got home was particularly unnerving. She'd been sleeping on her side with her arm protectively draped over Blake's shoulder, and John had been more than a little envious.

His mother's words kept haunting him. "And you're just going to let her go?"

How can I possibly hold on to her? He'd been uncivil to her all week; more than that, he'd made false accusations and fumbled over his apologies if he'd made them at all. What had come over him? He'd planned to stay quietly in the background while she worked through the situation with Phil, but who was he kidding?

He'd be a fool to sit idly by while Phil tried to move in on Maddy again.

He had to stop fighting with her and start fighting for her. With renewed resolve, he reached for the door. He would talk to Maddy before the crew arrived.

John was alone on the porch when Frank and the others showed up ten minutes later. He briefed his men on their various responsibilities for finishing up the roof. Puzzled by Maddy's absence, he finally put Burt in his pen and went to work.

They were essentially done when they came down at midday. Finishing touches would be completed by John and Frank, but the others were starting their weekend early. Maddy came out of her room while they ate their lunch, thanked them for their work, and avoided any kind of eye contact with John. He ate his sandwich and contemplated his next step with Maddy, while discussing the roof with Frank.

The afternoon moved in slow motion, as Maddy continued the endless process of unscrewing, bagging hardware, labeling and moving cupboard panels and drawers. Becky worked on her painting, leaving Maddy in relative peace. John and Frank came down while she was walking Burt, so she missed their departure. Sadly relieved that John was gone, she started to prepare herself for the fact that Phil would be back before long.

Maddy adjusted her position so that she could better see the ocean through the door and out of the window, and then promptly slipped down under the bubbles. She resurfaced and situated herself more carefully. She'd always wondered if one could enjoy both the beautiful view and the wonderful tub at the same time. Apparently not. She settled in for the soak, and closed her eyes.

As she tried to focus on what the evening with Phil might hold, all she could think about was John. All week long, he'd either been distant and removed, or downright mean. Last night was different, and she couldn't make sense of that either. Maddy blew a pile of bubbles away from her face in frustration, and another large pile quickly took its place; she'd overdone it with the bubble bath.

A voice broke into her less-than-satisfactory reverie, and Maddy sat up, alarmed. Becky had run an errand downtown, and she was pretty sure it was a man's voice, anyway. If Phil was in the house she would scream, not that anyone would hear her. For a sickening moment, she actually felt afraid, eyed her towel, and wondered how quickly she could get out of the tub and get dressed.

Then she heard the voice again. It wasn't Phil, it was John. *What's he doing here?*

She sat back in the tub and decided not to answer. He'd figure that she was gone with Becky, and leave. She didn't have the energy to talk with him or try to stay cool around him. She closed her eyes and willed herself to relax.

Let him worry a little and go away. Better yet, she thought with a half smile, let him come up and catch her bathing in her antique bathtub. That would give Mr. Restraint a little something to think about.

The smile left her face when she heard John call out again, this time from the stairwell.

"Maddy, are you up here?"

She listened, frozen in her bath. She glanced at her radio, silently cursing herself for the last-minute decision to play music to bathe by. Her heart rate went into overdrive when she heard John's footsteps in the hallway.

"Maddy?" He was at the door to the bedroom.

She couldn't believe it when she heard him closing the distance between them. She took a deep breath and held it as he came to the bathroom door.

"You are just determined to catch me in the worst possible circumstances, aren't you?" she asked with unbelievable calm.

John was dumbstruck. He looked at her, looked away, and then back again. A number of expressive emotions flashed across his face, and anger was among them. It was brief, but it made its appearance.

"Why didn't you answer me?" he asked. "I would never have

walked in on you like this." He turned his head away again. There was no other place to look in the bathroom, and it didn't immediately occur to him to walk back out.

"Well, John, I wasn't expecting anybody," Maddy answered evenly. The more agitated he became, the calmer she felt. "I really should be able to take a bath without having to explain it to the entire neighborhood, or my contractor."

A wounded expression flickered across his face. He looked down, and then back up at her, trying to separate her face from the rest of her. It shouldn't have been hard; with all of the bubbles, her face was about all that he could see, except for a little bit of her shoulders. He swallowed.

"Why didn't you answer me?" he asked again, trying to ignore the way her hair curled around her face, which was flushed from the bath, and maybe a little bit of anger. Whatever it was, it looked good on her.

"Why did you just walk into my bathroom?" she snapped.

"I don't know," John answered, genuinely perplexed. "I was worried. Your car was there and the front door was open, and Burt was in the front hall, and I'm used to just walking in…"

He was nervous and rambling. If Maddy wasn't in such an awkward position, she might have enjoyed it more.

"Maybe I wanted to be alone."

She was steamed. John wished it weren't so becoming.

"I'm sorry, Maddy."

Once more, he tried to look away, but there was nowhere else to look. He looked at the floor, at the ceiling, at the wall above her head. He met her eyes again. "I'm sorry I walked into your house, into your bathroom," he was really pained as he said this. "I heard the music and just followed it."

He looked helplessly at her, and Maddy started to feel a twinge of regret. Still, she wasn't ready for the fight to be over. She had to keep the argument going long enough for one of them to storm out of the bathroom. She hoped it would be him.

John turned and looked out into the bedroom, saying something under his breath that she couldn't quite hear. He held onto the frame above the door, and Maddy was struck by his physique, which was shown off to great advantage by that particular pose. He was surely unaware how broad his shoulders looked, or how trim his waist and hips, but Maddy was terribly distracted. It was her turn to try to look away. Her options also were limited.

"You know, you don't have to stay in here," she finally pointed out, thinking it might be best if he really did leave. "You're the one who walked in on me. I can't exactly get up and walk out while you're standing there."

He slowly turned around, and it was as though a different person faced her. He looked into her eyes.

"You're right."

Maddy thought the victory would be more satisfying. She wasn't sure she liked the look on his face.

"So?" she asked. Something had changed, and it wasn't in her favor. She sunk down a little under the bubbles.

John continued to regard her in silence before saying, "I would never try to find you in a compromising situation, but since I have, I'm going to take advantage."

Maddy looked at him wide-eyed.

John closed his eyes. "I mean, that while I have your attention, I have a few things to say to you."

Maddy relaxed the slightest bit, and he continued.

"I've behaved badly all week, and I'm sorry. I thought I could just stand back while you worked things out with Phil, but I can't. I don't want you to go back to him, Maddy. I love you and I want us to be together."

This would have been a nice time to touch her in some way, but that clearly wasn't an option. He put his hands in his pockets.

"I know you have unfinished business with him and I want you to have the freedom to handle it your way. I just want you to know that I'm going to fight for us, Maddy. For every reason he gives you to go back to him, I'll come up with five to make you stay."

Maddy, reeling from his unexpectedly sweet confession, shifted in the water and John's eyes widened in surprise. She slid down, noting that her bubbles were beginning to thin. He needed to pour his heart out quickly if she was going to exit this scene with any dignity.

"All week long I've fought with you, when all I really wanted to do was hold you and make you forget all about him. And then you made those references to my showing restraint like it's some annoying character flaw... Do you know how hard it's been to stay away from you? Do you know how difficult this is right now?"

He stopped, his words hanging in the air between them.

Maddy looked at her contractor, her heart pounding. She couldn't imagine what would happen to their list of bans if he took a step closer, and she was pretty sure they shouldn't find out.

"I think I'd better leave," he said, his voice uneven. He turned and walked out of the room, and returned a few seconds later. Maddy, her heart still hammering wildly, slid back down under her few remaining bubbles.

"Your sister's coming up the steps."

Maddy would have laughed at the expression on John's face, but there was no time.

"Shut the door and lock it!" she whispered frantically. "Otherwise, she'll just walk in."

John raised an eyebrow, but obeyed, maneuvering the door and its lock quickly and quietly.

"Maddy?"

Becky entered the bedroom and they could hear her crossing to the bathroom.

"Hey, Beck," Maddy's voice cracked.

"You okay?"

"Yep."

"Can I come in?"

"No!" It was a little too emphatic. "Sorry, I'm just taking a bath."

"Big deal. It's not like I haven't seen it all before."

Maddy and John watched the knob turn, holding their collective breath.

"Thank you for the implied compliment," Maddy parried, her eyes glued to the door, praying that the lock actually worked. The knob stopped turning, and she let out a quiet sigh of relief. So did John. "Go down the hall if you need the bathroom."

"I don't need the bathroom. You know John's back?"

"Really."

"Yeah. I haven't seen him, but his truck's here."

"Oh, well, maybe he's out in the shed or something."

"If I see him, you want me to send him up?" Her grin could be heard through the door.

John, who was studying the sink with considerable interest, shifted and looked at the wall.

"Very funny," Maddy answered.

"Maybe I'll just go look for him."

"Good luck."

"And I'll tell him you need him up here."

"Well, I *don't.*"

"I think you do. It would do you both some good."

"Becky, go away."

"I'll tell John you said hello."

"You do that."

"And I'll tell him that you're madly in love with him and that you want to have his children."

John closed his eyes and leaned his head against the wall.

"Well, Becky," Maddy answered hoarsely, looking up at the ceiling, "I don't think that will be necessary."

"Well, *you* won't do it."

"Consider it done."

"Yeah, right."

"Please go away so I can finish my bath."

"Fine. When's the dirtbag from Seattle showing up?"

"At five. What time is it?"

"Four-thirty. You'd better get ready."

"I will. Would you go find John and ask him what he wants?"

"He wants *you,* Maddy."

"Becky! Please, just go find him."

"Settle down. I will."

Becky's steps retreated and John started to turn.

"Don't you dare," Maddy hissed. "My bubbles are gone."

John stood very still, and then slowly pulled the towel off the rack on the door. He held it out behind him.

Maddy, unwilling to get out of the dubious protection of the water, said, "Just leave it on the chair."

He did so without a word, unlocked the door, and quickly left. Maddy reached over and picked up the towel. She stood in the bathtub as the water drained out, her heart pounding and her mind reeling.

There was no time to process her humiliation, only time to get dressed and deal with the next problem. It was the perfect state of mind to contemplate her evening with Phil.

He arrived promptly at five, and Becky answered the door with appropriate disdain. She had worked hard at detaining John until Phil's arrival, so she was ready for some fireworks when she led Phil out to the porch.

Burt began to growl, and John looked up, his face impassive as he considered the man who had broken Maddy's heart. Phil looked like he'd stepped out of a magazine, appropriately cloaked in labels and cologne.

John took a hold of Burt's collar. "It's okay," he said, walking the dog over to his pen and shutting him in. "Good dog," he said quietly, walking back up the steps.

"How's it goin'? John, right?" Phil asked, looking up briefly at John and then smiling at Becky.

"Fine, you?"

"Couldn't be better." Phil turned his full attention on Becky. "How've you been, Becky? It's been a long time."

"Fine. I'll go get Maddy."

Phil shrugged and looked out over the water while Becky went back into the house.

"Maddy sure found a nice piece of property out here."

"Yes, she did."

"How long do you figure before she opens shop?"

"There's still a lot to do. It'll be a while."

"Spoken like a true contractor."

"Well, Phil, I don't really know you, and it's not my place to discuss Maddy's business affairs with you."

Phil eyed John speculatively. "I'm sure she'll fill me in on everything tonight."

John picked up his papers and walked to the door, fighting the urge to spar with Phil. He reached for the handle just as Maddy was emerging.

Becky followed her sister onto the porch, and was very happy to sense a moment of palpable electricity between Maddy and her contractor. She just hoped that Phil sensed it, too.

John looked at Maddy in her jeans and blouse. He could still smell the bath oil she must have used, and it took an effort to greet her with equanimity.

"Have a nice evening, Maddy."

Maddy looked up at him, her face flushed. "You, too. Thanks for everything. The roof looks great."

He hesitated briefly. "You're welcome."

"Tell the boys I said hi."

"I will," he answered, finally moving past her.

"Oh my, it's warm out here, isn't it?" Becky fanned herself dramatically.

Maddy greeted Phil with admirable calm.

"Maddy, you look great."

Phil took a step toward her and she stiffened, putting her hand out between them. He looked down at her hand with a grin, and then shook it, keeping a hold of it as he led her off the porch toward the beach.

"Don't wait up!" he called out to Becky.

Phil surprised her with a dinner boat cruise.

Maddy, dismayed, faced her fear, figuring she'd have to deal with it sooner or later. The boat was large and festive, and once they were in the dining room, she could almost ignore the fact that they were on the water. This would be more difficult when they moved away from the dock, but she figured she'd deal with one crisis at a time.

Phil ordered drinks for them. "You really look good, Maddy. Life on the East Coast suits you."

"Thanks. It *usually* does." Maddy felt the boat begin to move.

Phil started talking about the old days, and how they'd started their business together. They got lost in the memories for a while, and even had a few laughs. When their dinner came out, Maddy decided to get to the point.

"It's been surprisingly nice catching up with you, Phil, but at some point we're going to have to deal with what happened between us."

Phil took a long drink from his second vodka and tonic. "I figured that would come up."

"Figured it would come up? Phil, we were engaged, and you left with another woman to start a business in another state. Did you not think I would remember that?"

"Well, it seemed like my only option."

"Excuse me?"

"You said you needed some space, so..."

"When did I say that?"

Phil's eyes narrowed. "In your rather colorful e-mail."

"*My what?*"

"You said you were having second thoughts, and you needed some time, space, whatever." Phil shifted in his chair as the uncomfortable truth began to dawn on him. "You didn't send me an e-mail, did you?"

Maddy looked at him, completely at a loss.

"Then what about the picture?" he asked.

"The picture from my desk?"

"Yeah, why did you return it?"

"The picture disappeared, Phil. I didn't give it back to you. And I would never handle our relationship through an e-mail. How could you think I would?"

"It had your tone," Phil protested. "Everything about it rang true."

Maddy's world had turned upside down, again. She was tired of trying to find her footing.

"Did it occur to you to ask me about it?"

"I was too angry. I couldn't believe it!" Phil's tone became heated with the recollection. "I mean, I knew we weren't perfect, but I thought we had a lot going for us."

"Then why didn't you talk to me?"

"I told you, I was angry, hurt," he added for good measure. "You know things had been a little strained between us and we hardly had any time together."

"That's the nature of the business. We both understood that."

"Well, you *had* been acting a little removed. I remember being angry, but not completely surprised by your e-mail."

Maddy looked at him thoughtfully. "It wasn't my e-mail, remember?"

"Right. Well, who would do that?"

"Think about it."

He ordered another drink while Maddy continued to put the pieces together. She almost preferred the version of the story in which he left without explanation. In the end, it didn't matter.

"So basically," she concluded, "you got your feelings hurt and replaced me with Kathy, who, incidentally, had access to my password…"

Phil looked out the window, processing this information.

Maddy stood up. "You chose not to fight for us, Phil."

"Where are you going? You can't leave."

"Yeah, I know that." The boat lurched and Maddy grabbed the table. She closed her eyes and took a deep breath. "I'm going to get some fresh air."

Phil started to get up from the table.

"Alone."

Maddy made her way out to the deck and looked out over the ocean, trying to hold the panic at bay. Why was it so different from the view from her porch? The boat lurched slightly, and Maddy acknowledged the difference with her entire, miserable body. She looked down and then over at the person standing a few yards away at the railing.

"Pastor Rob?"

"Ms. Jacobs? How are you?"

"Please, call me Maddy," she winced. "And not so good, I'm afraid."

"Me neither." He grimaced and walked slowly over to join her.

"I'm sorry. Are you here with Rachel?"

"Yes," Rob smiled a little. "And you're here with?"

A pained expression crossed Maddy's face, and Rob looked a little sicker. "I'm sorry, I shouldn't have asked."

"Oh, no, it's not that… I have an old boyfriend visiting."

"I see."

There was an uncomfortable silence, and then Maddy asked, "Where's Little John tonight?"

"Under the table."

"I'm sorry, where?"

Rob managed a grin. "He's sleeping in his car seat, and it's out of the way under the table."

"Oh, I guess that makes sense."

He turned to look out over the water and then closed his eyes. "This was supposed to be our first big night out together since Little John was born, and I'm afraid I'm not very good company."

"I'm sure Rachel understands."

"Yep. She's a keeper."

Maddy smiled at the endearment. "I guess I should get back to my… friend."

"Where's John tonight?" Rob regained a little of his energy and nerve.

I can tell you where he was a couple of hours ago. Maddy decided not to share this information with her pastor.

"Probably home with the boys," she answered. "Blake's getting over a cold."

"How does he feel about your friend's visit?"

Maddy looked over at Rob with a small smile. "And you're asking because…"

"I'm just nosy," he managed another grin.

"Well, I don't think either one of us is okay with it. It hasn't been a good week for us," she admitted. Looking out over the water began to have the same calming effect that it did when she was at home.

"I imagine that makes it hard working in your house together," he observed.

"Yeah, it's been a little awkward," Maddy agreed. "Luckily, they've been on the roof most of the week, so we've stayed out of each other's way."

"Where is your friend from?"

"Seattle," she replied. "We were engaged, but he broke it off. That was a year and a half ago. I decided to make a fresh start across the country, and he managed to find me."

"And what does he want now?"

"Good question. I'm still trying to figure that out."

"And you?"

"I just want to be done with the whole thing. I pretty much thought I'd gotten over it, then he shows up. Just when I thought I'd made my peace with it." She shook her head.

"You can't make peace, Maddy."

"You got that right."

Rob smiled. "God can give it to you, but it will involve forgiveness."

Maddy rolled her eyes with a smile. "You and your extreme methods." She sighed. "It's not like I feel that same pain anymore. It's just so confusing."

"We don't always have the luxury of waiting until the pain goes away to forgive someone. We sometimes have to forgive so that the pain starts to go away."

Maddy looked at a boat in the distance, trying to discern how many sails it had. "And if they don't ask for it?"

"I think forgiveness is much more about the healing God wants to give you," he answered, "whether the person who hurt you ever asks for forgiveness or not." Rob seemed to have forgotten his queasiness as he talked about what was clearly one of his favorite subjects. "Forgiving others frees us up to receive God's grace, to really be open to it in a way that we aren't when we're holding on to a lot of bitterness and unforgiveness."

"I held on to my anger for a long time," Maddy conceded. "It started to fade a little when I moved out here."

"And started coming to my church," Rob added smugly.

Maddy smiled. "I think you're all ganging up on me. Between you and John and Otis, and well, God, I haven't had a moment's peace about the whole business. The four of you are conspiring against me," she decided.

Rob nodded. "We've been planning this for months."

Maddy returned to the table, feeling slightly refreshed.

"Took you long enough. Did you go for a swim?" Phil had finished his third drink, and was signaling the waiter for a fourth.

Maddy sat down. "I ran into someone I know."

"I've been thinking."

Maddy folded her hands on the table. "And?"

"Seems like we didn't have a fair shot at our relationship. We were engaged, Maddy."

She sipped her wine. "I remember."

"And you were a great business partner."

"Thank you."

"Well, do you think we can try again?"

"The business or the relationship?"

Phil smiled. "You have to admit, we were a good team."

Maddy sat back, immune now to the smile that once charmed her. "What happened with Kathy?"

"She got another job in San Diego. Our business venture didn't work out, and neither did we; not that I was ever really serious about her."

That's supposed to make me feel better? "What are your plans?"

"I'm going back to Seattle. I've already got some consulting jobs lined up. Come back to Seattle with me, Maddy."

"You're not serious."

"I am. You could make a fortune on that house once it's fixed up."

"I like my house."

A new thought occurred to him. "Are you seeing someone?"

Maddy paused. "I was. I'm not sure where we stand right now."

"Is it your contractor?"

"Why do you ask?"

"He just looked ready to flatten me, or at least try," Phil

amended, "when I came over this afternoon." He took a long drink. "I was stupid enough to feel smug about being the one to take you out."

Maddy didn't think sympathy was in order, but she knew what was. "I'm not sure what happened to us, Phil, but whatever was between us is long over. We just need to forgive each other and move on." The words felt awkward, but it was, somehow, okay.

He looked at her and drained his drink. "That's it?"

"That's it."

He shook his head. "I thought you'd be more open-minded."

"I'm open-minded, but I'm not stupid." Maddy looked out of the window and noticed that they were approaching the pier. "Why don't you give me your keys and I'll drive you back to your hotel?"

He stood a bit unsteadily and managed a smirk. "Will you stay with me? For old times' sake?"

Maddy laid her napkin on the table. "Didn't then. Won't now."

Phil gave her a devilish grin, and Maddy took his keys.

twenty-five

Saturday was a workday for Maddy, which suited her just fine. She was emotionally exhausted, although a sense of peace hovered in the background, waiting to be explored. She decided to work on the cupboards while she let the events of the last week settle in her tired brain.

The process to strip the wood sounded terribly long and involved. She knelt down and looked at the compounds John brought in the day before, trying to remember the order in which to use them. A closer look revealed notes attached to the containers, with a reminder to be careful not to get any of the chemicals on her skin.

She smiled and looked at the first compound, a stripper of some kind, which was to be applied with a brush, and then scraped off with a putty knife. Maddy wrinkled her nose. *Sounds nasty.* John told her that this step might need to be repeated, and promised to work with her to let her know when it was time to move on to the next one.

She picked up solution number two, a liquid sander. It was to be applied with a brush and removed with a rag, the note explained. The third compound gave the wood a final wash and neutralized the other chemicals in preparation for priming. Maddy put that bottle down and sat on the floor. What had she gotten herself into?

Now that she'd removed the cabinet doors, she was pretty well committed to the task, and she wondered if it was really worth it to change the color of her kitchen. She sighed. There was no going back now. Getting up and opening the windows for ventilation, she found a good oldies station on the radio and got to work.

Becky got up relatively early, as she planned to be on the road before noon. She stopped in the fireplace room, complained about the smell, and insisted that Maddy come out to the porch to debrief before she left.

A light rain began to fall, and the women enjoyed the sight and sound of it as they sat together with their coffee. It seemed to wash the air of the chemical smells; a welcome cleansing.

"So?" Becky wasted no time. "What happened?"

"Well," Maddy began, "Phil explained why he left so suddenly, but I'm not really sure that it all holds up."

She recounted his story, mentioned her talk with Pastor Rob, and finished with fact that she'd dropped Phil off and still needed to return his car.

Becky sat quietly for a record amount of time. "I will concede that it's possible that Phil might not be as awful as I had originally believed."

"Or as smart," Maddy mused.

Becky smiled.

"It struck me, though," Maddy continued. "Whichever version is true, Phil wasn't willing to work at our relationship, and that's the bottom line. Our marriage would never have lasted."

"Not many people are willing to work at relationships these days," Becky observed. "It's easier just to move on to the next one."

"John said the sweetest thing, yesterday. He said he was ready to fight for me; for us."

Becky almost got tears in her eyes. "He said that? When? When did you talk to him?"

Maddy's mug froze midway to her mouth. "Yesterday."

"You said that." Becky looked hard at her sister. "Maddy?"

John reread the note with a heavy heart. He'd arrived a half hour later than the others Monday morning, and they were admittedly curious about its contents.

"What's up?" Frank asked.

"Maddy's gone up to Searsport for a couple of days."

Frank sipped his coffee and frowned. "Travis, you're not making the coffee anymore!" he called out to the porch.

"Not my fault. We need Maddy!"

"I assume everyone else is gone?" Frank asked John.

"She doesn't say," John replied. "I guess they must have left."

"When is she coming back?"

"Don't know. She just said she's doing more research at that B&B she visited earlier in the summer."

"I see." Frank wished he could say something to comfort his friend. "Well, let's get going on these cabinets. Maybe we can get them done before she gets back."

"Oh, my dear, those turned out beautifully! David, come see what Maddy's done! Oh, I forgot, he went into town. He always does his banking on Wednesday mornings. Bank's quiet, you know. And there's my dryer buzzer. Excuse me, dear."

Caroline Evans bustled down the steps to her laundry room. Maddy smiled and breathed in the fresh breeze that drifted gently through the window. It had been a good idea to get a change of scenery and clear her head. The elusive peace had finally started to take hold, and she felt like she could deal with her life again. She looked at her watch. It was probably time to start packing.

She walked into the front hall and jumped when the doorbell rang. She looked at the door and glanced back toward the kitchen. Mrs. Evans was still in the basement and would never hear it. She decided to answer it herself.

She opened the door and came face to chest with a crisp, clean polo shirt. She looked up and beheld the square, shaven jaw, hazel eyes – great eyes – and hair that curled in charming disarray around his ears. She couldn't help but stare.

"John."

"Hi, Maddy."

She stepped out onto the porch. "What brings you here?" It was a silly question, but she wanted to hear the answer.

He took her hands. "You do."

"I'm so happy to see you."

"I'm so glad to hear it." The drive up to Searsport had been a bit of a gamble.

"Um… Shouldn't you be fixing my house?"

"Someone left a mess in the kitchen, and I couldn't get anything done."

Maddy laughed. "I made a mess here, too. I learned how to make scones."

"No kidding?"

"And I learned all about tax laws for inns in Maine," she continued with satisfaction. "David Evans is very knowledgeable."

"You've been busy."

She smiled, then her look became serious. "Phil went home."

John nodded, waiting.

"And he's not coming back."

"Good." This simple response vastly understated John's relief.

"He wanted me to go back to Seattle with him." Maddy was still amazed at Phil's audacity. "He said I'd make good money on the house."

"Did he?" John almost choked on the words.

"But I told him I loved my house." Maddy took a step forward and ran her hands across John's broad, tense shoulders.

"I'm very happy to hear that." John's tense shoulders began to relax.

"And I love you, John." Maddy looked up into his eyes.

John looked back into hers and enveloped her in a crushing hug. Then he kissed her like he hadn't kissed her in ten long days, which, in fact, he hadn't.

The weeks that followed were some of the most interesting and challenging in Maddy's life. She had decided, with the Fordham family's encouragement, to have a grand-opening party on Labor Day weekend, so deadlines for projects became very real. Days were long and exhausting, and evenings were spent planning and recalculating, based on the day's accomplishments.

It took a full week to finish the kitchen cabinet job, but the end result was well worth the effort. The lighter color complimented the newly painted walls, and seemed to enlarge the kitchen, welcoming and reflecting the sunlight that streamed in through the windows.

Maddy's delight was in direct proportion to the discouragement she had routinely felt when the endlessness of the job got to her. This delight was considerable.

The following week saw the installation of new butcher block countertops and brick flooring, which was a much applauded recommendation of Bill's. Once this was accomplished, the new appliances were installed, and Maddy began to think that she might actually enjoy spending time in her kitchen. The pressed tin ceiling was restored, and a rack of copper-bottomed pans was rigged to hang over the central island. The kitchen's complete transformation lacked only three new stools and some decor.

With the kitchen virtually done, the adjacent room became a priority. After the fireplace was repointed and the molding in that area stripped and lacquered, the room got a fresh coat of paint and the floors on the first level were sanded and recoated. White-paneled wainscoting was installed in the parlor, sitting room and dining room, contrasting nicely with the newly-painted walls. The frieze could wait, but Maddy enjoyed being able to discuss these future decorating possibilities with such aplomb.

As room after room underwent transformation, Maddy tenaciously shopped yard sales, estate sales and antique stores for interesting furniture and pieces of art. Linda, good to her word, helped Maddy on the weekends, finding treasures like wall sconces, tassled pillows and needlework footstools. Within weeks, Maddy's Inn began to look like a real Bed & Breakfast.

Rainy weather delayed the painting of the shaker shingles and trim, but the crew had plenty to keep them busy inside. When a relatively dry spell was forecast, they dropped their indoor chores to work on the outside of the house.

Maddy continued with the accents inside, consulting Becky and her mother by phone when she needed creative input. She also spent the intermittent hour outdoors, keeping up with her gardens, and watching her house change before her eyes. The transformation from dingy green to white was stunning, and Maddy was thrilled to mark the painter's progress. Equally enthralling but less openly celebrated was John's increasingly bronzed torso.

It wasn't until just days before the grand opening that the progress they'd made finally hit home for Maddy. Blake and Parker were spending the evening at Karen's, so homeowner and contractor had a few hours alone to go through the house and take inventory.

It was as though Maddy walked through someone else's home, and saw everything for the first time.

The parlor and sitting room were outfitted simply but elegantly. The rooms lacked the glorious clutter of true Victorian style, but Maddy figured she had time to embellish. For now, the settees and armchairs, ottomans and side tables were well-chosen and inviting. The few pieces of art on the walls were local treasures, and she looked forward to adding to those, as well.

The dining room gave her particular satisfaction. The woodwork was beautiful, and the colorful glassware on display complimented the delicate tea set she'd bought for the newly finished sideboard. Truly remarkable was the pedestal table with gilt-stenciled chairs that she'd found at an antique auction. The crowning glory was a coffee dispenser that she'd ordered from a catalog specializing in antique-style fixtures with up-to-date function. No expense was spared when it came to keeping the coffee fresh and hot.

The kitchen was nothing less than stunning. Maddy put new dishes, bowls and vases in the glass-fronted cupboards, and the effect was colorful and welcoming. She also gradually filled her shelves and drawers, giving careful attention to the items on display in the cupboards without doors. She'd found her bar stools and several sturdy, but attractive rugs. Burt still had his comfortable mat in the corner; it was a nonnegotiable fixture.

The fireplace room was the one area decorated in contemporary style. Maddy decided her guests would need a cozy place to relax, and figured she'd be spending a good deal of time in there as well. The pillow-laden couch and comfortable recliners created just such a space. Bookshelves in one corner held games, puzzles and books, and a small entertainment center in the other corner housed the TV.

A walk through the bedrooms upstairs revealed the same comfort and style that was evident on the lower floor. The bedding, window dressings and even the area rugs celebrated the focus for the "shell room," the "lighthouse room," the "anchor room" and the "ship room." Simplicity was the overriding theme, and Maddy knew that improvements could always be made as interesting pieces became available. That would be part of the ongoing adventure.

She reveled in their accomplishment as she looked out over the water from the balcony of her old room, newly named "The Captain's Quarters."

John was reminded of their first walk-through almost three months earlier, and the awkward concern he'd felt for her when she'd leaned out over the railing on that first day. Now, as she did so, he felt no hesitation in pulling her back into his arms.

Maddy giggled. "I wasn't going to jump."

John kissed the top of her head. "I'll make sure of that."

Maddy leaned her head back against his chest and looked up at him. "The house looks amazing. Thank you for everything."

John smiled, enjoying her satisfaction in the renovation, and especially her proximity. It had been too long since he'd really held her. "You helped a lot. You should be proud."

Maddy turned and linked her fingers around his neck. "Thanks for being such a patient..." Her words were quietly interrupted. "Teacher," she managed with a grin.

"You're welcome," he answered, not yet willing to let go.

"Your mom's coming for the party, right?"

"Do we have to talk about my mother right now?" he asked, finding her lips again.

Maddy laughed. "What do you want to talk about?"

"I don't want to talk."

"Good thing we've been so busy, huh?"

"Good thing," John agreed, still determined to communicate without words.

"John?"

It took him a minute to respond. "Yeah?"

"Remember when you used to keep me at a distance when you kissed me?"

John acknowledged the lack of distance between them with little regret. "No?"

Maddy laughed and tried to back away. "It's a scary thing when I'm the strong one. We'd better go downstairs."

John reluctantly released her, but kept hold of her hands. He looked over her head at the water, drawing a deep breath.

"You coming?" Maddy turned to pull him through the doors.

"Where are you taking me?"

The glint in his eye almost made Maddy forget. She cleared her throat. "I'm taking you down to your truck, so you can go home and get some rest."

He gathered her into his arms one more time. Maddy lost all determination to make him leave, and this time John was the one to stop what he'd started. He looked into her eyes and then kissed her forehead.

"Okay, I'll go." He kissed her hand. "I don't want to, but I'll go."

Maddy smiled. "Yeah, you'd better."

They walked slowly down the newly finished front staircase, oblivious to the striking paintings that lined the freshly painted walls. Their feet passed over floors that reflected their images like mirrors, but they were only aware of the powerful point of contact between their linked fingers.

epilogue

Most of the guests had gone home, and Frank's family and the boys were finishing their game of Dominos. John smiled as he watched them lining up their tiles on the new kitchen table. He looked around the room with satisfaction; everything had turned out very nicely. The party had been well attended, and the guests were impressed. John was extraordinarily proud of this particular job.

He walked into the fireplace room and spoke briefly to one of Maddy's neighbors, who was just getting ready to leave. Doing a final walk-through, he made sure that Frank's family and his sons were the only guests left in the house, then made his way out to the place where he knew he'd find Maddy.

She was saying good night to Otis, and John smiled at the look of pride on Otis' face as he gave her a rare hug. John walked over to join them, and Maddy looked up with a smile.

"Otis is going to teach me how to make his famous muffins," she said happily.

Otis chuckled. "Your coffee is so good, no one's going to care what you make for breakfast."

"Thanks, Otis, but I'm still coming over Wednesday morning."

"I'll be ready. Good night, John." They shook hands. "You did a fine job on the house."

"Thank you. I had good help."

Otis smiled and waved over his shoulder as he walked down the steps to the beach.

John took Maddy's hand. "Let's go down to the water."

They walked carefully over the rocky sand. The moon was temporarily hidden behind a bank of clouds, leaving the beach in long, dark shadows. Arriving at the water's edge, they stood just beyond the gently lapping waves. John pulled Maddy close.

"So, you have guests coming next week."

"Yeah. Crazy, huh?" Maddy tucked into his side. "And your next job is…"

"In Portland."

"Wow, it's going to be really different around here."

"Yeah. Nice and quiet."

"I don't know if I'm going to like it."

John took a deep breath and reached into his pocket. "I should probably give you these." He started to detach her ring with its house keys on it from his.

Maddy watched with concern. "I don't mind if you hold on to them. You know, for emergencies."

John continued to separate the keys. "It's best if you have them."

Maddy didn't like the finality in his voice. "Well, if you think so." She put her hand out as he disconnected the ring.

He put the keys in her palm, holding her hand with both of his. "You'll take good care of these?"

She looked up at him, puzzled. "I've got a couple other sets."

"Not like these."

He dropped his hands and she looked down at her own. Something sparkled in the moonlight that now filtered through the clouds. The key ring held more than her house keys.

"John?"

"Maddy, I want you to be my wife."

She looked at him with happy wonder, then back down at the diamond ring – small, sparkling, perfect. She looked back up into his eyes. "Really?"

John laughed softly. "Really."

Maddy held up the keys with the ring on them. "I should probably try this on first."

"First?" John gave her his 'look' as he took the key ring from her hand.

Maddy smiled and hovered as he carefully disconnected metal from metal.

He elbowed her. "You're in my moonlight."

"Oh, sorry." She shifted slightly and watched as the ring came free.

John took her left hand in his. "So, you're thinking about it, right? Or is this step unnecessary?"

Maddy wiggled her fingers. "I'm thinking," she assured him with a laugh.

John slid the ring on, and Maddy emitted a soft sigh of pleasure.

"It's beautiful."

John stepped behind her and wrapped his arms around her waist as she held her hand out under the moonlight.

"It looks good," he observed.

"It does, doesn't it?"

They stood for a moment contemplating Maddy's hand, the ring and all that it symbolized. "I know it's complicated," John said and then turned her to face him. "For all practical purposes, you'll be a mother right away. It won't be easy for you." He stopped and took her face in his hands. "But it will be impossible for us without you." His earnest look finally gave way to a grin. "No pressure or anything."

Maddy linked her arms around his neck. "You're sure the boys are okay with this?"

"Absolutely. We've discussed it at length, and they want you to be part of the family. I had to arm-wrestle Parker to be the one to ask you."

Maddy laughed.

"So?"

She admired the ring as she held her hand up over John's shoulder. "So, what?"

John pulled her closer. "So, are you inclined to give me an answer, or do I have to resort to coercion?"

"Really, John. I'm thinking." She ran her fingers through the hair behind his ears, the diamond sparkling in the moonlight.

John's voice was a low growl. "Maddy…"

She giggled. "Well, and if I say no?"

John disengaged from her, leaned over, and untied his shoes. Maddy watched as he carefully removed them and set them aside. Realization dawned a moment too late, and she tried to jump out of reach. John was on her in an instant, scooping her up, and walking out into the water.

"John!" Maddy squealed. "You wouldn't!"

"Oh, I would." He continued to walk.

"Let's negotiate."

"Excuse me?"

"If I say yes, will you promise not to throw me in?"

"I wasn't really going to throw you. Maybe just drop you," John offered kindly. He took a few more steps. The water was now above the knees of his khaki slacks.

Maddy peeked at the water below and tightened her grip around his neck.

"I want you to be my husband," she whispered.

"Really?"

"Really."

John smiled. Maddy's face was an entertaining mix of happiness and just a little fear.

"I'm crazy about you, Maddy."

She smiled back and relaxed a little. "So, are you going to kiss me and seal the deal?"

"Oh, yeah," he replied, falling into the water.

About the Author

S. Jane Scheyder, a firm believer in romance, lives with her husband and five children in Connecticut. Born in Royal Oak, Michigan, she graduated from Valparaiso University in Indiana with a degree in Music Merchandising. Her first book, *The Other Side of the Pulpit*, was published in 2006.